IN PLAIN SIGHT

Fully camouflaged by his stealth suit, Holly silently moved unnoticed to one of the desks across from where the scientists were working. The computer came on, and he scrolled through the list of satellite programs. Holly went to the one he wanted: *Coordinate Selection Program.* Before he hit enter, he shut down the sound function—he didn't want to have the computer making noise while he was here. He slipped a disk into the hard drive and moved the cursor to *Download.*

The computer hummed quietly while he watched the file being copied.

Standing still like he was, his body was cooling and his faceplate continued to collect moisture. It was becoming distracting.

A moment later Holly was distracted by something else. A shout of alarm. He looked up. One of the scientists was standing behind the desk and pointing.

Straight at him.

Dead Rising

DEAD RISING

Jeff Rovin

BERKLEY BOOKS, NEW YORK

THE BERKLEY PUBLISHING GROUP
Published by the Penguin Group
Penguin Group (USA) Inc.
375 Hudson Street, New York, New York 10014, USA
Penguin Group (Canada), 10 Alcorn Avenue, Toronto, Ontario M4V 3B2, Canada
(a division of Pearson Penguin Canada Inc.)
Penguin Books Ltd., 80 Strand, London WC2R 0RL, England
Penguin Group Ireland, 25 St. Stephen's Green, Dublin 2, Ireland (a division of Penguin Books Ltd.)
Penguin Group (Australia), 250 Camberwell Road, Camberwell, Victoria 3124, Australia
(a division of Pearson Australia Group Pty. Ltd.)
Penguin Books India Pvt. Ltd., 11 Community Centre, Panchsheel Park, New Delhi—110 017, India
Penguin Group (NZ), Cnr. Airborne and Rosedale Roads, Albany, Auckland 1310, New Zealand
(a division of Pearson New Zealand Ltd.)
Penguin Books (South Africa) (Pty.) Ltd., 24 Sturdee Avenue, Rosebank, Johannesburg 2196,
South Africa

Penguin Books Ltd., Registered Offices: 80 Strand, London WC2R 0RL, England

This is a work of fiction. Names, characters, places, and incidents either are the product of the author's imagination or are used fictitiously, and any resemblance to actual persons, living or dead, business establishments, events, or locales is entirely coincidental.

DEAD RISING

A Berkley Book / published by arrangement with the author

PRINTING HISTORY
Berkley edition / January 2005

Copyright © 2005 by Jeff Rovin.
Cover design by Lesley Worrell.

ISBN: 0-425-18398-X

BERKLEY®
Berkley Books are published by The Berkley Publishing Group,
a division of Penguin Group (USA) Inc.,
375 Hudson Street, New York, New York 10014.
BERKLEY is a registered trademark of Penguin Group (USA) Inc.
The "B" design is a trademark belonging to Penguin Group (USA) Inc.

PRINTED IN THE UNITED STATES OF AMERICA

10 9 8 7 6 5 4 3 2 1

Prologue

The Washington Post

CAPE CANAVERAL, October 17—Weather is expected to be ideal for the inaugural flight of the new-generation space shuttle *Venture*. Commander Philip Boring will head a crew of five on a secret Air Force mission. Officials at both NASA and the Pentagon declined to discuss the nature of the payload, though Mission Director Brigadier General Rudolph Anastasia of Air Force Intelligence described it as a "revolutionary tool that will change the nature of how security efforts are undertaken."

One

Cape Canaveral, Florida
Monday, 7:15 A.M.

Captain Philip Wayne Boring sat in the crew compartment of the space shuttle *Venture*. The newest ship in the orbiter fleet, the vessel was perched on the back of its 184-foot-high main external tank, which was making its first and last trip into space. The MET would expend most of its thrust toward the end of the ride and be discarded high in the atmosphere, where it would burn up. The MET was girded by the two solid rocket boosters, the rockets that did most of the heavy lifting. The slender red SRBs provided just over seventy-one percent of the thrust at liftoff and during first-stage ascent. They were thirty-five feet shorter than the main external booster and, after being jettisoned, were recovered at sea and used again.

Boring had only recently joined the Air Force when *Challenger* was destroyed. The young flier was saddened by the tragedy, of course. He wept openly along with the other rookies and Air Force vets. But in the hours that followed, he had a different attitude about the blast than most people. He felt then that the crew of seven had died doing what they loved. They had died with their boots on. He would feel lucky to have that. Flying, making love, or sitting on a beach baking under the sun. If he died doing any of those, he would be content.

The shuttle stood proudly against the cloudless blue sky, its skin of 32,000 white and black tiles bright and well-scrubbed. The high-silica-content tiles ranged from one to five inches thick depending on their location and function. They were eight-by-eight-inch squares that kept the cold of space and the heat of the friction-intensive ascent and descent from reaching the underlying structure. These temperatures ranged from minus 250 degrees Fahrenheit to nearly three thousand degrees Fahrenheit.

The crew compartment where Commander Boring was seated was a relatively small, three-level section. The compartment was nestled clamlike inside the shuttle's forward fuselage—a twenty-four-foot-long wedge of pressurized, inhabitable space vehicle that sat in front of sixty feet of cargo bay. The two topmost sections of the forward fuselage were for the crew. Level one consisted of a forward and aft flight deck with six forward windshields, two circular overhead viewing windows, and two aft viewing windows. Below the aft flight deck was the mid-deck, which served as the crew's living quarters—if zippered sleeping bags attached to the face of a locker could be called "living," as Boring once quipped to the press. Below the mid-deck was the equipment bay. All three levels were connected by small interdeck openings with ladders that made them even snugger. The muscular six-foot-three-inch space veteran was lying on his back in the heavily padded forward left seat. There was a time when astronauts had to be under five feet eleven. It took nearly four hundred thousand pounds of thrust to lift the quarter-million-pound shuttle plus its engines plus the fuel into orbit—a gross liftoff weight of 4.5 million pounds. In the days of the Mercury, Gemini, and Apollo programs, with heavier structural materials and less efficient engines, astronaut size was a serious issue. The larger the passenger, the larger the seat and vehicle had to be. That would have added tens of thousands of pounds of fuel to the gross weight— plus more fuel to lift that extra fuel. Boring was glad that was no longer the case.

To Boring's right was his second in command, five-foot-seven-inch Pilot Astronaut Linda Karl. She was as tall as some of those early astronauts, every inch of her as full of "the right stuff" as John Glenn and Gordon Cooper. They shared twenty-four square feet of forward flight deck. Both astronauts were dressed in seventy pounds of altitude-protection suits, which were only called that by rookies. To the pilots they had always been and would always be space suits. The suits would be taken off once they achieved orbit, and included emergency oxygen systems, parachutes, and flotation devices. The pilots were snugly secured to the form-fitted seats by two shoulder harnesses and a lap belt. These restraints were in an inertial reel lock position. That would keep them securely in place during the shuttle's rattling ascent phase. If it were necessary for the pilots to change their position before they achieved orbit, toggle controls to the left of the seats could move them along two different axes. Behind the pilots was forty square feet of aft flight deck with chairs for two mission specialists.

In front of the two pilots were side-by-side work stations. These consoles featured displays and controls for maneuvering the vehicle throughout its mission. There were also HUDs—heads-up displays—which superimposed data directly on the window so the commander and pilot could read data during landing with minimal need for distracting head-down movement. The rotational hand controllers that managed the ship's roll, pitch, and yaw were located in front of the pilots' seats, with a third unit at an aft flight deck station. Whenever he held the stick, Boring felt as if it were part of his hand. And he knew every one of the buttons well enough to find them blindfolded, which was one of the training tests in the event that smoke filled the cabin. After all his flight time and training in shuttle simulators, he was sure he could fly the shuttle without any readouts. He could feel the bird. Feel it through his feet and up his legs, into his shoulders and down his arms into his hands. That connection happened now, at T minus eleven minutes—just over halfway through the shuttle's terminal count. That's when a built-in hold kicks in, lasting for ten minutes. It's there so ground personnel and flight controllers can attend to any unexpected glitches, discuss weather patterns, and check on the weather conditions at the transatlantic landing sites. In the event that a main rocket engine or major shuttle system were to fail before the shuttle had achieved orbit but after it was too far for an RTLS maneuver—return to landing site—the shuttle would land either in Moron de la Frontera, Spain; Dakar, Senegal; or Ben Guerir, Morocco.

Phil Boring always used that hold time to put mission and countdown details aside, bond with the bird, and go with whatever else relaxed him. Right now, it happened to be his sixth grade and the CGE that had almost sent him on the wrong lifetime trajectory.

Or maybe they just didn't anticipate that space flight would one day be able to accommodate big guys, he thought.

When Boring was a student at Forest Road Elementary School in Valley Stream, New York, he and the rest of his sixth-grade classmates took a State of New York Career Guidance Exam. The CGE was a nearly three-hour, multiple-choice questionnaire designed to point students in a vocational direction before they headed to high school. The test results would allow them to pick their electives with an eye on the future. Boring was an active, intelligent, technologically skilled young man. He was a master of Pong, then Space Invaders, and then the early Atari 2600 games. The results of his test pointed him in the vocational direction of being a video-game designer.

But there were a lot of areas the CGE didn't touch, details that slipped through the margins. There was no place on the exam sheet where he could tell the State of New York that he also liked to make and fly his own kites from scratch, or build and launch Estes rockets. Real-world, cloud-touching challenges that he could see, smell, and feel.

When Boring graduated from high school, he spent time in college. But he wanted to fly just like his kites and rockets, so he joined the Air Force and was placed in Air Education and Training Command. Because of his aptitude with computer games, Boring received both flight training and continuing education in the College of Aerospace Doctrine, Research, and Education. Though Boring never flew in combat, he worked in simulators testing war-fighting programs with an emphasis on future-wars scenarios. These simulated attacks against aircraft from both manned and unmanned orbital craft. His test results and extraordinary reaction time brought him to the attention of NASA. Under orders from the Pentagon, the space agency was secretly recruiting personnel to prepare for a time when Ronald Reagan's Strategic Defense Initiative was reactivated. People with Boring's skills would be needed both on the ground and in space.

Boring was twenty-five years old and a seasoned F-16 pilot when he entered the astronaut candidate program. It is an intensive one-year program that trains pilots and mission specialists for space travel. Boring did superlatively and flew his first mission two years later, serving as a pilot astronaut and second in command on a top-secret Department of Defense mission to deploy a new but conventional eye-in-the-sky spy satellite. Since then, Boring had flown two other DOD missions as second in command. Now, finally, he had his own flight to command. A five-man mission to put a new military satellite into orbit. One that was going to change the way the DOD collected intelligence.

The voice of Dean Michaels broke Boring's reflection.

"*Venture,* this is mission control. All systems are reading 'go' and we're out of hold."

"We copy that, Mr. Michaels," Boring replied. "Thank you for the finest word in the language."

The time for reflection and bonding with the *Venture* was past for now. Boring and Karl both turned their attention to the control panel. While Linda Karl reviewed the external component checklist with Co-Deputy Communications Officer Steve Sousa at mission control—covering boosters, fuel, communications systems, tracking and data network, and weather, among other things—Boring reviewed internal components with Sousa's partner, Alex "Flash" Gordon. These included everything from instrument lighting to smoke detection to payload status.

As the clock counted down and Boring okayed the security of their cargo, he couldn't help but think about the implication of what the *Venture* was carrying into orbit. Their payload would do more than change the face of intelligence-gathering. There were moral implications as well. A satellite that could do everything it could do—

Michaels's voice interrupted once again. "We're at five minutes and looking good," he said.

Dammit!

Commander Boring had been on mental autopilot for maybe two seconds. He was angry at himself; he knew better than that. He'd had his respite during the hold. Now he had to be *here,* present and thinking, alert for every moment of the countdown. All it would take to make this the first and last flight of *Venture* was one slipup—a small red warning light that he missed or an LCD readout that was off by a decimal point.

Boring continued to look at the numbers, listen to the data, watch for the green lights. He focused on the mission, not the payload.

Just over four minutes later, at T minus thirty-one seconds, Boring heard a gentle ping in his helmet com system. That meant the onboard computers' automatic launch sequence software had been enabled by the electronic launch processing system command. The *Venture* was his, though everything at this stage was fully automated. In quick succession, engines three, two, and one of the main propulsion system underwent a staggered ignition at intervals of 120 milliseconds. It was necessary that all three engines reach the necessary ninety percent of thrust at T minus three seconds. Otherwise, the launch monitoring system would trigger an automatic shutdown.

Boring watched the readout on the heads-up display. The engines fired exactly as they should. He immediately felt what the medics called the TSS—total sensory sequence. It was a familiar feeling to Boring, but no less thrilling than ever. He felt the seat vibrate. He saw the panels and reflections in his helmet visor move so slightly and quickly that they seemed slightly out of focus. Despite the fact that he was breathing suit-air, he could smell and even taste a change in the air as the oxygen molecules themselves vibrated and became slightly heated. His hearing was consumed by the roar that moved up the rockets, through the orbiter and his helmet, and into his ears. If anyone at mission control had anything to say, they would have to shout to be heard.

At T minus zero, the two SRBs were ignited. The four explosive restraining bolts blew off. The umbilical cords on either side of the spacecraft were retracted. The onboard master timing unit stitched on. Thrust from all the engines reached one hundred percent.

The ascent digital autopilot made certain that the SRB engine nozzles were moved into their correct positions from neutral to launch. The orbiter aerosurfaces were all securely locked in the launch position. At .03 seconds after SRB ignition, the *Venture* began its arduously slow climb. It rose at a dead vertical until the nozzles cleared the launch tower's lightning rod by forty-one feet. At that point the vehicle began a simultaneous roll, pitch, and yaw that was designed to carry it on its programed trajectory.

A thousand million man-made functions had taken place in less than half a minute. Intellectually, Boring knew that. But as the *Venture* began to accelerate and head into the darkening sky, he was aware of only one thing.

The tears that collected in his eyes as he seized one brief moment to contemplate the miracle, adventure, and responsibility that were his—*his*—to command.

Two

Lake Miasalaro, West Virginia
Monday, 7:16 A.M.

The sun cleared the high eastern mountains and presented Commander Amos Evans with a fresh and glorious morning. Evans had worked underground for so long that he'd forgotten what sunrises were like. For nearly ten years he'd worked in a Pentagon basement, and before that he was figuratively underground, working mostly at night in places where the cultures and language made the environment seem even darker somehow. Good mornings, like this one, made him thank God for life in general and for that day in particular. And for the moment at least, as he drank his morning coffee, Evans allowed himself to forget his dilemma. The problem of ultimate accountability.

The air was fresh and brisk as it brushed past Evans's face and slipped up the sleeves of his uniform. And the vision ahead was beautiful. It seemed like a painting; pale yellow light was sprinkled across the windswept lake surrounded by the muted greens and browns of the high hills. Blue-white skies were beyond. Evans felt a little sacrilegious wondering if this was what Eden might have been like—at least physically. And minus the coffee, of course. Evans's mentor, Father John, had once intimated in a private moment that Paradise might be a state of mind. If that were the case, then this was far from Paradise. Evans could not forget that as grand and beautiful as the scenery was, these hills and the cabins upon them had once been the home of the bloody, anarchic Huntsmen his team had destroyed.

Yet sometimes ground could be sanctified by the deeds done upon them, the thirty-eight-year-old Evans reminded himself. The deed didn't have to save a nation or a cause the way the Alamo had saved Texas or Gettysburg had saved the Union. Or like the unheralded place where a good man, a man alone, had saved Evans's soul and possibly his life.

Evans had grown up with his twin sister and single mother in Miami. His father Bryan rented fishing boats to tourists. One night late in 1970, Bryan Evans just didn't come home. They never found out whether he ran off with a client or got drunk and fell into the sea. Not that it mattered. He had rarely been home anyway.

Evans was six at the time. By the time he was eight he had joined the ruffians at school who became delinquent adolescents who became teenage criminals. Evans didn't mug older people the way his friends did. He had the good fortune, relatively speaking, to fall in with a gangster, Benny Hurwitz. Hurwitz thought the young Evans reminded him of the kid who played Dennis the Menace on TV. Hurwitz liked innocent-looking troublemakers, as he put it, and hired Evans to be an errand boy. Twenty bucks a run, which he spent on pool, pinball, and the young ladies. Ironically, working for Benny kept him out of the hands of the beat cops. If anything illegal was being done, it was Hurwitz and his boys who were doing it. Evans just carried empty duffel bags from the gym where Hurwitz managed fighters to the businesses where cash, jewelry, cruise tickets, hotel keys, and other items were placed inside. Then he brought the bags back again.

One day, Father John confronted Evans in a parking lot on NW 11th Street. It was just after two A.M. on a rainy Saturday morning when the elderly priest boldly walked up to the two-fisted, switchblade-packing kid after he'd picked up money from a bookie in a parked car. The car sped away and Evans tried to run. Father John reached out and grabbed him by the sleeve. Evans never imagined a white-haired priest would have that kind of grip. But he did. From playing stickball and guitar, the clergyman later confided.

Father John told Evans that his mother was worried about him. He also told Evans about how mobster Benny Hurwitz might seem like a powerful man and how working for him could be financially rewarding. But Father John insisted that there were more powerful figures and more rewarding quests if Evans would only come to church and learn about them.

Evans thought that sounded like what Benny called a frost job. Sweet icing on less than nothing special. What surprised Evans was that was all Father John said. No pushing, no promises, nothing else. But it was the way he said it that got the boy's attention. Powerfully, like one of Hurwitz's retired boxers who were now enforcers. And Father John said it even though he had to be aware that the bookie might have sent someone after him or Evans might even have stabbed him. If Father John was willing to put it on the line armed with nothing more than words and faith, maybe this *was* something the young man should look into.

Evans stole a sharp blue suit and black tie from a locker in Hurwitz's gym and went to church the following Sunday. The visit changed his life. There was something about the modest cathedral on NW 4th Avenue that made him feel safe. Not just from punks or from the father he was afraid might return someday. Evans felt as though he could show his fears and anxieties and not feel weak.

There was also something comforting about the way Father John commanded the church. Years later, at the old man's funeral, Evans was able to articulate it better. He said that Father John was like an officer addressing his troops. And Evans wanted to be one of those soldiers. Wanted it bad.

Evans stopped working for Benny Hurwitz. The gang leader was murdered less than six months later, shot in a beach cabana. Hurwitz, with all his bodyguards, was dead, and Father John, with none, was still standing. None, except for the Heavenly Host. That was a lesson the teenager never forgot. He began going to church every Sunday and turned to his neglected school studies. He went to work at a local fast-food restaurant and, unlike in his previous job, he contributed money to running the household. That felt good. He also did odd jobs around the church during his free time. For the first time in his life he was motivated by something stronger than the need to prove himself: the need to better himself.

Nearly a year after their first meeting in the parking lot, Father John introduced Amos Evans to a former parishioner who was home on leave—tall, dignified Lieutenant Harry Quint, USN. Quint told Evans all about the Navy and they corresponded over the next year. One week after graduating from high school, the young man enlisted. Swearing allegiance to God and country was the most moving experience of Evans's young life.

"Hey, there!"

Evans looked up the hill behind him. Victoria Hudson was walking down the dirt path. The young woman was tall and poised, her long brown hair spilling over the high collar of her white wool sweater.

"Good morning," Evans said. For the moment his doubts evaporated. This *was* Eden, complete with temptation.

"Good morning," she replied. "Are you one of those lucky people who doesn't have hay fever or attract mosquitoes?"

"No, but Colonel Lewis made this coffee and it's pretty toxic," Evans replied with a welcoming smile.

Evans wanted to ask how everything had gone in New York. Victoria had gone there to see a lawyer about her divorce. But it didn't seem appropriate to broach the subject. The young woman would bring it up if she wanted to.

"Have a good flight?" the commander asked.

"Very good, thanks," she said. "Never rode an Air Force mail plane before. Also had a good chopper ride from Langley with Captain McIver."

Captain Robin McIver was the group's liaison with Langley Air Force Base in Virginia. She and a hand-picked pilot ferried Stealth Warrior team members to a nearby clearing whenever necessary. Apart from the president and General Brad Jackson at Langley, McIver was the only one who knew that Commander Evans and his Stealth Warriors were here; even the pilot was kept in the dark. Whenever the team needed anything, from supplies to transportation, McIver was the one who provided or requisitioned it.

"Why was that ride good?" Evans asked.

"Captain McIver isn't the easiest person to get close to and I felt as though I connected with her a little," the young woman replied. "I found a way in."

"What was that?"

Victoria stopped beside Evans on the grassy slope and looked out at the lake. Her hair rose gently in the breeze; Evans smelled apricot. Before agreeing to lead the new Stealth Warriors unit, Evans had worked at the Pentagon's Defense Advance Research Projects Agency. He had been around a lot of scientists, a number of them women. But no one on the DARPA team had ever looked or smelled as sweet as Victoria Hudson. It might be sexist, and it certainly wasn't politically correct, but there it was. He breathed a little deeper.

"I found out that Captain McIver loves talking about the military," Victoria went on. "She has some amazing anecdotes about serving in Vietnam and about nearly getting court-martialed for beating up a male antiwar protester in Washington, D.C."

"Captain McIver's passionate about the Air Force," Evans agreed. "Every career officer feels strongly about the military, though maybe not for the same reasons."

"I'd have thought that patriotism or boosterism for one's branch were the main things," Victoria said.

"Usually," Evans said. "Some people just love challenges they can't get behind a desk, the discipline, even the danger." He looked at Victoria and grinned. "For some people, like Captain Holly, I think it may even be a little simpler."

"Oh?"

Evans grinned. "They just love big, fast hunks of flying machine. And they don't get any bigger or faster than in the Air Force."

Captain Peter Holly was one of the men who formed the Stealth Warriors team. Each man had been seconded from a different elite division. The thirty-two-year-old Holly had been a member of a newly commissioned U.S. Air Force group, the STARs: Stealth Team, Attack-Ready. The STARs were trained in all the cutting-edge stealth aircraft technology. Thirty-nine-year-old Master Chief Petty Officer Rodrigo Diaz was also part of a new fighting unit, the Coast Guard SHARCs—Sea, Harbor, and River Command unit. The group was responsible for seagoing electronic reconnaissance on and under the water. Colonel Matthew Lewis, also thirty-nine, was with the U.S. Army Delta Force, the 1st Special Forces Operational Detachment. He was a specialist in knife-fighting, tactical force infiltration, and "flashes"— lightning strikes. Twenty-nine-year-old Major Hank Taylor of the U.S. Marine medical corps held an advanced belt in the martial art of zujitsu and was schooled in PSY-OPs—psychological operations. Captain McIver was the liaison with General Jackson. Though the Stealth Warrior group had a van in case of emergencies—such as a night's leave whenever cabin fever set in—everything else they needed, including official travel accommodations, was requisitioned through General Jackson's office.

The team had been brought together by DARPA to test the new stealth field uniforms. The SFUs were prototype combat attire that blended, chameleonlike, with the wearer's surroundings. Victoria Hudson was one of the outside experts who had been hired years before to design components for the suit. A professor at New York University, Victoria had been brought down to help monitor the field tests. When the president and vice president were attacked by Huntsmen operatives, Evans and his team were uniquely positioned to go to the White House, find a way to end the threat, and then take out the Huntsmen command center. But because no one knew how much of the military-industrial complex was controlled by the Huntsmen, and how many allies the group had in the government, the president asked the team to remain together as his personal quick-response force. They were based in the former Huntsmen outpost high in the hills of West Virginia and worked outside the traditional military system.

"Well, my reasons for being here are certainly different from most people's," Victoria said. "To leave all the shit behind once and for all."

"Were you able to?" Evans asked tentatively.

"I was able to finish up my business with NYU, put my stuff in storage, and sit down with my lawyer."

"Is everything all right?" Evans asked.

"My husband, Stephen, is a misogynist who hates the very idea of me," she replied.

"What idea is that?" Evans asked.

"The idea that I was a busy professional instead of an attentive wifey," Victoria replied. "Unfortunately, no one told me those were the rules going in."

"Want us to stealth-attack him?" Evans asked. "I think some of the guys would like a few days in New York."

"Would you do that?" Victoria said.

"Actually, I was thinking about that very question before you got here," Evans said.

"You mean about beating some respect into Stephen?" she asked.

"No," Evans replied. "I was thinking about our responsibilities. I assume that anything we do as a unit will involve national security. But we have a unique power at our disposal. We haven't really discussed whether we should use that outside of a presidential order."

"To do what? Patrol city streets? Protect battered children?"

"Something moral," Evans said.

"St. War," Victoria said, smiling.

Evans shook his head. That was the nickname Captain McIver had given him after they finished their first mission. A man on a holy crusade against wrongdoing. *"Stealth warrior—St. War,"* she had said. *"Almost like it was destined."* Evans wasn't sure yet how he felt about the name. He couldn't tell whether or not Captain McIver and their teammates were teasing him when they used it. It hadn't been easy for some members of the unit to put aside the strong, traditional rivalries between the elite corps and serve under him. This was especially true for Major Lewis. For now, however, the commander was giving them the benefit of the doubt.

Evans looked up at the cabins that were serving as the group's headquarters. Below them were the bunkers the Huntsmen had used to train their paramilitary personnel.

"I guess I should be getting back," he said. "We've got to go prepare for Dr. Fraser."

"But not until tomorrow, right?" Victoria asked.

"Not until tomorrow," Evans assured her.

"Good. You scared me. I thought something might have changed."

"And if it had?"

"I need to decompress a little from Stephen before I take on the challenge of Dr. Fraser," Victoria said.

"You've got a day," Evans said.

Victoria made a face.

"Sorry," he said, "but I want to have the lab and computers up and running when he arrives. He's already shipped his hardware and software. It'll go in the com-shack."

"So I'll be sharing a room with him too," Victoria said.

"For now. Look," he said. "Most armies are only as strong as their supply lines. We're only as good as our tech support. I don't want to have something hit us and be unprepared to deal with it."

"Oh, something's going to hit all right," Victoria said. "A crackpot named Dr. Clark Fraser. Do you know how angry he was that I got sent down here for the field tests instead of him?"

"Yes," Evans said. "But he also knew we needed him in Washington. He was the only one who knew the whole picture in case we needed something fixed. It'll be all right, I promise," Evans said. He looked back over the lake. "This place can have a healing effect if we let it."

"You have more confidence in miracles than I do," Victoria said.

It was getting late, and Evans and Victoria started back up the gently sloping hillside.

Victoria was still obviously wound up about her husband, but she was also correct about Dr. Fraser. He had been one of the chief scientists on the SFU project. He was a brilliant man driven to micromanage the work of fellow scientists. And when he wasn't challenging the way coworkers did things, or admonishing them to work longer hours, he was driving them crazy by singing show tunes to his dead wife. But he got results. And in a world where high-tech dominance was power, results were all that mattered.

Results and the wisdom to use them ethically, Evans reminded himself. Which brought him back to the SFUs.

Commander Evans had a responsibility to both his commander in chief and to his own strong sense of morality. Hopefully, the two would never be in conflict. President John Gordon was an honorable man, as much as any politician could be honorable. Hopefully, he would never attempt to abuse the capabilities of the Stealth Warrior unit. Because, whether Evans agreed with him or not, Gordon was still his superior officer. And yet, the power they had at their command required the kind of checks and balances that one man, a president, could not provide. Even nuclear weapons had to be fired by someone other than the man who authorized their use. There was what the military called "an extra layer of conscience" that could overrule the chain of command.

As Evans walked back toward the hilltop he glanced to his left, toward the waterside cave that was being outfitted as a hangar. Because it was imperative that as few people as possible know of the team's existence, they were doing all the work themselves. For now, the Stealth Warriors' secret weapon, the sleek LHX-2B—the prototype stealth helicopter—was still at Langley housed in a windowless hangar that was guarded round the clock. The rocket-firing chopper was not to be moved without a direct order from the president to General Jackson. Evans could just imagine how that order had been received back at Holloman Air Force Base in New Mexico where the STAR wing was based.

Fortunately, that wasn't the commander's problem. As for ethical concerns, Evans knew that he would deal with them if and when conflicts arose. Right now there was the more pressing issue of being ready if and when the president called. The SFUs were complex, cumbersome pieces of equipment. The last time the Stealth Warriors had gone into battle, they'd barely had a chance to field-test their gear. The next time would be different. Evans had been drilling the team each day, three hours in the morning and two in the afternoon. The men were beginning to get the feel of moving in the thick, wet-suit-style uniforms. Of walking along walls and stopping in corners, out of direct light that might throw shadows. Of bending their knees when they walked to lower their center of gravity so they were as quiet as they were invisible. Of seeing through thick, polarized eyepieces that allowed them to see each other, hearing despite dampers that kept incoming messages from being heard by anyone outside the suit, speaking into sub-vocal communicators that picked up the softest whisper. If there were technical limitations, especially regarding heat and cold and working in water, he hoped those could be solved within the next few weeks by Drs. Fraser and Hudson working together. Indeed, perhaps the most important benefit of all over the past few weeks was living here, working together, getting to know each other's strengths, vulnerabilities, and idiosyncrasies. Learning to use the first, buffer the second, and live with the third.

And to be prepared.

The remaining Huntsmen had to be smarting after their defeat. Other subversive groups might be encouraged as they learned about the attack on the White House, an assault that had left the West Wing in near ruins and almost cost the president and vice president their lives.

Those too were Evans's problems. But he was glad of one thing at least. That he would not be dealing with the enemy alone. Like Father John, he had invisible allies beside him.

Three

Mrs. Hank Taylor, Sr., did what she did every day before leaving her Park Drive Manor apartment. She paused on her way out the door and glanced at the photographs of her son Hank, Jr., in what he jokingly called the Hank Taylor, Jr., Shrine. She looked at the color photographs and she smiled. The years had thrown the woman some surprises, especially when it had taken her husband's health and then his life far, far earlier than it should have. But overall, life had been good to her, especially where her boy was concerned.

There were shots of her handsome young son at the local dojo testing for his black belt when he was sixteen. There were photographs of him in his Marine uniform, and also posing with his parents on the tennis court, on the beach, and at his high school graduation. Hank, Sr., was so proud of his son that day. The first black student at Germantown Central High to finish in the top five of his class.

Her husband would have been so proud of his Hank today, a Marine medical officer and future—what? Surgeon? Specialist? General practitioner? Psychiatrist?

It didn't matter.

Hank loved people, had loved them from the time he was nine years old and first went to work in his dad's candy store. He had always been upset by the sick customers who came by looking for cough drops or aspirin or tissues. Hank wanted to heal them.

After lingering for a long minute, she left her sixth-floor apartment to walk down the corridor to the elevators. Mrs. Taylor's routine on Mondays was always the same. She would ride to the basement level, walk down the hallway past the small grocery store, the pharmacy, the beauty salon where she worked in the afternoons, the post office, and then enter the small ballroom. There, she would meet with other widows who lived in the building. One of them, Mrs. Pieczenik, a former concert pianist, improvised accompaniments on the piano. The other women, Mrs. Taylor included, sang. They taught each other songs from their childhood. Mrs. Byrne sang songs from her Irish youth, while Mrs. Colgani contributed songs from Sicily. Mrs. Greenberg performed and translated songs from the Yiddish theater in New York, where her father Martin had been a star. All Mrs. Bundonis knew were Christmas carols, so she sang those. Mrs. Taylor gave a strong accounting of songs from the Baptist church where she still performed in the choir. It was not only a delightful, very social way to start the week, but it was also a reminder of what all people had in common. Music as a means of expressing their culture, their past, their sorrow, their joy.

This morning, however, Mrs. Taylor did not make it to the singing club. She did not even reach the basement.

As she waited at the two maroon elevator doors, a white shawl pulled around her proud shoulders, a Hank Taylor,

Jr., Shrine smile still on her face, the stairwell door opened. She turned slowly to her left as two young men emerged. They were dressed in denim jackets, wool caps, and new Nikes. The men had scarves pulled around their mouths. They grabbed her, one by the head, with his hand over her mouth, the other by the arms. They pulled her back to where two other men were waiting on the landing.

One of the young men shut the fire door manually, taking care not to let it slam.

There were muted cries and dull blows to flesh and cloth. A shoe heel kicked the inside of the metal door, a sad, inarticulate cry for help. It struck once loudly, then once softly—an afterthought, or maybe it was an accident. There were several more blows and a few weak grunts. Then there was the soft sound of footsteps descending the stairwell.

There was a *ping* in the corridor. A moment later the elevator door slid open. No one got on. The sole elderly passenger in the carriage snarled something about inconsiderate people, jabbed the "close" button, and continued to grumble as the door glided shut.

The hallway was quiet.

Deathly quiet.

Four

It had been a near-textbook launch.

The *Venture* jettisoned its solid rocket boosters on schedule and on target. Main engine cutoff and external tank separation followed exactly on time. If the rocket burns had been too brief for any reason, resulting in a too low trajectory, the shuttle would have followed the transatlantic landing abort option. Instead, nearly nine minutes after launch, the shuttle was in a "normal trajectory" for orbital insertion.

As in most shuttle missions, the *Venture* would be required to execute several brief thrusting sequences. The bursts would push the spacecraft into the exact orbit required to deploy its cargo. These burns would be executed by the pilot using the orbital maneuvering system. The OMS is comprised of three fourteen-foot-long engines, liquid-propellant rockets that can be throttled anywhere from sixty-five to 109 percent of their rated power level in one-percent increments. Each engine can burn for a total of

7.5 hours and can be started fifty-five times. The rockets can be moved plus or minus 10.5 degrees in both the yaw and pitch axis for precision firing. Mission control gave Commander Boring the "go" to perform the positioning maneuvers.

A total of three short compensation burns were made at seven-minute intervals. No one of them was more than a second or two. The burns gave both Boring and mission control time to analyze the effectiveness of each burst and to determine the duration of the next. Forty-five minutes after liftoff, when the shuttle had reached the desired altitude and speed—which was slightly more than 25,000 feet each second—mission control gave Boring the go-ahead for a single "shakedown" orbit.

Meanwhile, with all the shuttle's systems functioning properly, Boring gave mission specialists Dr. Barry Gregg and Lieutenant Dave Havoc the okay to begin preparing for their extra-vehicular activity. Havoc, who worked for Air Force Intelligence, would run through a final systems check of the ESP satellite. He would make sure that the cargo had not been damaged during liftoff. The satellite had been secured with custom-manufactured cables, restraining bars, and thermal padding, and the satellite's systems had been designed to withstand normal launch vibration. Nonetheless, mishaps did occur. Before going out, Havoc would check to make sure the ESP was intact and secure, at least according to the instruments. While he did that, Gregg would prepare the suits. Once they were outside, Gregg would go over to the satellite and check the systems for deployment. Havoc would serve as his backup. The cargo was scheduled to be released from the cargo bay early in the fourth orbit, at five hours and ten minutes after launch.

By the completion of the second orbit both Dr. Gregg and Lieutenant Havoc reported that everything was functioning properly. Commander Boring gave them the go-ahead to undertake the EVA. Once the two mission specialists had suited up, there would be a final check of the suits and the systems within the cargo bay itself. They would make sure the doors were operating properly and that the exposed fuel and air tanks were intact. Even a slow, microscopic leak could send frozen particles into the bay that could puncture the suits or cause an explosion. That check would take approximately a half hour. Then they would be ready for their space walk and the deployment of the ESP.

The astronauts had a tradition back at the Manned Spacecraft Center in Houston, one that dated back to the second shuttle mission. Before a flight, the commanders of the previous shuttle mission and the next mission to go up made a handshake wager. They decided whether the orbital insertion or touchdown would be "prettier." Commander Anthony, who had taken the *Atlantis* up one month before, selected the orbital insertion. Commander Slotnick, who would be flying the *Discovery* in six weeks, picked the landing.

The orbital insertion had been a little masterwork, as good as space flight got. Which was fine with the competitive Boring because it gave him something to shoot for.

A touchdown that was even sweeter.

Five

Lake Miasalaro, West Virginia
Monday, 1:33 P.M.

Not only did it feel good to be out of the darkness. For Amos Evans it also felt good to be back in the field, working with an elite military unit. It felt very, very good.

For the ten years he spent as a Navy SEAL, Amos Evans had served on dozens of military and reconnaissance missions. He had gone into Turkey, Burma, Cuba, Afghanistan, Lebanon, and two dozen-plus other countries. Evans had also spent a great deal of that time as a solo op, penetrating foreign groups in order to conduct OSTE—on-site threat evaluation. Then came Desert Storm and the event that had landed him here.

Evans had learned that SCUD warheads were being stored in Al' Aziziya, fifty miles southeast of Baghdad. The missiles were tough to track once they got into the field on their mobile launchers, so he and his team went into the city at night. They found the missiles in a school crawl space and rigged a small charge to destroy the guidance systems. Unfortunately, the blasts were sizable enough to cause the warheads to blow. When they did, they took nearly half of the town with them. There were civilian casualties.

After the war, the military did not want to lose Evans. But the Iraqis made an issue of U.S. "war crimes" and the Defense Department decided to make a preemptive strike. They made an example of what they privately called Evans's "over-zealousness." But instead of court-martialing him, as the Iraqis demanded, they sent him to DARPA. It was all very quiet, no demotions, no publicity. It was what they called a "diplomatic sacrifice." Evans understood. He didn't hold it against the Pentagon for "taking him *in* from the pasture," as he put it. Amos Evans understood about martyrs.

When Evans first arrived at DARPA, he did not know which was worse. Being buried deep in the basement of the Pentagon, the military's top-secret research arm, was far different from anything Evans had known before. He was also frustrated by the slowness of research. It wasn't like getting intel from a spy or satellite, putting together a team, and taking out a target or enemy. At DARPA the target was more often than not a computer simulation that didn't work the way it was supposed to, or a senator who didn't understand why extra funds were needed to finesse that simulation into shape.

But as Evans came to know the work itself, he learned to love it. The research was designed to protect American lives and interests. Just as he did when he enlisted at the age of eighteen, he was proud to be a part of that process. Besides, it wouldn't be the first time he'd had to change his way of life. Nor, he'd suspected, would it be the last.

The SFU—the Stealth Field Uniform—was already in the works when Evans took charge of DARPA's Field Research Division. It became his pet project among the dozen or so for which he was responsible. Maybe that was because it was the only one that wasn't a destructive force of some kind. It was designed to undermine an enemy rather than destroy him. And it depended entirely on the skill of the person wearing it.

It was more like an angel than like hellfire.

The idea had first been conceived in 1980 by Dr. Fraser shortly after his wife died. Fraser was visiting his sister in Mystic, Connecticut. The family took a break from dull antiquing to visit the Mystic Seaport aquarium. That was where the chemist first saw the sargassum, a fish with sophisticated color-adaptive characteristics. Fraser began to wonder if there might be a way to move molecules along microscopic fibers to mimic the fish's abilities. He immediately returned to Washington and discussed the idea with his superior, General Orlando Vargas. Vargas was in charge of DARPA's camouflage division. Though the research unit had always discussed the concept of "stealth uniforms," the technology to create them, even a direction for that technology to take, was elusive. There was talk of using electromagnetism to bend light or chemicals to counteract pigmentation—all of it highly theoretical stuff. The idea of duplicating the abilities of chameleons and insects like geometrid moths was deemed possible but impractical due to the relative slowness of the transformation. But the sargassum fish seemed to make the switch much more quickly, in a matter of seconds. Fraser wondered if that process could be chemically accelerated. General Vargas was intrigued. He gave Fraser a small team and they began working on "The Griffin Project," a name the scientist had selected in honor of the protagonist in H.G. Wells's *The Invisible Man.*

Now, twenty-six years after Fraser's outing with the family, Amos Evans and his team were actually field-testing the first five SFU prototypes. It had been a long, arduous haul going from endless experiments with individual fibers in the lab to success with small swatches and now full suits. The plan had been to test them for a year, then go to a next generation of suits and begin deploying them to special forces in the early 2010s.

At least that *had* been the plan. Now, with the team serving as a special-ops unit reporting directly to the president, Evans wondered if they would ever be able to go back to the laboratory or to the mainstream military. That was one reason Dr. Hudson was here and Dr. Fraser was coming. To continue working on the stealth uniforms in secrecy. If the president was to have an effective "untouchables" force, they had to keep the Huntsmen and anyone else from learning about the group or their work.

Despite the cataclysmic events that had isolated them here, Evans was enjoying the challenge and the physicality. Even when he had been working for Benny Hurwitz, he liked being on the move. And he loved being outdoors, even if he and his team members *were* wearing suits that weighed sixty-seven pounds and had air-cooling systems that had been designed for operatives at rest, not people in motion. That was one of the first things Fraser and Hudson would have to work on. Effective air-conditioning.

Evans was standing on the small sandbar beside the lake. The cave was about one hundred yards ahead of him. Diaz and Taylor were moving along the edge of the water, trying to keep their balance on the rocky surface. Taylor had been wounded in the attack on the White House, and was moving a little more tentatively than the others. But he was young and in great shape and his recuperative powers were amazing. Lewis and Holly were up in the hills, roughly three hundred yards away. One of the problems the team had encountered during their first mission was functioning as a team. They were practicing coordinated attacks in stealth mode, staying in visual and audio contact while moving along different routes. The men were doing well, despite the heat inside the suits and the fact that their eyepieces tended to fog at times. For this exercise Evans was observing rather than participating.

The team had been working for several hours. Evans was about to call for a lunch break when he received a call in his suit headset. The incoming message was preceded by a short one-pulse tone. That meant the message was only being sent to him.

"Captain McIver to Commander Evans," said the woman's deep, cigarette-husky voice.

Evans turned down the suit-to-suit communications. "Go ahead, Captain," Evans replied.

"Sir, we just received disturbing news," she said. "This morning, Major Taylor's mother was badly beaten in the stairwell of her apartment building in Philadelphia."

Time seemed to slow down as Evans processed the words, imagined pictures to go along with them. Hank Taylor was devoted to his mother. The commander looked out at Taylor. He hated knowing that these were the last untroubled moments the officer would know for a long time.

"What's Mrs. Taylor's condition?" Evans asked.

"She's critical," McIver said. "Looks like they hit her with brass knuckles. She has five broken ribs, a broken hip and leg, and took a blow to the face that may cost her an eye. She also suffered about a half hour of internal bleeding before they found her. She's just come out of surgery. Camp Pendleton got the first call. It took a few hours for them to trace the major to DARPA and then to Langley."

"I understand," Evans said. He looked over at Major Taylor. The officer had deactivated his Stealth mode, come ashore and was executing graceful three-quarter turns by placing one knee behind the other, sinking low, and pivoting. When Taylor turned, he immediately aimed an imaginary gun and fired. "Do we know if Mrs. Taylor's going to make it?" Evans asked.

"I'm sorry but I don't have that information," McIver told him.

"Anything about who may have done it?" Evans asked.

"They don't know," McIver said. "But the attackers did leave something behind."

"What?"

"The name 'Django'—with a D in front," McIver informed him. "Cut in her right cheek with a knife."

"All right," Evans said. "Thank you."

"I'll put in a call to the hospital so Major Taylor can talk to whoever is attending his mother," McIver said. "Then I'll arrange transportation to Philadelphia. We'll get him up there ASAP."

Evans thanked her again.

"Do you want the call patched directly to his suit or—"

"Send it to the com-shack," Evans told her. "That will give him some privacy."

"Yes, sir," she said.

The commander walked toward the lake. As he did, he lowered the thick faceplate that was hinged at the chin. "Major Taylor, a moment!" Evans said into the helmet microphone.

"Yes, sir."

The African-American medical officer lowered his own faceplate. So did Diaz, who waded from the lake. Taylor's eyes were clear and bright, his skin beaded with perspiration. He was smiling broadly. This was going to kill him.

"I think I've got the turns figured out, sir!" Taylor said.

"I think you do," Diaz said as he slogged up behind him. "I didn't see a thing. That was pretty. Very pretty."

"Thanks," Taylor said. He looked at Evans. "See, sir, since the fabric is so stiff, the trick is that you have to get parts of it to turn gently instead of trying to force it all at the waist—"

"Major, that'll have to wait for a bit," Evans said. He

regarded the SHARC. "Would you give us a minute, Mr. Diaz?"

"Certainly, sir." There was a flash of concern in Diaz's eyes before he turned away.

Taylor looked at Evans. The smile faded a little.

People had always said there was a reassuring quality to Evans's voice. If that were true, he always imagined that he had picked it up from Father John. He hoped it was so. Over the years he had had to tell far too many wives or parents that their husband or son had been injured or killed.

"This doesn't sound good," Taylor said, his mouth downturned. "You're mustering me out."

"No," Evans replied. "This isn't military business."

"Not military?"

"It's about your mother, Major. She's in the hospital."

Evans gave Taylor a moment for that to register.

"What's wrong?" Taylor asked. "Her heart? Did she fall?"

"Someone attacked her at her apartment this morning," Evans said.

"Attacked my mother? How serious is it?" Taylor asked. "Do they know who did it?"

"We don't know very much," the commander admitted. "Captain McIver is putting in a call now. She'll relay it to the com-shack. She's also arranging to get you up to Philly."

"Do they know if it was a random attack? Do they have any clues, any evidence at all?"

"Just a name," Evans told him.

Taylor's eyes hardened. "What name?"

"Django," Evans said. He didn't tell Taylor where they found the name. "Does that mean anything to you?"

"Yes, sir, it does," Taylor said. His voice was flat, hard. He turned and started up the hillside.

Evans called over the rest of the team. He told them what

had happened and then they went up at a respectful distance. The quiet empathy they felt for Taylor was immediate and not unexpected. Evans had seen this before, usually when soldiers received Dear John letters or word that a close family member had died. But there was also a quiet, percolating sense of outrage. Whoever Django was, he hadn't just crossed a man.

He had crossed brothers.

Six

Dressed in his bulky white EMU—extra-vehicular mobility unit—Lieutenant Dave Havoc stood in the airlock just inside the open hatchway. The sixty-three-inch-wide, eighty-three-inch-long aluminum airlock was located in the mid-deck and was the shuttle's sole point of access to the cargo bay. Havoc watched as Dr. Barry Gregg stepped into the open cargo bay of the space shuttle. Inside the airlock, both men had been secured by handrail and foot restraints. Those grips and straps had allowed them to open the six latches on the egress hatch. Otherwise, when they applied pressure to the solidly fixed push-pull rods that controlled the door, the force would only have caused the men themselves to rotate. As soon as the hatch had been opened, the men had attached twenty-five-foot tethers to hooks on the outside of the hatch. Before releasing themselves from the interior restraints, they made certain the tethers were secure.

"How're you doing, Barry?" Lieutenant Havoc asked as Dr. Gregg slowly pulled himself out.

"No problems," Gregg replied in a low monotone.

"Does it feel like it did in the tank?" Havoc asked.

The tank was the huge indoor swimming pool where the astronauts had practiced their EVAs in suits just like these outside a life-size mockup of the shuttle cargo bay.

"Very much so," Gregg replied.

"Except there are no technicians swimming around," Havoc said. "Or mermaids, like the time you got too much oxygen."

He was trying to keep things light. Gregg did not reply.

Havoc's mouth twisted slightly. He had expected some enthusiasm from the man, just a little. Gregg had stepped out into space. But there was no sense of awe or reverence or even a gasp of *This Is So Cool I'm Gonna Shit My Pants.* No delay to suck it all down, the naked cosmos spread before him the way blue-black sky used to spread before Havoc in his G-33 StratoX. Nothing. Gregg's reaction only heightened the feeling that Havoc had had for some time. That Gregg was scared. The guy probably didn't belong in outer space. Havoc intended to keep a very careful watch on the mission specialist.

Physically, Dr. Gregg was as safe as a human being could be taking a walk in the void. Unless the computer scientist's suit was pierced by a micrometeoroid—which, at the speeds the shuttle was moving, would hit with force greater than a high-caliber bullet fired point-blank—or unless there were a catastrophic systems failure, which was unlikely, Gregg would be fine.

But the men had trained together for nine months. And as the training went on Gregg had become more and more withdrawn. Maybe he was becoming focused, as Dr. Wayne Campbell, head of the APET—Astronaut Psychological Evaluation Team—had suggested. After all, their cargo, the

ESP, was Gregg's pet project and he was sending it into space. Lives and national security depended on it, not to mention his own reputation.

Or maybe, as Havoc suspected, Gregg was just getting a wee bit scared. A former vice president of Research and Development for PS3, now Deputy Director of AFTIC—Air Force Technological Intelligence Collecting—the forty-seven-year-old Gregg was making his first trip into space. So was the thirty-two-year-old Havoc, but Havoc was a one-time test pilot. When he hit thirty he had segued into Air Force Intelligence, where he was responsible for debriefing "spylots" as they called the spy-plane pilots. But somehow, being a military man, Havoc felt a sense of confidence and entitlement. He was used to pushing the envelope. An egghead—one who had no sense of humor—was a different bunch of flowers.

So fear was Havoc's guess for Gregg shutting down. That happened a lot too. Even after the changes that had been made following the *Challenger* and *Columbia* disasters, the space shuttle was still a craft that had the very real potential to explode or implode, break up or burn up, get stranded in earth orbit or clobbered by a piece of space junk. It could just be that emotionally and psychologically, Gregg was not one of the right-stuff boys. Ironically, though, fliers and mission specialists tended to stifle their jitters as best they could or they'd be benched from their once-in-a-lifetime chance to go aloft.

When Dr. Gregg had fully cleared airlock—which was where the EMUs were stored—Havoc moved into position, like a parachutist waiting to make his jump. He peered out. The two sixty-foot-long doors to the cargo area had been opened as soon as the shuttle achieved orbit. They were at maximum spread, just over 175 degrees each, and had been opened to allow the deployment of the radiator panels that rejected accumulated heat and gases generated by the ship's environmental and life support systems.

Havoc's amber-tinted dome-helmet was full of sounds. There were communications between Commander Boring and mission control. There were his own shallow breath and the loud drumbeat as his heart compensated for the lack of gravity and worked to push blood to his lower extremities. And there were occasional beeps and pings from the various systems, sounds that let him know that they had been activated or were functioning properly.

Havoc watched Gregg a moment more. Then he started to move through the hatchway.

"I'm coming out," Havoc said.

"Copy," Gregg replied.

Not even a "Good luck," Havoc grumbled to himself. Well, there was always one raw egg in the squad. Commander Boring and the others were cool, so it had to be Gregg.

Havoc had to twist to get through the hatchway without snagging any of the nozzles or joints of his stiff suit. It went pretty much the way they'd rehearsed in the water.

Maybe being out in space did or didn't blow Dr. Gregg away. Havoc didn't know and he didn't care now. As he stepped out and stood under the canopy of forever, Havoc leaned his body back slightly so he could turn his face spaceward. The sounds in his head and the shuttle itself and Gregg's self-absorption all seemed so small and pathetic.

That's the universe out there, he thought as hovered just inside the payload bay. Not just the sky at night with its gentle light and soft twinkling. All those episodes of Carl Sagan's *Cosmos* he'd watched when he was a teenager came back to him. Those were stars, brighter and more intense without the atmosphere to diffuse them. Each of them was a nuclear furnace consuming itself and the ghosts of whatever matter or life comprised the first generation of stars and planets and possibly even civilizations. It was more humbling than the hardened flier had imagined it would be.

Wow, he thought. Just fucking *wow.*

"You two all right?" Boring asked.

"Affirmative," Gregg replied. As the first one out, Gregg was always supposed to be the first one to respond to a general query.

"I'm A-OK," Havoc replied. "Damn, this is impressive. Nice ship, POCC, but good work, God."

"We reject the top billing, but thank you, Lieutenant," replied Merton Hood of the Payload Operations Control Center operated by NASA's Marshall Space Flight Center in Huntsville, Alabama. Once the astronauts stepped into the cargo bay, communications had switched from mission control in Houston to POCC.

Lieutenant Havoc turned his eyes from the star-splashed heavens to the *Venture*'s payload, the ESP. Using handholds on the side of the cargo bay, he walked himself over, following Gregg. Havoc was already accustomed to microgravity conditions, thanks to both the near-zero-G conditions underwater and also to flights in the padded fuselage of a modified KC-135 jet aircraft, which simulated weightlessness during twenty seconds of parabolic free fall. The sensation was a lot like holding a helium balloon, except that you were the balloon. Each muscle had to work harder to do what it did with the help of gravity. And things that he took for granted on earth, such as his arms hanging down or his hair staying flat on his head—or scratching an itch, which he couldn't do in this suit—were different here.

Hand over hand, the men drew themselves toward the cylindrical six-thousand-pound satellite. The thirty-six-foot-tall gold-paneled ESP was sitting on the shuttle's remote manipulator system. The RMS is a robot arm capable of deploying or retrieving payloads. It also serves as a ladder for crew members who need to reach all sides of the cargo.

The RMS is operated from a display and control panel in

the aft flight deck crew station. Dr. Humphrey Curtiz was back there waiting for the go-ahead from Lieutenant Havoc to raise the ESP from the bay. Havoc manually released the straps and braces that held the graphite and aluminum RMS in place, since its own considerable vibrations during launch could hurt the cargo. When he was finished, he radioed Curtiz to raise the arm. The fifty-foot-three-inch arm began to unfold toward the heavens, powered by DC motors that wouldn't have had the strength to move it under earth's gravity. The arm was jointed like a human arm, one that had been stripped to the bone.

Not quite human, Havoc thought. Anyone who believed that space was for robot explorers didn't get it. It was a place where artists, writers, reporters, homemakers, and children should go as well as scientists. People who could grasp and communicate the sense of wonder and adventure that lay out here. Hell, he was just a flyboy and this was pushing him into poetic thoughts and vocabulary he didn't know he had.

As the arm rose into the dark skies, the ESP shined dully from the reflected glow of the earth. The satellite's small, black rocket booster was hidden in stark shadow. Once the satellite had been released, a command from earth would nudge it into the proper orbit.

After twenty minutes the ESP had cleared the cargo bay. With Havoc's help, Gregg released his tether from near the hatch and reconnected it at the base of the arm. When it was secure, Gregg used the handholds and foot restraints to climb toward the satellite. The lieutenant remained behind, standing at the bottom of the arm. Havoc had no function other than to help Gregg if something went wrong or if the scientist became snagged on something or disabled.

The ESP was held in place by a series of lever-locked clutches that resembled pliers. As soon as Gregg had ascertained that the satellite's booster rocket was free of debris and had checked the onboard systems readout, which would confirm the "A-OK" readings that Havoc had received inside, he would climb back down. Curtiz would then release the satellite. The arm would be retracted and, assuming that everything was still functioning properly, Gregg and Havoc would return to the airlock. The shuttle would withdraw from the site, the ESP rocket would be ignited, and this portion of the mission would be completed.

Upon reaching the satellite, Gregg looked at the readout. It was located beside a solar panel on the ESP's underbelly. There were four horizontal lines of bright red numerals. Below them was a keypad. As chief scientist on the ESP project, Gregg had designed the keypad to be part of the satellite. Since computer systems on earth were always changing, he felt the ESP should have the capacity to be reprogrammed. Not from earth, which would make it easy for foreign powers to corrupt the system, but from here. Just haul it in and reconfigure the software or upgrade it. For the foreseeable future only the United States would have the capability to pluck the satellite from space and perform those functions.

Gregg began punching in numbers.

"Is something wrong?" Havoc asked.

"I'm not getting a readout from the gamma line," Gregg answered.

"POCC, what are you reading about gamma line?" Havoc asked.

"We're getting a normal display down here," Campbell replied. "What about you, Curtiz?"

"Normal back here," Dr. Curtiz replied from his aft station.

"Maybe a bulb shook loose at your end, Barry," the POCC officer suggested.

"I have a feeling that's exactly the problem," Gregg said. "I'm reversing the lights for beta and gamma lines—"

"Whoa!" Curtiz said. "I just lost everything!"

"Ditto at POCC," Campbell said.

"Hold on," Gregg told them. "There's something screwy in here."

"Could you be a little more specific, Bar?" Campbell asked.

"Checking," Gregg replied.

Havoc waited anxiously, barely breathing. That was all they needed: some two-buck piece of plastic screwing things up. All of a sudden that was more important than the whole goddamn universe hanging over his head.

It was slow going working a keyboard in space. Not only were the thick-fingered gloves clumsy to work with, but Gregg would have to generate momentum from the shoulder for each push of a key. There was no "typing down" and no gravity to help.

"I think I have it," Gregg said.

"You sure as hell do," Curtiz said. "Nice going. We're back on-line."

Lieutenant Havoc's breath came back.

"Here too," Campbell said.

"I'm starting to get some glow in the gamma line," Gregg said. "It was just a loose jack. The clip is okay, though, and I put it back."

"Good work," Campbell said. "We've got all systems 'go' for prime and fire."

Dr. Gregg inputted the code to prime the rocket that would send the satellite into space. Then he climbed back down the arm. The scientist was breathing heavily from the exertion of the climb.

Havoc gave him a smile and pat on the shoulder. "Nice job," the lieutenant said.

Gregg appeared even more preoccupied than before. Maybe he was tired or maybe it was just working through the final moments of seeing whether years of work were going to pay off.

Havoc helped Gregg back to the handholds along the side of the bay. The men returned to the airlock. When they were safely inside they shut the hatch. However, they remained suited up. Dr. Curtiz would be releasing the satellite from inside. If there were a snafu of any kind, Havoc and Gregg would be able to go right out and fix it.

But there were no snags. The satellite was released. The shuttle pulled away with a two-second burn of its engines.

"It's looking good!" said the POCC officer. "We're on schedule for ESP orbital insertion burn in fifteen minutes."

Havoc stood back and let Dr. Gregg watch through the small airlock window as the satellite receded slowly into the darkness. This was his baby, his moment. Over the scientist's shoulder Havoc could see the gold exterior of the ESP shine brightly, even as it shrunk to the size of a thimble.

Havoc began removing his EMU. The men had to get out of the airlock before the burn could take place. If something went wrong and the ESP exploded, there would be an extra wall of protection on the other side of the airlock.

"You'd better hurry," Havoc told Gregg through the headset.

Gregg began removing his suit slowly, mechanically. Havoc kept his headset on as he listened to the countdown. The ESP burn was in five minutes. Havoc helped Gregg out of the suit and then they stowed it alongside his own in the EMU compartment. They climbed through the interior hatch into the aft flight deck. Dr. Curtiz was at the controls, preparing to execute and follow the satellite orbital maneuver.

The three men floated in the small compartment. Gregg watched the closed-circuit television display from the cargo bay while Havoc looked out the small, overhead trapezoidal window. The lieutenant couldn't see the satellite. Just space. But when the ESP booster ignited there was a pure, arcing flash of white, blue, and orange at the right

Seven

**The White House
Monday, 2:07 P.M.**

All things considered, there was something extremely cozy about working at home.

At least, that's what being at a desk upstairs in the White House made President John Gordon feel like. That he was home. Though the Oval Office was still part of the president's "house," the formality of the office itself and the seriousness or awe of the people who came there, not to mention the gravity of the topics discussed there, made it seem worlds away.

The assassination and coup attempt organized by the Huntsmen had seriously damaged the West Wing and underground situation room of the White House, as well as the missile silos that protected the Executive Mansion from aerial attack. Repairs were being made quickly and the external structure was nearly enclosed. Though the Oval Office, cabinet room, and surrounding chambers had suffered only minor damage, it would be another week before the wiring and plumbing would be complete and at least some of the staff could move back in. Complete restoration work would take well over a year.

Until then, the president and his executive secretary, Laura Richmond, were nestled in his large book-lined study in the third-floor living quarters. Their desks were on opposite sides of the room. The president faced a small window that looked out on the Washington Monument. Laura faced the door. Chief of Staff Jane O'Brien was working down the hall in a parlor that the president used to receive guests. The rest of the staff was scattered in offices throughout the Old Executive Office Building, to the west on 17th Street, and the Treasury Department Building, to the east on 15th Street. Tunnels to both buildings allowed White House staff to move between them without going outside. Meetings, when they were conducted, were held mostly on the phone or in one of those two buildings.

The fifty-eight-year-old president was a short, wiry former New York police commissioner with dark brown eyes and a thin mouth. He was once described by *Time* magazine as "Jack Nicholson without the edge," though people who did stupid or selfish or partisan things in his administration often experienced that edge. Gordon believed in the people and he believed in serving all those people, not special interests or fashionable trends.

The president was just finishing a conference call with the Senate majority leader and the head of the foreign relations committee when the study door opened. Executive Secretary Richmond looked up as Chief of Staff O'Brien walked in. The forty-three-year-old O'Brien was the five-foot-two-inch former Director of Regulation and Certification for the Federal Aviation Administration. The woman's round face was usually impassive beneath her short brown hair. Today it was pale with her eyes wide and startled. She was slightly out of breath.

"Mr. President!" she said urgently as she entered the room.

The president turned his swivel chair around and hung up the phone. "What's the matter, Jane?"

O'Brien took a short, steadying breath as she walked around Laura Richmond's desk.

"Mr. President, shortly before completing its fourth orbit, the space shuttle *Venture* lost all of its main and backup computer systems," she told him.

"Is the crew all right?" the president asked.

"For the moment," O'Brien said. "But if they can't restore power in approximately half an hour, they'll freeze."

"Shit. What are their chances?"

"We don't know yet," she said.

"What happened?" the president asked.

"The crew had just deployed a military satellite when everything just went down," she said.

"Which satellite?" the president asked.

"The Electronic Surveillance Post," O'Brien replied. "I spoke with DOD. It's an Air Force project, designed to crack and upload data from dedicated computer systems back on earth."

"Did it crack the shuttle?" the president asked. There was an edge of disgust in his voice. He knew about the ESP and he knew that it was designed to read unshielded systems, computers that were outside complex electromagnetic barriers. But the ESP was designed to read, not disable.

"They're checking to see if there's any way activation of the satellite could have affected the shuttle's systems," O'Brien told him. "I'm told they had a problem while getting the ESP out of the cargo bay and now they're having trouble contacting it."

That didn't sound good. Nine times out of ten "having trouble" turned out to be a permanent state.

The president felt as though he had walked into a

dream. It was tough to get his bearings, to wrap his mind around the idea that the space shuttle could be stranded in orbit, that a team of men and women could die there. And to *know* they were going to die there—how did one deal with that? He brought his mind back to earth. To a place where he could help.

"How many of the *Venture* astronauts have spouses and children?" the president asked.

"Three of the five," O'Brien replied.

"Have they been informed?"

"Not yet," O'Brien replied. "This only happened a few minutes ago. The crew is just breaking out flashlights and oxygen on board, still trying to get a handle on things at their end. Sir, we don't want to cause any premature alarm. This may be fixable."

In the past, civilians weren't informed of what NASA and the military called "unresolved situations" unless there was a good chance that things would not be resolved successfully. The media knew because they had reporters at the Manned Spacecraft Center and the Cape. They would release limited information at first, not so much to keep the public in the dark as to keep calls from flooding in and distracting NASA and the families of the astronauts. To "prep" the public, as they described it, journalists would describe an electrical problem, communications snafu, or watch-and-wait situation. But those rules were drawn up before home satellite dishes allowed people to eavesdrop on open communications between earth and the shuttle.

"I want them told and I want to talk to them immediately afterwards," the president said. "The press is going to find out something's up and I don't want the families hearing about this from CNBC."

"Of course," O'Brien said. "I understand."

"Was there any sign of trouble on board, anything to indicate that this could happen?" he pressed.

"Are you asking if the crew or ground control got careless?" O'Brien asked.

"That's exactly what I'm asking," the president said.

"I was told there was some trouble with the satellite they were launching, that it went dark for a half a minute or so," O'Brien said. "But no one was in danger and the systems came back on and were functioning normally."

The president shook his head. "Let me know about the families and anything else you hear," the president said.

"Yes, sir."

The president's chief of staff left the room. Laura and the president looked at one another.

"Get me General Rogers, please," the president said. General Jesse Rogers was the unflappable chairman of the Joint Chiefs of Staff. "Then put me through to NASA mission control and get ready to place calls to the families of all the astronauts."

"Yes, sir."

"And one more thing," he added. "Call the chaplain. Ask him to say a prayer for the crew."

Richmond said she would.

Gordon turned back toward the window. There were times when the president had felt vulnerable—battling with Congress, trying to keep information from the press, and being trapped in the situation room by the Huntsmen. But this was the first time as president that Gordon had felt helpless. Whether this turned out to be sabotage or carelessness or an unforeseeable accident, there was only one thing he could think to do.

As he looked out across the rich green lawn and the ellipse, he said his own quiet prayer.

Eight

Commander Evans waited outside the cabin while Major Taylor made his call. The rest of the team had gone to the barracks. The five cabins had been built by the late Huntsman leader Bernard Schiller, code-named Axe. They were constructed on the hillside, along a series of ridges that overlooked the lake. The land had been settled by Schiller's parents over seventy years before and had become theirs under the provisions of the second Homestead Act. Now the cabins and the hillside belonged to the United States government, seized according to the Terrorist Property Reclamation Act. There was one cabin for each member of the team. Evans slept in the shack that had once belonged to Axe. The cabin was situated beside and just below the communications shack at the top of the hill. The cabins had not yet been reconstructed to accommodate the needs of the unit—storage space for the SFUs, personal computers to stay in touch with family and friends—but they had cots and bathrooms and that was enough for now.

Major Taylor hadn't bothered to close the door. Evans stood a respectful distance away, not listening but wanting to be there if Taylor needed anything. Evans also needed a moment alone to think. He knew Major Taylor. He knew *all* his men and he knew where this was going. The question was how to keep it from going there the best and cleanest way possible. When he was in the SEALs, one of the three things they taught him when debriefing a soldier was not to promise to send him back to the scene of an emotionally devastating action. "Purpose" was a better stimulus than "revenge." Taylor was going back, Evans couldn't help that. But he could control how he went back.

After just a few minutes, Taylor hung up and walked toward Evans. He had removed the glove from his right hand and stood in the doorway undoing the Velcro wristbands on the other glove.

"Are you all right?" Evans asked. It was a hollow question, he knew, but it was all he could think of to say.

"I've been better, sir," Taylor said.

"How is she?"

"In and out of unconsciousness," Taylor replied. He removed the glove and began unbuttoning the collar that held the hood in place. "The doctors are still running tests. The MRI was inconclusive." He choked. "She's got some broken bones in her leg that are going to need rods to put back together."

"Do the police have any idea what happened?"

"They do now," Taylor said.

"What do you mean?"

"One of the bastards cut a name in her face," Taylor said. He had to take a breath before continuing.

"Django?" Evans pressed. The second thing the

SEALs taught about debriefing a soldier was not to let an emotionally distraught man sit and think. Whatever was upsetting him was healthier on the outside than on the inside so clear heads could consider it instead of one muddled head.

"Yes, sir."

"Did that give the police a lead on finding the people who did this?" Evans asked.

"Not immediately," Taylor said. "It wasn't the perp's name."

"I don't understand."

"Before coming down here I had a run-in with some punks in the parking lot of my mom's building," Taylor told him. "They were listening to a Django Reinhardt jazz tape while they waited to make a drug deal."

"And you sent them running."

"Yes, sir," Taylor replied. "But somehow they found out who I was and came back. That was the name they left behind. Django. Cut on my mom, in her skin, like she was a fucking tree—"

"You don't have any other family up there, do you?" Evans asked. The third thing the SEALs taught about debriefing was that whenever someone got in too deep emotionally, it was best to try to direct the subject even slightly from the heart of the upset.

"No, sir. Just some close family friends. I'm going to meet them at the hospital." The major looked into the taller officer's eyes. "Commander, I know this is an important time for the team and I don't like bailing on you—"

"You're not bailing," Evans assured him. "If anything, I feel like we're bailing on you."

"On me?"

"We should be up there, helping you," Evans said. "In fact, I'd feel better if Colonel Lewis went with you."

"The colonel? Why, sir?"

"For support," Evans said.

"I have that, sir," Taylor replied. "I told you, we have friends there."

"I know," Evans said. "Friends for helping you get around the city, for making sure that your mother is taken care of. That isn't the kind of support I'm talking about."

"What then? The colonel isn't exactly Mr. Compassion."

"No, he isn't."

Taylor's eyes suddenly hardened. "Wait a minute, sir. You're talking about a chaperon. You're sending the colonel to keep me in line. Well, forget it. No one's going to stop me from doing whatever needs to be done."

"What needs to be done?" Evans asked.

"Sir? I need to nuke the scum who did this to my mother."

"That's not going to happen," Evans told him.

"It absolutely is, sir," Taylor assured him.

"You're not thinking clearly, Major—"

"I don't really care, sir," Taylor replied. "I'd resign my commission before I agreed to back off."

"Then do it," Evans said. "Now."

"Don't push me, sir."

"I'm damn well going to push!" Evans said. "If you think you're going to lone-wolf these people—"

"People? They're animals—"

"The law doesn't agree with you, and I'm not going to have one of my men roaming around breaking laws, looking for revenge."

"This isn't about revenge, it's about justice."

"It's about revenge," Evans said, "and revenge makes a man reckless and sloppy. The Viet Cong used to sacrifice small units so they could follow the enemy back to base and get a larger prize. Let the police find these people. The system will take care of justice. And failing that, there's the ultimate judge—"

"Which works fine for you, but not me," Taylor said.

"I can't wait for God to wring their fucking necks—"

"Enough, Major!"

Taylor pulled himself back. "I'm sorry, sir. But you don't understand. These aren't soldiers, they're punks. And if I let this go, if I let *them* go, I won't have any self-respect."

"You won't have any self-respect if you follow through," Evans assured him. "You know you can stalk them, kill them. You have to be better than that."

"Forgive me, sir, but that's real easy for you to say. It isn't your mother they busted up."

"No, it isn't," Evans said. "That's why I can see past this and that's why I'm asking you to trust me. We made a pledge to the President of the United States to do a job here. If you do anything that forces you to renege on *that* promise, that puts you on trial or sends you to jail, you'll do more than lose your self-respect. You'll expose this unit and you'll lose my respect. Giving in to anger, to emotion, takes no backbone at all. But fighting it, Major. *That* takes character."

Taylor was silent.

"And is becoming a vigilante the way to help your mother?" Evans asked. "Do you think she's going to want to come out of the hospital and find her only son in jail?"

"What you're saying isn't wrong," the major said. "But what I'm saying isn't wrong either."

"No," Evans agreed. "I just hope you'll pick the path that's right for more than just you."

Taylor looked away.

"I'll have Captain McIver make the travel arrangements," Evans said. "I'll contact you in your cabin, let you know when she'll be here."

"Thank you, sir," Taylor said.

Evans nodded and Taylor saluted. Then the major headed toward his cabin. Evans followed at a distance. He wasn't sure he had gotten through to Taylor. And though he didn't want to lose two men, he was certain now that he couldn't allow the major to go up there alone. He would tell McIver to arrange passage for two. Then he'd have a talk with Colonel Lewis. The colonel wouldn't like his instructions either, but Evans had a feeling that he'd do the right thing when it came down to it. Lewis was not emotionally involved, and he would put the well-being of a fellow soldier before other considerations.

As Evans walked toward his cabin to phone Captain McIver at Langley, he hoped that he was right. Lewis was also one of the most explosive soldiers he'd ever met.

Evans also hoped for one thing more.

That the president didn't need the Stealth team before Lewis and Taylor returned.

Nine

In the vacuum of space an object in motion keeps moving.

Though the bulk of its systems had shut down, the space shuttle *Venture* continued to orbit the earth. While it did, Commander Boring had instituted a series of emergency procedures. First, he cut off all communication with earth to conserve battery power. Next, he ordered the mission specialists to put on their space suits and return to their seats. Sitting still would conserve oxygen and would buy the crew extra time by letting them survive on the air supply of the EMU.

Working calmly but quickly, Boring and Karl went through the checklist of everything that might have gone wrong. For the primary and backup computers to have all gone down—not even drawing on battery power, which they were designed to do—would require a catastrophic failure in the master control system of the shuttle's computers. Perhaps a solar flare or ion barrage from the sun.

Possibly a storm of micrometeorites that had penetrated the ship's hull and disabled or shorted key electrical systems. Whatever it was, the temperature was falling steadily and there was not going to be a lot of time to find the problem, let alone fix it if and when they did.

That was when Boring made a command decision. Either they would spend time and the ship's fast-waning power looking for an answer that might not come, or they could attempt to return to earth. Boring checked the battery display. They had enough power for a deorbit burn. An educated guess gave them approximately thirty-six minutes of air. A landing would take about thirty minutes from the time the shuttle hit the atmosphere. He wanted to go for it.

Even in simulation, no one had ever attempted to land the space shuttle off one of the practiced flight patterns and without the benefit of at least some computer assistance.

Looks like this'll be the time, he thought.

The first thing Boring would have to do was let Houston know he was coming in. The Tactical Air Navigation system—TACAN—provided range and bearing data when it reached an altitude of 145,000 feet. When it descended to twenty thousand feet, more precise information about slant range, azimuth, and elevation was provided by the Microwave Scanning Beam Landing System—MSBLS— that, if necessary, could also guide the shuttle to a hands-free landing. If the computers could be restarted by that point in the descent, Boring and Linda Karl would not have to do everything manually. Hopefully, mission control could also guide them to a landing site.

The space shuttle was roughly the size of a DC-9. It would be able to land at most major airports, assuming Boring could position the shuttle to reach one and the tarmac could be cleared in time. It would also be extremely helpful if the landing field had Precision Approach Path Indicator lights, an electronic visual aid that told pilots whether they were coming in at the correct glide slope. Unlike conventional aircraft, the space shuttle approaches the ground at a twenty-degree angle, more than six times steeper than the three-degree slope of most jet planes. This is the result of presenting only the heat-resistant bottom of the aircraft to the atmosphere. Otherwise, the fires generated by the heat of reentry would incinerate the craft, similar to the way *Columbia* burned up. The shuttle lands without engines and, due to the placement of the windows, without a clear view of the airfield. Without PAPI lights or a computer, it would be difficult for Boring to make certain the wheels were the first thing to touch the ground.

So while keeping the radio on would consume power, Boring had no choice but to do it. Before switching his radio on and going into an abbreviated countdown, he turned to Linda.

"We are going to land," he said. "Our craft appears to be intact and we have our skills. We'll find a place to set down. We can do this."

Cool and focused, she flashed him a strong thumbs-up, then turned her eyes toward the viewport in front of her.

Boring adjusted the mouthpiece of his headset and turned the radio on. They were over the Indian Ocean at that point, which meant the shuttle would be coming down somewhere in or near North America. That was good, in terms of having ground support available to them. Boring told Linda to use the reaction control system rockets to maneuver them to deorbit attitude. That would position the shuttle for the belly-down "dive" into the atmosphere. Then he informed Houston what he was going to do. Mission control didn't comment on the plan other than to tell him they understood and would wait to hear from him. They added that ground personnel studying the *Venture*'s problem still had no idea what had caused the computers to go down. That made Boring feel better about what he was attempting to do. Trying to save their lives rather than allow them to die in space.

The commander went into a thirty-second countdown to burn. The propellant management subsystem became operational. The values were all operated electrically and pneumatically and could be controlled without the help of computers. Liquid oxygen and liquid hydrogen began to flow. Linda would have to fire the rockets manually. Boring told his pilot to give him a two-minute, thirty-second burn. He wanted to try and get out of orbit in one long burst instead of the usual three or four that were used to fine-tune their position. Each start-and-stop of the engines would cost him power he could not afford.

Linda fired the orbital maneuvering system engines when the countdown clock reached zero. The rockets decelerated the ship with a retrograde burn, and the crew felt the first G-forces they had experienced since achieving orbit. The view from the pilot windows changed from black space to a hint of blue spilling up from earth's atmosphere. There was a glint of red from the blazing OMS rockets.

Boring took control of the descent. It was a two-stick operation, with the left stick controlling roll and yaw and the right stick controlling the angle of descent. Ordinarily, Boring and Linda would be interfacing with the guidance, navigation, and flight control software using their CRT displays. But that was primarily to ensure that the shuttle reached its prime landing site at Cape Canaveral or its prime alternate site at Edwards Air Force Base in California. Right now Boring was hoping to get through the atmosphere. He'd worry about setting the shuttle down when they reached the stratosphere.

Since there were no inclination gauges to watch, Commander Boring closed his eyes. He had brought the shuttle down hundreds of times in the simulators. He knew how it felt. Early in training he had discovered that landing the

shuttle was not unlike snowboarding, which he had done as
a kid when visiting his grandparents in upstate New York.
He knew in exactly what position the fuselage needed to be
when it entered the atmosphere. Wings level, fuselage tilted
just so. He maneuvered the shuttle until it *felt* right. If they
hit the atmosphere correctly, with both the vertical component or "angle of attack" and horizontal component or
"sideslip angle" precisely right, they would be well positioned to make it back. It would then be a matter of Boring
and Karl using the seven aerodynamic control surfaces to
keep the shuttle at the proper angle. If not, if they hit the atmosphere wrong, the shuttle would either bounce back into
space like a stone skipping across a pond or they would
burn up within a matter of seconds.

The G-forces increased as they sped back to earth. The
temperature had dropped considerably. Boring could just
about see his breath.

The burn ended.

The *Venture* slapped the outer fringes of the atmosphere
and continued to fall. The G-forces increased as gravity
pulled on the shuttle. Boring felt it pushing him back and
down into the seat. The straps tightened automatically to
keep him snug. At the same time the crew compartment began to heat very quickly. He opened his eyes. The air outside the window turned wispy red, like the aurora borealis
in crimson. As he watched the flames and felt changes in
the sea of air beneath them, Boring made incremental ad-
justments on the stick controls. A slight tug with the left-
hand control to adjust the angle of attack, then watching
for the aurora to even out. A slight shift with the right-hand
control to even the sideslip angle as the thickness of the air
changed. Linda Karl was watching the temperature, clock,
and altimeter readouts, which were still operating. She was
alert and ready to perform additional functions at Boring's
command.

Boring's actions became automatic. He would feel the shuttle shift, feel it in his backside and spine. His arms would work accordingly. His eyes would see the fires shift slightly to one side or the other. His hands would compensate. No thought, just action. Less than ten seconds had passed since they started through the exosphere. It would take fifteen minutes to make it through the upper levels of the atmosphere.

It was going to be a long, long ride home.

Ten

The White House
Monday, 2:29 P.M.

President John Gordon was on the phone listening to the communications between NASA mission control and tracking stations around the world. Since the *Venture* began its descent there had been no communications at all from the vessel. That was to be expected, since the highly charged ionosphere prevented radio signals from reaching the earth. But this situation was obviously different from previous space flights. Not only the spacecraft was at stake. If it survived, but not intact, anything in its flight path would be in jeopardy.

The president's heart was punching the bottom of his throat and the inside of his collar was growing cool with sweat. He prayed fervently for the safe return of the spacecraft. When Gordon played basketball in high school, he had been sidelined with a knee injury for just over a month. Sitting on the bench, he learned one very important fact: It is much more difficult being a helpless observer to something than an active participant. He had not been this concerned when his own life was at risk during the recent attack on the White House.

Suddenly, Executive Secretary Laura Richmond turned to him. "Mr. President, General Rogers is on line three."

"Thank you." The president punched the button. General Jesse Rogers had told Gordon that he would call as soon as the Department of Defense had information on the status of the satellite *Venture* had put into orbit. "What have you got, General?"

"Nothing good," the deep-voiced Rogers told him. "Something definitely happened to the ESP satellite shortly after it was released."

"Was it accidental or intentional?"

"We're leaning toward sabotage, sir," Rogers said.

"Jesus, General." The president immediately thought of the Huntsmen, the group that had attempted to kill him and Vice President Catlin. The cabal had successfully infiltrated numerous areas of the government and the military. Perhaps hitting the ESP and limiting the Pentagon's intelligence-gathering capabilities was part of a master plan.

"NASA analyzed the shuttle's data records from the moments before the computers shut down," Rogers went on. "*Venture* was hit with a severe electromagnetic burst that affected only the computer systems. And at literally the same time, DOD lost control of the satellite."

"Why couldn't that be a result of the satellite malfunctioning?" the president asked.

"Because telemetry is still being received from the ESP," Rogers told him. "The readings are perfectly normal. It's what they call 'dead rising,' when a satellite continues to orbit the planet without responding through established contact parameters."

"I see. What's the next step?" the president asked. "Is the ESP a danger to other satellites?"

"Unfortunately, we won't know that until they can figure out what caused the electromagnetic—" Rogers paused. "Wait a minute, sir. We're getting something on the shuttle."

Just then, the president noticed CNN cut away from tape of that morning's shuttle launch to anchor Ross Belvera. There was an inset of a reporter talking to him from the Manned Spacecraft Center. The president reached for the remote and punched up the volume.

"—picking up radar blip of what may be the shuttle," reporter Yuri Lincoln was telling Belvera.

"They think they have the shuttle," General Rogers said. "Long-range radar at Elmendorf AFB in Alaska has acquired the blip."

"I know. I just saw it on CNN," the president said. "Have there been any communications?"

"Only briefly, sir," Rogers said. "The ship appears to have come through the atmosphere intact. Speed about normal, nearly twice the speed of sound. This is incredible, sir."

"You told me Commander Boring can fly without electronics, but can he *land* the shuttle?" the president asked.

"Hold on, sir," Rogers said. He was speaking with someone.

The president tried not to think of the options they might be facing in the next few minutes. The shuttle was not engine-powered in the atmosphere. It was essentially gliding to earth. He knew that standard operating procedure during a shuttle reentry was to fly in a big wide S pattern and let the atmosphere brake the ship on the way down. He did not know whether that could be done entirely without onboard computers.

"That's an affirmative on the manual landing," Rogers informed the president. "The only difference is that in manual mode Commander Boring and Pilot Karl are going to have to 'feel' the airstream. They'll have to work the wing elevons and rudder pedals manually to bring her down. It's difficult but it's doable. There are still two big problems, however," the general went on. "The first is to ascertain what condition the shuttle's life support systems are in. The computers *do* control that. Boring isn't certain exactly how much air they have left since the monitors are off-line. Unfortunately, even if they get low enough, they can't just open a window. The airflow would destabilize the craft."

"Understood. What's the second problem?"

"The *Venture*'s well north of where it needs to be to set down in Florida or California," Rogers informed him. "It's about two hundred miles southwest of the Aleutians instead of over the Pacific heading toward the Baja Peninsula. Boring doesn't think he can swing the ship south without the computers to help navigate. It's all he can do right now to keep it level."

"Which means?"

"At nearly mach-two, the *Venture* should reach the continental coast in roughly five minutes," Rogers said. "After that it will go into its final descent. I'm looking at a computer simulation now. Current projections put touchdown somewhere in the northern Midwest. Excuse me, sir—if you can hold the line we've got some new information coming in."

While the president waited, he watched as CNN switched to a live picture of the space shuttle, captured by an airborne camera crew in Seattle. The image was shaky and indistinct, showing the *Venture* as a small black shape against the misty blue-white sky. There was a contrail of water vapor behind the ship as it sped through the atmosphere. At this height the shuttle was slowing fast. Yet it was still generating sufficient air friction to evaporate airborne water droplets.

"Mr. President, they're saying that a number of airports could conceivably accommodate the spacecraft," Rogers said. "Denver, Chicago, St. Paul, and Minneapolis. Mission control's looking at O'Hare as the most likely site. If Boring has the ability to fine-tune his approach and the weather isn't a problem, that gives him the most runways and the most room. The problem is it's especially windy there right now. He's going to have a very bumpy ride. NASA's working with the FAA to immediately clear the air lanes of traffic. They're landing all commercial and military airplanes ASAP or diverting them to the south. They're also sending airplanes back to the gates to clear the runways."

"General," the president said, "we're letting the shuttle come in toward a metropolitan area. Across several of them actually."

"Right now we don't have a choice, sir," Rogers said. "Boring doesn't have enough control to turn the shuttle back to sea and ditch in the Pacific. A manual turn that extreme, at this level and speed, would cause the shuttle to invert and send it out of control. It could hit any number of cities along the western coast."

The president knew what was coming. He didn't like it.

"Sir, we're going to have to consider the option of aborting the reentry," Rogers said.

"You mean shoot it down," the president said. He wanted to be very clear about that.

"Yes, Mr. President," Rogers said. "That is the current position of NORAD." Once the outward-looking eyes against a Soviet attack, the North American Aerospace Defense Command now monitored all flights entering and within American airspace. In the aftermath of the September 2001 enemy attacks they were the firewall against aerial attacks. Only the president could countermand a NORAD decision.

"How soon will that decision have to be made?" the president asked.

"We don't have a lot of time," Rogers said. "Maybe six or seven minutes from now, when we have a better idea of the shuttle's trajectory and the condition of the crew."

"Who would handle the operation?" the president asked.

"F-16s from the 611th Combat Operations Flight are being scrambled out of Elmendorf," Rogers told him. "They'll swing across the Gulf and intercept the target over the Cascades."

"It's not a target yet, General," the president pointed out.

"I'm sorry, sir," Rogers said.

"What are they armed with?" the president asked.

"Sidewinder missiles," Rogers told him.

"All right," Gordon said. "I'll want the joint chiefs in on this."

"They're standing by, sir," Rogers said. "I've got a call from our aeronautics people. I'll be right back, sir."

Gordon thanked the general, then punched the phone back to mission control. They had raised the shuttle again and were talking to Boring. With relative calm, the commander was describing the condition of the shuttle. The commander said that he and Linda Karl were struggling to keep the ship steady. They had already shut down life support in the mid-deck where the mission specialists were wearing their EMUs. Boring felt that would give him and Karl enough oxygen and heat to complete the mission.

No one talked after that. They were listening. Waiting perhaps for Commander Boring to give them some clear indication about what to do. It would be easier, they knew, if any abort requests were to come from him.

A moment later General Rogers came back on the line. "Sir, we've calculated the trajectory and fuel reserves of the shuttle."

"And?"

"None of the scenarios is encouraging," Rogers said. "They've got the shuttle going down anywhere from around Billings, Montana, to Chicago."

"Based on projections," the president said.

"Yes, sir," Rogers said.

President Gordon watched the shuttle on CNN. The calculations did not take into account the human factor. Boring had already done things no one had anticipated. He'd deorbited a virtually dead shuttle and he was still flying. He might surprise them again.

"Where are the F-16s now?" the president asked.

"They're within seventy-five seconds of achieving Stinger range," Rogers informed him. "That will occur at five miles due west of the shuttle. They'll close in to a range of a half mile."

"What's the delay time after launch?"

"Three miles a minute," Rogers said. "If we wait until the shuttle is much lower and it starts an uncontrolled descent, we may not have time to abort."

"What about debris?" the president asked.

"We anticipate seventy- to eighty-five-percent destruction in the blast," Rogers said.

"Which means we'll still have tons of debris raining down."

"That's correct, sir," Rogers said. "That's still less than the intact shuttle itself."

"All right," the president said. Gordon's voice was calm even though he was not. "We're going to take this moment to moment. Every update you get, I want it too."

"Yes, sir," Rogers said.

The president held the phone tightly as he turned back to the television. Laura was also watching. The shuttle image was larger now. Each sudden wobble of the delta wings, each sputter or shift in the contrail caused the president's throat to tighten, his palms to grow even damper.

Is this the moment the shuttle is going to go down? he wondered. How many lives on the ground would the president's hesitation cost?

"Mr. President," Rogers said suddenly, "the simulation

software's given us an update. We've got him coming down in the Chicago area."

"Do you know exactly where?"

"Not yet," Rogers said.

The president continued to watch the TV. He prayed for a moment. Then he did the only thing his conscience would let him do.

General Rogers acknowledged and said he would relay the order.

Eleven

Lake Miasalaro, West Virginia
Monday, 2:30 P.M.

The door to Lewis's cabin was open, but Evans rapped on it anyway. The major was inside taking off his SFU. It was a difficult process, since the wearer had to make sure to touch the suit only under the flaps that concealed the zippers and snaps. Otherwise, oil from the fingertips would stain the fabric and leave a highly visible smudge. He also had to make certain that the suit pieces hung only on their specially constructed hangers. Lint and threads picked up from bedding or seat cushions, even dustballs kicked up from the floor, might cling to the suits and be perfectly visible when it went into stealth mode.

Colonel Lewis was facing the door. There was a cot behind him and an unstained oak desk to the right, near the window. The chest in which the SFU was stored was standing at the foot of the cot.

Lewis stood just under five feet nine, most of it strong,

cable-thick muscle. The dark-eyed officer looked up when Evans knocked.

"Come in, sir," Lewis said.

The colonel's tone was formal and he did not initiate conversation. He made only brief eye contact. The tough Army officer hated having to answer to a Navy man, and Evans knew and understood that. Lewis continued to remove the SFU as the commander entered.

Evans slipped off the small headphones he was wearing. He let them rest around his neck. "Major Taylor just spoke with the doctors in Philadelphia," Evans said.

"How is Mrs. Taylor?" Lewis asked, still not looking up.

"Not well," Evans told him. "Major Taylor is going back to Philadelphia to be with her."

"Right," Lewis said. "You know, I was thinking about that just now. We don't have a personnel pool to draw from. When we start working on surveillance and combat tactics we'll have to engineer a down-one option—"

"Down two," Evans said.

"Excuse me?"

"I want you to go with him," Evans said.

Lewis looked up. "To do what, sir?"

"To keep him focused," Evans said.

"On what, sir?"

"On what he's going up there to do," Evans said.

Lewis smiled humorlessly. "You want me to babysit him, sir?"

"I've told you what I want you to do," Evans replied.

"Yes, sir, you did," Lewis said. He continued to remove the SFU.

Evans said that he'd let Lewis know the travel arrangements, then turned to go.

"Sir?" Lewis said.

Evans turned back. "Colonel?"

"Are you sure you want me to be the one doing this?" Lewis asked.

"Yes."

"I see, sir," Lewis said. He glanced at the bowie knife he kept in a sheath on his night table. "Because if it were up to me, I'd just as soon bring Mrs. Taylor a couple of scalps instead of flowers."

"This isn't about what you want," Evans reminded him. "It's about what's best for the Taylors and for the team. Now, can you do it?"

"Yes, sir," Lewis said.

"Thank you, Colonel," Evans said.

As the commander turned to leave, he heard Captain McIver's voice in his headphones.

"Commander?"

"Yes?" Evans said as he slipped them on.

"Sir, we're going to have to put Major Taylor on a train," she said. "No flights are taking off from any landing strip in the East."

"Why?" Evans asked.

"They're keeping civilian and military runways open for air traffic turning back from the Midwest," McIver told him. "The backup may last well into the night."

"What's happening in the Midwest?" Evans asked.

"The space shuttle is off course, crippled, and heading for the Chicago area," she told him.

Twelve

15 miles from 45°N, 95°W
Monday, 1:47 P.M., CST

As the space shuttle sliced through the air above the Amer-
ican heartland, Commander Boring had made two requests
to NASA. First was that the Air Force be prepared to shoot
the shuttle down before it neared a populated area. Through
mission control, DOD replied that those preparations were
being made. Now, just a few minutes before touchdown,
Boring was uncertain whether he could reach O'Hare or
land there with precision. He was coming down fast, nearly
350 miles an hour, which was over a hundred miles an hour
faster than he should be traveling. Without computers to
handle the S turns and help maintain the angle of descent, all
of which were preprogrammed, he had probably been off
just a little. A few hundred feet on each turn, a half-degree
too steep—those would have been completely acceptable
in a powered aircraft or in a sailplane. But in a ship of this
size and weight, the difference could be catastrophic. Thus,

with about three minutes to go, Boring requested that the landing be terminated.

NASA reported that the president would not execute the operation. He had given the following order: Commander Boring is instructed to bring the shuttle home safely.

The veteran space pilot was too busy trying to control the ship to argue. Boring acknowledged the order, then shut down the heating system at five thousand feet to conserve what little battery power they had left. It was twenty-two degrees in the compartment. The air supply was thinning. Boring felt as though he were sitting on a beach in the winter as the sun went down and the temperature of the sand, sea, and air sucked the warmth out of him.

And he still needed to find a place to set down. That decision would have to be made soon before the shuttle made the decision for him.

"Mission control, where is *Venture* relative to Scott AFB?" Boring asked. His voice was rattling. They were encountering turbulence.

"Their radar is down," Dean Michaels replied. "O'Hare puts you at 120 miles due north of Scott."

"I don't have 120 miles in me," Boring said. "I'm going down in about thirty, max."

"Given your current rate of descent we concur," Michaels replied.

"What about O'Hare, or Chicago Midway?"

"O'Hare's thirty-five miles to the north and Midway's fields aren't long enough," Michaels told him.

As the shuttle continued to fall, the air thinned. The thermal currents, which began to diminish after noon, provided even less support than they did at higher altitudes. Boring felt control of the shuttle slipping out from under him. The speed and angle of descent were becoming more pronounced.

As the nose dropped, the overhead windows lowered.

When they were almost directly in front of Boring he saw something in the distance. Something he might be able to reach, especially if he kept the landing gear retracted to reduce air friction. Even if he couldn't land safely, at least he'd be able to avoid collateral damage on the ground.

"Mission control—I may have a landing site," Boring said. His teeth were chattering. Yet in spite of the cold he was perspiring along the neckline and down his sides. His palms too were greasy with sweat. His breath was causing the windshields to fog around the edges.

"What is the target?" Michaels asked.

Boring didn't answer. The shuttle was losing altitude quickly and he was busy trying to keep it airborne. Linda Karl was losing her fight with the wing elevons. The batteries had begun to die and the hydraulic actuators were slowing. Boring compensated by using the rudder pedals to bank into the head wind. It gave them a tweak of a lift each time he nosed from port to starboard.

"*Venture,* do you need us to do anything?" Michaels pressed.

"Negative!" Boring yelled as the rattling grew louder. They were nearly parallel to the ground instead of nose-up twenty degrees and they were still coming in too fast. Fortunately, the target zone was huge.

If he could reach it.

Thirteen

Lake Miasalaro, West Virginia
Monday, 2:48 P.M.

Commander Evans and the remaining members of the
Stealth Warrior team gathered in the com-shack and
watched television. As the gleaming white craft descended,
the image grew larger and clearer. Evans listened to the
broadcast of the sonic booms as the shuttle sped over the
counties of Bureau, La Salle, Kendall, and Will and headed
toward Chicago. According to the newscast cutaways, people were abandoning their cars in the city proper, leaving
the streets and heading into basements, Cold War air raid
shelters, and other underground areas in case the *Venture*
came down in the street.

"They're lucky in one respect," Captain Holly said.

"About what?" MCPO Diaz asked.

"There probably wasn't a lot of fuel left in that ship,"
Holly pointed out. "If the commander can't set her down,
whatever damage occurs will be from the crash itself."

"At the speed they're going, that's gonna be pretty

severe," Diaz said. "And who knows what kind of stuff they could hit. Oil tanks, a power plant, the bottom of a skyscraper."

"God, please get them down," Holly said.

Evans quietly seconded that.

Victoria shook her head. "Whatever happens, I can just hear the doomsaying after this."

"What do you mean?" Diaz asked.

"The environmentalists are all going to cry, 'What if this had happened while it was still carrying a plutonium-powered satellite? Lethal radiation would be everywhere.' "

"Well, it would be," Diaz said.

"There's risk in everything humans do," Victoria said.

"And I'm not saying space exploration isn't worth that risk," Diaz added. "But Chicago would be like the Forbidden Zone in *Planet of the Apes*. Nothing but busted-up landmarks and mutants for decades."

"It'd be our own fault," Holly pointed out.

"How so?" Diaz asked.

"We need the rapid-response containment force that NASA's been pushing for," he said. "But Congress won't spend the bucks, the dumb bastards. Mega-billions to rebuild Iraq, a piss-stream to secure a human presence off-planet which includes ground support for the effort. Those are the people the environmentalists should be PO'ed at. The answers to human survival are *in* space."

"Amen to that," Victoria said. "Which is another thing that'll happen, regardless of whether the ship gets down safely. The bleeding-heart myopics will all resume their mantra, 'All this money wasted on outer space research when we have problems here on earth.' They'll resume the whining using the very satellites and computers developed for the space program."

"Hey, at least the space program gets serious funding," Diaz said.

"Serious?" Victoria said. "Only for military programs. The exploration stuff is okayed as a cover for what really matters to Congress. Spying and weapons in earth orbit."

"At least NASA still gets money for that," Diaz said. "I've been writing congressmen and petitioning superiors for years to do more about exploring and colonizing the sea, using the oceans to develop food and electricity. Nothing ever happens."

"The oceans will die with the rest of the planet," Victoria said. "The answer is space. We've got to move away from where we first crawled out from."

The debate went on. Evans only half-listened. It was probably good for the others to be able to vent, but he couldn't get involved. All he could do was pray for the shuttle crew and try to imagine what Commander Boring was going through. Command was a tough enough responsibility. To be in command of this mission, at this point, was unimaginable. Boring had to be working on heightened instinct and survival senses with a hint of intellect to keep it all greased. Maybe a touch of religion, which so many people found in crisis situations.

Evans hoped so. As the shuttle dropped lower and lower, its speed relatively undiminished, Evans knew something else. That Boring would need a miracle to bring the bird in.

Fourteen

Chicago, Illinois
Monday, 1:51 P.M.

Commander Boring had never been to Chicago. He had always intended to visit. He wanted to check out the Billy-goat Tavern and see the Second City troupe perform. But he'd never gotten around to it until now. The irony was awful, though Boring didn't have time to think about it.

As Boring tried to control the shuttle, relentless winds batted the craft's delta wings from side to side. Just keeping the *Venture* stable was taking most of his attention.

Boring had decided to try to follow the Chicago River for three reasons. First, if the shuttle went down prematurely, it would hit mostly water. Second, there were no tall buildings on the river. He had been sufficiently high to avoid the fourteen-hundred-foot-tall Sears Tower on his southerly approach. Now he was under one thousand feet and that was no longer possible. Third, the Chicago River flowed west from Lake Michigan. The commander could concentrate more on flying than on navigating through the vapor-hazed window.

"Seven hundred feet and descending at twenty FPS," Linda Karl informed him, her voice steady.

Twenty feet per second was too fast. That would put the shuttle down in a little over a half minute, short of Lake Shore Drive and the murky waters of Lake Michigan.

"Fuel cell reading," Boring demanded.

"Two kilowatts," she replied.

What he was considering would leave the shuttle with no power at all. But he had no choice. "Burn the aft RCS till shutdown!" Boring ordered.

Karl acknowledged and did as she was told.

The reaction control system was designed to provide thrust for attitude and velocity changes in orbit. There was a kick and a muffled roar as the rockets engaged in the back of the shuttle. The nose came up slightly, and Boring used the translational hand controllers to try to nurse the shuttle up on the vertical axis. He gained them a little altitude before the engines closed down along with the batteries. The RCS had burned for just a little over a second. The air circulation in the compartment went off. The shuttle was eerily silent. They could hear the whistle of the wind as they nosed back down.

"Altimeter shutdown," Karl said. "The last reading was seven hundred and forty feet."

The burn had given them a boost of fifty feet or so. With complete loss of elevon and rudder control, that might not be enough to get them to the lake.

"Be ready for emergency egress!" Boring said.

Without power he couldn't communicate the command to the mid-deck. But if they managed to reach water, the crew there would know what to do. As soon as the shuttle came to a stop, one of the mission specialists would open the emergency hatch and pull a lanyard to inflate the emergency egress slide. Boring and Karl would escape via the left overhead window. The outer pane was designed to

come free by pulling a T handle located forward of the
flight deck center console between Boring and Karl.

Though Boring held onto the controllers, the ship was
no longer under his control. The *Venture* was nosing down
fast, and Boring hoped that it didn't invert on its way
down. But the burn had had its desired effect. The shuttle
passed over Lake Shore Drive with forty feet to spare. It
twisted to the north, toward Streeter Drive and the Navy
Pier beyond.

He could see the dim shape of the cruise boats ahead as
the shuttle twisted to the port side and simultaneously
nosed down.

Traveling at 215 miles an hour, the *Venture* hit the shallow water with a crack that shook the windows of surrounding buildings. The foredeck's own windows were
punched in and the shuttle kept going. Sand, glass, and
structural matter rushed in, covering Boring and Karl and
killing them instantly. A moment later the nose of the shuttle stopped moving forward. But the fuselage and tail kept
going. The vessel flipped over, its tail section coming down
on a cruising yacht and slicing the *Robinson* in two. Waves
surged upward followed by steam as water washed against
the still-hot belly of the shuttle. The Pier's four-masted
schooner *Windy* was moored beside the yacht. It rocked vi-
olently, nearly tipping over as the waves battered it east,
and then losing one of its masts as it rocked west with the
backwash and smacked against the pier.

The *Venture* settled on its back. The lower portion of the
ship was still exposed. Patrol boats of the Marine Division,
Special Operations section, of the Chicago police department's Special Functions Group sped toward the scene.
Except for distant sirens as fire engines and other emergency vehicles raced to the shore, the site was quiet.

The space shuttle's emergency hatch was just above the
waterline. The door blew open on the lakeward-side of the

craft as the *Venture* filled with water. It began to sink lower into the silt. Three space-suited figures emerged through the steam and smoke. Dr. Curtiz tried to make his way to the front of the shuttle. Boring and Karl had not been wearing space suits. They might drown as water rushed in. But the thick steam made it impossible to see and the churning waters made it difficult to maneuver with the suit on. The other crew members grabbed him and they huddled together in the water. Large and small bubbles slipped from under the fallen shuttle as if the water was boiling. The astronauts bobbed on the choppy waters, buoyed by their airtight suits.

Less than a half-minute later the first of the patrol boats stopped nearby. Several officers in wet suits jumped into the water while others threw life preservers to the astronauts.

Within fifteen minutes helicopters from the Coast Guard's 9th District Marine Safety Office had arrived. Active-duty underwater specialists trained in rescue and rapid field physical care went into the shuttle to assist police units. The debris was thick and the escaping air continued to generate thick, blinding sheets of bubbles. It took another twenty minutes for the heavy torches and vacuum hoses to arrive. That allowed the Coast Guard team to draw off sand and cut through the crushed structural debris. It was nearly ninety minutes before the bodies of Commander Boring and Pilot Karl could be reached, and another ten minutes before they had been removed. It was a small consolation for the rescue team to know that the two had died on impact.

The other crew members had been airlifted to the Louis A. Weiss Memorial Hospital on North Marine Drive. Remarkably, the mid-deck of the space shuttle had not suffered very much damage and the mission specialists were all in good shape. Every one of them could not stop talking about the miracle Commander Boring and Pilot Karl had pulled off.

Everyone except for Dr. Gregg.

He was dazed and he was hurt. But in his lucid moments he was one thing more.

Astonished.

Fifteen

Lake Miasalaro, West Virginia
Monday, 2:52 P.M.

Commander Evans, Victoria Hudson, Peter Holly, and Rodrigo Diaz were still watching the TV coverage of the shuttle's approach to Chicago. Evans had not yet removed his SFU; there hadn't been time to change and he didn't want to leave until he knew how this turned out.

The squarish com-shack used by the Stealth Warrior team was little changed from when the Huntsmen communications chief, Mack McQueen, had been stationed there. There was a thirty-two-inch Zenith TV beside the window in the north wall. Along the west wall, heavy oak shelves were crammed with computer, radio, and telecommunications equipment. There was also a fifteen-inch radar screen that tapped into an early-warning post higher in the hills. Some of the equipment had been built by McQueen and some of it had been bought from Russian dealers who had redirected it as the system was being shipped to St. Petersburg from a decommissioned listening post on the Chukchi

Peninsula, near the Bering Strait. The Russian equipment had been bolstered by technology bought or appropriated from American firms that had been designing com-systems for the aborted Strategic Defense Initiative program during the Reagan years. Neither Diaz nor Victoria could see anything that needed updating. The only equipment that had been added was a TAC-SAT secure phone that the president could call directly. The mobile unit sat on the gunmetal desk in a black plastic case that was about the size and shape of a videocassette recorder.

Like most of the other cabins around the lake, the comshack was built of cinder block, painted flat white. It was cold and uninteresting. It didn't have the smell of aged West Virginia oak that permeated Evans's cabin, the cabin Axe's parents had built over eighty years before.

As the team watched the TV, the phone beeped—the landline, not the TAC-SAT. Victoria took the call. It was Captain McIver. Victoria handed the phone to Evans.

McIver said that she had dropped Taylor and Lewis off at Union Station in Washington, D.C. The men—the two "very, very unhappy men," as she described them—were catching the Acela to Philadelphia. Evans thanked the Air Force officer. Absolutely nothing was easy where the Stealth Warrior unit was concerned. Not the personalities from different elite forces, not the lack of depth in personnel that Lewis was concerned about, and not the cabin fever they all knew could hit them at any time. But serving as liaison between the team and the outside world was especially difficult. There hadn't been time for McIver to drive out. So she'd stopped what she was doing to requisition a pilot and chopper and fly to Lake Miasalaro. They'd rendezvoused in a clearing a quarter mile from the base. Because the Stealth Warrior team did not officially exist, the pilot could not know who they were picking up or why. Besides, it would not do for anyone to see military vehicles prowling around the area, either by eye or by satellite. There were still Huntsmen out there, and they might have access to satellites that the military used to watch American militia and paramilitary organizations. General Brad Jackson at Langley had been given a standing order by President Gordon that McIver be allowed to tend to "The St. War Project" whenever the need arose. That had created some tension between McIver, the general, and other high-ranking officers at Langley. But McIver didn't care what other people thought. Like Evans, like the other soldiers and the two civilians who had committed themselves to this undertaking, McIver only cared about one thing.

Doing what was right.

When McIver hung up, Evans returned to watching the shuttle drama unfold on TV. He stood off to the side, his long arms loosely folded. The shorter Diaz was beside him. Though aircraft had been grounded throughout Illinois, cameras located on the tops of various buildings around town were recording the spacecraft's dramatic descent.

Victoria was sitting on the edge of the desk, beside a computer to which all the equipment was hardwired. The only other items on the desk were the telephone, her own laptop, and several long plastic storage units that contained diskettes that Evans had brought from DARPA. All the specifications and research for the SFUs was on those disks. The plastic units were closed and could only be opened with a keypad located on the front. If an incorrect number were entered, a battery pack would send an electrical charge through a metal strip that touched the tops of all the diskettes. Everything on them would be erased.

Captain Holly was standing on the opposite side of the cabin from the other two men. The Air Force pilot was hugging himself tightly. The Texas-born Holly had been talking to himself as the shuttle descended—talking to the *Venture* really, alternately telling the shuttle to do what it was made to do and to give the commander a break.

"Ride, you sumbitch," Holly said loudly. "Don't go lame."

Holly was taking this all very personally, and Evans understood that. The captain had met Boring once at an Air Education and Training Command seminar. Though they were there for different reasons—Holly's expertise was in stealth aircraft, and he was there to give engineers a pilot's perspective on the latest designs—Holly and Boring had enjoyed one another's "I'm here to push the envelope" attitude. Testing technology in simulators and on computers was a good start. But the only way to really move aeronautics forward was, as Holly once put it, "To put that stuff in a plane and see if it'll fly."

The pilot shot up his fist in triumph when Boring, hanging perilously low over Chicago, nursed a short burn from his engines. That gave the shuttle the bump it needed to reach Lake Michigan. But the elation turned to concern, then sadness, then dejection as they watched the shuttle do a slow, ugly backflip into the lake. Holly knew from the way the nose hit hard, in shallow water, that Boring and his pilot could not have survived. He said so, but stayed to watch the recovery efforts. He did that more out of respect for the crew than curiosity. Commander Evans, however, did not give up hope. He would not, not until the bodies were removed. That was just the way he looked at things.

Shortly after McIver called, the TAC-SAT phone beeped. Evans looked at Victoria.

"It's more than the shuttle," she said.

Evans nodded. He turned and picked up the flat receiver. "Commander Evans here, sir."

"Commander, you know about the shuttle."

"Yes, sir."

"We have a situation," the president went on, "one that caused the shuttle to come down the way it did. One that's apparently going to get a lot worse. I'm forwarding an E-mail we received here a short time ago. We're going to be discussing it here but I want you to have a look at it. I'm also sending along a file on the shuttle's cargo."

Victoria had already punched in the secure access code that would allow them to receive the president's E-mail. Holly and Diaz asked permission to have a look as it came through. Evans granted it. The three of them gathered behind Victoria and read the terse communication.

"Lord in heaven," Holly said as he looked at it.

It was indeed more than the shuttle.

Sixteen

The Northeast Corridor
Monday, 3:35 P.M.

The train sped north along the industrialized mid-Atlantic coast. It stopped in Baltimore, Maryland, before heading northeast toward Wilmington. The next stop after that would be 30th Street Station in Philadelphia. It was a short ride that seemed endless, and Taylor knew why.

Thought. Thought slowed everything down.

Hank Taylor was looking out the window, but his mind was not on the view. Offices, factories, and waterways flashed by, but all he could see was one thing: the faces of the bastards he had confronted in the parking lot of the Park Drive Manor apartment complex. He was remembering them, trying to recall every detail he could, even the smells in the car. Fast-food smells. Cigarette smells. Liquor smells. He was etching the details into his brain. He could still feel himself standing there, thinking about what he'd have to do to take them out—

"Fuck!" he snarled as he punched the headrest of the seat in front of him, jabbed it hard.

"Hey!" yelled the occupant as the chair bounced. The beefy young businessman rose on the armrest, turned around, and glared at the man who had struck the seat.

Taylor glowered back at the man. He didn't see a young executive looking down at him. He saw the arrogant eyes of all those punks in the parking lot. They were glaring at him from the darkness of their car. He wanted to close those eyes, their mouths—

Lewis was sitting in the aisle seat. He reached his arm across his companion, all the way to the window, gently restraining him. "Reel it in, tiger," Lewis said softly but firmly.

"Excuse you!" the businessman said.

"I'm sorry, sir," Lewis said. "It won't happen again."

"It better not," the businessman replied. "Next time I get the conductor and your friend will be—"

"Sir," Lewis said, "go back to your laptop before you get *me* mad."

The businessman huffed and turned around. Taylor's entire body was taut. His eyes had dropped and he was staring at the back of the seat.

"Taylor?" Lewis said. "Are you all right?"

Taylor looked at the square-jawed colonel. He could see the coiled strength under the colonel's windbreaker. Then he looked back at the window.

"I'm okay, sir," Taylor said. Even though the men were officially civilians until they returned to base, the young medical officer had felt compelled to acknowledge the other man's rank. He had to watch that. You never knew when another on-leave soldier might overhear them, start talking to them, push the conversation into places it wasn't free to go.

"Are you sure?" Lewis asked.

"Yeah," Taylor said.

Lewis sat back, but he continued to regard Taylor. "Who was it?" the colonel asked.

"Who was what?" Taylor replied.

"Who were you punching at?" Lewis asked Taylor. "Was it one of those punks?"

"Who else?"

"I don't know," Lewis replied. "Maybe the commander for sending me. Maybe you."

"Me? Why would I be punching at me?"

"I'm not sure," Lewis said. "I get mad at myself a lot, usually when I don't do something as well as I should. I was thinking you might be mad at yourself for being somewhere else while all this was going down. Or maybe for being the trigger in the first place. I don't know."

Taylor looked at his fist, which was still tightly balled. He wondered if Lewis might be right. The anger was just a big, surging mass inside him.

"What I *do* know is that you better calm down," Lewis said. "Punching seats doesn't help anything."

"No, it doesn't," Taylor agreed. "Thank you."

"You're welcome," Lewis said.

The young African-American turned and looked back out the window. The world continued to blow past the high-speed train, layer upon layer of *things*. Taylor looked at the scenery now. Some of it was too distant to see clearly, some of it was too close and moving too fast to make out at all. Taylor let his eyes focus on nothing in particular. It was all in his head anyway. Everything he needed to see. The faces of the punks.

The more he thought about it, the more Taylor wondered if Colonel Lewis was right. Maybe Taylor was partly angry with himself for having started the whole damn thing. For having gone into the parking lot that night and chasing the drug dealers away. It wasn't the wrong thing to do. Each time he came home on leave the area around the building had gotten a little worse. After everything his mother had done for him, working long hours at the apartment building's beauty salon to help put him through medical school and make their apartment "our sweet little nest," as she used to call it, Taylor had gone down there to try and *keep* the apartment sweet. And quiet. And safe.

Maybe you should have anticipated how low these animals would go, he told himself. Yet if he hadn't done something, his mother might have been hurt eventually, if not by these people, then by someone else. *And what about the simple morality of doing the right thing?* he asked himself. He wondered what Evans would have to say about that. That he shouldn't have gotten involved? That he should have left it up to the police or God?

Hank Taylor balled his fist even tighter, then relaxed it. He tried to relax himself. Hitting the seat again wouldn't do any good. Taylor closed his eyes and did what he used to do as a young student, a *zujitsu-ka,* at Master Ruiz's dojo. First, he reflected on the system's motto. *A zujitsu-ka must be gentle in life and ferocious in combat.* Then he did what he and the other students used to do after class. They would sit on the floor, close their eyes, and picture the moves they had learned. That would help them to remember the kicks and blocks and strikes. They would apply the moves mentally, reinforce whatever the body had learned.

Right now Taylor pictured himself using his black-belt skills, employing rapid-fire combinations of a palm-heel strike, an elbow strike, a roundhouse kick, and a bear claw rake to the eyes. A hip throw to put his target on the ground and a heel on the throat or back of the neck.

A snap.

Taylor felt the anger subside. He started to crash as he thought about his mother. But he knew where the rage was and he knew something else.

That he would have no trouble getting to it again when the time was right. No trouble at all.

Seventeen

With the television droning in the background, the four members of the Stealth Warrior team studied the president's E-mail. Their mood had changed considerably since it arrived. Suddenly, the four of them were no longer observers in this event but participants.

The message was not what Victoria had been expecting. She thought there would be a threat of further attacks unless money was paid or prisoners were freed or some other demands were met. It was nothing of the sort.

Victoria knew that Evans and Holly were waiting for her to speak. She was the one with the computer degrees. Only she didn't know what to say. She read the memo again.

Mr. President:
  At midnight tonight, the world will be introduced to the organization known as Estate when our website goes on-line and is open to subscribers.

Our group has taken control of the Electronic Sur-
veillance Post satellite. We have reprogrammed the
ESP to be able to read, reconfigure, or close down any
electronic system on earth. You cannot approach the
satellite. Any attempt to terminate its operation from
earth orbit will result in a failure identical to the one
that shut down the Venture. *Any attempt to close down*
the satellite from earth will fail.

At that point there was a short memo attached to the
E-mail. It was from Air Force Mission Director Rudolph
Anastasia. General Anastasia indicated that less than an hour
ago, at 1503 hours, an attempt to fire the ESP's orbital adjustment rockets with a command from the Cape Canaveral
facility did not succeed. Attempts to reestablish contact with
the satellite were ongoing but, to date, none of those had
been successful either.

The E-mail continued:

To demonstrate the extent of our abilities, we will
activate the ESP at nine P.M., EST. We will shut
down computer activities in the following localities:
The White House and Capitol, the British Houses
of Parliament, the Kremlin, the Japanese National
Diet, and the German Parliament.
The blackouts will last for exactly thirty minutes.
We strongly suggest that you keep the reasons from be-
coming public knowledge to prevent panic. The general
populace need never know what has happened. We will
deal with uncooperative powers on a per-nation basis.
Those responses will be longer than thirty minutes.
They will be most severe.
As long as the governments of the world do not in-
terfere with the activities of Estate, there will be no
hostile acts on our part.

"This wasn't written by a well-educated individual," Victoria said.

"How can you tell?" Evans asked.

"The grammar and some of the usages are awkward," she said. "They remind me of college papers I've read."

"The writer could be an uneducated sociopath and still be a genius," Diaz observed.

"Or a smart kid who's in over his head," Evans said.

"It reminds *me* of something from that old TV show," Holly remarked. "The one where they said, 'We will control the transmission. . . .'"

"*The Outer Limits,*" Diaz said.

"That's the one."

"Well, whoever they are, they're pretty confident," Evans said.

"Probably with good reason," Diaz said. "I once set out target beacons in the North Atlantic for satellites that were forerunners of the ESP. All they had to do was hit very precise targets with a laser beam. They didn't have to read any data. They were powerful. And precise."

"How did the satellites find their targets?" Victoria asked.

"With internal maps," Diaz said. "We sent coordinates to the onboard cameras and they zoomed in on targets."

"Those had to be pretty precise maps," Evans said.

"They were," Diaz told him. "We used data provided by National Reconnaissance Office satellites. The spacers—which is what we called the space lasers—were able to focus down to one and one-half meters if they had to. They hit anything in that target area."

"So the ESP has a way of doing that," Evans said. "It zeroes in on a computer system and accesses the memory."

"Sounds like it," Diaz said. "And moving the computer to another location won't do any good. Back then they were working on a way of targeting computers using data sent via E-mail. I don't know exactly how it worked, but I'm sure they've made improvements since then."

"That part would be frighteningly easy," Victoria said. "If Estate is a sophisticated enough website it could use servers, E-mail, online yellow and white pages, hack billing sites, do anything to get to specific computers. They could probably reach ninety percent of the world's computers that way. Mark them with viruses of some kind, something only the ESP would pick up. Then, of course, they'll have access to all the computers involved in the Estate subscriptions."

"That's great," Holly said. "So somebody else can do what AOL does all the time. Gum up my PC."

"I'm more worried about this 'Estate' thing," Diaz thought aloud. "Who the hell are they?"

No one answered. Victoria just shook her head slowly.

"And look at this bull," the pilot muttered. " 'No hostile acts.' What do they think the attack on the shuttle was?"

"I don't think that was an attack," Victoria said.

"Whoa. You don't think these people were responsible for what happened?" Holly asked.

"Oh, I think they were responsible," Victoria said, "but not directly. Look here." She pointed to a passage in the E-mail. "It says, *You cannot approach the satellite.* They claim to have been involved with the other acts and threats but not with that."

"Meaning what?" Evans asked.

"That there must be some kind of electronic defense system in the satellite itself," Victoria said.

"Like an electronic shield?" Evans said. "What do they call those, electromagnetic pulses?"

"Exactly," Victoria told him. "I don't think that whatever happened to the shuttle was active aggression. I'm guessing it was a result of being exposed to that system."

"That still smells like an attack to me," Holly said.

"Frankly, that's not important right now," Evans said. "Only the United States and Russia would be able to get to the satellite physically, so I doubt a shield like that was actually designed into the system. It was probably hardwired into the satellite by one of the contractors and ushered through whatever checkpoints there are along the way."

"The Huntsmen?" Holly asked.

"They still have people in the military-industrial complex, so it's possible," Evans said.

"I'm not so sure of that," Victoria said. "Something this big would have to have been in the works before Axe and his group struck."

"The Huntsmen go back nearly ninety years," Evans pointed out. "They could have been working on this years ago."

"Commander, I think what Victoria is saying is that there wouldn't have been a need for the Huntsmen to attack the White House if they already planned to usurp the ESP," Diaz said. "The satellite would have rendered a coup redundant."

"Maybe the ESP maneuver was a backup plan," Holly said, "something it would have been easier to do if the Huntsmen already owned the White House. Or it could be like one of those old-time battles where the guy carrying the flag goes down and someone else picks it up."

"I still think they were independent actions," Diaz said. "Something this sensitive would only have been known to a handful of people. The Huntsmen used coercion and muscle, a lot of it, to get what they wanted."

"I agree," Victoria said. "And I think that controlling the world's computers makes everything else secondary."

"Like controlling a nation's water supply," Diaz said. "Get that and nothing else matters."

"All right," Evans said. "Let's assume the Huntsmen and Estate are not affiliated. Where does that leave us?"

"That depends on what the ESP can do," Victoria said. "Controlling the world's computers would allow them to shut down electrical grids, defense systems, financial activities, communications, transportation—everything. So we need to get as much information about that as we can. Specs, uplinks, anything."

Evans picked up the TAC-SAT receiver. "Hopefully, someone has hard copy of that information. I'd hate to think that the people running the ESP have already erased the data from Pentagon hard drives."

Victoria looked at Evans as he punched his code into the box followed by the president's direct number. She was scared, which was sad and ironic. This was the kind of job she had always dreamed of. Being involved with cutting-edge science instead of teaching slack-jawed students at New York University. Interaction with the President of the United States instead of the head of the NYU school of computer sciences. Wrestling with international issues instead of interdepartmental ones. Working beside and being impressed by a charismatic leader like Amos Evans instead of living with and being disappointed by a charming phony like her soon-to-be-former-husband Stephen.

But now that Victoria was on the inside, it was discouraging. She had always assumed that the government had "special ways" of dealing with problems like this. That persons, experts, were in place to deal with every possible configuration of danger. They weren't. The Air Force was stymied and they had built the damn satellite. NASA was surprised and they had inspected, loaded, and launched the damn shuttle. Apparently, she and Evans and the rest of the Stealth Warrior team were "it" as far as crisis management went. The president's last and best hope to fix things. And the group was largely untried, still getting to know their equipment, their limitations, and each other—feeling their way in the dark. It was not only discouraging, it was frightening.

On the other hand, maybe they did have the one advantage that made them uniquely equipped to deal with this, Victoria told herself. If the Huntsmen or the backers of this Estate undertaking were DOD or NASA insiders, who better to take them by surprise than an unheralded, unknown unit outside the system? And she and Evans and the others *were* all professionals. Maybe the ideal contingency for a situation like this was to have the best people available and improvise. That thought gave her a little hope.

A very little.

The president came on the line. Commander Evans told Gordon that they had read the E-mail, then asked him about the ESP and Estate. Evans listened while the president spoke. A few minutes later the commander hung up. His expression was grave.

"This is not good," Evans said. "Mr. Diaz was only partly right. The ESP satellite was not only designed to read signals from dedicated systems. This new model was designed to read, infiltrate, and change dedicated computer programs if necessary. The president is having the data scanned and E-mailed to us."

"Dedicated," Holly said. "You mean stand-alone systems. Not connected to anything else?"

"Right," Evans said. "President Gordon says that NASA has no idea how the satellite's response mechanism was altered, though it was apparently an inside operation."

"Why apparently?" Victoria asked.

"Because the ESP was designed only to be able to access one earthbound system at a time," Evans said. "One PC, one rocket guidance system, one spy satellite. If these people can hit multiple systems at once, as they say they can, they had to have made improvements to internal components."

"Without NASA knowing it?" Victoria asked.

Evans nodded.

"But wouldn't the Air Force have incorporated that

technology into the ESP if they knew it existed?" Victoria asked.

Evans just looked at her. She had answered her own question even as she asked it. *If they knew it existed.* The good news was that meant there was a brain trust of some size and intellectual heft outside the Pentagon. It might be possible to locate that.

"The president's advisors say it's going to take days of studying the satellite's design log to even begin to understand who did this, how, and what the ramifications might be," Evans said. "Obviously, we don't have that long."

"Does the president have any idea what Estate is or who these people are?" Victoria asked.

"None," Evans said. "The decryption people at the Pentagon and the CIA are working on the E-mail to try and trace it."

"Good luck," Victoria said.

"Why 'good luck'?" Holly asked.

"The E-mail transmission could be coming from anywhere on earth," Victoria said. "It probably came through the ESP, so there's no way of tracking it backward." She thought for a moment. "Though I wonder if there are daemons we can check on."

"If there were what?" Holly asked.

"Daemons," Victoria said. "Programs stored on computers that weren't aware they were harboring a virus. If so, the program that was used to take over the ESP could have been planted in a NASA computer months ago."

"And triggered by a timer?" Evans asked.

"Or remotely," Victoria said. "It may even have been placed in the computers of subcontractors and slipped in that way."

"I'm not sure about that one," Diaz said. "A rogue program to rewrite an entire satellite's systems—that would be a lot of data to try and hide."

"What about hiding it on board the satellite itself?" Evans asked.

"Possibly," Victoria said. "But then you'd need someone on-site to activate it, one of the astronauts."

"Why?" Evans asked. "Couldn't a command like that be beamed up?"

"Again, you'd have the problem of sending the sheer bulk of data uninterrupted," Diaz said.

"It would be very risky," Victoria said. "With all the tracking of the shuttle that goes on around the world, an outside signal would almost certainly be detected and pinpointed."

"You know, I wonder if one of the astronauts *did* do this," Diaz thought aloud.

"Knowing that the shuttle would go belly-up under him?" Holly said. "He'd have to be crazy, and NASA's head boys would have picked that up in the psych tests."

"Crazy," Diaz said, "or resolute."

Victoria shook her head. "We're still looking at a lot of ground to cover and no good place to start."

"Well," Evans said, "the president told me he'll share whatever information comes to him. He and his advisors are hoping to get more information when Estate goes online—"

"Logistically, I'd love to know how the bastards are working this," Victoria interrupted. "I mean, the satellite is in earth orbit, shielded from approximately half the globe at any given time. How can it infiltrate dedicated systems on the *other* half of the globe?"

"Maybe it took control of other military satellites and created some kind of earth-orbiting web," Diaz said.

"They could also be using dishes or aircraft to bounce the signals around," Holly suggested. "Something like a squadron of AWACS flying tag-team, always airborne."

"Even so, there should be traceable transmissions coming off the ESP," Victoria said. "And any transmissions, even encrypted ones, should be readable in time. Estate wouldn't leave themselves open to that. There's got to be some hidden method of communication, something we're missing."

"What's the difference how open these people are if they can shut down computers at will?" Diaz said. "Any attack against the aircraft would be deflected. Can you imagine a Tomahawk missile having its internal guidance mucked up and running wild?"

"Except that wherever there's a signal there's a way to block it," Victoria pointed out.

"Again, not without retribution," Evans said.

"Also, not if it's an RVS," Diaz said, "a randomly vacillating signal. Cracking those is not as easy as you might think. Again, when I worked on seagoing buoys the Air Force used as test targets for their satellites, guidance signals were sent from satellites to help airborne missiles find the targets. I used every trick I could think of to try and impede the impulses. Even when I succeeded, Air Force intelligence would send up some new command and close me out the next time. And I didn't have a missile coming at me. I had all the time I needed to try and break up the signals."

"Maybe you didn't have the right tools," Victoria said stubbornly. She hated being told that something "couldn't" be done, especially by a man. That was a holdover from Stephen.

"I was usually working off a medium-endurance cutter homeported at SHARC tech headquarters in Guam," Diaz said. "Big vessel, lots of gear. It had all the right tools."

" 'Big vessel, all the right tools,' " Victoria said. "A man's answer to everything."

Evans gave her a look.

Diaz noticed Evans's expression. "But I'm sorry, sir. Victoria. I didn't mean to get sidetracked like that."

"It's all right," Evans said. "Everything you two have said helps. It tells us what we and the White House pretty much suspected, that a technical fix isn't going to be easy."

"That being the case, sir," said Holly, "what does the president want us to do?"

Evans looked at his watch. "Before Victoria sidetracked us," he said, "I was about to say he wants two of us to go down to Cape Canaveral, try to find out if anyone there is involved with this plot."

"Sorry about that," Victoria said.

Evans winked at her.

"I've been down to the Cape, sir," Holly said. "I know my way around there pretty good."

Evans nodded. "Good. Mr. Diaz will go with you. You've got a little breathing room before you have to be there. We'll get you quarters at the space center. Pack the SFUs—if you have to say anything, tell people you're there to test out a new kind of extra-vehicular suit. I'll stay here and work with Victoria, let you know what else the president learns about the group."

"Yes, sir," Holly said.

"I'll let Captain McIver know she's got more travel plans to arrange," Diaz said.

"Why don't you get ready, Mr. Diaz," Victoria said. "I'll make the call."

"Sure," he said with a smile. "Thanks."

It was a small peace offering, meant more for the commander than for Diaz. Puzzles and missing information frustrated her. She shouldn't have taken that, and her divorce, out on Diaz.

The men left, and the commander watched the CNN coverage of the shuttle crash while Victoria made the call to Langley. Captain McIver was actually pleased to be given something to do. The mood at the base was extremely low after the shuttle crash. The *Venture*'s Commander Boring and Captain Karl were both Air Force. Every flier took the loss personally.

"Captain McIver will bring them to Langley and have them flown out of there," Victoria said when she was finished. "Air traffic is still backed up all over but she can squeeze them through."

"Thank you, Victoria," Evans replied. His voice was low and his eyes were shut.

"Are you angry at me?"

"No," he said.

"Are you all right?"

"Sure," he answered after a long moment. "I was just saying a prayer for the pilots."

"Oh," Victoria said. "Sorry."

"Those two pilots did an amazing job," the commander said as he opened his eyes. "Not just getting the shuttle back, but making sure it didn't land in a populated area. Just amazing."

"What will happen to the shuttle?" Victoria asked.

"NASA will want to keep it intact for the investigation," Evans told her. "My guess is they'll set up cranes and put the shuttle on a scow, float it to deeper water. Then they'll probably transfer it to a Navy vessel for transport to the Atlantic and a trip back to the Cape." The officer turned to Victoria. "Your turn now. Are *you* all right?"

"More or less."

"You were getting pretty angry before," Evans said.

"I know and I'm sorry," she said.

"Are you sure you don't need more time off?" he asked.

"I'm sure," Victoria insisted. "I'd rather work."

"Is there anything I can do for you?" Evans asked.

"Truthfully?"

"Of course."

"I've been thinking about your offer to go to New York and teach my one-day-to-be-former-husband how to treat a lady," Victoria said. "If you're serious, that would improve my mood considerably."

"I wasn't entirely serious," he admitted.

"I was afraid you'd say that."

"But don't worry about him," Evans said.

"Why not?"

"He'll get what he deserves."

"You think so?" Victoria asked. "Unfortunately, I don't have your faith in divine justice."

"That's not what I meant."

"It isn't?" Victoria said. "Because if you want to talk about divine justice, then let's talk about it. Old Testament justice. You know, an eye for an eye, a tooth for a tooth. Stephen's guts ripped out an inch at a time as payback for everything he's done to mine."

Evans shook his head. "Why are all my people so angry?"

"Why?" Victoria asked. "Because look at what happened to Mrs. Taylor. Decency and honor and courtesy are dead. Where have you been living? Scratch that," Victoria said. "You've been working for DARPA where the real world doesn't intrude. Well, Amos, during those years you were away everyone in the world got really, really selfish. And ugly. And those who didn't got really fed up with those who did."

"But we don't need to respond in kind," Evans replied.

"*I* do," she said. "I don't believe that God is going to punish Stephen."

"He doesn't have to," Evans insisted. "Your husband has lost you. *That's* his punishment. He just doesn't realize it yet."

Wow, she thought.

Coming from anyone else that would have been a line.

But Amos Evans wasn't like that. And it sure put things in perspective.

Victoria turned and walked back to the desk. Did her footfalls always sound so loud?

"Well," Victoria said.

"Well what?"

"I sure don't have a comeback for that," she said.

"You don't need one."

Touché again, Victoria thought. Jesus, she was handling this poorly. She sat behind the desk. She just wasn't used to this kind of support. In classes, kids challenged her because who knows more than a nineteen- or twenty-year-old? At home it had been Stephen. When she started consulting for DARPA it had been Dr. Fraser. Now Diaz.

But Rodrigo Diaz isn't Stephen, she reminded herself. Neither is Dr. Fraser or the other members of the Stealth Warrior team. If Evans wasn't right about Stephen—that he was too selfish and narcissistic to care about anyone but himself—one thing was true. Every difference of opinion was not necessarily an attack on her. This group was about achieving goals. It was about one for all and all for one. She had to remember that.

"So Stephen loses by getting what he wants," Victoria said. "I'll have to take your word for that. The bastard seemed pretty happy when I left him."

"He won't be so happy next time," Evans said. "Deserters always find out that running away is the problem, not the solution. I've seen your good qualities, your devotion, intelligence, courage, compassion. You just said that not everyone has them. Stephen will miss you. Believe me."

She wanted to. God, how she wanted to. As she looked into his dark eyes, she also knew that wasn't all she wanted.

"We have work to do," Evans said suddenly.

It was as if he'd turned a flashlight on. The mood

snapped. Maybe for the best because he was right. They did have work to do.

The commander walked toward the desk and looked down at her from behind the monitor. "Apart from the ESP data, is there anything else we need from the White House?" Evans asked. "Computer terrorism isn't an area I've had much experience in."

"There's nothing I can think of," she said. "If it's okay with you, I'd rather not concentrate on areas NASA and the Pentagon are probably already studying, like how the satellite software was changed from 'spy' to 'impede,'" Victoria said. "Maybe Diaz is right. Maybe we can't blanket-protect computers from signals on the way down from the ESP. But whatever safeguards these people may have put in place, there still might be a way to stop the signals on the way up. That's what I want to look into."

"What do you need to do that?" Evans asked.

"Time," she replied. She looked at the monitor and shook her head slowly. "This E-mail they sent is so damn confident. Either they're convinced we'll never locate the source of the signal, or if we do, that we'll never be able to block it. But I'm going to," she said. She looked back at Evans and smiled. "And that's not anger, by the way. It's determination."

"I know," Evans said, smiling back. "Look, I'm going to my cabin to update Colonel Lewis. Let me know if you need anything."

"I will," she said.

He walked toward the door.

"Amos?" she said.

Evans stopped and looked back into the cabin. At that moment Victoria felt very safe.

"Thanks," she said. "Having someone give a damn after Stephen—it means a lot to me."

The commander smiled and left the cabin.

That wasn't exactly what Victoria had wanted from Evans. She'd wanted him to turn back to her and embrace her and make the hurt go away. She had wanted him to hold her ever since she got back from New York and saw him standing on the hill, alone but somehow not alone.

Reliable. Strong. *There.*

She wasn't going to get that from Evans—at least not now. But at least she no longer felt so alone, and at the moment that mattered too.

A lot.

Eighteen

Germantown, Pennsylvania
Monday, 4:45 P.M.

When he was a child, Colonel Matt Lewis was never very close to his parents. An Army brat, he lived in Alabama, Texas, New Jersey, Virginia, Germany, and Italy—all in the space of twelve years. Lewis's father, Fine—that was really his name, given to him by a helluva proud mother—was also a colonel. He was an in-your-face kind of guy who kept pissing people off and getting moved around. Lewis's mother was a singer who, when Lewis was ten, decided to go on the road as a backup singer for some dirty-haired country music guy. Lewis didn't know whether it was because she needed to sing or needed to get away from his father. And he never got to ask her. She died in a bus accident three months into the tour.

The elder Lewis never remarried. He never even brought another woman into the house. He just read his books on military history, watched military shows on TV, chain-smoked hand-rolled cigarettes, and went to off-base parties by himself. Just about the only time he and his son spent together was when they hunted, and that was more about military strategy than about father-son camaraderie. The one fun time Lewis could remember was when they were stationed at Fort Dix in New Jersey. They took a side trip to Philadelphia to see Independence Hall and the Liberty Bell. The junior Lewis was about fifteen at the time. It was a frigid winter day and the city was deserted. While they were walking quietly toward the waterfront, his father puffing cold air and cigarette smoke, they happened to pass Benjamin Franklin's house—at least, a "ghost structure" of it. A skeletal white framework had been erected in a more or less empty lot for the bicentennial in 1776. All that remained of the actual house were excavation pits covered by thick plastic panes. Inside one could see some basement floors, a bit of foundation—and the brick conduit of Benjamin Franklin's privy. The pipes for his toilet. The two Lewises looked at each other and started laughing. Somehow they knew the irreverent statesman would have appreciated that.

When Colonel Fine Lewis died of cancer of the esophagus, the twenty-year-old Lewis didn't have any regrets that he knew about. He didn't dislike his father; Fine Lewis was what he was and his son had accepted that. But they certainly hadn't been close.

Not like Hank Taylor and his mother. Lewis didn't know what was more upsetting: standing next to the sedated woman in the bed or standing next to her son. Most of the woman's body, her head, and her face were bandaged. The parts that weren't covered were discolored and swollen, and her arms were in braces. Yet there was still a very special dignity about the woman. Lewis couldn't explain it; maybe it was just the *idea* that she had survived this attack that gave him the impression. But it was there.

Her son was a different story. Hank Taylor was like a zombie, alive but dead. The men had arrived at the 30th

Street Station and taken a cab directly to the Germantown Hospital and Medical Center at One Penn Boulevard. As they neared the hospital, the rage that had gnawed at and then exploded from Taylor in the train seemed to vanish. It was replaced by concern, then anxiety, then this complete crash. Taylor looked and behaved as though someone had anesthetized him. Part of Lewis found that weak and unacceptable. He wanted to grab the major hard, shake him, and tell him to deal with this. That's what Lewis would have done with any soldier in the field to keep him moving, fighting, focused. But he didn't do that, partly out of respect for Mrs. Taylor and partly out of a desire to give her son the benefit of the doubt. Lewis had never had anyone care enough for him to care back. Maybe no one would have understood *him* sharing a laugh with his dad over Ben Franklin's crapper either.

Lewis and Taylor didn't stay at Mrs. Taylor's side very long. Hank was afraid that his outrage would generate tension she might feel. He had to do something about that. A family friend, Mrs. St. Martin, had been there when they arrived. She'd been sitting with the unconscious Mrs. Taylor, talking to her and reading her favorite sections of the newspaper—the funnies, the advice columns, even reading the clues aloud as she worked the crossword puzzle. Mrs. St. Martin wept when she told Hank Taylor how she normally went down to the auditorium with Mrs. Taylor for their singing club, but hadn't this week because she'd been on the phone with her daughter Heather and hadn't gotten off in time. Major Taylor told the woman not to be angry at herself. He said this probably would have happened some other time, or if she had been there, maybe both women would have been attacked.

Mrs. St. Martin said that she was going to stay with Hank's mother for another few hours. She offered Hank her car. He graciously accepted and said that he would come back for her around nine.

Before leaving, Taylor asked one of the nurses to let him see his mother's chart. He read it. Her vital signs had been steady, which was encouraging. Then they stopped to talk to Mrs. Taylor's neurologist, Dr. Baker Canterbury. The doctor told them that the MRI didn't reveal any obvious brain damage despite the severe concussion; they would just have to wait and see what happened. Taylor thanked him and left.

As they rode down the elevator, Lewis asked if they were going to the Germantown police so that Taylor could tell them more about what had happened in the parking lot and possibly find out what *they* knew.

"There's no point in that," Taylor said.

"Why not?"

"The police won't tell me a damn thing," Taylor said as they left the elevator and walked toward the front door. "And I don't want to help them find these assholes first."

"Hold on," Lewis said. "You know the commander's orders."

"Yeah, I do. But we're civilians for right now."

"Not really," Lewis said sharply.

"Look, Colonel," Taylor said. "I'm going to find these fucks. That's my priority. Whether I tear them up or not, I want the option. And I can't do that unless I find out where they are."

"Yeah, well, I have priorities too," Lewis replied. "Following orders. And you're not giving me a lot of wiggle room."

"No one's telling you to disregard them," Taylor said. "You want to try and stop me, go ahead."

Lewis's expression darkened. "Don't make this personal, Taylor."

"I'm not," Taylor replied. "I'm just outlining the options.

Either you fight with me or against me, that's all. I guess the question you have to ask yourself is if you fight against me, are you fighting for Commander Evans or for the dirt I'm looking to clean up?"

Lewis thought for a moment. Then he swore to himself. *Goddamn this man.* And goddamn Evans for putting him in this position. He was in the field with a member of his unit. He couldn't turn on him.

"What's the plan?" Lewis asked.

"We're going to talk to someone who knows the street," Taylor said. "An old friend of mine."

"Then what?"

"Then we'll see," Taylor said.

"Fine," Lewis said. "I'll let you go that far at least."

As they reached Mrs. St. Martin's Toyota, there was a beep from the pocket of Lewis's windbreaker. The colonel removed his USMail device. Each member of the team had one. The palm-size unit was a portable, government-issued E-mail delivery system. Unlike cell phones, whose signals could be picked off, USMail was encrypted and completely secure. While that limited the amount of information that could be sent and also slowed both the upload and download time, it also meant that sensitive information could be sent into the field. If an immediate follow-up communication was necessary, it could be made on a ground line.

Lewis read the message.

"What is it?" Taylor asked.

"The president called Commander Evans," Lewis replied. His voice was a deep whisper. "There is a strong belief the shuttle was sabotaged and whoever was behind the accident is going on-line with a new—'challenge' is how the commander puts it."

"I wonder what that means."

"I don't know," Lewis said. "Holly and Diaz are going to Cape Canaveral to investigate a possible source of the sabotage. He wants us on-base by late tomorrow morning in case they have an update."

"Why don't you go now, Colonel?" Taylor said.

"Because that's not how the order reads," Lewis replied.

"I know, sir," Taylor said. "But that's because the commander didn't think I could take care of this situation myself—"

"If the commander wanted us there now, he would have asked for us to be there now." The colonel pressed the acknowledge button. That would send a quick, simple "message received" notice to Commander Evans. "Let's do what we can while we can," Lewis said. He put the USMail unit away and snapped his fingers several times. "Let me have the keys. I'm driving."

Taylor handed the leather key case to Lewis. The colonel unlocked the door, popped the locks, and the men climbed in.

Now Lewis resented being here even more. His first drill instructor once told him that being a soldier was like being a baseball player. If the manager told you to lay down a bunt to get on base and let the next guy homer, that's what you did. If your CO told you to handhold a grieving soldier instead of hunt for saboteurs, then that was what you did.

At least for another dozen or so hours. Then he was going back to West Virginia, where, hopefully, his teammates would have learned where the saboteurs were hiding. Then they'd be able to answer the "challenge" with a time-tested Delta Force–style response.

One that left the idea of "rematch" out of the question.

Nineteen

In one sense the timing was extremely fortuitous. In another sense it was not.

Captain Holly had been hoping to be able to fly himself and Diaz to Cape Canaveral in an F-16B trainer. Unfortunately, the Air Force had a C-141A StarLifter scheduled to make the trip with spare parts for NASA's fleet of two-seat T-38 jets, which pilot astronauts used to maintain flying proficiency. So, for the umpteenth time in his career, Holly climbed into the cargo bay of a transport plane to go where he was needed. He and Diaz helped each other aboard with the chests containing the SFUs. Moving them was a two-person operation not only because of the weight of the suits, but because of the added weight of the rods and plastic bags used to contain the SFU elements during shipping.

MCPO Diaz was his usual outgoing self during both the van ride to the field and the wait for takeoff. He was extremely talkative, throwing out thoughts and ideas about the ESP puzzle. At least it was more interesting than his story about Diogenes the Cynic in his bathtub, which was the most memorable part of their first plane trip together.

The men sat side by side on the uncomfortable unpadded benches that lined both sides of the spare, cavernous fuselage. This particular StarLifter had been configured for fore-to-aft space since most of the spare parts were packed in long crates. That meant the more comfortable "actual seats," as they were called, had been removed.

"I wonder if there's any connection between the 'E-S' in 'Estate' and the "ESP" in the Electronic Surveillance Post acronym," Diaz was saying as the engines fired up.

"Why would there be?" Holly asked.

"Well, it might be possible to disguise a signal destined for the ESP satellite if it were written in code and hidden as a signal for, say, 'Estate Program' or 'Estate Portal.' See what I mean?"

"I see," Holly drawled. "But if their operation is that low-tech—"

"No one would ever suspect it," Diaz cut in. "That's why it'd be so pretty. Suppose you've got a few thousand computers communicating with this Estate, whatever it is. A message could be encoded for the satellite and never picked up by us."

"As a computer-to-computer transmission that could work, I guess," Holly said. He was yelling now to be heard over the thunderous roar of the four Pratt & Whitney TF33-P7 turbofans. "But the data still has to get from all those computers into space, to the satellite."

"That's true," Diaz said. "That would take an uplink, which could be traced back to the source." He rattled his fists in frustration. "God, I would love to know who these guys are. So damn cocky. Hey," he said, brightening. "Maybe there's a clue in that."

"In what?" Holly asked.

"Who's the cockiest kind of person you can think of?"

"The cockiest? A thoroughbred horse breeder," Holly answered.

"Really? Not, like—oilmen?"

"Nope. Or cattlemen. I knew both kinds in Texas," Holly replied. "Horse breeders've got money, know lots of rich folk, and travel all over the world. And the ones I knew had all kinds of attitude up the wazoo."

"They probably do a lot of Internet scouting and trading—"

"And studding," Holly said.

"What do they study besides horses?"

"I said *stud*ding," Holly shouted. "Making romantic matches for their horses. There's good money in that."

"Gotcha," Diaz said. He shook his head. "Y'know, this approach isn't going to work. I'm sure there are a lot of cocky people who'd want to take over all the world's computers."

"Yeah," Holly said. "The more likely guy would be some kind of techno-geek. A joker who does this for the thrill or the challenge. To stick out his tongue at the big boys."

"And there are a million of those," Diaz said.

Holly leaned back against the fuselage. The metal was warm from the plane sitting out in the sun, and the entire wall was vibrating heavily. A leather strap hung above Holly's head to the right. He wrapped it around his hand. Though the men wore seat belts, this would keep him from slumping onto Diaz as the plane took off. Holly looked past the crates that filled the fuselage. A half-dozen other crew members were sitting on the opposite bench. Bright light flashed across them like lightning as the huge plane rose slowly, laboriously, almost as though it wasn't going to get off the ground. Holly saw the grim set of the men's faces. The loss of the shuttle was with them all. Going to the Cape only made it worse. And Holly knew it probably hadn't hit them yet. Not really. It was still hovering on the outside of the soul, like a cold night that hadn't quite gotten through your skin. It would be a lot worse when it did.

"I don't believe that," Diaz said suddenly.

Holly looked at him.

"A techno-geek didn't do this," Diaz went on.

"What makes you say that?"

"I was just sitting here thinking about the space shuttle," Diaz told him.

"Me too," said Holly. "I guess we all are."

"Naturally," Diaz said. "And we're sick about it. Well, a techno-geek would be disgusted too. He'd love big sleek hunks of sophisticated machinery. Bringing down the space shuttle wouldn't fit the profile of a person like that, it would be a sacrilege."

"I don't know about that," Holly said.

"Why?"

"Well, people have love-hate relationships with things," Holly said. "There've been times I've wanted to crash planes into mountainsides 'cause I hated the hell out of 'em."

"But you didn't *really* hate them," Diaz said. "They frustrated you. And you didn't crash them, and not because you were in them."

"No," Holly said. "All I'm saying is that there are people who don't have an emotional firewall like I do. Maybe somebody got screwed out of a government contract to work on the shuttle or its cargo. Or he didn't win a Nobel prize and some NASA guy did."

"I suppose."

"Or maybe it's none of that," Holly went on. "A cyber-Joe might not feel so bad about destroying real-world stuff. Who the hell knows?"

"That's all true," Diaz said sadly. "It also doesn't put us closer to having any clues."

"Not yet," Holly agreed. "But we took out the last big

shot who thought he could run a coup on us. We'll get this one too."

"I'm usually not an optimist, but I hope you're right," Diaz said. "We have to get them."

"Maybe if you give your brain a rest something'll come to you," Holly suggested.

"I can't work that way," Diaz told him. "I've got to dig at problems until they're figured out."

"Like a raccoon in a trash barrel," Holly suggested.

"Exactly," Diaz replied. "And if I don't paw through the thing it just sits there. Then all I can think of is how much it smells."

The Air Force pilot reached into the pocket of his denim shirt and took out a stick of gum. He offered some to Diaz. "You should chew on this. It helps me relax. Might help you too. And it smells better than chewed dog toy too."

"Thanks, no," said the Coast Guard SHARC. "I need to focus. No distractions. Just the problem."

"But you may not have enough information yet to find the answers you're looking for," Holly said. "That's why it might be better to rest."

"Maybe it is better," Diaz said. "I'm just not built that way."

The seaman leaned back and stared at the ceiling. His mind left the building. Holly could see it in the MCPO's eyes.

Okay, the flier thought. It takes all kinds to make a world.

Holly unwrapped the piece, folded it into his mouth, and looked back across the crates. The colors of the fuse-lage fit his mood. They were drab, mostly grays and greenish-browns all bleeding into shadows. The blazing white light coming through the small windows made the interior seem even darker. He thought about the awful TV image of the *Venture* on its back in the water. Surreal, *un*-real, just like the threat they were facing now. It was funny.

He and Diaz were going to face the threat using suits that effectively rendered them invisible. That idea didn't seem strange because he understood the technology and knew the people inside the suits.

And then it occurred to him. Maybe that's part of what Diaz was trying to do. Give the enemy a face, an identity, a motivation. Even if it all turned out to be wrong, it might help to strip away the strangeness and mystery of what was happening. And if it were right—

"Diaz?"

"Yes?"

"Chew out loud," Holly said.

"Huh?"

"Talk to me about what you're thinking," Holly said. "Maybe you're right. You never know what I might spark to."

"Sure," Diaz said, smiling.

The master chief petty officer said he was thinking about whether other satellites or satellite functions had ever been co-opted by outside personnel. He would ask Evans to find that out from the president.

That was a good idea, Holly thought. And the fact that the enemy might have had to field-test the thing made sense. It also did something else.

It made them seem just a little less invulnerable.

Twenty

**Lake Miasalaro, West Virginia
Monday, 5:50 P.M.**

It was good to finally get out of his own SFU.

He had kept the suit on to see how long he could endure it comfortably. Even at rest soldiers could be in training. Besides, Evans liked being in combat mode. It was an anvil for his soldier's spirit and it made him feel as if he were an active part of the military again. The commander also didn't mind the discomfort of the suit. Suffering, as the Bible said, was the road to perfection.

Still, it was refreshing to take the SFU off.

Evans stood in the center of the cabin as he removed the pieces of the uniform. He was amazed at how much more snug the SFU was from when he'd first started wearing it. That was because carrying around the weight of the suit every day had caused muscles all over his body to bulk out. Not significantly, but enough to make a difference in the fit. It wouldn't be long before the extra mass would restrict their mobility.

The question of more absorbent undergarments was something they'd also have to address. The men perspired a great deal in the suits. Over long periods of time—more than just the few hours they wore the suits now—that could become a serious problem. The suit circuitry was insulated from the sweat, but the men were not, and the cotton long johns they were wearing now just didn't absorb enough moisture. DARPA had been working with new "wicking" materials for submarine crews, fabrics that drew away dampness through capillary action. A Pentagon study in 1999 revealed that underwater units tended to sweat the most because of both the close quarters and the constant danger from other submarines, geologic formations, icebergs, surface vessels, bad weather, and even whales. Fabrics like Stelon and Sutex were already being manufactured to draw away and retain one-hundred-percent moisture. Evans would contact Dr. Fraser before he left and see if the scientist could have some of those sent down.

All of this was important, but it passed through Evans's mind in a moment as he started removing the suit. He moved on to the more immediate issue, which was finding out who was behind the Estate and figuring out how to stop them. Not "if." Failure wasn't an option. He glanced at the digital clock he'd placed on the mantel over the fireplace. Though he had his own computer, he wanted to be with Victoria so they could study the ESP problem together and review whatever new data came in. She was a smart, determined woman. Part of him wished she could forgive her husband, while another part of him wished he could squeeze the idiot's neck. Not long enough to kill him; just enough to get his complete attention. Hold him there and look in his frightened eyes and say, *"Apologize to the lady for having hurt her and don't do it again."*

Evans finished removing the SFU suit and long johns. He showered and put on his sweatshirt and jeans. As he

pulled down the gray Navy sweatshirt he experienced something he didn't like. He was no longer thinking about the
Estate and the stealing of the ESP. He suddenly felt very
alone.

Which probably isn't so surprising, Evans told himself
as he continued to dress.

Evans was out here in the mountains in relative isolation,
out of contact with the "real" world. It was even less real
than the basement of the Pentagon, where at least he had a
home to go to—a home he had rented out to college kids
from Georgetown before coming here. He missed it more
than he thought he would; it was the first home he'd had as
an adult. Then there was Taylor's bond with his mother.
That exposed Evans to feelings, very *strong* feelings, that
he never quite got to share with his own mother. He'd been
too young, too immature to appreciate Helen Evans, and
she had left this world far too early. Taylor's intense devotion did remind Evans of what he'd felt for Father John, and
right now he very much missed the priest's guidance and
friendship.

Then there was working closely with Victoria. More than
anything, that made it clear to Evans that he *was* alone.

Not that there hadn't been women in Evans's life. There
had been, when he was a very young man. A lot of them.
Some of them were older women who hung around with
Hurwitz. Very few of those were the bubble-headed moll-
types that the movies pictured "gang girls" to be. Some were
aging strippers or bar girls who worked in local clubs after
having spent their best years in Las Vegas. Most of them
were wise and droll and very sexual. Some of the women
were divorcees with children and dull nine-to-five jobs. Several were married women who were miserably bored with
upper-middle-class suburbia; Evans always knew who those
women were by the sunglasses and hats they wore at night

so they wouldn't be recognized. And by the white lines where wedding rings were worn during the day.

Many of those women thought the young Evans was cute. They arranged to meet him in the same places they often met Hurwitz, in out-of-the-way bars or hotel rooms or even dark beaches. They taught Evans things, things he never read about in the copies of *Playboy, Nugget,* and *After Hours* that Hurwitz left lying around. He liked those women for their minds, souls, and needs. They tended to be very hungry sexually.

Then there were teenage women who had homes or waitressing jobs or classes to go to but didn't want to. They were restless, unhappy young women who enjoyed the night life and guys with money or drugs or pull—"heft" was what they called it back in Miami. Evans was happy to be with them, to spend money on them and give them attention and sanctuary from whatever they didn't want to deal with at the moment.

Ironically, all of the women, young and old, had helped to prepare Evans for the military. He learned to take orders from the more experienced ladies and how to give them to the younger ones.

Victoria is somewhere in the middle, he thought. But she was also unique in his experience. For most of his life the only people Evans had really gotten to know were gangsters or soldiers. Victoria was a person. And as a person, she reminded him that he was wrong about something. By the time he broke with Hurwitz, Amos Evans thought that he had done everything he could do with a woman. That wasn't true. He had never felt anything deeper than affection for any woman in his life. By the time Father John had turned Evans's life around, the young man was preoccupied with God and then the military. On those rare occasions when he actually thought about marriage, the idea appealed to him, but he never found the time to pursue it or the right person to pursue it with.

Until now.

Evans grabbed his boots from beside his footlocker and sat on the edge of the bed. There was something about Victoria that made him want not to be alone. He had been feeling that before she went back to New York, and he had been thinking of her while she was gone. That surprised him. He had worked closely with smart, attractive women at DARPA and in the Navy, yet none of them had touched him the way she had. Like many of those teenaged girls he once knew, Victoria was hurting and needed strength, help. *His* help. She also had the maturity and intelligence most of those other girls had lacked.

He happened to glance at Axe's old desk, which was hand-carved with figures of warriors from all eras of history. Among the figures on the front was an Arthurian knight. Evans thought of Sir Lancelot, Arthur's favorite and most trusted knight. He thought of how Lancelot's desire to protect Queen Guinevere led to love and passion and a closeness that virtually destroyed Camelot. That gave him pause. A friendship might complicate his working relationship with Victoria. It could also create tension between the two of them if things went wrong, or jealousy among the others if by some happy chance things went *right*.

And then there was the possibility that he was out of his damn mind. Victoria might not be interested in him "that way." Maybe she only wanted his support. He was her commander and long-time coworker. Who else could she turn to?

Unfortunately, relationships were not an area where he had a lot of hands-on experience. But like the less emotional issue of new long johns for the Stealth team—he smiled as he thought of the segue from the sublime to the practical—the question of how to deal with these feelings would have to wait. There was a battle to fight and, just as it did in wartime, a conflict for survival had a way of shutting everything else down. Even thoughts of women.

Tugging on his boots, Evans left the cabin and headed back toward the com-shack.

Twenty-one

Germantown, Pennsylvania
Monday, 5:59 P.M.

Taylor left the car in Mrs. St. Martin's spot at Park Drive Manor's indoor garage. Then he and Colonel Lewis walked the short distance to the zujitsu dojo, which was located on the third floor of a narrow brick building on West Harvey Street.

Though the streets were less friendly now, with punks on the corner and homeless people where there had been none before, Taylor still saw the neighborhood's charm. The 19th and early 20th century facades, some of them restored, sat close to the sidewalk with flowerpots and dolls in the windows. The tall thick oaks whose roots had split the concrete framed the walk from the roadside. Though the owners of the homes and the musical tastes of the loiterers changed with time, the quaintness of the setting did not. Taylor did not let the people ruin the place or the memories—memories of coming here every day after school from the time he was nine until the time he went away to college.

When Taylor and Lewis reached the building, they entered the vestibule. The linoleum tiles were nearly worn to the wood underneath, but the black and white wall tiles were clean and there was no trash on the floor. Taylor pressed the buzzer beside 301. A strong, high voice crackled over the speaker.

"Oss?"

"Oss," Taylor said, offering the traditional Japanese greeting. When stated as a question it meant, *"Do you understand and will you obey?"* When uttered as a response the word meant, *"I do understand."* *"Sensei,* it's Hank Taylor and Colonel Matt Lewis."

The door buzzed and Taylor stepped in followed by Lewis. The men hurried up the old wooden stairs. Without even thinking, Taylor did what he had been instructed to do the first time he came. He bent his knees and lowered his center of gravity as he climbed. The stairs barely creaked. Sensei Ruiz believed that everything was training, even climbing a staircase as silently as possible.

Lewis ascended on the balls of his feet, not as quietly.

The smell of incense was strong and comforting as they neared the third floor. Wherever Taylor went in the world, that smell immediately brought him back to this place and gave him a sense of peace. The door of the dojo was open. There was a bench beside the door. The men sat and removed their shoes and socks. It was both a sign of respect and a practical matter. Students worked out in bare feet to strengthen their toes and toughen their soles. Pebbles, glass, and splinters of wood tended to hitchhike in on shoe bottoms.

Master Frank Ruiz came from his small office. The eighty-eight-year-old *sensei* had a round face and swarthy, leathery skin from the four years he had spent in the Pacific with the Fifth Fleet during World War II, then studying for another decade in the spartan Shaolin temple in Wutai, China. Since returning to the United States in 1955, Master

Ruiz had lived at this dojo, sleeping on a bedroll he kept in the small dressing room. He wore a black *gi* and a red-and-black belt signifying his grandmaster status. Taylor had last seen his *sensei* several months ago, shortly before being ordered down to Langley.

Taylor locked his elbows at his sides, held his fists out, and bowed to the slender, white-haired grandmaster. Master Ruiz bowed back slightly and then the men embraced. They both stood tall as they did. The *sensei* had made it a practice that every student embrace every other student at both the start and end of class. One could not be afraid of full-body contact and practice martial arts. And they were not permitted to bend, however much taller one student was than another. *Sensei* did not want them getting into the bad habit of being off balance when coming into contact with another person.

Sensei smiled as he stepped back. The spindly man squinted at his pupil. "It's good to see you, though I am sorry to have heard about the circumstances."

"Thank you, *sensei*," Taylor said. The major turned and presented Colonel Lewis.

Lewis saluted, then stepped forward and offered his hand. "It's an honor to meet you, sir. Mr. Taylor has told us a lot about you."

Master Ruiz shook his hand and held it for a moment. "You're a knife fighter," he said.

"Yes, sir."

"And a good one," Master Ruiz added.

"How can you tell any of that, sir?" Lewis asked.

Master Ruiz rubbed Lewis's palm midway between the base of the colonel's pinkie and the wrist. "The skin is very hard here. That's where the knife hilt toughened it."

Lewis smiled. "And how do you know I'm good, sir?" he asked.

"Your posture, for one thing," Master Ruiz said as he released Lewis's hand. "You didn't lean forward to shake my hand. A good knife fighter stays balanced. He never knows when he has to catch or step away from a victim. Also, you didn't blink when you approached me. That was trained into you. To wait for the other fellow to blink before moving."

"I'm impressed, sir." Lewis smiled.

Master Ruiz looked back at Taylor. The *sensei*'s eyes were failing but Taylor was amazed at how much they saw. He himself felt naked right now, but it had nothing to do with vision.

"How is your mother?" Master Ruiz asked softly.

"She's critical, *sensei*," Taylor replied. "Unconscious with a severe concussion, broken bones, but no other internal trauma."

"She will recover?"

"It's too early to say, *sensei*," Taylor replied. "But my mother will probably survive. How much mobility she regains and whether any of her mental faculties have been impaired—it's too early to tell any of that."

"I see." Master Ruiz nodded and continued to look at him.

"*Sensei,* do you know why they did this?" Taylor asked.

"I've heard things, and there has been speculation," Master Ruiz said. "Several young students from your mother's building heard things. I'm told they or their parents saw things from the window."

"I'll tell you what happened," Taylor said. "A couple of months ago I tore into some punks selling drugs in the parking lot. They were in an old black Cadillac. I didn't know who they were, only that they didn't belong there."

"But they knew who you were."

"Apparently. Or they found out," Taylor said.

Master Ruiz nodded. "So you came here to talk to the Street Cleaners to see if they knew anything about the gang, *oss*?"

"Oss, sensei," Taylor replied. "I thought some of them might come to the six-thirty class."

The Street Cleaners were former gang members who had left their various gangs to form a civilian patrol unit. They had first organized twenty years before and Master Ruiz trained them for free—as long as they stayed out of trouble and gave at least three hours a week to the unit.

"Some of the Street Cleaners will be here, but I've already spoken to them," Master Ruiz said. "They have a good idea who it was you chased from the parking lot that night. One of them lost an eye because of your attack. Two of the others had their arms in casts."

"They pulled weapons," Taylor said. He felt as though his insides had been set on fire. He wanted these people. Bad. "Who are they, *sensei?*"

Master Ruiz stepped a little closer. "I see this terrible thing in your eyes, Mr. Taylor."

"I know, *sensei,*" Taylor said.

"But you're not doing anything to control it," Master Ruiz said. "Our system is about controlling yourself, your body, your opponent. You're feeding this furnace of yours."

"I'm sorry," Taylor said.

"As am I," Master Ruiz said. He stepped back. "But I also taught you that you can't fight your instincts. So I'll tell you what you want to know. They believe the attackers were members of a gang named Moonshot."

"I've never heard of them," Taylor said.

"They sell heroin," Master Ruiz said. "Instead of moonshine they call it moonshot."

"Pushers with a sense of humor," Lewis said. "That alone makes me want to hand them their heads."

"Do you know where they hang out?" Taylor asked.

"They work from a parking garage on Front and Gatzmer Streets," the *sensei* told him.

"Do the police know that, Master Ruiz?" Lewis asked.

"They do," the martial arts master replied. "But Moon-shot has been a difficult group to stop. The dealers and distributors have known one another for years and earn a great deal of money. No one breaks rank and the weapons they carry are all legal. The boss claims to be a political refugee from Armenia and that he needs the protection. They pay the parking fee, conduct their business, and then leave."

"I don't understand, master," Lewis said. "They can be watched, videotaped. The police should be able to do something."

"Apparently, the gang members trade drugs and money by switching cars," Master Ruiz replied. "There are different teams and different cars. The only car that's always the same is the Bentley that belongs to the leader. There's no law against trading vehicles and no reason to approach them, especially if the tags and emission stickers are current and the lights are working correctly and they have paid the fee to enter the lot."

"And do the police know about their possible involvement in the attack on Mrs. Taylor?" Lewis asked.

"They were informed," the grandmaster replied. "But there appears to have been only one witness to the attack and that was Mrs. Taylor. Frankly, more people saw Mr. Taylor assault the men in the car. There were the men in the car and several others from their windows."

"The Moonshot gang probably didn't press charges because they don't want trouble," Lewis speculated.

"*Sensei,* can you tell me what time these animals usually meet?" Taylor asked.

"Between ten o'clock and midnight," he said. "Then the drivers with the drugs disburse. They go to places like Park Drive Manor to deliver their poison to smaller distributors."

"What are there, about a dozen gang members in the lot while all this is going on?" Lewis asked.

"I'm told there are three to five people in each car, twenty or more gang members," Master Ruiz said.

Lewis shook his head. "Not great odds."

"I don't care about the rest of them," Taylor said. "My fight is with four of them."

"*You* may not care about them, but Master Ruiz told you they're a tight band," Lewis said. "If someone attacked one of your dojo brothers or sisters, wouldn't the fight be with everyone?"

"We have honor," Taylor replied.

"And they have a business to run," Lewis said. "From what Master Ruiz said, it sounds like they've got an old team that won't want to lose personnel. Besides, I'm not so sure they'll even fight you."

"I won't give them a choice," Taylor said.

"I don't know about that," Lewis said. "I don't want to piss on your party, but they may have a choice you're not counting on."

"What do you mean?" Taylor asked.

"These guys obviously aren't careless," Lewis said. "There are probably rival drug dealers out there. I'll bet they leave their cars in shifts, no more than one group at a time. If somebody comes after one group, the other guys are still in the cars and can call 911. What choice would the police have except to arrest whoever's attacking them?"

"This is ridiculous!" Taylor said angrily.

"It gets worse," Lewis said. "I'm betting you won't even be able to follow just the four sons of bitches you want."

"Why not?"

"If I were dealing drugs, I'd post lookouts around the perimeter to watch for a tail," Lewis said.

"Fine," Taylor said. "Let them do their recon and call it in and have the police come to their rescue. I'll still have enough time to go in there and take those four shits out."

"You do that and you won't be getting back to where

you need to be by tomorrow morning," Lewis pointed out.

"What did you do, work out a script with Commander Evans?"

"No, Major. This is common sense," Lewis said. "It's about duty—"

"To who?" Taylor snapped. "My country or my mother? What am I supposed to do, nothing? Let these animals get away with what they did?"

"That isn't nothing," Master Ruiz pointed out.

"You're right, *sensei*. It's cowardice!" Taylor said.

"It's a *choice*," Master Ruiz replied. "The right choices don't always suit us, Mr. Taylor, but they're still the right ones."

"Letting this go isn't the right choice," Taylor said. "Why doesn't anyone see that but me?"

"Because we are seeing clearly," Master Ruiz said. "You know you *can* beat them, *oss*?"

"*Oss, sensei*," Taylor replied. "But I didn't start this to prove anything."

"Why did you start it?"

"To clean up the world a little," Taylor replied. "To teach them manners, courtesy. I won't feel right unless I finish it."

Master Ruiz's mouth turned up imperceptibly. "I see. Above all, we want you to feel right."

Taylor shut his mouth tightly. He felt like a kid again, being quietly disciplined by his teacher. The Marine medical officer looked at Master Ruiz and then exhaled through his nose.

"I deserved that, *sensei*," he said. "This part of it isn't about the world. They hurt my mother. They're going to pay."

"I understand that," Master Ruiz said. "But there's one thing you should consider."

"What is that, *sensei*?"

"Do you know Robert Mallon?"

"Yes," Taylor said. "He's one of the Street Cleaners, works on the docks during the day. I met him the last time I was here."

"That's right," Master Ruiz said. "Mr. Mallon also patrols that area at night. He heard from someone who works at the garage that the only reason Moonshot didn't kill your mother was to make sure you came down to visit her. Coming here, the gang was certain that you would seek them out. And seeking them out, you would be trapped very much as Mr. Lewis has described. Tell me. If that comes to pass, how will you feel then?"

"Stupid," Taylor answered honestly. "*If* it comes to pass."

"Nothing is certain," Master Ruiz replied. "But don't forget what you learned your first day here. When you attack, if your opponent is trained he can use your momentum against you. And you never know if or how your opponent is trained, do you?"

Taylor said nothing.

The grandmaster extended his hand to Colonel Lewis. "Mr. Lewis, thank you for coming."

Lewis clasped the grandmaster's hand with both of his. "Thank *you,* sir. I hope to see you again."

"I would like that," Master Ruiz said. "Tell me. Is Captain Hirt still instructing at Fort Bragg?"

"Yes, he is," Lewis said. He was openly surprised. "Sir, how did you know I'm from Bragg?"

"You have a 1st Special Forces Operational Detachment insignia on your watch," he said.

"That doesn't mean I'm from Bragg—"

"I've read Captain Hirt's interviews in magazines," Master Ruiz said. "He believes in training fighters to use their left hand since most soldiers are taught to defend against a right-handed attack. I noticed that the skin of your left hand is as tough as your right."

Lewis smiled. "Damn, sir. You ought to be giving the lessons there. I'll give him your regards."

Master Ruiz smiled, then turned to Taylor. The men embraced.

"I love you, Hank," Master Ruiz said into his ear. "But I believe this to be true: If you deny them what they want you will win. *Oss?*"

"*Oss, sensei,*" Taylor replied.

The two men turned and quickly left the dojo. They sat on the rickety old bench in the hallway, put their shoes on in silence, then hurried down the stairs. They stepped into the street. The sun had dropped behind the buildings and there was a slight chill in the air. Taylor glowered at the street. He remembered a time when he used to come out of here feeling better about himself. Right now he wanted to break something. Anything.

"You were lucky to have trained with him," Lewis said. "He's an exceptional man."

Taylor nodded.

"So you want to hear what I think?" Lewis asked.

"Sure."

"I think we should go back to the hospital and visit with your mother and Mrs. St. Martin for a while."

Taylor looked around for something to punch. A little newspaper stand, a mailbox, a street lamp. He was angry at the *sensei* for having made him feel headstrong. This wasn't about being impulsive. It was about rage. Rage that was completely justified.

Don't transfer that to Master Ruiz, he cautioned himself. *He was just looking out for you.*

"Taylor?" Lewis said.

"Yeah."

"Let's go back there, okay?"

"Yeah," Taylor said. "I'm going to drive to the hospital,

pick up Mrs. St. Martin, bring her home, then head downtown to Front Street."

"What?" Lewis said.

"I'm going to the Moonshot garage," Taylor said.

"Man, didn't you hear a goddamn thing your *sensei* said
up there?" Lewis asked.

"Every word," Taylor assured him. "I even heard the
words that weren't said. But I have to go. I don't know what
I'm going to do, but I can't let this sit. I *won't* let it sit."

"What if I order you not to go?"

"You won't," Taylor said. "That's a cheap way to win
and you don't play cheap. If I don't go to that parking lot,
I'm not going to be worth shit to anyone. Not to me and not
to the team."

Lewis shook his head. "Man, I'm as all-for-revenge as
the next Special Forces guy. I'll drink blood with the
Vikings. But think about what we're looking at here. What
we're risking."

"I can't see that far."

"I can. I can see you losing it, losing your cool and
tracking skills, and tearing into these guys. Which is why I
should fucking order you not to do this," Lewis said.
"Commander Evans asked me not to wear rank up here, but
he didn't order it."

"Then order me," Taylor said softly. "You want me to
go back with you, I'll go back."

"And the catch is . . . ?"

"That is isn't going to accomplish a damn thing," Taylor
said. "You'll be bringing damaged goods back to base."

"I thought you were a pro, not a candy-ass."

Taylor made a face. "You don't get it. What do you
think, I would go back down there and sit and wring my
fucking hands, 'Ooooh, I got ordered around and I'm so
fucking sad'? No, man. I'm afraid I'll go back and go after
some guys Evans wants and have a Moonshot flashback

and take someone's head off. You *know* what a gutful of mad is like, Colonel. You know it doesn't go away just 'cause you tell it to." Taylor looked at his watch, angled it so he could see in the streetlight. Then he hunkered into the settling darkness. "Look, I'm going back to the hospital to get Mrs. St. Martin. You coming?"

"Yeah," Lewis said. "I'll drive. Don't need you having road rage and not hitting any of your targets."

The men walked with Taylor a few paces ahead. As they rounded the corner the side of the dojo building was visible. Taylor felt eyes looking down on him from the window. He didn't look back. There was no need. He had suffered enough reproval for one day.

And then something strange happened. It was like a very gentle tap on the shoulder.

It suddenly occurred to Taylor that there was something missing from his thought process, or his reaction process, or whatever the hell was happening inside his head. Something he hadn't bothered to consider in all this. Something that made his fists open just a little.

His mother had been attacked, but it wasn't her eyes looking down from above. It was the *sensei*'s.

His mother was still alive.

Twenty-two

**Lake Miasalaro, West Virginia
Monday, 6:00 P.M.**

Evans entered the com-shack, where Victoria was still
seated behind the computer. The recovery of the shuttle
was still on the TV, though she had muted the sound.

"Anything?" Evans asked.

"I haven't seen any banners or pop-ups yet," she said. "I
was just about to do a search on Estate."

Victoria keyed in the word and waited, her fingers
poised above the keyboard. Evans bent over her. There was
a website. Victoria clicked on the hyperlink and went there.
She was told that the website was "under construction."

"To hell with that," she said. She began typing.

"What are you doing?" Evans asked.

"If a site's going to be open for business soon, it's probably very nearly done," she said. "What I'm doing is relatively simple. It's using B2C to reach us. That's a new
business-to-consumer server."

"And?"

"I'm going to change the clock on our computer and send a signal, through B2C, saying that it's a minute past midnight. That should tell the program that it's open for business and let us see what's there."

"That seems a little too easy," Evans said.

"It *is* easy," Victoria replied. "Like I said, that only works if a site is nearly ready and waiting only for a clock trigger. If the site isn't ready, it won't let me in no matter what time it is."

Victoria finished resending the request. The site opened. It downloaded quickly.

"I'm impressed," Evans said.

A flag filled the monitor. But it was not like any flag Evans had ever seen. It was moving slowly, as though waving in the wind, but it quickly morphed from the flag of one nation to another—the United States to Canada to Iceland and on through the flags of Europe, Africa, Asia, South America. There were at least three different flag images each second.

As Evans and Victoria watched, rapt, the screen changed. There was a scroll with mock-calligraphy on it. The large, bold legend on top said *Statement of Emancipation*. Commander Evans read the body copy:

"I, the undersigned, believe in freedom. Freedom to be one or to be many. Freedom to study the universe and explore the self. Freedom from boundaries and controls."

There was a space for an E-mail address at the bottom. Victoria typed in a personal address. Only asterisks appeared on the screen.

"Now they know who you are," Evans said.

"No, they don't," she replied. "I used one of Stephen's addresses."

"No prisoners."

"No prisoners," she said. "It was one he used to chat with women in the tri-state affair rooms. He doesn't know I know about it. If they want to play games in his computer, that's fine with me."

After a moment, they moved to a second screen. There was another simulated scroll. Below it was a form.

> *"Welcome to the future of commerce, communication, and personal security. By filling out the form below, you will have free and immediate access to a revolution in computer living, the most powerful mega-ring on the web."*

"What's a mega-ring?" Evans asked.

"I'm not sure," Victoria replied. "A ring is a series of linked websites about similar topics. But I've never heard of a mega-ring."

"It must be a larger ring."

"No," Victoria said. "A ring is a ring, no matter how many sites are linked. My guess is it's a series of interrelated rings, synergistic in some way."

"That makes sense," Evans said. He felt stupid. He knew he shouldn't because this wasn't his field, but he felt a little slow anyway. He looked over the form. It had spaces for name, address, telephone number, profession, age, sex, and information about the immediate family. "What does their Statement of Emancipation sound like to you? I mean, does it sound legitimate?"

"It sounds almost like every other self-hyped site, hyperbolic and sounding very, very exclusive," she said. "Sites like that always promise the sky to get you to sign on for a low weekly fee."

"Like carny barkers," Evans said.

"Exactly. Once they get your credit card number the

fee is self-renewing. Canceling is a pain in the butt."

"But it doesn't look like these people are asking for a fee," Evans pointed out.

"Maybe that comes later," Victoria said. "There's always a fee somewhere in the site. There has to be."

"Can you hack them, find out who's behind it?" Evans asked.

"Not if they're equipped to shut down any computers that interfere," Victoria said. "It may be easier to let them come to us."

"How?" Evans asked.

"By filling in the form," she said as she started typing.

Victoria entered information about her husband, making up some of it to keep from having her name anywhere on the form. She gave him a fake wife, Emy, and changed his address. Then she pressed "Submit."

The form was rejected instantly.

"Holy shit," she said.

"What?"

"They knew I was lying," she said.

"Okay. Maybe they have access to some kind of database," Evans said.

"Obviously," Victoria replied. "But how could they be so sure their information was accurate unless they had access to multiple sources, and very *recent* multiple sources?"

"And if they already had the information, why ask for it again?" Evans wondered.

"To see if I was lying?" Victoria suggested. She input the correct information about Stephen's wife and address. This time it let her register. "I'll be damned," she said. "They want to keep us honest."

"But we still don't know what they're offering," Evans said.

Then the screen scrolled down one more space. It asked for the name of Stephen's elementary school.

"I don't know that," Victoria said.

"Probably no one but Stephen would," Evans said.

"In theory, yes," she said. "This is a control question. Estate already knows the name of his school, probably from his high school records. They don't want people who are pretending to be other people. They want confirmation so that only the people who are really interested sign up." She sat back. "They're not looking for money right now. What they're looking for are loyalists."

"For what, though?" Evans asked.

Victoria sighed. "It looks like there's only one way we're going to find out what the nature of the revolution is." She sat up, went back to the keyboard, and hit the back-key. That returned her to the sign-up screen. She began inputting her own information using her New York address. "What the hell," she said. "They're not going to find me there."

When she finished, the control question appeared. Evans and Victoria both stared at the monitor. This time the question was different.

" 'Where did you earn your PhD?' " Victoria read. "Interesting," she said. "I wonder why they didn't ask Stephen where he got his law degree."

"Probably to mix things up," Evans suggested. "It wouldn't be difficult to find out where a person went to school, but you couldn't anticipate every question."

"Good point," Victoria said. She typed "New York University" and hit "Enter." Almost at once her application was accepted.

Evans wasn't sure what would come up next. He half-expected more chest-thumping to convince potential subscribers to pay for some service.

He was right. Estate wanted money. But what they offered in exchange stunned him.

Twenty-three

**Cape Canaveral, Florida
Monday, 8:11 P.M.**

During World War II, German rocket scientists led by Werner Von Braun developed the V2 rocket program. The V stood for *Vergeltungswaffe,* "retaliation weapon." Captain Holly never understood how "retaliation" applied to a weapon used to bomb innocent Londoners while they slept, but he wasn't the one who named the rocket. Immediately following the war, parts for captured German V2s were brought to a desert storage facility near Las Cruces, New Mexico. So were the rocket scientists who, wisely, had chosen to surrender to American forces rather than to the Soviets. For years thereafter the nascent American missile program was run from the White Sands Proving Ground.

As the scientists continued to improve the load-bearing capacity and range of the rockets, more room was needed. In 1949 the Joint Long Range Proving Ground was set up at the deserted Cape Canaveral in Florida. On July 24,

1950, the new two-stage "Bumper" rocket was the first one to be launched from "the Cape." The Army Ballistic Missile Agency was established in 1956 to manage the growing arsenal of rockets. The agency continued this mission until 1958, when the National Aeronautics and Space Act was signed by the president, establishing the National Aeronautics and Space Administration. While the ABMA continued to develop and manage payload-bearing missiles for the national defense, NASA was charged with creating research rockets for "flight within and outside the earth's atmosphere." Those flights were launched primarily from Cape Canaveral.

The Cape has grown enormously since the days when the 140,000 acres of marshes were dotted with unimposing gantries and small blockhouses. Today, six thousand of those acres are occupied by the Kennedy Space Center, the hub of Cape's activities; the rest of the Cape is a wildlife sanctuary. Bisected by Kennedy Parkway and NASA Parkway on the west shore of Banana River and by Cape Road and Industry Road on the eastern shore, the space center is the home of launch pads—including 39A and 39B, formerly used to send men to the moon and now used for the space shuttle—test facilities, research labs, hangars, a shuttle landing strip, an Air Force station, the huge Vehicle Assembly Building—one of the largest man-made structures on the planet—and the smaller Satellite Assembly Building. There is a sprawling visitors' complex that offers tours and seminars as well as hosting exhibits of space memorabilia, including a collection of historic boosters in the Rocket Garden, an IMAX movie theater, a full-scale replica of the space shuttle *Explorer,* and even a space-themed playground.

The place certainly felt a lot more like Disney World than the last time Captain Holly was here. He could see that even from a distance as they climbed from the open door of the towering cargo plane. Not that he minded. Holly was completely in favor of anything that could be done to promote selling the exploration of outer space to the taxpaying public.

The StarLifter had landed east of the Kennedy Space Center, at the Air Force Station situated directly on the Atlantic coast. It was located just north of Port Canaveral, which was where the booster recovery ships were moored. Holly and Diaz were greeted by Air Force liaison Captain Jessica Ryan. There was a heightened state of security following the shuttle crash. Despite their top security clearance, both men had to be logged in at Ryan's office.

"I was informed by General Jackson's staff that the nature of your mission is top secret, something having to do with new equipment," the tall, slender African-American officer told them.

"Yes, ma'am," Holly replied.

Ryan's mouth twisted unhappily as a pair of Air Force "newbies" loaded the trunks into a black van. "Well, that's fine for General Jackson and both of you. But I've got to put something in my daily report that doesn't send up a flag at KSC operations."

"What kind of flag would our being here send up?" Diaz asked.

"They might think you know or suspect something about the shuttle crash that the space agency doesn't and will want to talk to you," she said. "To forestall that I'm going to tell them that you're just here to support our own security unit—which, I gather, is not that far from the truth."

"No, it isn't," Holly said.

Captain Ryan looked at the trunks as they climbed into the van. "Those are pretty big grips," she said.

"You should try carrying them for a while," Holly said. "Weight seems to multiply."

"Is that the new equipment?"

"It is," Holly said.

"Will it be installed here?"

"No," Holly replied.

Ryan waited for him to say more. He did not. With the two newbies sitting in front, the van started off. The growl of the engine covered the short, uncomfortable silence.

"What about radioactive components?" Ryan pressed. "Anything hot in there?"

"No," Holly told the officer. "Why do you ask?"

"NASA uses plutonium here to power some of the satellites," Captain Ryan said. "They've got Geiger-L counters hidden all over the Cape to prevent theft and help track what supplies they do have. If there were any radiation, you might set off alarms."

"Not to worry," Holly said. "But if we did have them, they'd be sealed in lead. How would the Geigers pick them up?"

"That's what the L stands for," Ryan replied. "They were developed during the Manhattan Project for security but not used much. A Geiger-L unit reacts to the particular density of lead as well as to the radiation itself."

"I see," Holly said. "Tell me something, though. What other hidden security systems do they have here?" He knew a good deal about the set-up but it never hurt to ask.

"Cameras, motion detectors at the labs and construction sites, guards who scan the IDs," she said. "Pretty much what you'd expect in places that aren't used around the clock like the intel services are."

And pretty much what a saboteur would expect, Holly thought. When he was test-piloting stealth aircraft, security included things he only found out about later. The best, he thought, was that one of the water jets in the shower contained oil with tiny amounts of phosphorous. The substance clung to his skin and hair. If Holly went out at night, he positively glowed in night-vision goggles. That made it easy for Air Force security officers to track him after dark, make sure he wasn't hanging out with foreign agents.

The men were given all-access security badges at Ryan's office. While they were there, Holly glanced at the roster on the duty officer's computer. The shifts changed at one A.M. Holly and Diaz would make their move just before then, when eyes were on clocks instead of doorways.

Once the brief check-in process was completed, the two men and their gear were driven over to a guest room in the Air Force barracks. The first-floor room was white, with two beds on opposite sides of the small area. The newbies told the men where to find the mess hall and showers. When they left, Diaz lay down on the bed. Holly unpacked the secure TAC-SAT phone he'd brought to communicate with Evans. Then he went to the two large windows and opened the blinds. He looked out on a short expanse of lawn and road, beyond which was the Atlantic. He was glad they were on the ocean side of the barracks. It was quieter than on the base side. After sitting in the loud, echoing StarLifter for hours, Captain Holly was enjoying the quiet.

Unfortunately, the silence didn't last long. MCPO Diaz did not know the meaning of "down time."

"Do you think the captain was telling the truth about security measures?" Diaz asked.

"About the technology being relatively unsophisticated?" Holly asked.

"Right."

"Absolutely," Holly said. He raised the window and continued to stare out at the ocean. The cool, surprisingly strong breeze was invigorating and the sea air smelled refreshing. "With all the budget cuts NASA has suffered over the past few years, they don't have all the security they should have," Holly added. "But that wouldn't have affected the ESP."

"Why not?"

"The satellite was Air Force," Holly said. "Security would have come out of *their* budget and the Air Force takes that stuff very seriously."

"So if the satellite was preprogrammed to go bad, not remotely hijacked from earth, it was probably done by someone who already had heavy-duty security clearance," Diaz said.

"That'd be my guess," Holly told him. "But we don't know at what stage of the process that happened. It could have been done by one of the subcontractors, whichever one wrote the software."

"Agreed," Diaz said. "But there would still be checks. The Estate people would have needed someone here to make sure those systems reviews didn't turn up any anomalies."

"Good point," Holly said as he turned from the window and sat on his own bed. He lay back. Something was bothering him. Something that suddenly made him wish he weren't here.

"Where would the satellite have been assembled?" Diaz asked.

"The Satellite Assembly Building, which is on this side of the river," Holly said absently. He was trying to understand his discomfort. "After that, it would have been taken over the bridge to NASA Parkway and over to the Orbiter Processing Facility. That's where it would be married to the shuttle."

"The last checks on the ESP would probably have been done at the assembly building," Diaz said. "But someone still could have made changes in the software at the orbiter facility. Maybe slipped a new microchip in somehow. I say we work backwards," he said. "Start by having a look at the orbiter building and see if there's anything over there that doesn't smell right."

"Makes sense," Holly said. There was a night table between the beds and a small dresser at the foot of one bed. The captain reached over and set the clock for midnight. "I'm going to have a rest till then. How about you?"

"Sounds good," Diaz replied. "I saw a candy machine outside. I'm gonna grab a few Snickers for later. Don't want to have our stomachs growl and give our invisible selves away."

"Makes sense." Holly smiled. "You know, we ought to have that written into the instruction manual."

Diaz left the room. Holly stared at the bright white ceiling and thought about the space shuttle. It made him sick. Yet that wasn't what was bothering him. Not deep inside. It was something else.

This place? he wondered.

As the ocean broke in the distance and the blinds fluttered in the wind, it suddenly occurred to Holly exactly what it was. The sound reminded him of something he'd been told during one of his trips here. That the name "Canaveral" came from the Spanish words for "old" and "edge." This place was the "old seacoast," and it had been so for hundreds of years. Except for one brief period. Cape Canaveral had been called Cape Kennedy for ten years, until 1973. That was when the locals decided that the space center was honor enough and that the coast's Spanish heritage should be reacknowledged.

After their last mission, data had been confiscated from Axe and Holly had learned that his father had been one of the Huntsmen back in the 1960s. President Gordon and Vice President Catlin were not the only officials the Huntsmen had attempted to kill. They had also plotted and carried out the assassination of President Kennedy in Dallas. Afterwards, ashamed about what he'd done, Lane Holly took his life.

It was Kennedy's vision and commitment that had allowed NASA to flower and put a man on the moon. Being here, thinking of the part his father had had in the death of that president, was like a knife lodged in Holly's soul. He struggled to hold back tears of sadness and shame. He wished that he had been more than just a child when all of that was happening, that he had been able to talk to his father and help him.

The tears came, and he turned on his side so that his back was to the door. He didn't want Diaz to see.

It was too late to help Lane Holly, but it was not too late to make sure that these new killers were stopped.

And they would be.

Stopped dead.

Twenty-four

Lake Miasalaro, West Virginia
Monday, 8:46 P.M.

During the ten years since Victoria Hudson first went on-line, she'd seen some strange things on the Internet. Sick sites; bizarre attempts to scam people out of money; and sometimes combinations of the two. But she had never encountered anything like Estate. And though she and Commander Evans had read everything on the website, she still wasn't quite sure what to make of it.

The deal it offered was simple. Once the user had signed up—the way Victoria had—they would be sent a download of additional information. Then, if they agreed to the terms being offered, which included a subscription fee, a free laptop would be sent to them. The new computer would come bundled with 512 MB of RAM memory, dual-channel DDR2, 5DRAM at 533 MHz and a DVD burner.

"That's a lot of juice for a giveaway," Victoria said, looking over the specs.

"How much would that cost in the marketplace?" Evans asked her.

"Maybe two thousand dollars," Victoria said. "But they can't ask for that much as part of the subscription deal. There aren't enough gullible people to buy that blind."

"Obviously, the Estate people intend to make their money back somehow," Evans said.

Victoria nodded. "They're probably going to offer additional downloads of their own software, their own servers, browsers. That'll cost."

"You signed up," Evans said. "Why aren't you getting the initial download they promised?"

"Because those won't be available until midnight," Victoria replied. "It's one thing to fool the computer and get into the website. Webmasters even anticipate that hacker-geeks will break in to get a first look at something new. Some of them count on it to get some buzz going in the chat rooms. But the material itself won't go on-line until then."

"I see. What I don't understand is if the material can be downloaded, why send out new hardware?"

"If I wanted to be paranoid, which I am, I have to wonder if they're planning on using the ESP somehow to shut down every home computer but their own," Victoria said. "Maybe there's a chip in their computers that makes it immune."

"I thought of that," Evans said. "Again, why not just make an antidote to the ESP that's downloadable?"

"Sometimes prophylactic programs work better if they're hardwired," Victoria said.

"Better," Evans said, "but to the tune of five thousand dollars a person? What if millions of people sign up? Who has the money to invest billions of dollars building computers?"

"Well, not everyone would sign up at once," Victoria said. "And if there's a charge for software, the Estate people can use that money to build the additional machines."

"Maybe," Evans said. "There's still an expensive tooling-up process."

"Perhaps not quite so much if the people are already in the business," Victoria pointed out. "The people who are behind this are the people who hijacked the ESP. They obviously know the business."

"True," Evans said. "Is there any way you can find out who they are by hacking deeper into the website?"

"I'll give it a try," Victoria said. "But all I did was shoot an arrow over the castle wall. Getting *to* the website and getting behind it are very different things. There are probably all kinds of safeguards built into the system."

Evans looked at his watch. It was ten minutes to nine. "I wonder if there's one thing we can do."

"What?" Victoria asked.

Evans thought for a moment. Except for the gentle hum of her computer, the only sound Victoria heard was a wind from the lake. It sighed past the door on its way up the hillside. Though the Stealth War team was connected electronically to the rest of the world, she felt very isolated. Vulnerable.

"The people who hijacked the ESP and the people behind Estate are on the same team," Evans thought aloud. "Whatever they're planning to do to the computers at the White House and elsewhere will take place in a few minutes. Do you think there will be some kind of spike in the system somewhere?"

"You mean a power surge?" Victoria asked.

"I don't know—maybe that isn't the right word. They told us where they're going to attack. Can we pick one of those places and watch for incoming from the ESP, a shutdown signal of some kind? Maybe we can identify the frequency and figure out a way to block it."

"In theory, yes," Victoria said. "But I'm sure every government specialist will be doing exactly the same thing.

They know where the ESP is and they'll be tracking it."

"Then I'm not understanding something," Evans said. "Even if we can't stop the satellite, why can't we protect computers from the signal coming off it—or the signals going to it?"

"To answer the first question, the Estate people may slip the shutdown messages to the target some way we're not expecting," Victoria said. "Maybe using the same wavelength as TV or radio receivers, cell phones, maybe even radar systems in the White House or wherever."

"Can they do that?" Evans asked.

"Absolutely," Victoria said. "It doesn't take a complex signal to close something down. As for why we can't intercept the signals on the way to the satellite, I'm guessing the Estate people may use other space platforms as relays—like mirrors bouncing light."

"Are you saying they'll send the signal to another satellite or two first?" Evans asked.

"If they've done their homework they can brainwash dozens, even hundreds of satellites," Victoria said. "A lot of the computer specs are available to whoever wants them. The ESP may have already transformed internal computer systems of other satellites. We call them 'slave systems.' They're allowed to work autonomously until they're needed."

"That could be why there's been a couple of hours lag between the Estate group taking over the ESP and when they're shutting down the targeted computer systems," Evans said.

"They need tooling-up time," Victoria agreed. "Though I have to admit, I've got a weird suspicion about what these people are really up to."

"What kind of suspicion?"

"That they're like magicians who are going to use sleight-of-hand to make us all believers," Victoria said.

"They make a point of warning everyone that a virus of some kind is coming. So everyone shuts down their computers as a preventative measure, to keep them clean. It has the same effect as shutting the systems down themselves."

"But that scam would only work once," Evans said. "In order to make Estate work, these people need to have *real* control."

"True," Victoria said. "But maybe by shutting the computers down, we tip them off about what systems are vital to us. You know those old mystery shows where a burglar would call some rich guy in his mansion and tell him his safe had been robbed? Then the caller would watch while the millionaire moved Lord Rushton's portrait to check the safe—"

"And by so doing revealed where the safe was."

"Exactly," Victoria said. "The ESP was designed to read dedicated computer systems. Maybe it's up there watching to see where we go, what we try to protect from them."

"Except for one thing," Evans said. "They've already demonstrated that they can get into secure systems."

"I missed that. When?"

Evans went to the computer and backed up several screens to the E-mail from the White House. "The president's computer can only receive E-mail once it has passed through a screening process," Evans told her. "In essence, the E-mail is taken off-line and then sent to him via an internal system."

"A screened host firewall," Victoria said. "That makes sense."

Evans shook his head. "I'm afraid this attack is real. And that being the case, there's got to be a way to spot it."

Victoria stared at the Estate home page and then checked her watch. It read 8:53. The blackout was due to hit in seven minutes. It frustrated her that she didn't have any idea how to watch for the carrier wave. Usually, intercepting a signal was a matter of turning the satellite dish to a section of the sky and watching for the transmission code that identified a particular broadcaster—a series of pulses that was unique to that source, like a bar code on consumer goods. There had been a great deal of research in that area to try to scramble signals being received by smart bombs—shut them down or cause them to detonate before they hit American targets. That was part of the initial Strategic Defense Initiative research that was still ongoing. Maybe the ESP was a part of that, called something else in order to get around Congressional bans on SDI spending. There had also been a lot of work done in both the private and military sectors on what were called "quantum cloaks," a laser pulse broadcast so faint that most scans missed it. Except the receiver at which it was directed.

"Maybe I'm missing something here," Evans said. "But if the signal is getting into dedicated computers, it'll *have* to come off the ESP. So even if we can't read the broadcast as it's going up—"

"We should be able to read it coming down," Victoria said. "In theory, that's true. But if there is a blast code, which is a signal that can get through anti-hacker firewalls or in this case into a dedicated system, you can't look at it without getting in the way—"

"And that will shut you down," Evans said.

"Correct," Victoria said. "You're dead before you can even start to read the blast code."

Victoria looked at her watch. There were five minutes to go. Why was it that having a person next to you could be inspiring at some times and debilitating at others? Right now having Evans beside her made each passing minute seem like an additional weight.

"Wait a second," Evans said more to himself than to

Victoria, as though he were thinking aloud. "How long will the shutdown signal have to run?"

"For as long as the computers are supposed to stay shut down, I'd guess," Victoria told him. "Otherwise, they could probably be rebooted and turned back on right away."

"But systems watching for the signal would be on beforehand," Evans said.

"Probably," she said. "Scanning the skies, looking for signals heading toward the ESP or coming from it."

Evans looked at his watch. Then, quickly, he reached for the phone.

"Who are you calling?" she asked.

"The Air Force put the ESP into space," Evans said. "They know where it is and all the codes that were programmed into it. They're going to be watching for any hint of those access codes in signals going to it."

"I'm sure all the codes have been changed," Victoria said. "Otherwise, it would be easy for the Air Force to see them coming and to see where they're coming *from*. The military satellites would read, say, password Alpha-Beta-Gamma-Whatever coming from Main Street, U.S.A., and every space eye would be turned toward the source. For that matter, depending on how sophisticated the Air Force satellites are, they may be able to sweep the skies and read every signal headed spaceward at exactly nine P.M."

"That's exactly my point!" Evans said. He punched a number into the phone and waited. "If you wanted to slip a signal to a satellite unseen, wouldn't you hide in the sunlight?"

"I don't understand."

"You might use the satellites looking *at* the ESP to get to it," Evans said. "You might piggyback into space on that signal."

"Makes sense."

"The Air Force built and is monitoring the ESP from Florida," Evans said. "What if the hijackers have people at Cape Canaveral?"

"So do we," Victoria said.

And she was glad then, very glad that Evans was here.

Twenty-five

The White House
Monday, 8:58 P.M.

The president hung up the phone. He had just received a briefing from NASA Director Steve Bender about the medical condition of the *Venture* astronauts. Lieutenant Dave Havoc was in the best shape of the three survivors. There were broken bones but no internal injuries. He was conscious and lucid. Dr. Humphrey Curtiz was in the worst condition. He'd suffered a collapsed lung, a gross concussion with likely traumatic brain injury to the frontal lobe, and a pair of fractured vertebrae. There was some question about whether there had been damage to his spinal cord. At present he was undergoing computerized tomography scans. The prognosis was good for his survival, but nothing more.

The status of Dr. Barry Gregg was somewhere between that of the other two men. The scientist had broken ribs and third-degree burns on his hands and face, suffered when he worked open the egress hatch through flames. He had suffered a mild transient concussion and, while conscious, was sedated. He spoke, mostly incoherently, about the mission, the satellite, and "the team."

The president was grateful that two of the three surviving astronauts would almost certainly be able to lead normal lives. But the prevailing emotion was sadness for the brave commander and pilot who had died and for the mission specialist who might well be crippled for life.

As president, John Gordon was not unfamiliar with tragedy. During his years in office he had been presented with intelligence reports that had tested his belief in God. Reports of sadism resulting from ethnic hatreds, awful war injuries—skulls and faces sheared away without death resulting—bacteria, chemicals, and radiation tested on prisoners of war in Eastern Europe and the Near East. But there was still a kind of scrim between Gordon and those horrors. Photographs and printed documents were a filtering system that kept an emotional distance between the president and the horror. The crash of the *Venture* was much more personal. The president had met Commander Boring and had been to a recent shuttle launch. He knew how hard the people worked, from the astronauts to the ground crew to the scientists at the Manned Spacecraft Center in Houston. And he knew that this was going to be one of those frozen moments of horror for the American people. He had already gone down to the Rose Garden and made a short speech praising the efforts of the commander and his crew. He had said that the reasons for the accident—which were as yet unknown to the public—were going to be exhaustively investigated and that this would not be the end to the American space program.

"We owe it to these heroes, and to generations yet unborn, to continue the work that took these brave people to the far frontier. . . ."

That wasn't just a platitude. John Gordon believed it and would fight for it against the budget-cutters on the Hill.

But whatever the situation, however grave or upsetting, there was a certainty: The president never had long to dwell on any one thing. Two minutes after he hung up with Steve Bender, as Laura Richmond was turning to remind him that it was nine o'clock, the monitors of the two computers in his office went black, the fan behind the computers died, and the room became eerily silent.

The president and his executive secretary looked at one another. She picked up the phone.

"It's working," she said.

The president shut his computer and tried to reboot it. Nothing happened. He noticed that the light on the monitor was still on.

"So is the TV screen," the president said. "They hit the computers, just as they said they would. Laura, please ask Jane O'Brien to get me reports from the other targets."

"Yes, sir," Ms. Richmond replied.

The president's chief of staff had been briefed on the contents of the message from Estate. He wanted to know if all the sites had gone down as the E-mail said they would. While the executive secretary placed the call to Ms. O'Brien's temporary office, the president called General Rogers. He wanted to know immediately if the blackout had helped the Pentagon find the people who had sabotaged the ESP. Earlier, there had been some debate among the Joint Chiefs of Staff about putting police and FBI offices nationwide on a heightened alert status so they could move as soon as any clues were known, possibly before the shutdown ended. It would be easier to prosecute the perpetrators if they were captured in the act. Though that idea had been abandoned as impractical, FBI Director Tom Patrick was also on the line. If they got a clue, and if there were time, he would immediately put the appropriate field office on the case.

The ominous silence continued. Jane O'Brien called to say that the blackout had also struck, as forecast, in London,

Germany, Moscow, and Tokyo. Still on the line, General Rogers asked one of his aides if the think tanks they'd consulted had come up with a reason why France, China, India, and other major nations had been spared.

The answer was that they didn't know.

"What's your thinking on this, General?" the president asked.

"Well, our first reaction, sir, was that the attacks were a virtue of proving they could strike simultaneously in several different time zones," Rogers explained. "Then we thought that there might be a connection with techno-terrorists based in those countries. NASA's intelligence people think it might have to do with sending a warning to space-faring nations, but France and China were spared any direct attacks."

"Maybe they're afraid of Beijing," O'Brien suggested. "No one's afraid of France."

"That's possible," Rogers said. "It's also possible that one of those nations is behind it. They certainly have the technology. But our thinking right now is along a different line. We believe that the five countries represent the most likely source of subscribers to whatever this Estate website is."

"Interesting," the president replied.

"That could make the site politically motivated rather than financially driven," O'Brien suggested.

"Exactly," said Rogers. "We've got a team trying to find a common denominator between the five countries. Any movements that have touched them all, religious groups, cults, anything."

"What kind of cult would have the resources to do something like this?" the president's chief of staff asked.

"According to David Van Dyne there are several that have very successful international business fronts," Rogers said.

Van Dyne, a former Chairman of the Securities and

Exchange Commission, was the hard-nosed director of the CIA's International Business Investigations Department, the so-called White Collar Witch-hunters. Among other things, the IBID worked closely with the FBI, Interpol, and other international police organizations to find and break money-laundering schemes.

The president thanked the team for their ideas and good work, then hung up. He took a moment to phone the first lady and catch up on her day. When she asked if he had eaten and he told her that he had not, she said she was bringing a Cobb salad over. He thanked her, then asked Ms. Richmond how much longer she intended to stay. She was a good woman with a devoted husband and she should be with him more often.

"I'll leave as soon as the computers come back on," she said. "If there's a problem, I'll have to go get the printouts of all our phone numbers and addresses in case they're needed."

The president smiled at the fifty-three-year-old woman. She had fine gray hair worn in a bun, clear, pale skin, and the bluest, most compassionate eyes he had ever seen.

"Thank you, Ms. Richmond," the president said to her. "I hadn't thought of that."

"You've had other things on your mind," Ms. Richmond said as she turned back to her desk.

The president sat back to await the first lady and the return of the computer systems. There were another nine minutes to go, according to his watch. The phone beeped. Ms. Richmond answered. It was the vice president. Chuck Catlin had been assigned to liaise with the leaders of the other countries named in the Estate E-mail. He was reporting on the last of those conversations, with United Nations Secretary General Eiji Tsuburaya of Japan. Mr. Tsuburaya wanted to know if the United States expected to be able to recover control of the ESP.

"I told him what I told the other foreign leaders, that we are working very hard on that problem and on finding out who is behind Estate," Vice President Catlin replied. "Is there any news on that?"

The president brought the vice president up to date on what General Rogers and the others were thinking and doing.

"It is an interesting mix of targets," the vice president said. "Old democracies and new ones."

"Yes, three of them totalitarian states during the last century," the president added.

"I'm not sure any of that is relevant," the vice president said. "They may simply be those computers that the ESP is currently able to hit."

"Hopefully, we'll find that out," the president said.

The vice president hung up and President Gordon looked at his watch. There were four minutes left. The phone beeped again. Ms. Richmond answered.

"It's Mr. Bender," she said.

The president picked up the phone. "Yes, Steve?"

"Mr. President, I'm sorry to have to tell you this but we've lost Dr. Gregg," Bender said.

"Dr. Gregg?" the president said. "I thought he was doing all right."

"He was," Bender replied. "It looks as if someone might have given him the wrong medicine—"

"What?"

Bender's statement—his confession, actually—just hung there unwanted. Of all the things the president had heard today, those words were somehow the most horrific.

"Don't tell me that, Steve," the president said angrily. "Don't tell me that your people screwed up."

"It may have been a miscommunication—"

"How? For Christ's sake, Steve, this wasn't a rocket trajectory you were calculating—"

"I know, Mr. President," Bender said. "Dr. Gregg's physician in Florida was consulted on his condition and E-mailed data from the flight. Even brief exposure to weightlessness affects blood flow and has to be factored into dosages of any medication. It appears as though a number with a misplaced decimal point came through from the Cape."

"Christ, Steve," the president said. "Jesus Christ."

"Mr. President, I don't know what to say," Bender went on. "You'll have my resignation, of course."

"Like hell!" the president snapped. "You don't slink away like that."

"Mr. President, I wasn't—"

"You're going to ride this one out, Steve. Ride it right through the inquiries. You can start by making an announcement about Dr. Gregg personally. Tell the truth and take the heat. Then find out who's responsible and get them here tomorrow. I want to fire them myself."

"Yes, Mr. President."

"Is his mother at the hospital?"

"She is," Bender replied.

"Make sure there's enough security to give the woman her privacy," the president said.

"There will be."

"And I don't mean a half-assed job," the president told him. "I want it done right."

"It will be."

The president hung up. Actually, he slammed the phone down. For years critics had said that NASA stood for "Not A Serious Agency" and "Never A Straight Answer." Gordon had refused to accept that—until now. He was embarrassed for the nation, for the government, and most of all for the thousands of good people who worked at the agency. And he resented the added burden this placed on them all while they were dealing with the threat of the ESP and Estate.

The president looked over at Laura Richmond. The woman was staring back at him.

"We lost Dr. Gregg," he said quietly.

"His poor mother," she said. "That poor, poor woman."

A moment later the first lady arrived with a food tray. She looked lovely and reassuring. Seconds after that, the computers winked back on. There was a sudden semblance of normalcy. But it was only superficial. Which was okay, for the moment. The president was going to have to issue a statement in time to make the ten P.M. news. It would be a good opportunity to assure the nation that the normalcy was real, to tell them again that all would be well.

Platitudes, he thought.

The president hated lying to the nation, but America was a place where people liked going to bed feeling safe. So did the stock market. Telling lies—or rather, withholding the truth—was better than causing domestic or financial panics. And the truth about the ESP would do that.

The first lady sat down on the opposite side of the desk and the president told her what had happened. She took the news stoically, as was her way. While the president was speaking, the first lady reached across the desk and took her husband's hand between both of hers. Her touch was warm and soft and comforting. Wherever they were, whatever the circumstances, it always made the president feel as if he were home.

Unfortunately, Gordon could not afford to stay there. He needed to bring Amos Evans up to speed and see if his team had learned anything about Estate. He also needed to talk to the Secretary of State and his foreign policy advisors about other issues that had been on the back burner since the shuttle accident. Military flare-ups between China and the separatist province of Fujian on the East China Sea. Brewing civil war in Mauritania on the west coast of Africa, unrest that threatened to dump tens of thousands of refugees into

Morocco. Territorial squabbles off the coast of Antarctica, of all places, between Russia and Canada involving the discovery of oil.

Reluctantly, the president asked his wife and Ms. Richmond to excuse him for a few minutes. The president did not want anyone, even the first lady, to know about the Stealth Warriors. Some of what concerned him was the security of the team; the fewer people that knew about them, the safer they were. Keeping it from the first lady was a different matter. The secret unit had been authorized to use whatever means necessary to protect the nation and the president. If the team were ever found out and investigated, Gordon did not want his wife to have knowledge of their existence.

The women left, closing the door behind them. The president placed the call.

What he heard from Amos was not what he was expecting.

Twenty-six

Germantown, Pennsylvania
Monday, 8:59 P.M.

His mother was alive. . . .

It was in the car, on the way back to the hospital, that Hank Taylor started to question what he intended to do. Until a few minutes before, what he had been determined to do.

Lewis remembered the way they had come, and reversed it without asking for help. As he drove, Taylor just sat in the passenger's seat staring out at the dark night and into his soul.

The idea had been to give Mrs. St. Martin her car, visit his mother, then head out to where Moonshot hung out and take the gang apart. Limb by limb, stinking joint by joint. The major felt that he owed it to his mother and to family honor to *punish* those who had attacked her, not let them off. Yet they hadn't killed her. Taylor wasn't about to praise them for that, but he still had his mother. The realization that she was still here softened his rage a little. At least, it was enough to make him question himself.

Rage and honor on one side, gratitude on the other. He didn't see how he could reconcile these different feelings.

He thought briefly about Commander Evans, "St. War," and the fact that Evans had somehow been able to handle being a devout Catholic and a special-ops soldier. Taylor hadn't talked about it a lot with Evans because they'd been extremely busy over the past few weeks. In addition to that, the commander was a private man. He was happy to talk about Catholicism and faith in general, but much less so about his own life and faith.

Still, Evans had once allowed that he found it possible to deal with the conflict by prioritizing. *"God comes first,"* he had said. He went on to explain that while he had killed for his country, he had never murdered anyone, which was what the commandment forbade.

In Taylor's case the hierarchy was also quite clear. His mother came first, the Stealth Warriors came second, and medicine came third. Taylor himself came fourth, and the question he had to ask himself was simple. It was the same one Lewis had posed.

Who was the counterattack really for?

His mother wouldn't want it. His unit wouldn't benefit by it. And to hurt people went against the Hippocratic Oath. The last time, in the parking lot of Park Drive Manor, they had threatened him first. If he went after them it would be bald aggression.

But they shouldn't be allowed to get away with it, he thought. What they'd done was evil. *And yet—*

It started to rain. Drizzle smeared the streetlights. The car turned a corner. The hospital was just a few blocks away. It towered over the small, old houses on the street.

"So?" Lewis said.

Taylor looked at him.

"You still got a mad on?" Lewis asked.

"I don't know," Taylor replied. He looked back out the window. The rivulets of water were bright and clean. Simple, like too few things in life. "This morning, when the commander told me what happened, I got this emotional thing going. I kept it cranking on the train, in at the hospital, with *sensei*. I *was* mad. Madder than I've ever been."

"What about now?"

"Now . . . I don't want to give it up. It isn't only payback. There's honor to think about."

"But you're spent," Lewis said.

Taylor looked at him again. "Yeah, I'm feeling pretty drained."

"Abort Syndrome," Lewis said.

"It's exactly that," Taylor replied.

Abort Syndrome was when soldiers were put on red alert, stayed at high readiness for an hour or two, then had to stand down. The intense level of preparedness and the increased adrenaline flow resulted in a proportionate emotional, mental, and physical crash.

"I've always believed that honor isn't necessarily in the acting," Lewis pointed out. "Sometimes it's in the restraint."

"But how do you know when it's restraint and how do you know when it's eating shit?" Taylor asked.

"One of them tastes really, really bad," Lewis said. "The other one doesn't necessarily sit well, but it sits right."

"Are you saying you'd give this up if you were me?" Taylor asked.

"If I were you? Yeah," Lewis told him. "I'd let this go. For one reason, if nothing else."

"What's that?" Taylor asked.

"You're too caught up in it," Lewis told him. "You'd make bad calls, emotional calls."

Lewis parked the car in the short-term spot near the

emergency ward and they went in. Because it was after visiting hours, only immediate family was allowed into patients' rooms. Mrs. St. Martin was waiting in the lobby adjoining the emergency ward, knitting.

Taylor apologized for being late. Mrs. St. Martin told him it was all right. She said that this was exactly what she'd be doing if she were home, except that the television would be on.

"And this is far more interesting than *ER*," she said.

Taylor smiled at her.

Since he couldn't go upstairs, Lewis said that he would like to drive Mrs. St. Martin home. Then he said he would come back for Taylor.

"You'll be here, won't you?" Lewis asked.

"Of course he will," the woman said sharply. "There's nothing around here worth going to." She looked from Lewis to Taylor. "Where else would you be, Henry?"

Taylor shook his head slowly. "Nowhere, Mrs. St. Martin." He looked at Lewis. "I'll be right here when you get back."

Lewis nodded once.

Mrs. St. Martin rose. She bundled up her yarn and needles and began putting them in a large paper shopping bag. "I must have missed something," she said to herself. "My daughter does that all the time. Says things to her friends that I don't understand, that I'm probably not *supposed* to understand. But that's okay. I don't need more things cluttering up my poor head. I've already got enough in there already that I don't want."

Lewis took the shopping bag from Mrs. St. Martin, gave her his arm, and escorted her from the hospital. She was still complaining about all the things she had in her head as they left.

Taylor went upstairs. The intensive care ward was fluorescent-bright but quiet. Taylor went to his mother's room and sat in the chair beside her bed. The woman was still unconscious. She seemed thinner than before. Maybe it was just the nighttime darkness in the room, but the shadows seemed deeper on the parts of her cheek, eye socket, and wrist that he could see. He wanted to touch her, to hold her hand, but was afraid he might dislodge the intravenous tube or the monitors that were attached to her fingers. So he sat there hunched over, the chair turned toward the bed, his elbows on his thighs and his hands hanging between his legs. He looked at his mother lying motionless on the bed. She looked as though she was asleep, but she wasn't. She was unconscious. He could tell by the shallowness of her breathing and the absence of any eye movement.

Warm tears built along his eyes and quickly spilled over.

"I'm sorry I started this thing," Taylor said quietly. "And I'm sorry I wasn't there to protect you. It's like a sickness." He shook his head. "I can't stop picturing them hurting you. I don't know whether I'm beating myself up with that or keeping the hate alive or what, but I'm having trouble with it, Mom. I really am. I want to bust them up, hurt them back. But Colonel Lewis is right. I don't think I can do that. I'd go gorilla on these guys and get myself in trouble. Then I'd let you down and my unit down and who knows where this would go from there. I don't want you to think less of me. I just hope that when you get better you'll tell me you forgive me. Because I can't."

Taylor sobbed openly, and continued to weep as he sat there looking at her. He thought back on his life, on his mother's life, on how he wanted to spend more time with her when she got out of here. Maybe she would move to West Virginia so they could be closer. Perhaps Mrs. St. Martin would go with her. Things cost a lot less than they did in Philadelphia. They could buy a house together, have a garden, enjoy warmer weather and a slower lifestyle. Get away from the gangs.

A young nurse rapped on the half-open door. "Time to take the eleven o'clock readings," she whispered.

Taylor wiped his eyes. He smiled at her as he stood and moved the chair out of the way.

The nurse smiled back as she walked in on cat's feet, quietly and gently. She looked at the monitor on the wall beside the bed. "Has your mother moved or said anything?"

"No," Taylor said. He glanced at his watch and frowned. *How had it gotten to be eleven o'clock?*

Excusing himself, Taylor went down the hall to the pay phone. He dropped in a quarter and phoned Mrs. St. Martin.

"Hello?" she said.

"Hi, Mrs. S," Taylor said. "Sorry to call so late."

"Is anything wrong?"

"No, no—Mom's the same. I was just wondering. Has my friend Mr. Lewis left yet?"

"Quite a while ago," she said. "Isn't he with you?"

"No—"

"Well, that's strange," Mrs. St. Martin said. "Let me think. He left—oh, it was exactly an hour and five minutes ago. Mr. Lewis was very kind. He saw me to my apartment door, came in and called a cab, and then he was gone."

Goddamn him, Taylor thought suddenly.

"Oh, and he took something to eat," she added. "Several slices of American cheese. Do you think he's all right?"

"I do, Mrs. S," Taylor replied, "but I've got to run. I'll talk to you in the morning."

Taylor hung up. He hurried back to the room and kissed the bandage across his mother's forehead.

"Hang in there," he said quietly. "I'll be back in the morning."

Taylor left the room, phoned for a cab, then went to the

lobby and waited. *Of course,* he thought. He should have seen this coming. Lewis had done exactly what Taylor would have done in his place. Lewis had helped him get to the high road, then put himself on his own high road: taking up the commitment of a friend and making it his own.

Lewis had gone to see Moonshot himself.

Twenty-seven

Lake Miasalaro, West Virginia
Monday, 9:33 P.M.

Commander Evans was still in the com-shack. He was conferring with Captain Holly by phone.

Holly had reported that he and Diaz were waiting until after lights out before proceeding. Evans had just finished sharing the thoughts he and Victoria had about a possible starting point for their investigation when the president's line beeped. Evans told Holly he would call back if he had anything else to report.

The president told Evans that all the targets on the Estate list had been struck, as the E-mail had threatened. He also told the commander about the loss of Dr. Gregg. Evans asked how the scientist had died, and the president told him. Gregg's death did not hit Evans the same way it had affected Gordon. Evans hadn't known the mission specialist personally. Emotionally, he was able to fold the death into the whole tragedy. But there was something else that stood out. Something that refused to be folded away.

"Mr. President, I may be taking a really wide swing here, but there's a coincidence that doesn't sit well," Evans said.

"What's that?"

"How certain are you that Dr. Gregg's death resulted from data contained in a downloaded file?" Evans said.

"Very certain," the president replied. "Why?"

"What if that download was intentional?"

"Are you talking about assassination?"

"Yes, sir. The misinformation could have been placed in the file at Cape Canaveral or it could have been placed in the file after it left the Cape."

"Placed there by who?" the president asked.

"By the people behind Estate," Evans told him. "Placed in the computer by the ESP."

"Why?"

"Because that would dovetail with something else we've been considering," Evans told the president. "That the takeover of the satellite was probably an inside job."

"We've been talking about that too, but we haven't begun to narrow down the possibilities," the president said. "I still don't see what that has to do with the killing of Dr. Gregg."

"Suppose no one expected Dr. Gregg to make it back to earth, not even Dr. Gregg himself," Evans said. "Suppose someone was afraid he might say something incriminating."

"Hold it," the president said. "Are you suggesting that Dr. Gregg was involved in this operation?"

"I can't rule it out."

"Commander, our astronauts go through an exhaustive series of psych tests every month. Stress levels, emotional adjustment, attention span. Researchers look for any sign of self-destructive behavior."

"I know that, sir."

"If Dr. Gregg were trying to hide something, it would have shown up."

"Not necessarily, sir," Evans replied. "I worked with and sometimes against rogue forces in Kuwait and Iraq, men and women who were fanatics. They were also some of the coolest, most rational people on earth. They had to be or the police would have spotted them."

"Would a rational man have agreed to fly on the shuttle knowing it was going to be shut down in orbit?" the president asked.

"He might," Evans said. "Dr. Gregg wouldn't be the first person to die for a cause."

"Is that what you think Estate is?" the president asked. "A cause?"

"I don't know what to call it, Mr. President," Evans said. "They're an international group with access to deadly force, and they're definitely pushing some kind of an agenda."

"They could also be just a sick bunch of hackers."

"Sir, we've had an early look at their website," Evans told him. "These people seem to have put a great deal of thought into developing a following on-line. They certainly don't look like hackers."

"And what do hackers look like?" the president asked.

"Gadflies," Evans replied. "Hackers either want to get in and out of a system unnoticed or they want to cause complete chaos. Shutting down a few government systems for a short period was more than some lonely sociopath's diversion. It was a shot across the bow."

Victoria couldn't hear what the president was saying, but she gave Evans a thumbs-up for his definition. That made him feel good considering the beating he was taking from the president. Not that he blamed Gordon for his frustration. For one thing, the president barely knew Evans. They had been forced together by circumstance and there hadn't been time for a shakedown cruise. Perhaps more importantly, this was coming so soon after the showdown with the Huntsmen. The last thing anyone wanted was to face the prospect of more moles in government agencies. Moles who could be working for the Huntsmen, foreign governments, or some other group. But the Stealth Warriors had been commissioned to help seek out subversive elements and Evans intended to do that.

"All right," the president said. "I don't want to waste time debating this. Let's assume Estate is what you say is it and Dr. Gregg is what you say he is. How do we prove or disprove it?"

"I assume the satellite was closely monitored all the time it was in space," Evans said.

"Of course."

"I'd like to get records of that data," Evans said. "Commands may have been sent to the ESP from a station on earth or even in space. If Dr. Gregg did not have access to that site, we might be able to eliminate him as a suspect."

The president was silent.

"Sir?" Evans said.

"I can get you that data except for a brief period when the satellite shut down," the president told him. "It lasted about half a minute."

"When?"

The president replied gravely, "When Dr. Gregg was getting ready to release the ESP."

Evans was not happy to hear that. Sometimes vindication comes at a terrible price. "Does NASA know why or what happened?"

"No," the president said. "But I'll get an update and brief you as soon as possible."

"Thank you, sir."

"Commander, I hope you understand my feelings about this. We're talking about a man who is already being called an American hero. I still don't want to believe it."

"I understand, sir," Evans said. "I'll move carefully and I won't let this go any further without the strongest evidence."

"How will you do that?" the president asked.

"There may be some answers at the Cape," Evans said. "Evidence that won't destroy the memory of Dr. Gregg, but may protect it by finding out who was behind him . . . and Estate."

Twenty-eight
Cape Canaveral, Florida
Monday, 9:50 P.M.

Evans called the napping Holly and Diaz to let them know about the thirty-second blackout and Gregg's death. The two calls from Evans sent Rodrigo Diaz and Peter Holly in a different direction than they had intended to go.

Before the calls, Diaz had two theories about why the ESP went bad. The first was that someone had installed guerrilla chips in the system, a component that was timed to activate when something else happened—for example, the firing of the satellite's positioning rockets. Technologically, that made the most sense, especially with the bulk of data that had to be uploaded. The second theory was that someone had activated rogue programs on existing chips after they were installed. That would have been tougher, since the programs would have had to be buried inside other programs and then brought out. Since storage space would have been at a premium, the rogue programs would have to have been very concise. They couldn't have been more elaborate than a series of commands to force the satellite to listen to uploads coming from somewhere else.

Unfortunately, there were problems with both of those theories. Actually, they were the same problem.

Even allowing that there had been access to the satellite prior to its being launched—which apparently there had been—NASA maintained careful logs of who checked, double-checked, and then triple-checked programming or the satellite components before and after they were assembled. To cover their tracks, saboteurs would have had to erase those files. Because the ESP was an Air Force spy satellite, the log was recorded on disks in computers situated in the Satellite Assembly Building vaults. According to Captain Holly, these bomb-proof shelters were thirty feet underground and guarded around the clock. The walls were lined with Mylar and lead shielding to prevent anyone from using electromagnetic pulses to erase the data. Backup disks were made automatically. Every day these disks were flown to the Pentagon via the Air Force's heavily guarded intelligence pouch and locked in a safe.

The disks en route could have been attacked and erased by the ESP. But even with the SFUs activated, Diaz and Holly would have had a difficult time getting to the master disks at Cape Canaveral. Saboteurs would have had an even tougher time. Diaz couldn't imagine that any group undertaking to tamper with the ESP would have left a data trail like that. Especially when Air Force techies could reconstruct the sabotage and find out who was behind it. Erasing it with the ESP wouldn't have been possible. There was no way the satellite could have penetrated the computers in that bunker. The Estate guys would have to threaten some other exposed site to be allowed access to those disks to cover their trail. Even then, the government might call their bluff, accept the collateral damage, reconstruct the hijacking of the ESP, and find a way to shut it down.

The possible involvement of Dr. Barry Gregg changed things, however. Through him, Estate had direct access to the satellite and a possible means of getting around the checks and balances. Especially if more than Gregg was involved in the sabotage.

Captain Holly was standing beside the low-lying dresser. The only thing on it was the TAC-SAT phone. MCPO Diaz was sitting on the side of the bed. Holly had just finished relaying to him what Commander Evans had said. Both men were silent for a long while.

"If Dr. Gregg changed the programming during that thirty-second blackout, there would be no record of his actions except on the satellite itself," Diaz said. "If Dr. Gregg weren't coming home, no one would ever have known who did this or how."

"An untraceable crime," Holly said.

"So it probably won't do us any good to try and access NASA's logs," Diaz said.

"To the contrary," Holly said. "That'll only keep us from where we should be searching—Dr. Gregg's quarters." He looked at his watch. "Lights out is at eleven. Why don't we have a look at the target area. By the time we come back and get suited up, the grounds will be a lot quieter."

Diaz agreed.

The men went outside. Gantries were lit in the distance to warn off low-flying aircraft, and a cool, edgy breeze rolled in from the ocean. The wind and salt air invigorated Diaz as they always had. But beyond that, there was gloom and a palpable sense of disconnect. The Air Force personnel the men encountered were bundled in their own quiet thoughts, their own despair. Salutes offered to Captain Holly were sharp but perfunctory.

Their destination was Building G. The plain, white, two-story structure was less than a ten-minute walk away, located between the Satellite Assembly Building and Industry Road. The men went inside.

Because Commander Boring had been Air Force, Holly was allowed to go to the pilot's quarters. It was located on the first floor, down an L-shaped corridor. The tradition among test pilots was to leave money behind that would go to the widows and children of fliers. Because Boring wasn't married, it would go to some kind of memorial at the Cape. A shrine had already been set up at Boring's room, an inverted flight helmet on the floor with a photo of Boring taped to the door below his nameplate. Each of the men dropped a twenty-dollar bill into the helmet, then Holly knelt for a moment in silent prayer. Though their visit was to scout out the building, there was nothing insincere about Holly's quiet tribute to his fallen comrade. Diaz bowed his head for a moment and then looked down the hallway. He saw what was obviously Gregg's room two doors down and noted exactly where it was. Because the scientist had been a civilian there was no shrine, though someone had tied a black ribbon around the doorknob. It was a sad, elegant gesture.

Holly was subdued as they walked back to their quarters. For a few minutes at least, their mission had been forgotten.

The chests containing the Stealth Field Uniforms were standing upright on the floor at the foot of each bed. The men inputted their passwords on the keypads and the latches popped open on either side. The heavy lids were on small ball-bearing wheels. The men eased them open.

Even though he'd been working with the SFU for several weeks, the Coast Guard SHARC was still thrilled to be around it. He removed the foam-rubber padding that surrounded the suit.

The SFU looked like a solid blue wet suit with bulges covering pouches for equipment. Each suit was comprised of twenty-six separate panels. The fabric in each panel was woven of light-reflective material synthesized from proteins contained in silk from the ampullate gland of araneid spiders. These panels were comprised of three layers. The topmost layer was a loose weave. The silk's reflective properties at this layer acted as receptors. The remaining two layers were implanted with two components. One was the bioengineered chromatophores, color cells based on the chemical processes of the sargassum fish, with sophisticated color-adaptive characteristics. These cells changed color and were what gave the suit its chameleonlike capacities. The other component was the digital data globules, microscopic liquid microprocessors that relayed the color information from one panel to another. These flowed through the threads that held the panels together. The threads themselves were transparent stitching fibers hollowed to 1/30th of an inch and undetectable to an observer further than eleven inches away. They functioned with extraordinary precision and speed as the environment around the soldier was recorded by the outermost layer of the suit and data was relayed by the hollow fibers to the second and third layers of fabric on the opposite side of the suit—front to back, back to front, side to side, top to bottom.

The entire process was known as SLD—strategic light dispersion—and was engaged by controls built under the armpits of the suit. They had been placed there to protect them from damage if the wearer fell or was struck by something. Standing still, the wearer was completely invisible from every angle and perspective, even in bright daylight. Walking slowly, the wearer was virtually invisible in a twilight or darkened-room situation. Outside, in sunlight, the SFUs created a kind of rippling effect due to the slight delay in the SLD. The effect was similar to that of heat rising from a hot road. Shadows could also be problematic in the strong sunlight.

There was a holster on the right hip and a tool kit on the left. The flaps looked as though they had been vacuformed around the pouches and covered them completely. The tool kits contained a small screwdriver, Swiss army knife, ten feet of copper line for jumping electrical connections or setting up trip wire, a small flashlight, and a compact digital camera. It was up to the soldier what kind of gun he carried. Diaz preferred a Sig-Sauer P228 9mm semiautomatic pistol. He did not intend to have to use the weapon here, but kept it just the same. He undressed and removed the main body of the suit from its specially constructed hanger.

Diaz put on absorbent long johns, climbed into the SFU legs carefully, then pulled on the body and the attached headpiece. The tight fabric of the cowl pinched his forehead and ears, but he had learned to like that. The discomfort helped to keep him alert. Diaz did not yet raise the thick faceplate, which resembled a form-fitting mouse pad. Once that was on, the suit became very hot very quickly. That was the reason for the long johns.

The mouth had porous spots so the wearer could breathe, and large blue eyepieces that ran from the bridge of the nose nearly to the ear. Looking through these polarized lenses was like looking through dark sunglasses. They also enabled SFU wearers to see other SFUs as faint shadows. There were small subvocal receptor radios built into the throat piece, just under the jawline. They picked up the softest whispers and broadcast them to the other suits. Sound dampers in the ear-coverings kept incoming audio messages from being heard by anyone outside the suits. The uniform contained other dampers in the chest, sides, and back that absorbed the sound of the wearer's respiration and heartbeat.

Once the SLD capacity was engaged, it would seem as

though a curtain were being drawn across the wearer from the outside in.

When both men were dressed, they raised their face-plates and pressed them in place.

"Audio?" Captain Holly asked.

"Perfect," Diaz replied.

Diaz moved his arms around and took a few steps. It felt different walking here than it did on the hills and along the lake. He had gotten accustomed to sloping and uneven surfaces. Here the suit actually seemed lighter. That was because the weight rested squarely on his shoulders instead of on his sides, back, chest, or arms depending upon the angle of his body.

Holly walked toward the window. They had decided to go through the darkness rather than the corridor where the refraction caused by the suits in motion might be noticed. "You help me out, then I'll help you," he said.

Diaz acknowledged. He turned off the light while Holly opened the window. The men shut the SFU trunks, then activated the stealth mode of their suits. There was a low, whispering hum that was audible inside the suit as a very low electrical charge caused the chemicals to become active. Apart from the sound, there was no other sense that anything had changed.

The window was a little over three feet up. In order to get over the sill Holly brought a wooden chair over to the window. Meanwhile, Diaz laid a pillow on the sill so the SFU didn't pick up any dust. Then Diaz steadied the pilot's arm as Holly stepped onto the chair. He turned his back to the window, knelt on the sill, and eased outside. Diaz followed him. Holly took the pillow and tossed it back inside, then lowered the window.

They had agreed that Holly would take point, and the men started out with Diaz walking several paces behind. He would keep an eye on the captain to make certain his shadow wasn't visible whenever they passed close to a light source.

They reached Building G without incident. Soldiers they passed didn't seem to hear them or notice them. They went to the window outside Gregg's room and, after listening to make sure no one was inside, they worked open the window latch with the screwdriver. Together, Holly and Diaz lifted the window slowly. Holly raised his flashlight and shined it inside. He shielded the bulb with his left hand so that anyone who happened to be looking from the quad would not see a light seeming to float outside the window. The room appeared to be just the way Dr. Gregg had left it.

With a boost from Diaz, Holly climbed into the window. Then he turned and helped Diaz in. Diaz shut the window behind him, closed the shade, and drew his own flashlight. Holly made certain that the door was locked. Then the men walked around.

The room was pretty much what Diaz had expected. It was neat, awaiting the occupant's return to the Cape. Three suitcases had been stowed in the closet. Jackets, shirts, and trousers were hanging above them. Shoes were lined up on the floor. In the bathroom, Gregg's toiletries were all packed in a kit. The towels were folded and hanging from racks.

"Looks like he was expecting to come back," Holly said.

"Or wanting it to seem like he was," Diaz said.

"True," Holly said. "I'll start with the suitcases. You check the desk drawer and dresser."

Diaz decided to start with the desk. It was simple and uncluttered. There was a lamp, a cell phone, a desktop phone, and a laptop. The cell phone wasn't plugged in for recharging. That seemed odd. Maybe Gregg just forgot. The laptop was shut, and Diaz reached for it. As he did he saw something he wasn't expecting. He called Holly over.

"What is it?" Holly asked.

Twenty-nine

Philadelphia, Pennsylvania
Monday, 10:01 P.M.

Colonel Lewis had done a number of extremely unpleasant things in his thirty-nine years.

For most of his military career he was no more or less unorthodox than other members of Delta Force. They were trained to be aggressive and he never disappointed, not his superiors, his comrades, or most importantly himself. In his early twenties there were the occasional run-ins with COs whom he detested and whom he found ways to strike at without them knowing it. Those were always on the level of frat-boy pranks, such as substituting tea for scotch or vodka for water in an officer's private stores or sneaking into the bathroom and mixing Elmer's glue with their shampoo. A shot fired across the bow, Lewis called them. A warning that they were taking advantage of men and matériel or pursuing a personal vendetta or prejudice. That their priority was not the squad. He never struck at or through mistresses, recording or photographing private rendezvous, since that might have attracted attention and ruined the COs' careers. Then there were struggles with members of other elite forces with whom Delta was exceptionally competitive. Those were mostly barroom dustups with Marines and SEALs, brawls that no one ever owned up to when the MPs would arrive.

The real life-changing unpleasantness came during Lewis's "flashes" in Desert Storm. The flashes were a half-dozen lightning-fast missions behind enemy lines. They were the actions that changed the then-lieutenant's definitions of duty and patriotism. They also changed the twenty-four-year-old. They changed him from tough to ruthless, from experienced to seasoned, from a committed fighter to a veteran killer. He did not regret any of the things he had done in the course of accumulating intelligence. Not the assassination of enemy officers to steal maps, the sabotage of aircraft to cover the theft of undeveloped spy film, and even the kidnaping and abuse of wives and daughters to expedite interviews with husbands and fathers. The United States hadn't provoked that damn war, Iraq had. But Matthew Lewis had not murdered people outside the arena of combat. Though his conscience was clean, his hands were not.

Yet this thing he was about to do was going to be the most unpleasant thing he had ever done. Unlike his other activities behind enemy lines, this was going to stain his soul.

Colonel Lewis had left the cab and moved silently along the dark and deserted waterfront at Penn's Landing. The air was tinged with the smells of fish and diesel fuel. The odors had to be coming from somewhere north or south of here since this section of the Delaware River was not heavily trafficked by ships. It was mostly a starting place for tourists who came over the Benjamin Franklin Bridge from Camden, New Jersey. They parked their cars here and then headed west, into the historic district.

Tourists and drug dealers, he thought angrily.

Lewis had learned all of that by engaging the driver in conversation. The colonel didn't know much about Philadelphia and didn't like going into an area not even knowing which way was north.

Now Lewis knew. He also knew that the parking lot was two blocks south of where he'd asked the driver to leave him. And he knew one thing more. He had to act quickly. He had to be finished here before Major Taylor figured out what he was up to. All the debate about the risks of being caught and detained, of doing what his mother would want him to do—that had been good for Taylor. It had helped to bring him to the point where he needed to be, which was to discourage him from acting rashly. But that had failed to do the one thing that gnawed at Colonel Lewis. It had failed to right the wrong that had been done. And that was something Lewis couldn't live with. The question was how to do that without revenge becoming an accelerant, without it causing more violence against the people who lived in Mrs. Taylor's apartment complex.

Lewis thought he had a way.

The colonel walked on the west side of Front Street, which was the side where the lot was located. To his left, on the east side of the street, was Interstate 95 and the river. It was all open and exposed there. Here, at least, there were buildings, shadows, doorways, fire escapes, and alleys. He noted them all. They were places to hide if something went wrong.

Lewis passed Ionic Street. Gatzmer was next. He could see the plain concrete structure of the parking garage ahead. It was three stories tall. The mostly empty tiers were lit by naked fluorescent bulbs. The cab driver had told him that the entrance to the garage was on 2nd Street, but Lewis didn't want that. The Moonshots would be parked in that direction, so they could either make a getaway or see new arrivals. He didn't want them to see him. Not until he was ready to be seen. He noticed security cameras on the columns, one on each side.

There was a firewell in the back of the garage. It was a concrete silo without windows. After making sure his US-Mail device was set on vibrate instead of beep, Lewis entered and climbed to the third floor. There, he used a handkerchief to unscrew the bulb in the stairwell. Then he cracked the metal door slightly and looked out.

There were eight cars on the enclosed upper deck. Five of the vehicles were dark. They probably belonged to workers at one of the nearby restaurants. Beyond those five cars were three occupied vehicles. The engines were running but the lights were off. They were parked side by side, about one hundred feet away, facing the ramp that led back to the street. None of the cars was a black Cadillac. Lewis didn't expect them to be. The men in the Cadillac, the ones Taylor had attacked, were subcontractors. They would come here for drugs and then go somewhere else to sell them.

The car in the middle was an off-white Bentley with dark-tinted windows. Obviously, the expensive foreign car belonged to the Moonshot kingpin. Like a pimp, his accoutrements probably commanded respect in the street. However, the way the cars were parked suggested that sometimes respect wasn't enough. Though he assumed the windows were bullet-proof, gangs today packed everything from rocket launchers to armor-piercing shells. In case of an attempted hit on the leader, the other two cars would offer some cover. But they were parked far enough apart so that the doors could be opened. This would allow the occupants of the center car to run if they had to. If any of the gang members had trained in the elite forces—and Lewis knew that many street kids did—they might also know that this was a tactic taught for military maneuvers in the desert. If soldiers in Humvees or staff cars were ever caught in enemy gunfire, they could open the front and rear doors to create a "box fort." The double doors on each provided enough armor to protect the men behind it against most automatic weapons and hand grenades. The maneuver could also be executed with Jeeps and other two-door vehicles facing nose-to-rear, though then the barricades were only one-door deep.

Still crouching, Lewis reached into his pocket. He withdrew the four slices of American cheese he had taken from Mrs. St. Martin. He unwrapped them carefully so the cellophane would not make noise. Then he wadded the cheese into a lump. He worked it in his hand for a short while until it was malleable, then put it back in his pocket. Opening the door a little more, he eased out, shut it behind him, then quickly made his way from the stairwell to the nearest unoccupied car. He squatted behind it and looked out. There was another empty car to the left, but he wouldn't bother going for that one. The parked cars were about sixty feet away. If he stayed very low he wouldn't show up in their rearview or side mirrors. And he wanted to get there as quickly as possible.

He assumed there were three men in the back seat of the middle car. There might be fewer, but not more. The man in the middle was probably the boss, protected on both sides. It didn't strike him as strange that the head guy was on-premises. From helping to train FBI agents who worked undercover in Colombia and in the former Soviet republics, Lewis knew that small-time drug dealers always went out "on calls" to make sure they got all the cash that was due them and that customers got all the drugs they had been promised.

Bending his arms and tucking them into his chest, Lewis lay flat and did a pencil roll toward the car. He went over and over, using his shoulders to generate the turns, and reached the trunk of the Bentley unseen. He crouched very low, pulled the cheese from his pocket, and snapped it into three pieces. He put two of the pieces back in his pocket. Then he drew the bowie knife from its sheath under his left arm and moved carefully to the driver's side of the car. He put the tip of the knife against the left rear tire and shoved it deep into one of the treads. He pushed it three inches deep. The tires were not run-flats used by embassies and government officials. If they were, the knife would have struck metal bands. Reinforced tires provided a hard, noisy ride. The boss obviously had his priorities. Lewis removed the knife, took the wad of cheese, and pushed it onto the puncture. Then he turned to the passenger's side and repeated the procedure on the right rear tire. When he was finished, he sheathed the knife, stood, and walked between the cars on the passenger's side. He rapped gently on the window of the Bentley. The colonel could tell from the thickness and grainy look of the pane that it was a thick polycarbonate. Bullet-proof, as he suspected.

The knock startled whoever was inside. He heard rapid motion and gun safeties being unlocked. Lewis knew they wouldn't fire inside. The bullets would ricochet all over. The colonel raised both of his hands head-high and looked at the man in the middle of the backseat. He was a bony Slavic-looking man in his middle thirties. He had short black hair and even blacker eyes. His mouth was straight and thin-lipped. He was dressed in a white suit and shirt, no tie.

"I need to talk to the boss," Lewis said.

The young man sitting on the passenger's side, next to the boss, was a swarthy green-haired youth with a nose-ring, half-shut eyes, and an Uzi in his young fist. He cracked the window slightly. "Get the fuck away, man. Where'd you come from anyway?"

Lewis cocked his head toward the stairwell.

"Yeah, well go back there, jerk-off," the kid said. "Leave us alone."

"Just a word with the boss and then I'll go," Lewis replied. "It's important. It's about four of your guys."

The young man turned and looked at his boss. After a moment the Slav nodded once, just slightly. The young man opened the door and got out. So did a burly man in the front passenger's seat. While the green-haired youth held the Uzi on Lewis, the other man frisked him. He removed the bowie knife and Lewis's wallet. He handed both of them to the boss. The leader of Moonshot put the knife on his left side, away from Lewis, as he studied the wallet's contents. Then he set the wallet beside him and motioned to the green-haired youth for Lewis to get in. The colonel stepped around the young man and eased into the Bentley. The leader stared ahead as Lewis sat beside him.

"What do you want to tell me about my men, Colonel Matthew Lewis of Fort Bragg, North Carolina?" the boss asked. He spoke in a heavily accented voice free of emotion or any real interest.

"They beat up an old lady to get at her son," Lewis said.

"I heard about that," the boss replied. "Your friend had no right interfering with my operation."

"All he wanted was a little quiet, not to fuck you up," Lewis said. "But their beef was with him, not with her. What they did was chicken-shit."

"Even if I were to agree with that, Colonel Lewis, what do you want me to do?"

"Make it right."

"What is 'right' to you?" the boss asked.

"The guys who did this have to turn themselves in to the police."

"No," the boss replied.

"That wasn't a request," Lewis said. "It was an order."

"Really?"

"Really. They won't rat you out," Lewis said. "I've heard they're loyal."

"Loyalty isn't the issue. I need them," the boss replied.

"Too fucking bad," Lewis said.

"This conversation is ended," the boss said.

"Not quite," Lewis replied. "I despise what you do for a living but I don't have time for a war."

The leader looked at him for the first time. "I could kill you now and this would be over."

"Really?" Lewis said.

"Really," the gang leader replied. "A very short war."

"Short, but not in the way you think."

"I kill you and drive away. What could be shorter?"

"For one thing—and there are two—this place has security cameras. They'll see my body."

"They can't see past the darkened windows," the leader pointed out.

"They won't have to," Lewis said. "You'll be stuck with me." He pulled the third piece of cheese from his pocket. "See this?"

The boss looked. The other men snickered.

"Cheese?" the boss said. "You're going to stop me with cheese?"

"I made holes in two of your tires and filled them with cheese. It's an old boot camp trick—we used to do it to staff cars from other services. The driver doesn't feel the air leak out. The wheels start to turn, the cheese gets crushed, turns particulate, falls out. Your tires will die before you reach the street. You'll have to abandon the car. The police will find it *and* my body, which'll leave you in a tough spot. On the other hand, if you do the right thing, your boys will be able to put the spare on, rustle up another new tire, and fix you up without a problem."

"They can do that and ignore you and where would you be then?" the leader asked.

"Back to being at war with you," Lewis answered. "Which leads me to the second 'thing.' I've got shock troops behind me. With flat tires you won't stand a chance against them. I'm offering you a chance to handle your own people and avoid that."

The boss looked ahead again. Lewis couldn't see the driver's gun but he knew from the man's quick, low breathing—"psyched" breathing, they called it in Delta Force—that he was ready to use the weapon at a nod from the leader. The heavyset man on the other side of the car was more relaxed, but then he wouldn't be the one to act. Not with their boss between them. The kid outside would also be afraid to fire for fear of hitting their boss. So Lewis concentrated on the man in the driver's seat. The gun would have to be raised to be fired. If Lewis saw the man's shoulder rise, he would move toward him. Gunmen never expected that. The colonel would have a better-than-even chance of getting the weapon and taking the boss hostage. He could live with those odds if it came to that.

The leader reached to his left and picked up Lewis's knife. "Did you really cut my tires?" the leader asked.

"Try driving to the ramp."

The man looked into Lewis's eyes. Then he returned the knife and Lewis's wallet. "I agree to what you ask, but not because of your threats. Because of your courage. And because my men should not be cowards. They should have beaten your friend in the parking lot."

"Whatever," Lewis said. What the dirt-bag really wanted was to prevent the chance of a war and save face in front of his other men. Lewis would give him that. He got out of the car, then stopped suddenly and stuck his head back in. "One more thing. Find some place other than Park Drive Manor to do your stinking goddamn business."

The leader said nothing. But Lewis knew he would comply with that too. A man who had blinked once would blink twice.

Lewis walked away. When he was back on the street he

would USMail Taylor and let him know where he was—if he hadn't figured it out already—and tell him to get a cab and meet him at Independence Hall. He didn't want the major showing up here and mucking things up.

As Lewis headed down the stairwell, he told himself that he had done what he came for. Intellectually, he knew that. He'd nailed the pigs who had beat Mrs. Taylor and he'd kept Hank out of trouble. In the military that was called AT-TEC—"Acceptable Terms To End Conflict."

And yet—

Spiritually, Lewis felt as bad as he knew he would. He'd effectively made a handshake deal with a killer of children. If his hands were dirty before, they were stained now with the blood of innocents. He wondered if he could live with that. For the first time in his life he wondered if patriotism and the welfare of others was worth the price he had just paid.

Thirty

While waiting for Diaz and Holly to check in, Commander Evans left Victoria at the computer and went to the mess hall. It was a small bunker near the river, one that the Huntsmen had used to store ammunition. It was now used to store supplies. There, Evans used a small electric range to make grilled cheese sandwiches with mayonnaise for himself and Victoria. He started back to the com-shack through the clear, cool night carrying the sandwiches, two bags of potato chips, and two cans of Coke on a tray.

It was a good feeling preparing food for someone, taking care of them in a domestic way. Though one aspect of it did seem a little strange. Victoria was waiting for intel from the field while he had been in the kitchen, cooking. The role reversal was alien to Evans. Yet he found that he liked it. Being kind to others was not something he had ever gotten to do a lot of in the military. And not for the reasons he had worried about when he first started his military career.

When Evans first joined the Navy, Father John had helped him to reconcile war and faith by understanding that struggle was often necessary to defend just rights or exact reparation for the violation of rights by another force. Ironically, though, his most trying battles and ferocious enemies were not limited to foreign soil. When he first came to the Pentagon, Evans had fought with his DARPA superiors for putting his research team in a section of the basement that had clear water running down the walls, brown water running in the sinks, and rats and cockroaches running across the stained, warping floor tiles.

Evans told his superior at the time, the late General Orlando Vargas, that he was willing to die for his country but didn't see the sense of being killed *by* his country. Vargas agreed not to stand in Evans's way. Stonewalled by the Pentagon's budget overseers—who had to fight Homeland Security for funds they needed for planes, tanks, ships, and munitions, the equipment that kept them tightly bound to the private sector and future jobs, consultancies, and kickback—Evans took his complaints all the way to the Secretary of Defense. He forced health inspections that, in addition to the problems he had described, also found lead paint in the walls and unhealthy levels of asbestos under them. The renovations cost the Department of Defense over half a billion dollars, money that had to come from the existing budget. The work was complicated by the fact that the Pentagon had been designated an historical landmark. All the repairs and changes had to be made without harming the building's exterior, which added tens of millions of dollars to the expense.

The crusade made it impossible for Evans to get promoted out of the basement. But he accepted that penalty and made the best of his time there, wondering if God had another purpose for him. It turned out that He had. And the irony was that here, at this new base, Evans was finally able to act with the kind of charity he had always desired.

Victoria was staring at her computer when Evans walked in behind her. The blue screen was flashing a small red and white "Working" banner and her hard drive was spinning. After a moment the banner disappeared and text began to download on the monitor.

Evans placed the tray on the desk. He leaned over Victoria. "What's happening?" he asked.

"Holly and Diaz found Dr. Gregg's laptop," the young woman told him. "The computer was on when they entered his room. It looks like he forgot to turn it off the night before."

"Any significance?"

"We don't know," she said. "We don't think he was working because the computer wasn't jacked in and there are no disks in the room."

"Then why would the computer be turned on?" Evans asked.

"Maybe Dr. Gregg was reading to put himself to sleep," she said. "All Diaz found on the computer's hard drive was an E-book, the unabridged *Ben Hur*. Diaz is downloading it to me now."

The commander was quite familiar with the sprawling novel. It was about the tragic destruction of the friendship between a Jewish man and a Roman officer, the crucifixion of Jesus, and the fate of early converts to Christianity. Evans had read the novel about fifteen years before, not only because he was interested in the roots of his faith, but because it was written by a military officer, General Lew Wallace. *Ben Hur* was a massive, dated novel, no longer widely read. He understood how it could put someone to sleep.

"You know what's strange about this?" Victoria asked as she studied the download.

"What?"

"Have a close look at the text," she said.

Evans regarded the monitor. The text was appearing every few seconds in ten-page chunks. He selected one block and read it.

"Help them, O my Messala! Remem
ber our childhood and help them. I—
Judah—pray you." Messala affected
Not to hear. "I cannot be of fur
ther use to you," he said to the offi
cer. "There is richer entertainment in
the street. Down Eros, up Mars!" With the
Last words he disappeared. Judah under
stood him, and, in the bitterness of hi
s soul, prayed to Heaven. "In the hour of th
y vengeance, O Lord," he said, "be mine
the hand to put it upon him!" By great
exertion, he drew nearer the offi
cer. "O sir, the woman you hea
r is my mother. Spare her, spa
re my sister yonder. God is j
ust, he will give you mercy for mercy."

"Notice anything strange?" Victoria asked.

"The page formatting is off," Evans said.

"It's way off," Victoria told him. "And it isn't just the bad line breaks," she pointed out. "There are no paragraphs and the dialogue isn't separated from the descriptive prose."

"Could that be a transcription error from whatever program he was using to what we're using?" Evans asked.

"No," Victoria said. "I'm using exactly what Dr. Gregg used to store the novel, a book program called Town Hall Forum3. I'm wondering if the word breaks may be significant. If there could be some kind of code in the last letters, or in every other last letter."

"It's possible," Evans agreed, "but before we try to find patterns in the text, we need to download a copy of the novel from another source and run a comparison. See if there's anything hidden in Dr. Gregg's version."

"Good idea," she said. "This should be done downloading in about five minutes. When it's finished I'll go to readbookonline.net and get another on-line copy there. I'll have the lines justified left and right, set them in the same type-size, and run a comparison to make sure all the words are the same."

"If everything stacks up, then we can isolate the last letters of each line and look for some kind of message." Evans shook his head. "Did they check his E-mail address book?"

"Yes," Victoria said. "It's empty. And Diaz said that Dr. Gregg wasn't jacked in, there was no wireless link, so he couldn't have been sending delayed E-mail to anyone."

"Yet he left the computer on," Evans said. "Was it running on batteries?"

"No. It was plugged in."

Evans watched as another section of text appeared. The pages scrolled through quickly as it downloaded.

"It's almost midnight," Victoria said. "We're going to want to go back to Estate, see what new information there is on-line."

"All right," Evans said. He was still studying the download. The download had stopped immediately after a new chapter had begun. "Look here," he said. "Even the chapter headings are run together with the text. It's like a solid block of text, hundreds of thousands of words carved—"

He stopped suddenly.

"What is it?" Victoria asked.

"Can you scroll back to the beginning?" he asked.

"Sure," she said.

"I mean fast, the way it was downloading?"

Victoria hit auto-scroll and the pages began flashing upward at seven pages each second.

"Is that too fast?" she asked.

"No," Evans said. As he watched, he turned his head to its side and stared at the right side of the screen. It looked as though he was watching a mountain range flash past.

"That's what it is," he said to himself.

"What is it?"

"Anyone who found the program would think Dr. Gregg was reading a novel," Evans said. "They would think that he downloaded and the justification came out funny. But that's not it at all."

Victoria cocked her head to the side. "Amos, what am I missing here?"

"The oscillograph," he said.

"Excuse me?"

"Peaks and valleys," he said.

"You've totally lost me."

Evans straightened up. "The edges of the lines are a transmission. Dr. Gregg couldn't have input a changed program into the ESP without it being seen. But he might have had time to input target coordinates."

"I suppose so," she said. "It depends on how the ESP finds computers. We'd have to check with the Air Force, see what targeting system they used—the serial number, geographic location, that sort of thing."

"Suppose Dr. Gregg went into the cargo bay and targeted the ESP to read his own computer," Evans said. "Suppose it read the right side of this manuscript, which isn't really a manuscript but a wavelength—"

"A wavelength to which the satellite was reprogrammed to respond, overriding whatever radio control the Air Force had over it," Victoria said excitedly. "Yes, that's possible." She looked at the manuscript of *Ben Hur*. It was nearly scrolled back to the first page. "You'd need a text that was large enough to contain a full description of the new wavelength it was supposed to obey."

"A text like *Ben Hur*," Evans said.

"But even so, telling the ESP to read a new signal would still leave it vulnerable," Victoria said. "If the new wavelength were discovered the site could be shut down."

"We should give Diaz a call," Evans said. "Maybe he can use equipment at the Cape to beam this signal back to the ESP, make a few changes, screw things up for Estate."

"I don't think that will work," Victoria said.

"Why not?"

"If your theory is correct, then all Dr. Gregg's computer did was redirect the ESP to look elsewhere for its new instructions. The ESP wouldn't respond to Gregg's computer anymore."

"Couldn't we duplicate this wavelength?" Evans said.

"Yes, but I'm saying that duplicating the wavelength probably won't help," Victoria said. "All the wavelength did was to direct the ESP to listen to signals from some other site. We have no idea what that site is or what wavelength the satellite might be using."

Evans slouched. "I see. For a second I thought we had 'em."

"Let me work on this," Victoria said. "I'll see if I can find that wavelength in any official government radio logs. I'll let you know if I find anything."

"All right," Evans said.

The commander left the com-shack. As he headed back to his cabin the phone from the White House beeped. Evans took the call. "Yes, Mr. President?"

"Did I wake you, Commander?"

"No, sir," Evans told him. "We were working on an interesting lead. We think we know how the satellite was corrupted."

"Really?"

"Yes, sir," Evans said. "Victoria will forward that data."

"Excellent work," the president said. "We're going to need all the information we can get."

"Why? What's happened?"

"Have you had a look at the Estate website since it's gone on-line?" the president asked.

"Not yet, sir."

"Please do," the president said ominously.

Thirty-one

Cape Canaveral, Florida
Tuesday, 12:01 A.M.

It was dark and extremely quiet in Dr. Gregg's room, which was now lit only by the bluish glow of the laptop. Rodrigo Diaz was afraid that his stealth uniform would be too heavy for the swivel chair, so he stood at the desk beside the bed, his face pale in the light as he watched the last of the text download. The communications system of the SFU was uplinked to the phones at the base. Diaz had plugged Dr. Gregg's computer into his suit's equipment jack to transfer the data. When he was finished, he removed the computer jack, shut the laptop but left it on, and reconnected the SFU's voice function. As Holly finished checking the contents of the room, Diaz listened as Victoria Hudson explained what she and Commander Evans thought about the contents of Gregg's computer.

"You're saying the satellite essentially connected the dots of the last letters or punctuation in each line to create a pattern," Diaz said.

"Correct," Victoria replied.

"But if that were the case, then anyone could use radio antennas to do a sky-scan, find the signal, and figure out a way to block it," he said.

"Not if the source were no longer using it to send commands to the satellite," she said. "Maybe they told the satellite to tune into another machine to get its marching orders."

"Good point," Diaz said. "So even if there is a signal embedded in this novel, we probably can't use it to ram new commands through to the ESP."

"Right. The satellite is probably no longer receiving traditional analog radio communications. I'm thinking it's all digital now."

"You're probably correct. In which case we're a little bit more screwed," Diaz said.

Holly was standing by the door. He was listening to the conversation through his own headset, but also kept an ear open for any activity in the corridor. "Why should it matter whether the signal is analog or digital?" he asked. "Isn't a signal still a signal?"

"Yes," Diaz said. "But digital signals are like a spray of salt instead of Silly String. Digital signals are numbers and there are gaps between them. They mix with other digital signals and are tough to spot."

"As long as they get to the receiver in the right sequence, they can be broken up any way the sender wants," Victoria said.

"I see," Holly replied.

"Mr. Diaz, is it possible the ESP is using some kind of satellite link to relay signals all over the world?" Victoria asked.

"It's possible," Diaz said. "NASA maintains a secure Tracking and Data Relay Satellite system. Right now that system consists of five satellites in a very high orbit over the equator. That not only gives them access to a large part of the earth's surface, but to any satellites in a lower orbit—which means most satellites."

"Perfect plan," Victoria said. "Usurp them all."

"Just like that movie *Invasion of the Body Snatchers,*" Diaz said. "Take them over and reimprint them one by one by one."

"I wonder if Gregg had any accomplices here," Holly said.

"I doubt it," Diaz said. "He wouldn't have left the computer on if he had. He would have entrusted it to someone else, someone who could shut it off and erase the only clue we've found."

"Good point," Holly said.

Diaz stared at the computer. In all his years of working with technology he had never met a system so clean. There were no disks and nothing except the book on the hard drive. No E-mail, no old files, nothing.

"You know, I just realized why this computer is so clean," Diaz said. "Dr. Gregg didn't want the ESP sucking up any hidden files that might have polluted the system or eaten up memory."

"So the ESP isn't pinpoint precise when it goes into a system," Victoria said. "It can't read or delete just one file."

"Apparently not," Diaz replied.

"Does that mean we could send a virus up if we knew what computer it was going to mind-read?" Holly asked.

"Unlikely," Diaz told him. "Most of what the ESP is doing now is the opposite of what it was apparently designed to do. The satellite is sending out commands to shut systems down."

"Hold on, I just thought of something," Holly said. "The shuttle was alive until the ESP was activated."

"Yes. But what good does that do?" Diaz asked. "Gregg programmed the access code for his computer directly into the satellite. It swallowed that information directly from this laptop. The shuttle was out of the loop."

"Not necessarily. I used to fly tracking missions to test new satellite targeting systems," Holly said. "Their antennas are aligned to transmitters on earth. Before the ESP would have given itself up to outside control, its antenna would have to have shifted away from the Cape Canaveral Air Force Station to whoever is controlling it now."

"But how can we find out where that is?" Diaz asked. "We can't read signals coming from the ESP and we certainly can't see the damn satellite with enough precision to know where the antenna is pointed."

"That's what I'm saying," Holly told him. "The information was on board the shuttle."

"What?" Victoria said.

"It's there, on the shuttle that Commander Boring wasn't *supposed* to be able to bring home," Holly said.

"Where on the shuttle was it?"

"In the Mission Data Recording Unit, the shuttle's black box," Holly said. "In the event of a catastrophic failure the MiDRU freezes the data at the point of failure and disconnects the box from the main systems so it isn't overwritten by malfunctioning signals."

"Shuts it off how?" Victoria asked.

"With Mylar shielding to protect it from exactly what happened," Holly told her.

"And that's something the saboteurs probably didn't plan for," Diaz said. "The black box was supposed to vanish with Dr. Gregg and the rest of the shuttle."

"A black box which will show the new position of the ESP antenna and possibly the location of Estate," Victoria said.

"With any luck, yes," Holly said. "After saving the astronauts, the MiDRU would have been the first thing salvagers tried to retrieve. When they bring it on home it'll be heavily guarded—I can't imagine anyone getting to the box while it's en route."

"Can't Estate shut down whatever plane it's transported in, cause it to crash?" Victoria asked.

"Sure, but to what end?" Holly said. "It's a black box. It'll survive. It's like the goddamn Terminator. Nothing on earth can kill it."

"Where will the MiDRU be taken?" Diaz asked.

"They took the boxes of *Challenger* and *Columbia* to the Intelligence Processing Building on Cape Road," Holly said. "But that was a civilian mission. After a military mission the black box is supposed to go to the Pentagon, to whichever service was running the operation. In this case it would be the Air Force's Aerospace Intelligence Department."

"Where they'll remove the data from the shielding," Victoria said. "The ESP has probably already targeted the computers there to kill them and whatever is plugged into them."

"I don't think so," Holly said. "Hasn't the military already seen what the ESP can do to unshielded systems in the White House and those other places? They'll take it to some ultra-secure area where the data is protected from electromagnetic interference."

"So the Air Force will get the location of the antenna and take Estate out," Victoria said. "End of story."

"Shit," Diaz said suddenly. He felt his gut tighten as he stared at the blank computer screen. "Shit shit shit."

"What's wrong?" Holly asked.

"We may be thinking about this the wrong way," Diaz said. "We're looking at the ESP as the ESP."

"I don't follow," Victoria said.

"The secure computers in the basement of the Pentagon and Cape Canaveral are protected from eavesdropping and erasure," Diaz said. "In theory, that would protect them from the ESP. But those computers are not dedicated systems. They're linked by cable to computers at military bases around the world. The ESP can target a computer anywhere else and send a program into the Pentagon. They might be able to erase the shuttle data as soon as it's loaded."

"They can if they have the *Venture*'s MiDRU code," Holly told her. "And I'm sure that's something Dr. Gregg, with his security clearance, could have gotten with no problem."

"I'm not seeing the problem," Victoria said. "Won't the original black box data still be safe?"

"That won't matter," Diaz said. "The investigators will look at the data on their computers, see nothing, and think there's nothing *in* the black box."

"Again, all we have to do is warn them," Victoria said.

"We can't," Diaz told her. "Whoever did this might have accomplices in Washington. For all we know it could be the Huntsmen. We *know* those people are still out there and we don't want them coming after our team."

"Don't you think this matter is a little too serious to be worried about *our* future?" Holly asked.

"I *am* worried abut the mission, not about us," Diaz told him. "The Estate backers, whoever they are, don't know that we know what's going on. We're invisible in every sense of the word. If we go to the Air Force and tell them what we suspect, we'll be as helpless as the Pentagon to stop Estate from whatever it's planning."

"Diaz is right," Victoria said.

"Commander Evans has to get over there and try to get the box or the data before it's destroyed," Diaz said. "Victoria, you'd better brief him. We have a job to do here."

"What job is that?" Holly asked.

"We've got to assume the commander can get to the

black box and learn the coordinates for the ESP's antenna realignment," Diaz replied. "But that's not going to do us any good unless we have a map we can use to precisely identify those coordinates."

"Gotcha," Holly replied. "So you and I are going to Air Force mission control to get those maps."

"Exactly," Diaz told him. "Do you know the way?"

Holly said he did.

Victoria clicked off and Diaz raised his faceplate. He was spent, both physically and mentally. He felt as he did on long, lonely boat voyages when he worked outside under the baking sun all day, testing new equipment, then "relaxed" by playing a computer chess program in his bunk or reading some weighty sea tome like *Moby Dick, Billy Budd,* or something else by his favorite author, Herman Melville. As Ahab said in *Moby Dick,* "The lightning flashes through my skull; mine eyeballs ache and ache; my whole beaten brain seems as beheaded, and rolling on some stunning ground." Diaz had nothing left; his arms wanted to hang where they were and his brain wanted to shut down, take a short drop into "the lap of Morpheus," as his grandfather Jose used to put it. Jose Diaz was a fisherman in Guaymas, Mexico, a lover of Greek and Roman poetry and the man Rodrigo's mother Katy had always said her son reminded her of most. Jose died pushing himself too hard, trying to save a fellow fisherman whose boat was overturned in a storm after they'd already spent a full day at sea.

Jose didn't have a choice then and his grandson didn't have a choice now. As Melville also wrote in *Mardi: and a Voyage Thither*—words Diaz recalled often when he felt that he was overworked—"Toil is man's allotment; toil of brain, or toil of hands, or a grief that's more than either, the grief and sin of idleness."

Yet this was more than toil. This was more than the salt

in his veins and the unsteadiness he felt on land always driving him back to sea, even at the sad expense of his marriage. This was a different kind of love and duty. He had to protect the nation his parents had adopted and made their own.

And he would.

Thirty-two

Hank Taylor stood in the dark between Independence Hall and the Liberty Bell Pavilion Mall. He had been there for nearly half an hour, practicing the ritualistic zujitsu *katas* both to calm himself and to stay focused. But each block and punch, every step and kick, all the turns and stepping into stances had an edge that normally wasn't there. Even Taylor's measured breathing and abdomen-tightening exhalations were angry. That was because people were standing in the darkness and laughing at him, calling him a coward. The animals that Hank Taylor hadn't taken down on his own.

Taylor had already been in a taxi on his way to the parking garage on Front Street when he received Colonel Lewis's USMail message. The E-mail told the major to go to Independence Hall and wait on Chestnut Street. It was not a request but an order.

Even so, Taylor hadn't wanted to obey it. Lord God, he hadn't, which was why Lewis had made it an order. From the moment back at the hospital when Taylor had realized the colonel had gone to take care of Moonshot himself, the Marine medical officer had wanted to get over there and crack whatever skulls the Delta Force leader might have left relatively intact. He couldn't believe all the colonel's talk about keeping his nose clean had been a ruse.

Around him the city was quiet. Except for the odd restaurant and movie theater, Philadelphia had always shut down at the close of the business day. Taylor was crouching low in a perfect horse stance, legs wide and bent at the knee, feet parallel while his thighs took all of his weight and he sat "on air." He was running through the soft blocks, protecting the groin, blocking to the sides, raising his hands to stop an overhead attack—

Taylor heard someone approaching from the east. He paused and looked in that direction. Colonel Lewis had a distinctive tread, a step that was forefooted rather than heel-first. It was easier to sink, lower the center of gravity, and walk in silence that way. It was definitely Lewis coming.

Taylor rose from the horse stance. He stood and faced the man coming toward him as a chilly breeze slipped across the mall. It was strange having a person here instead of ghosts. His troubles and the rage they caused seemed to shrink back to human-sized.

"Dead town you've got here, Major," Lewis said when he was just a few yards away.

"No deader than usual," Taylor replied. "Or is it?"

Lewis reached the major. Except for some whitish dirt on the sleeves of his windbreaker and jeans, he looked no different than before.

"It's no deader," Lewis replied.

"What happened?"

Lewis looked over at Independence Hall. "When I was a kid moving from base to base with my family, I lost myself in my dad's history books. It gives me a chill to stand here." After a moment he looked back at Taylor. "Do you know anything about the debate they had over the first draft of the Declaration?"

"Not really," Taylor replied.

"And you don't want to talk about history, do you?"

"No, sir."

The colonel looked around. "Where can we get a cab down here? I'm tired."

"There are a couple of hotels a few blocks in that direction," Taylor said, pointing behind himself to the west. "Toward Rittenhouse Square. We can tag one there."

"Let's do it," Lewis said.

The men started walking in that direction.

"You gonna talk to me?" Taylor asked.

"Sure," Lewis said. He sighed. "What happened back at the garage was a chat with the head of Moonshot. We came to an agreement. He promised me that his guys were going to turn themselves in to the police and I promised him that our team wouldn't go to war with his group."

Taylor stopped. "You negotiated with a drug dealer?"

"Yeah, I did," Lewis replied. He looked back at Taylor. "We get what we want, he gets what he wants, and the four fucks who ambushed your mom get what they deserve. It's a clean, surgical strike. Now come on," he sighed. "I need to crash."

"You think that's a good deal?" Taylor said.

"Good as we were going to get," Lewis replied.

"Then why is it sitting really bad with me?" Taylor asked.

"Because you didn't get to break their fucking elbows, that's why," Lewis said. "And you know what? Neither did

I. There was a moment of 'yeah' when I got him to bend, when everything worked the way I planned. But after I left I started wishing I could have hurt them all slowly, busted every one of the two-hundred-odd bones in their frigging bodies. But the boss guy wouldn't have fought back. Not that way. Not a way that would have let the police into his car. He'd have turned the cops loose on us, or he would have turned up the heat on the people at Park Drive till we cried uncle. So I got in his face a little and then gave him a way out. It was the best way to handle this. At least it was the best way I could think of."

"And you think this kid killer is going to live up to his promise?" Taylor demanded.

"I do," Lewis replied. "That dead-eyed cocksucker is like every other Third World strong-arm warlord I've ever faced. He wants to protect his position, his empire, his income. That comes before everything, before loyalty." Lewis stepped closer. "Let me tell you something. What I was asking you about the Declaration of Independence—I asked it for a reason."

"What reason is that?" Taylor asked.

"Before the South would ratify the Declaration, there was a big fight about slavery," Lewis told him. "The Northern colonies wanted it abolished back in 1776 and the Southern colonies didn't. After many superheated sessions in the Continental Congress, the South won. And you know why? Because abolitionists like Benjamin Franklin and John Adams realized they had to secure a consensus on independence first. They had to make a deal with the devil."

"So what are you telling me? Are you saying you're Benjamin Franklin?"

"What?"

"Are you 'Great White Fathering' me?"

Lewis seemed surprised. "What the hell are you talking about, Major Taylor?"

"Are you telling me that I have to eat shit today because one day I'll see how you really set me free?"

Taylor knew he was way off target even as the words came from his mouth. But he didn't apologize. He was pushing Lewis because he was pissed off and there was no one else to push.

"Goddam you, Major," Lewis said. "Goddam you to hell. I ought to take you down for that."

"Go for it," Taylor was surprised to hear himself say. And again, he knew he said it because he was looking for a fight. He wanted to shout and strain every muscle he had and even take a beating until he was spent. But part of him was also smart enough to know that he wasn't thinking clearly. He was exhausted, frustrated, and pissed off, and that was an explosive combination.

" 'Go for it,' " Lewis muttered. He jammed his hands in his pockets. "Against a guy who wants to fight 'cause he's mad. I don't think that would help either of us. What I was trying to tell you was that the good guys always win eventually. That's all." Lewis turned. "The only thing I'm going for is that cab. You coming, or are you going to stay here and shadow-box?"

"I'm coming," Taylor said. "And Colonel? I'm sorry."

"Yeah."

"I mean that."

"I know you do," Lewis said. "That's why my hands are in my pockets. Not because they're cold."

As they walked in silence, Taylor felt the anger leave him and weakness settle into him. Because he knew now it wasn't Lewis he was mad at, or even the pusher and his punk army. He was only mad at one person. He was angry at himself for starting this whole damn thing. All he'd had to do that night was call the police and they'd have chased the car away. Instead, he went outside looking to mark his territory. And he did.

He'd marked it with his mother's blood.

Thirty-three

Lake Miasalaro, West Virginia
Tuesday, 12:03 A.M.

With the TAC-SAT phone in his left hand and the grilled cheese sandwich in his right, Commander Evans hurried along the dirt path to his cabin. The insects were subdued tonight, no doubt because the migrating nighthawks and native whippoorwills were unusually active, fighting a seasonal turf war. The whippoorwills rarely flew, except to feed. Evans had considered it a God-sent sign when he first noticed that they were here. When resting on dead leaves— which they did most of the time—the nearly foot-long birds were nearly invisible.

Evans ate and thought while he walked. He was not thinking about Estate, but about how this situation was straining the resources and energies of his team. They'd been on the go all day with no end in view. At some point, Victoria, Holly, Diaz, and even he would have to stop and rest. He was annoyed that he hadn't thought about this kind of mega-geographical crisis before now. They'd spent so much time working on the SFUs that they hadn't done enough work to set up a strong technical support system linking the computer, communications, and intelligence resources of the base with Langley. Most of what they were using were Huntsman hand-me-downs. The equipment had been reprogrammed and debugged by Victoria; the team hadn't wanted to start using the computers and discover that all the information was simultaneously being downloaded to another Huntsmen cell. The equipment was all state-of-the-art, but there wasn't a lot of it. The Huntsmen were basically a militia with "HUMINT" resources—human intelligence in government, military, and industrial offices. Obviously, Evans would have to make sure the com-shack had more access to the Internet than a single phone line and one computer.

The current situation also underscored the fact that the team didn't have enough staff to handle large-scale emergencies. While the Stealth Warriors were the right size for a strong, mobile strike force, they were not set up for crisis management. Getting Dr. Fraser over here would help, though not much. Ideally, Evans needed additional support staff, not more "techsperts."

Those thoughts left, for the time being, as Evans entered his cabin. He switched on the light, sat at his desk, and put the TAC-SAT down on the desk. He booted his computer, went on-line to the Estate website, and accessed the page using Victoria's password.

The initial download of information that had been promised when Victoria signed up was waiting. Evans read it. He read the material the way he used to read dispatches from the front during Desert Storm. The dimensions of Iraqi death and destruction had been so overwhelming that the information only registered on the surface of his brain. Evans came to regard it as an emotional desensitizer, something to

keep him from being overwhelmed by the nature of the
work in which he was involved.

Evans's reaction to what appeared on his monitor was
the same. The facts and substance registered. But the substance of the message and its implications were so vast he
couldn't immediately process them.

Congratulations!
   *By signing up with Estate you have become a
leader in world commerce and self-determination.
When you receive your new hardware and software
package you will be able to join an on-line government that will free you from having to pay taxes, serve
in the military, attend off-line schools or universities,
or seek justice in costly and biased courtrooms.*
   *Welcome to Estate, the on-line nation of peace,
independence, and prosperity for all. Further details
will be included in your membership package.*

Evans read the message through several times. It struck
him that they referred to belonging to Estate as a membership. From everything he had just read, what they were really talking about was something else.

Citizenship. Estate wasn't just a name. It was a concept.
E state. The electronic state.

Evans logged off and phoned the president.

"You've seen the site?" Gordon asked.

"Yes, sir."

"You want to know what's frightening, Commander?"
the president asked. "For the past three years the FBI has
been sitting on a top-secret white paper about the possibility of an on-line government. The Tapestry Group in
Boston did a joint study with M.I.T. about the probability
of such a thing coming into existence. But it was a problem

they didn't think we had to worry about for another ten to fifteen years."

"They didn't foresee the ESP or anything like it," Evans said.

"No one did," the president said. "We didn't anticipate some individual or group stealing technology that could be reconditioned to control all other technology. We didn't foresee someone using that to make life so comfortable that average people, good people, would surrender liberty to what amounts to a dictatorship in exchange for not paying taxes or fighting wars."

"Sir, that isn't all America means—"

"To you, God bless you," the president said.

"To a great many Americans," Evans replied. "We don't know that people will sign up."

"We believe they will absolutely," the president said. "There's going to be a core group that wants to try 'the next thing,' so they'll be in the first wave. We've been doing a few projections here, imagining everything Estate can do to coerce the people who don't sign up. They can cause systems slowdowns and failures, target individual computers of influential columnists, politicians, and business leaders as well as larger electronic grids and communications services."

"And they may not even know what hit them," Evans said.

"They won't," the president agreed. "We suspect that anyone who tries to move against the Estate people will get hit. Even if they don't, business and civic leaders can't stand up to mass fear. This isn't a Microsoft-style monopoly. The template we're using is the gas shortage of 1974. When gas became scarce, people were willing to pay whatever it cost to get it. People will sign on whatever dotted line it takes to get their computers and cell phones and bank accounts back."

The president had sounded tired earlier; now he sounded

beaten. Not that Evans blamed him. The future he and his staff had been imagining did not look very pleasant.

"Did the Tapestry people suggest any possible perpetrators in their report?" Evans asked.

"No," the president told him. "I just had a look at it. They followed the trends of on-line banking, on-line voting, e-mail, all of that. They said it was inevitable that political 'entities' would form, but didn't speculate on what sector would produce them. We've got theories here that range from the military to private individuals to the Huntsmen. We've got theories but no leads."

"Except for Dr. Gregg," Evans reminded him.

"Except for a dead man," the president agreed. "We're going over all his telephone and travel records for the past five years. He took a few vacations—Las Vegas, Atlantic City, New York, that sort of thing. Following up on that is going to take a while and we're not sure we have a while. Estate may already be cleaning up that data if they haven't already."

Evans's phone beeped. He asked the president to hold on while he picked up the other phone. Victoria quickly briefed him about what she had discussed with Diaz and Holly about the shuttle's black box. Evans asked her to stay on the line while he went back to the TAC-SAT.

"Mr. President," Evans said. "Can you find out if and when the shuttle's black box will be arriving at the Pentagon?"

"It's already there," the president told him. "It arrived about ten minutes ago. Why? Is there a problem?"

"There could be," Evans told him. "We believe the data contains important information about how to combat the ESP, information which may be targeted by the ESP as soon as it's downloaded."

"What data?" the president asked.

"The coordinates of the ESP's new antenna alignment,"

Evans told him. "That will pinpoint the location of the terrorists."

"I'll have the Air Force stop the process immediately," the president said.

"No, sir, just have them delay it," Evans said. "If Estate has personnel inside the Pentagon, stopping it might raise a flag."

"Then delay it to what end?" the president asked.

"So we can get the box out of there and protect the data," Evans said. "Take it somewhere Estate couldn't possibly know about."

"Your base."

"Yes, sir."

"It'll take you at least ninety minutes to drive to the Pentagon," the president said. "I can order them to wait, but what do I tell them you're doing there?"

"I won't be the one joining the investigation," Evans told the president. "I want Dr. Clark Fraser in on it. He worked for me at DARPA. He was going to be joining us here tomorrow. He lives a few minutes away from the Pentagon and he has highest security clearance. I'll call him. If he's not still at the Pentagon, I'll have him get right over."

"What's his AOE?" the president asked. "It'll be more credible if I have something to tell the group leader—"

"Fraser's area of expertise is biochemistry," Evans said. "Tell them your science advisors want him there in case there was microbial contamination—anything to slow the team down and get Dr. Fraser inside."

"You've got it," the president said. "Once he's in, what then?"

"I'm working on that," Evans said. "Let me get him over there first, then we'll work out the details."

"It's in your hands," the president said.

Evans thanked him. Then he turned to the desk phone and called Dr. Fraser on his cell phone. This wasn't going to be easy. The eccentric fifty-nine-year-old scientist worked in ways and sometimes in dimensions that weren't the same as everyone else. Since he wasn't military, Evans couldn't order him to go. He had to try to position this in a very particular way. He also had to try to keep Fraser from questioning everything, which the scientist was inclined to do.

As the commander waited for the scientist to pick up, he went over to the chest containing his SFU. He was busy working on a separate track of his own.

"Hello?" Fraser muttered. The scientist sounded groggy or distracted. It was often tough to tell the two apart.

"Clark, it's Amos Evans."

"Amos, it's funny you called," Fraser said, his spirits rising audibly. "I've been sitting here reading that pamphlet you gave me, Pope Paul's *The Acts of the Apostolic See*. You guys have got to be kidding about—"

"Clark, where are you right now?" Evans asked urgently.

"Where am I?"

"Where *are* you?" Evans repeated.

"I'm in my laboratory transferring data to diskettes to bring with me," Fraser told him. "Why?"

"I need you to do something important," Evans said.

"What?" Fraser asked.

Though this was an open line, Evans had no choice but to tell him what he needed. He just wouldn't tell him everything.

"I need someone who can go upstairs to the AF's Aerospace Intel room and keep the shuttle's black box from being opened for as long as possible," Evans told him.

"The black box from the *Venture,* the shuttle that went down today?" Fraser asked.

"That's right," Evans said.

"A little out of my line of work," Fraser said.

"I wouldn't ask if it weren't desperately important," Evans said.

"What am I supposed to do, use physical force?"

"I hope that won't be necessary," Evans said. "I want you to talk to them, Clark. Tell them it's contaminated. I've seen you bust chops at DARPA—bust theirs."

"I only do that with bureaucrats—"

"These are going to be military officers and they aren't going to be happy," Evans said. "Pay them back for every general who's ever cut costs on you. But keep that data in the box and shielded as long as you can. If you can get it away, so much the better. I wouldn't ask if I didn't think you could do it."

"Flatterer. How long will it be necessary to keep this up?"

"As long as possible," Evans said. "Look, time is not on our side. The president's holding up the process for us."

"Why doesn't he hold it up altogether?"

"There are reasons," Evans said. "Please. Will you get over there and take care of it?"

"Yes," Fraser said. "And what will you be doing? Not praying, I hope. I don't put much credence in that."

"Not praying," Evans assured him.

The commander said he would talk to the scientist later and hung up. He had a lot to do and very little time to do it. But he hadn't quite told Fraser the truth just then.

In addition to everything else, he *would* be praying.

Thirty-four

**Cape Canaveral, Florida
Tuesday, 12:23 A.M.**

Back in Dallas, where he grew up, Peter Holly's best friend was Chuck Free. Chuck was a music nut, from pop to blues to jazz. He taught himself to play piano and guitar, and Holly had once helped him build his own synthesizer. Free didn't say much; he let his instruments talk for him. He was fifteen when he got his first gig, backing three classmates who formed a girl group known as the Three Little Pegs. They dressed like farm girls, sang country western, and built themselves a pretty decent following. After graduation the group became TLP, became the opening act for several well-known singers, and Holly lost touch with Free. He had always meant to look him up again.

What had always struck Holly as strange was how important Free was to the group, yet how apart from it he seemed. He kept the beat, set the key, yet he always stayed in the background. He seemed to like it there, just making his music and doing his thing. Holly had been thinking a lot about his old friend the past few weeks because he had been feeling the same way ever since joining the Stealth Warriors. Not that he was necessarily in the background, but he certainly was different. Taylor, Lewis, and Evans were all shock troopers—the first to go behind enemy lines where they surgically neutralized enemies, ordnance, and supplies. Diaz was a tech guy who also got out there and set things up, testing or arranging communications in places where they'd be needed for current or future action.

Holly was the only member of the team who wrapped himself in a machine. He wasn't ashamed; test-piloting was hazardous. Flying missions was dangerous. But there was a godlike sense that came with being airborne. And also, strangely enough, a sense of cleanliness. There was no mud, no seawater, and if a flier started to perspire, he changed the environment in his suit or cabin. Since the start of the Stealth Warrior unit Holly had felt different, a little intimidated, and somewhat disconnected from the others. At the same time that gave him impetus to think in the ways he'd seen the others think.

There was one thing more that set him apart from the rest of the team members. As far as Holly knew he was also the only member whose father was a traitor. He had something to atone for.

All of this weighed on Captain Holly as he made his way through the night wearing the SFU. He had the same sense of omnipotence that he did in the air. Airmen passed nearby without seeing him or Diaz. But the pilot was very much aware of how relatively slowly he was moving on the ground. How his body moved in parts, arms swinging, weight shifting from leg to leg, instead of being hurled forward, up, or down—sometimes in combinations—all at once. Holly wasn't certain that the others had adapted to the stealth uniforms any better than he had. But their shadowy invisibility had to be an improvement over what the soldiers were used to, hiding behind walls or under trucks in "enemy" territory. For him, the entire experience was new. But, as his Aunt Ruth used to say, the Lord giveth and sometimes the Lord taketh. Though the men had been working out in the SFU for several months now, neither Holly nor Diaz had gotten accustomed to carrying around the extra sixty-plus pounds. It was tiring work.

However, Holly was energized by a plan he'd been developing about how to get inside mission control. As they neared their target, the elements seemed to be inclined to cooperate with what he had in mind.

The grounds on the Air Force side of the Banana River were mostly short-cropped lawns with narrow paved walks. The men stuck to the walks lest someone notice the grass sink under their weight. Holly walked several feet ahead of Diaz, thinking how strange it was to be this close to the ocean on a warm night and to hear the wind through the external audio sensors but not to feel it because of the suit. He led the way to the Air Force mission control building, a sprawling, white, one-story structure that stood off Cape Road near the tarmac where they'd flown in.

"Do you know where the mapping data is kept?" Diaz asked as they neared the building.

"Negative," Holly replied. "But it won't be difficult to find. The security post will have a directory."

The entrance was just coming into view.

"I don't see any guards," Diaz said. "I'm guessing the door's going to have an access-card lock. How do we get past that?"

"I'll show you," Holly said.

They made their way toward the well-lit entranceway. As they neared the building, Holly stopped at a freestanding newspaper dispenser that contained copies of the base newspaper, *The Canaveral Eagle*. He looked around. He and Diaz might be invisible, but the newspapers weren't.

No one was nearby. He opened the door. The top paper fluttered briskly in the wind. He reached in and removed a copy. They continued toward the building.

"What are you going to do with that?" Diaz asked.

"Have it blow someplace inconvenient," Holly replied.

There was a security camera above the door. It was pointed down but away from the door, toward the walkway.

"Stand right there," Holly said, motioning Diaz toward the wall between the door and a window. "They've got fish-eye lenses in these things that can see all kinds of directions."

Diaz did as he was told. Holly removed a page and handed the rest of the newspaper to Diaz.

"Hold this in case I need it," Holly told him.

"I still don't get what you're going," Diaz said.

"You know about sailing mythology," Holly said. "Who was the giant the Greek seamen blinded?"

"Polyphemus," Diaz said. "Ulysses and his crew put out his eye and then overcame him."

"That's exactly what we're going to do," Holly said.

The wind whipped the newspaper sheet around as Holly edged toward the door. The camera wouldn't see him. But in just another step or two it would see the newspaper. He was going to have to move swiftly.

Back in flight training one of Holly's instructors tested the balance and coordination of potential pilots by using the "sheet music" technique. Students had to place one sheet of typing paper on each open palm and then move the palms around—up, down, diagonally, and sideways with sufficient speed so that the papers wouldn't slide off. At the same time they had to sing a song of the instructor's choosing, from "The Star Spangled Banner" to "Off We Go into the Wild Blue Yonder." It was difficult to concentrate on all three things, which was the point. Pilots had to be effective multitaskers.

Holly learned to be very good with the sheets of paper. His skill was about to pay off.

As Holly approached the glass door, he held the big sheet of newspaper flat in his right hand. He began moving the hand around so that the paper appeared to be floating upward. The maneuver was a little cumbersome in the SFU but, fortunately, Holly wasn't going to have to do it for very long. He quickly raised his arm and the paper with it, bringing the sheet closer to the camera in movements that simulated the wind. If the security unit ever played back the videotape, it would appear as if the newspaper blew toward the camera. Finally, Holly placed the newsprint against the lens. He held it there.

"I'm confused," Diaz said.

"They can't see."

"But we're not breaking a window or anything else."

"We don't have to," Holly told him. "There are always two guards on security. One of them will have to come out and clear the newspaper from the camera. When he does, we'll ease in."

The wait was a short one and Holly was glad. The suit added weight to his arm and holding it up wasn't easy. After about two minutes, the pilot saw a solemn young officer walking casually along the tiled corridor. Holly recognized the winged-earth patch on the man's sleeve. He was a second lieutenant, a member of "Seven Phoenix," the technology police of the Air Force Office of Special Investigations. Because of the sensitive nature of the work done down here, the notoriously grave "heavy artillery personnel," as they were sometimes referred to, were always present. The young officer wore a small black nameplate that said "Passo."

The second lieutenant looked through the door to the left and right. Then he looked up.

"Yeah, it's a newspaper," he said into the small microphone he wore on his shirt collar.

Passo removed the access card from the clip on his vest pocket and slipped it into the slot beside the door.

"You stay put," Holly said to Diaz over the subvocal microphone. "I'll handle this."

"Roger," Diaz replied.

The AFOSI officer used his foot to prop open the door, then replaced the access card. He carried a flashlight in one of his belt loops, right beside a holstered automatic. He stuck it through the crack in the door, shining it at both sides. When Passo was satisfied that no one was hiding there, he stepped part of the way outside. He continued to hold the door open with one foot while he twisted around and reached up to remove the newspaper. As he was about to grab it, Holly let go. The paper hung there for a moment while Holly drove the bottom of his foot into the back of the officer's knee. The security guard fell backward to the walk and landed directly below the camera, though his foot was still inside the door.

"Crap!" the officer cried.

"You all right?" a voice said through a speaker to the side of the door.

"Yes," the officer said. "My knee just gave out."

"You need help?"

"No," the officer said as he got up. "I assume you got that on digital."

"The whole thing, Mr. Passo. Your graceful paper-snatching is now part of the base security record."

"And I didn't even get the newspaper," Passo said disgustedly. "It blew away by itself."

"We record that as a 'mission accomplished,'" the voice said with a little laugh.

Passo brushed himself off, then went back inside. He shut the door solidly and checked to make sure it was locked. Then he turned and walked back down the corridor.

Holly watched the officer go. The pilot was standing

inside the doorway. He'd stepped in over Passo while the officer was lying on the walk.

"Diaz?" Holly said.

"Still here."

"I'm looking at the access panel here," Holly said. "Not good news."

"Why?"

"Some of the panels also have keypads so visitors can input the day-code and leave," Holly told him. "This one doesn't. We'd need an access card to get it open again."

"Are you going to try and get one?"

"No," Holly said. "I'm going to find the map room myself. What I need you to do is sit tight out there and talk me through any technical problems I have accessing data."

"That's not going to be the fastest way to get the job done," the Coast Guard SHARC pointed out.

"Maybe not. But trying to pop the door could take even longer."

"True," Diaz said. "Well, I'm impressed you got in at all. I wouldn't have thought to do what you did."

"Thanks," Holly said.

"Stay in touch," Diaz told him. "Let me know where you are and what you're doing in case there's a snafu."

Holly promised that he would, then turned and started down the deserted hallway.

The captain stuck to the sides of the corridor, out from under the fluorescent lights where he might cast a shadow. There was a security camera at the far end of the hallway and he didn't think it would pick up the faint shadow he cast here.

Holly looked from side to side as he moved ahead. At least the rooms were tagged here just as they were at Holloman and other air bases—Accounting, Infirmary, Civilian Personnel Human Resources. And none of them required special access. But that didn't mean he was home-free.

According to the colored floor molding Holly was still in
the blue zone, the general offices. Still, at least he wouldn't
have to waste time on a computer looking for the building
directory once he entered the red zone. Those areas were
typically in the center of the building and he headed in that
direction.

The building's central air-conditioning didn't make the
suit any cooler. Sweat trickled around the corners of Holly's
eyes, and he realized he should have raised his faceplate and
blotted his forehead before he came in. Now he'd just have
to deal with it. At least there was one thing in his favor. That
pat on the back from Diaz had felt damn good.

Holly rounded the first corner. The building was constructed concentrically. He stopped as a night worker walked
down the hall heading into the red sector. Holly reflexively
held his breath, though that wasn't necessary; the woman
passed without spotting him. As her footsteps echoed away,
he continued toward the red zone.

Holly had a plan for getting into the map room. He would
pound on the door and someone would either let him in or
call security. He would pound again when security arrived.
The guard would have to open the door to check inside.
Once that happened Holly would be in.

Unfortunately, when he reached the red zone he realized that he was going to need a different plan. A much different plan.

The red zone security was nothing like he expected.

Thirty-five

Lake Miasalaro, West Virginia
Tuesday, 12:56 A.M.

After Commander Evans left, Victoria went to the Estate website herself and read the details of what the service was offering. She was alarmed but not surprised. The rapid intrusion of computer technology in every aspect of society had left the world vulnerable to exactly this kind of terrorism or temptation, however one chose to look at it. What did surprise her was that it wasn't the work of a hacker, which was what she had always anticipated. It was obviously the work of a cabal whose members had talents in different areas.

Victoria didn't linger long on the Estate site. She had other work to do. Dr. Gregg probably did not have the scientific chops to execute this operation. Even if he did, would he have put it all in motion and then allowed himself to go down with the ship? Victoria remained on the Internet and did a search for information about Dr. Gregg and his past. Though she could have gotten access to his official

files, she wondered what they would find in there. Anyone
who had been planning to execute a coup like this would
probably have done his best to eliminate the paper trail to
his past or to any colleagues.

*Unless Dr. Gregg has no colleagues in this, just a com-
puter and the ESP running the whole thing,* Victoria thought
ominously. She didn't really believe that, and yet—

When Victoria was growing up on a farm in rural Ver-
mont she used to read a lot of science fiction. Everything
the local library stocked, from the space operas of Edgar
Rice Burroughs to the poetics of Ray Bradbury, from the
far-sighted hard science of Isaac Asimov and Arthur C.
Clarke to the militarism of Robert Heinlein. The possibilities inherent in the future seemed limitless, and she
couldn't wait to graduate from high school, get to college,
and become a part of building that future. Then she
learned about the realities of the present, things like budgets and cutbacks and the glass ceiling for women. But
even as she worked in her chosen field of micromolecular
electronics, the future loomed tall. She knew that even the
relatively sophisticated process of moving molecules
along microscopic grooves and creating molecular computer chips was still an interim technology, just like the
current generation of silicon chips. The real chip of the future would be bioengineered, a cyborg mix of the living
and the artificial.

What if that were already happening? What if Dr. Gregg
had created some kind of mega-link with supercomputers
around the world?

*And what if you get some sleep before you do any more
research?* she told herself. Maybe then she wouldn't be all
over the map with Arthur Clarke-ish flights of fancy.

There were 352 mentions of Dr. Barry Gregg. She nar-
rowed the search by adding the word "college." If someone

were planning an operation this big, he would probably only trust people he had known for a long time.

Victoria found 241 mentions of Dr. Barry Gregg and college. She went to the sites until she found the schools he had attended rather than simply visited as part of a group or lecture series. The first one was the University of California, Berkeley. She ran an advanced search, which gave her ninety-eight mentions of Dr. Gregg and the Berkeley campus. An additional search eliminated post-graduate lectures he gave there as well as cites of the school in his curriculum vitae. She refined the search to his undergraduate years, and found twenty-one references. She started visiting each of them. In less than a half hour she had compiled a list of twenty-two fellow students as well as three professors. The name that interested her the most, however, was one that she had heard of: Professor Charles Shannon-Crabbe, head of the university's Instructional Technology Program.

Located in a Victorian house in the southeast sector of the campus, the TTP was an experimental division of the school's Institute of Science and Technology. It was founded to design and create models for the use of technology in teaching as well as "pilot projects" to assist governments and the communities that depended on them.

Victoria knew about Professor Crabbe because he was a leading computer scientist who had disappeared ten years before, after a scandal involving several young female students and sexual activity. Though Victoria knew that there was nothing unusual about professors and students becoming intimate, this situation reportedly involved orgies at Professor Crabbe's off-campus apartment. He was forced to resign and vanished from the academic radar. However, many of his early publications about artificial intelligence were still regarded as authoritative philosophical guidelines. *He* probably wouldn't have found Victoria's fears about a supercomputer taking over the world that far-fetched.

You really need to get rest, she told herself as she returned to her Internet research.

Victoria word-searched Professor Crabbe and, unfortunately, came up with just one other mention—a news blurb about an altercation in Atlanta as he attempted to board Delta flight 740 with three large pieces of carry-on luggage. It was after Christmas, crowds of people were returning home, and space was scarce. Crabbe and an unnamed male companion were arrested, though the charges were subsequently dropped.

Or maybe eliminated by hacking? Victoria wondered.

The young woman looked over the list of the other names she'd pulled from sites where Dr. Gregg had been mentioned. The only other name Victoria recognized was Marcus Forte, a wunderkind Manhattan and Atlantic City billionaire-media-magnate-playboy. In 1999, Forte had hosted a high-tech turn-of-the-millennium conference at his then-new Salzburg Hotel to show the world that he was a visionary instead of just a profit-minded billionaire-media-magnate-playboy.

You failed, Marcus, Victoria thought as she read the article from *New Jersey* magazine's on-line archive.

The presence of two dozen international geniuses like Dr. Gregg, even at a high-profile turn-of-the-century event, did not enhance Marcus's reputation. It could not undo years of profit-making and the building of a broadcast empire founded on sex. It started with sex-based game shows, sex documentaries, pushing-the-envelope cable programming, and interactive on-line sexual activities. The latter caused Forte Communications to be sued by several states for prostitution, even though no physical contact was involved. Not only did Forte win the class-action suit, but it gave him the idea for the satellite-only channel Hooked-In, which offered round-the-clock coverage of legal prostitution activities in Nevada and Amsterdam. The faces of the johns were digitally removed and they were given a discount for allowing their activities to be broadcast. Only customers who bought Forte dishes could receive the programs. Hooked-In made Forte's privately held company one of the most lucrative media corporations in history.

This was getting her nowhere. Victoria's eyes stung and her brain was getting sluggish. She extended her heel and used it to drag over the wastebasket by the side of the desk. She swung her chair around, crossed her feet on top of the trash can, and happened to notice the sandwich Evans had brought. She picked it up and took a small bite. It was cold, but it was food.

Victoria chewed and shut her eyes.

She cursed her husband just because he entered her mind.

She swallowed the grilled cheese and opened her eyes, looked for the Coke. Then she realized something. Professor Crabbe had had that run-in at the Atlanta airport on December 29, 1999.

Curious, Victoria sat up and checked the computer to see where that Delta flight had been bound. Number 740 was a New York–bound flight. She wondered if Crabbe had been headed to that conference and been delayed or side-tracked or maybe disinvited after the altercation. Or maybe he'd made it and, because of the Berkeley scandal, wasn't listed as an official attendee.

And why would it matter in any case? she asked herself. A Crabbe-Gregg reunion was hardly noteworthy.

Maybe because she *was* tired and her instincts were talking louder than her brain, Victoria felt as if there were something here. She just didn't know what it was. Nor

Thirty-six

Arlington, Virginia
Tuesday, 12:59 A.M.

Dr. Clark Fraser moved quickly along the empty halls of the Pentagon basement. His white lab coat swirled around his legs as he improvised the elements he would need. The necrotizing faciitis. The B3 soap. While the right side of his brain worked on that, the left side "told" his wife about the task Commander Evans had given him. A job that meant he not only had to deal with people, he had to dominate them.

"I don't have to tell you that I'm not looking forward to this," the barrel-chested scientist said to the spirit of his wife as he neared the Air Force computer center. *"Sanctioned bullying is still bullying. It's something we do when language and ideas and communication fail. Or are inconvenient."* Fraser didn't like to think of the higher processes of his species as disposable.

Fraser began humming the song "Some Day" from *The Vagabond King*. His wife Lydia had been a singer, a lyric soprano, and was a fanatic about Broadway and movie musicals and operetta. Before meeting her Fraser had never been interested in music. But her passion for music and her love for him somehow, magically, brought the two together. Now they were inseparable. And for more reasons than just the beauty of the music.

Even though Lydia Fraser was physically deceased, talking to his wife brought Dr. Fraser more solace and reward than speaking to most "carnates," which was what he called living individuals. While she didn't answer him in speech, she communicated intangibly. Her voice infused the songs that were theirs and her spiritual smile gave him solace in a sullen world.

And he was convinced that it was not all in his mind.

Fraser had numerous theories about life, death, the infinite, and beyond. Few of those theories were quantifiable or verifiable, not even remotely. But he held them no less strongly because of that. Sometimes faith and dreams were all a scientist had to go on. Like when he was a kid growing up in Silver Spring, Maryland, and would find roadkill on his way to school. He would stop and look at the squirrel or bird or snake and wonder why an impact should destroy "it." He understood that the vessel, the body, got "busted up" as his older brother Kyle used to put it. But that didn't explain where the rest of the creature went. The instincts, the drives, whatever memories it had, all the intangibles. He didn't understand that when his grandmother died either. When he was a young teenager in the late 1950s, he began to explore the beatnik world of bohemian expression, which led him to study mysticism and dreams as a means of trying to find a way to the next level of understanding. When he decided to take up biochemistry in college, Fraser found that meditation and trances were often the road that led to the next discovery. He stayed away from drugs and drink because they clouded the mind and painted false pictures. He also avoided organized religions like streptococcus. Their spiritualism was like the wheel ruts in the Oregon Trail, deep and inviolable. But inspired visions were different. Despite what some of the hard-science boys thought, such visions were snapshots of the goals to which scientists built rational bridges.

It was Fraser's meditation and reflections, combined with scientific study and readings and contemplation in mysticism, that brought him to his theory of life and death. Aldonza, the kitchen maid adored by Don Quixote in *Man of La Mancha*, had gotten it partly right. The world *is* essentially a dung heap and we're all maggots that crawl on it. But that isn't the entire story. Unlike dung heaps, the earth is comprised primarily of metals and oxygen, all of which conduct electricity. The brain conducts thought and self-awareness through electrical impulses. Those impulses have to go somewhere when the body stops working.

Dr. Fraser believed they went into the earth, where they were stored and perhaps redirected into the brains of those who were receptive to them. Right now Lydia's essence was stored in Fraser's own mind along with her music. He knew because she made her thoughts known there. The only people who understood that were those who had loved ones in their own brains—not that it mattered whether anyone else got it or not. It did not alter truth.

And on days like today, when a numbing disaster like the *Venture* had occurred, it helped him to process the idea that all the skills and learning and experiences the astronauts and mission specialists had were not really dead. They were just downloaded to Mother Earth.

Only her presence, her support, gave him the courage to put one foot ahead of the other, to do what he was about to do. Even though she wouldn't approve of the bullying, she would support what needed to be done.

All I wanted to do was to start work on the "webvest," he muttered to himself. The webvest was a lightweight

bullet-proof vest made from a superstrong new protein
called BioIron. The protein was found in the milk of goats
that had been bred on an old Air Force base in New York's
Plattsburgh. Thanks to the addition of bioengineered spider genes to the goat embryos, the protein had the proportionate strength and elasticity of spider silk. In theory, all
garments made with the protein could become bullet-proof.
It was one of those military creations that could help to
spawn a billion-dollar consumer spinoff industry. Fraser
had wanted very much to help launch that.

But no. He was going to work with Victoria Hudson on
a lake in the middle of the wilderness. *After* he finished
spying.

The Air Force's Aerospace Intelligence Department was
located in the basement of the Pentagon. It was two floors
above DARPA and two floors below the Tank. The Tank
was where the Joint Chiefs of Staff met. Also known as the
Gold Room, the Tank got its nickname during World War II,
shortly before the Pentagon was built. At that time the Joint
Chiefs of Staff—then known as the Combined Chiefs—met
in a basement of the Public Health building. The hallway
that led to the room was so snug and dark that an officer
once remarked it was like entering a tank. The name stuck.

There were two armed guards waiting outside the AFAID
room. Dr. Fraser showed them his top-security access card
and then used it to enter. The metal door clicked open.
Fraser suddenly felt a rush of concern. He had set his sights
high, on the biggest challenge Evans had presented. And
though he didn't want to let the commander down, the
guards' weapons made it very unlikely that Clark Fraser was
going to be doing any black box stealing today.

The AFAID room was about the size of an elementary
school classroom, with white walls, fluorescent lights, and
rows of computers sitting on five long cafeteria-style ta-
bles. Some of these computers were linked with the

NRO—the National Reconnaissance Office, which monitored most of America's spy satellites. Some of the computers interfaced with air services of other nations; others were tied to different United States intelligence agencies. There were no windows and there were four speakers, one on each wall, that constantly droned medium-loud eighties rock 'n' roll—Pat Benatar, Duran Duran, Loverboy, and the Cars among others. That was to prevent anyone from using electronic listening devices to eavesdrop on discussions. The noise in the Air Force, Army, Navy, and Marine intelligence department wings effectively protected the Tank in the center.

In the back of the room, against the far wall, was a four-tiered lab table. It had a black marble top and pine shelves. In addition to a projection microscope, video and acoustic equipment, a sink, and both thin latex and heavy rubber gloves, there were vises, tools, and racks of chemicals. Sitting in the center of the tool section was a charcoal-gray box about the size of a small safe-deposit container. The box was made of four-inch-thick steel covered with a recrystallized silicon carbide fire-resisting shell that was itself another two inches thick.

Three tech staff officers, all colonels, and a brigadier general were gathered around one of the computers in the center of the room. If Fraser had to classify his first impression of the men, it was "impatient." The officers were talking quietly; they stopped when Fraser walked in. The small size of the group obviously meant that whatever happened to the shuttle was being explored and disseminated on a very strict need-to-know basis.

Translation? Fraser thought. The Air Force suspected that the *Venture* was a victim of sabotage, with the possibility that there were still perpetrators afoot. Commander Evans probably thought so too, or he wouldn't want to keep the box from all these people. It wouldn't surprise

Fraser to learn that Evans knew more than these men did.

The ranking officer, Brigadier General Rudolph Anastasia, was a giant of a man, at least six feet six. He had the biggest hands Fraser had ever seen on a human. He was seated on the edge of a table. His voice was raspy and his manner was loutish. Fraser could tell that he was a "blue collar" officer, a big-lunged man who had not come through college and the officers' training corps, but had bellowed himself up from tech sergeant or thereabouts.

Brain over brawn, Fraser reminded himself. If ever there were a time and place to prove that, this was it. He had already thought about what he was going to do and he got into it. Fast.

"The prodigal son, I presume?" the brigadier general asked disgustedly as Fraser approached.

"I'm Dr. Fraser," the scientist said as he strode over.

"Yes, we met several years ago."

"We did?" Fraser said.

"About EVA suits for space walks," Anastasia said.

Fraser didn't remember. Not that it mattered. He was a man on a mission. He stopped, looked from the men to the flight recorder, then walked over to the lab table. He pulled a pair of latex gloves from the dispenser. As he pulled them on he went over to the black box. It was time to go into his dance.

"Has anyone touched that with their bare hands?" Fraser asked.

"What?" General Anastasia asked.

"The flight recorder," Fraser said. "Has anyone handled it without wearing protective gear?"

"I did," Anastasia said. "So did those two MPs when they brought it here over a half hour ago. Why?"

"Weren't you briefed?" Fraser asked. It suddenly occurred to the scientist that he'd better find out what they knew. He didn't want to say anything that contradicted whatever the president may have told them.

"No," Anastasia told him. "We got a call from the president himself to wait for you to get here before we opened the Mission Data Recording Unit. You're here. Let's get on with it."

"I'm afraid it's not going to be that simple," Fraser said. "I need you to go to the infirmary and wash your hands thoroughly with B3 antibacterial soap. If they don't have any, send over to the main infirmary." Fraser was proud of that. They wouldn't have B3 there. That would delay the process even more. "And don't touch your eyes or anything else until you *get* there."

"Dr. Fraser, I don't have time for this bullshit."

"Excuse me?"

"We lost some fine pilots today," General Anastasia said. "That little box may tell us how and why. I'm not leaving this room unless you tell me what the hell's going on."

"What's going on may be a bioengineered form of necrotizing faciitis," Fraser informed him. He picked the box up with his fingertips and examined it carefully along the seams. "My BE group has been working on it downstairs—a bacterium designed to eat through rubber and plastic insulation and short-circuit electrical impulses traveling through wire."

That much was true. DARPA was working on the so-called electricity-eating bug. But it was nowhere near the testing stage.

"And that's relevant because . . . ?" Anastasia pressed.

"Samples are missing from my laboratory," Fraser went on. "There's a possibility that someone may have placed them on board the shuttle. We need to sterilize the box before we open it. Otherwise, one of the bugs may slip inside and attack the data."

The men were silent.

"If you're worried about a bacterium why didn't you bring a decon team?" one of the colonels asked.

"Because *I* was the one who noticed the missing test tube, *I* was the only one here, and the bacterium isn't airborne," Fraser replied impatiently. The biochemist was starting to lose it—the act, the script he had written in his head. Lydia was the performer, not him, he wasn't very good at improv. "Decontamination personnel will meet me back at the BE lab to clean the flight recorder. Then it's all yours. Now please. Let's get this taken care of."

Anastasia hesitated. "Something isn't right here," he said.

"I'll say!" Fraser snapped. "You have orders from your commander in chief and you're ignoring them!"

"The president told us to wait until you got here," Anastasia said. "You're here. He didn't say anything about a decontamination process for us or the flight recorder."

"He didn't know," Fraser insisted.

"The *president* didn't know?" Anastasia said.

"My bioengineering program was need-to-know," Fraser snapped. "The president didn't need to know. Now let's get this taken care of!"

Anastasia shook his head. "You know what? My bullshit radar is showing a big brown blip."

"Call the president," Fraser demanded.

"I may," Anastasia said.

"Right. He's got nothing better to do than worry about your bullshit radar," Fraser said. "Look, we're talking about a thirty-minute delay at most. And that'll last even longer if we keep this up."

"This isn't only about the delay," Anastasia angrily insisted. "It's about the president knowing something and you knowing something and me not knowing something."

"You're being paranoid," Fraser said.

"It comes with intelligence work," Anastasia replied. "I

supervised the construction of the ESP. We ran microbial and decon tests. They came up clean. You're saying we missed something. I want to know how and why."

"That's what we're trying to find out!" Fraser shouted, holding up the flight recorder.

"I'm thinking you already know," Anastasia said.

"Pardon?"

"Did you piggyback something into earth orbit, something that fucked my shuttle mission all the hell up?" Anastasia demanded. "Do you want to get to the flight recorder to destroy data because it's going to tell us exactly what you did up there?"

"DARPA had nothing to do with this," Fraser insisted. "We're trying to find out who did."

"We?" Anastasia asked.

"We," Fraser said. "My fellow scientists, me, the President of the United States."

"If you didn't place it there, how did you track the missing bacterial agent to this particular mission?" Anastasia asked.

"I said we're only exploring the possibility," Fraser said. *Oh, Christ,* he thought. *Christ, Christ, Christ, this is getting way out of control.*

The brigadier general slipped off the edge of the table and jerked a thumb at the computer. "Pull up your file."

"What?"

"Show me the goddam computer file on your necrotizing germ," Anastasia told him. "I want to see the data log and the report on the theft. We've all got alpha-level clearance. Come on. Move it."

Fraser's bowels were tightening. He was about to get busted. Not only was there no file, he couldn't even bring something up and pretend it was the file he'd just described.

"General, you're leaping to some very weird conclusions," Fraser said. "I don't know the president. I've never met him."

"Neither have I, which is why I don't understand him calling me now," Anastasia said.

"Look. I came here to see if—not how, but *if*—the microbe that was stolen from my laboratory *might* be responsible for shutdown of the space shuttle. It's conceivable. This is all still very speculative."

"Why are you backpedaling?"

"I'm not—"

"Show me the file, Dr. Fraser," Anastasia demanded. The brigadier general was walking toward him slowly. The other men had risen and the guards were facing the lab table. "If someone else fucked with my mission and killed that crew, we'll deal with them together," Anastasia said. "But if this was a black ops deal with my mission and crew as guinea pigs, then I want to know here and now. I want to know if it was illegal and I want to know if the president knew."

Fraser knew he shouldn't have agreed to do this. Anastasia was stressed from the day's events. Fraser's coming here hadn't helped. To the contrary. His own transformation was not unlike environmental zoological holometabolism, a sudden, unexpected change. A brilliant, confident scientist had become a quaking man-without-a-clue. It was bad enough that he'd blown this. Now he wanted to get out before he was so cornered that he had to tell the officer about the Stealth Warriors.

Fraser only hoped that Lydia wasn't watching.

Anastasia stopped walking. He was standing between Fraser and the door. "Assuming the flight recorder is contaminated, what needs to be done?" the general asked.

"We need to take it to my lab and wash the exterior with B3," Fraser said.

"Why didn't you bring the soap here?" Anastasia asked.

"Because we need 1600 milliliters and—it's *late,*" Fraser protested. "I left in a hurry. I wasn't thinking."

"Is that why you told us to go to the infirmary instead of to your lab?" Anastasia asked.

"Yes," Fraser said.

"Let me have the flight recorder," Anastasia said.

Fraser handed it to him.

"I don't believe most of what you just told me, Dr. Fraser," Anastasia said as he tucked the box under his arm. "But the president wants you involved in the investigation, so we'll play this string out. We're all going to go to your lab. And if I don't find B3 soap and a tub to use it in, these guards will escort you to a place where you will, I promise, come very clean."

"I can't believe I'm being treated this way," Fraser said.

"It's been a rough day all around," Anastasia said. "You're lucky I'm doing this at all."

"Maybe *I* should be the one calling the president!" Fraser shot back.

Anastasia did not reply. With the general in front, the colonels behind, and a guard on either side of him, an extremely anxious Dr. Fraser was escorted into the corridor. As they marched him to his office he couldn't focus on a single song. And then one popped into his brain. One that he wished would go away.

It was "The Impossible Dream." Not the heroic version sung by Don Quixote, but the closing arrangement the prisoners sang to Cervantes as he was being led to the Inquisition. . . .

Thirty-seven

Cape Canaveral, Florida
Tuesday, 1:17 A.M.

Captain Holly stared through the visor at the steel doors of an elevator. He was frustrated because he was stonewalled. He was angry at himself because this was not something he'd anticipated.

"Mr. Diaz—I'm a little screwed here," Holly said.

"Talk to me," Diaz said.

"The red zone is located underground," Holly told him. "In order to get to the map room I have to ride the elevator. In order to get the doors to open I have to pick up the telephone, stand under the security camera, and let the guard downstairs see who's calling."

"Can't you wait until someone comes along and then slip in?"

"Yeah. I can also waste a lot of time waiting." Holly walked several yards past the elevator and looked down the hallway. The corridor was just like the others he'd been through.

"You know what?" Diaz said. "I was once on a new San Clemente–class tanker for a joint operation with the Navy. We had to be dry-docked because the only way up from the engine room was an elevator."

"Your point, Mr. Diaz?" Holly said. *Lord, this man loves to talk.*

"The Navy had to refit the ship to put in stairs in case of a fire," the Coast Guard SHARC said.

Holly stopped walking. "Of course. There has to be a fire well somewhere down there."

"Exactly."

Holly looked around for a fire alarm. He saw the distinctive red faceplate just ahead and headed toward it as quickly as the heavy suit would allow. He moved with a lumbering jog with his body bent forward and his arms chugging hard. Holly reached the glass-faced alarm, tripped the switch, then stood back against the wall to get out of the way. Only then did it occur to him to look up. Many government buildings had sprinkler systems. That was all he'd need, water falling everywhere and outlining his invisible shape.

There *were* sprinklers. Holly hoped they were thermostat- or smoke-driven so they wouldn't go off.

The captain heard the alarms sounding upstairs and also below. He wished he could take off his headpiece and listen for the sound of doors or footsteps on concrete stairs.

Only one office door opened in this section of the corridor. Two men exited, looked around tentatively, then decided to leave. A moment later two guards rushed past in the opposite direction. One was talking into a radio and the other was carrying a fire extinguisher. They spoke for a moment with the two office workers. Then the guards went ahead, toward the fire alarm. Their shoes crunched on broken glass when they arrived.

"There was definitely a 'pull' at station twelve," the guard with the radio said.

"No one's left the building or called anything in," said the voice on the other end. "Check the offices."

"Roger that," said the guard.

The two men started checking all the offices in this section of the building, looking for the fire. As soon as they went around the corner, Holly moved away from the wall. He had to find the stairwell.

He heard a heavy door slam in the distance. That had to be it. He started moving down the corridor as quickly as possible. People were hurrying in his direction. They were civilians. Obviously, the military personnel were waiting for confirmation that there was a fire. The door from which the civilians had emerged was a green metal door just a few yards away. Holly hurried toward it and waited in the center of the hall. He hoped that the door opened again soon. He didn't want to waste time figuring out how to get in.

A moment later he heard one set of footfalls. The door groaned open and a woman stepped out. Holly knew the door would close quickly, so he moved toward it as soon as the woman emerged. He caught the door by the edge, swung through, and let it close behind him. He walked down two flights of stairs and reached another door.

A locked door.

Suddenly the alarm stopped.

Shit, Holly thought. No one else would be leaving the secure area. And no one would be coming back down via the stairwell. Anyone who'd be returning to work would use—

Holly swore again, then turned and hurried back up the stairs. He hesitated at the door, listened to make sure no one was coming, then pushed it open. He hurried down the corridor to the elevator. He arrived just as a man and a

woman were getting back in the car. Holly bopped the edge
of the door as it started to shut, and it slid open again.

The people inside looked at each other.

"Must've been me," the woman said.

She stepped deeper into the car, away from the sensor in
the door. Holly moved into the opposite corner. He was
breathing heavily from the run, and was glad for the strong
whir of the overhead fan and the slight groan of the coun-
terweight. He was convinced the occupants would hear him
otherwise. The car descended smoothly and swiftly. When
the door opened, the woman exited followed by the man.
Holly slid out behind them.

The captain found himself in a brightly lit corridor identical to the one upstairs save for the forced air vents along
the tops of the walls. Without windows or doors, the air supply down here would have to be replenished regularly. A
guard sat to the left of the door. On the glass-topped desk
were a security monitor, telephone, and computer. A fire
extinguisher was sitting on the floor beside the chair. The
guard, a slender young African-American, had obviously
been conducting the fire search down here.

"A false alarm, it looks like," the guard declared as the
coworkers returned.

"Some kind of joke?" asked the woman.

"More likely an accident," the guard said. "Someone
must've stumbled against the alarm and didn't want to own
up to it."

That's as good an explanation as any, Holly thought. It
took a special kind of individual to fly multibillion-dollar
test planes. That wasn't only because you could kill yourself with an attention-lapse that lasted a nanosecond, but
because there was only one person to face the "I-may-have-
screwed-up" music if the plane crashed and you didn't go
down with it. Even if it were the plane's fault, one of the

countless flaws inherent in any new technology, the pilot was plagued with the idea *"If only I'd done this or that differently."* Air Force desk jockeys were a different breed. They liked to have the option of hiding. Otherwise, they'd be up there with the real risk-takers.

"Probably Captain Orjuela tapping the motor oil again," the woman remarked.

"Been a long day here," the guard replied with a forgiving shrug. "Some people are falling over without taking a drink."

She cocked her head down the hall. "The generals stayed?"

"All of them," the guard told her. "Nothing's going to pull them out of there tonight."

"Either that or they'd rather fry than have to face the next few months," the woman said.

When the woman and man left, Holly walked behind the security desk. The guard was annoyed and muttering to himself. Holly didn't blame him. It was okay when he criticized the military, but he hated when civilians did it. Especially smug civilians.

Holly watched as the guard scrolled down the personnel board. He typed on the keyboard, "In 1:29 A.M." beside the names Suze Samuels and Matt Mazer, and hit save. Holly leaned closer. According to the log both employees worked in the SMU, the Satellite Monitoring Unit. The map room was probably located there. Holly turned and followed them down the corridor.

He was no longer sweating inside the uniform. The forced air must be air-conditioned. Now that he thought about it, the long johns he had on under the suit were starting to feel a little cooler. The SFU itself must be cooling. A moment later he started to see a bit of condensation on the fringes of the faceplate. Apart from obscuring his peripheral vision slightly, Holly wondered if the haze would be visible from the outside.

Holly heard voices behind double doors down the hall. Probably "the generals" in what looked like a conference room. They were searching for answers they weren't going to find.

The captain slipped into the SMU room behind the two civilian workers. The big, open room reminded him of a newsroom at a newspaper—with a few differences. There were over a dozen desks with computers, fax machines, shredders, encryption and decryption units, and a pair of large plasma-screen wall monitors. The televisions were blank now, but were probably used to generate high-resolution images from satellites.

Only the two workers were here. A number of employees had probably been reassigned to the ESP project. If everything had gone as planned, they would have been calibrating or downloading data from the ESP tonight. That obviously wasn't going to be happening. These two must be watching an older Air Force satellite. So many of those were aging fast, their technology outdated or orbits decaying. If they couldn't get the ESP back, military intelligence was going to be hurting. It was a shame Holly couldn't just tell them why he was here and ask for the map files that had been programmed into the ESP.

Suze Samuels got herself a Coke from a small refrigerator in the back of the room. Holly moved around the perimeter of the room. He shadowed the woman as she went to her desk. She sat down and inputted her password, VIRTUA3. The menu came up, a white drop-down screen on a cobalt-blue field. She scrolled down to HISPASAT 1A. She got a view of the earth from 35,778 km above 0 degrees 1 minute N, 29 degrees 56 minutes W. The entire Atlantic Ocean was visible. Bright night lights were visible along the coast of South America; North America was barely on the monitor in the top left corner. The woman moved the cursor to a point northeast of the Cuban coast and zoomed in. While she waited, she brought up a view that had been taken the night before. Obviously, Suze's job was to run through the Air Force satellites and compare images to record troop or weapons movements in world hot spots. If she found any changes, she would probably forward the data to the appropriate military functionary, who would then analyze the information to see if it was something to worry about.

All the computers in the room were on. Holly located the surge protector that provided power to Suze's computer. It was bolted to the floor behind her desk. He extended his foot and used his toe to kill it.

"Hey!" the woman shouted as her screen went black. "My computer just died."

"Mine's okay," her coworker said. "Check the connection."

She got up to do so. That would shut her out while he used her password. It was regulation to have a backup, and he would use that to get back on. Then he went to one of the desks away from where Suze and Matt were working. He leaned over the chair and inputted Suze's code. The computer came on. The monitor looked strange, the image rolling because of the polarization of the faceplate. It was almost like watching a TV screen that had been filmed. Holly scrolled through the list of satellites and selected ESP. Before he hit enter, he used the keyboard to shut down the sound function. He didn't want to have the computer pinging or clanging while he was here.

A menu appeared on the monitor. There were fifteen selections. Three of them were marked with red Xs: *Orbital Element Status, Targeting Adjustment,* and *Data Response Time.* Holly went directly to the one he wanted: *Coordinate*

Selection Program. He slipped a disk into the hard drive and moved the cursor to *Download.*

The computer hummed quietly. He watched as the file was copied.

His body kept cooling and his faceplate continued to collect moisture. It was becoming distracting.

A moment later, Holly was distracted by something else. A shout. He looked to his left. Suze was standing over the surge protector near her desk and pointing.

At him.

Thirty-eight

Germantown, Pennsylvania
Tuesday, 1:30 A.M.

Colonel Lewis couldn't sleep.

Taylor had offered him the bed in his mother's room, but Lewis preferred the creaky sofa bed. For one thing, the room smelled of baby powder or whatever flowery perfume she used. For another, it was a real bedroom. Too much comfort made a man soft. Besides, with the big living room windows that looked out on acres of treetops and whatever part of Philadelphia was spread out beyond, with a bright moon over all, he felt almost as if he was out in the field. And that was always where Matt Lewis was happiest.

Right now the colonel needed something that made him viscerally happy. What he'd done for Taylor had gratified him intellectually. But it was the only time in Lewis's life—the *only* time—he had ever used détente instead of a knife or shoulder throw or trip wire to take an opponent down. Contrary to fashion in this post-Iraq age, when diplomacy was typically preferable to military confrontation, Lewis didn't find it satisfying. However expertly a compromise was worked out, it was still a trade-off and not a victory. It was like weeding without pulling the damn thing out by the roots.

Lewis looked at the illuminated clock on the stove in the kitchenette. It was creeping toward two A.M. He shook his head and lay back. Since he tended to be up at dawn, he was rarely awake past eleven. This was frustrating. The issue of whether he'd copped out today was bugging him a lot, even more than it had right after he'd left the Front Street garage. Lewis forgot who it was that said, "Compromise makes a good umbrella but a poor roof." But that certainly applied to what had happened today. And Matt Lewis hated leaving things half done.

If it weren't so late, he would call the base and find out what was going on. There had been no messages from Commander Evans, so Lewis assumed that, for the moment, everything was under control. He wondered if there were any new developments in the shuttle crash. He felt a little pathetic lying here thinking about his problem in the long shadow of what had happened to those lives, those families, and the future of space exploration. Not to mention the threat from whatever might be behind the crash.

Lewis looked at the ghostly-white walls, at the moonlit photographs in the Hank Taylor, Jr., Shrine. The colonel felt a pinch of envy and wondered if maybe this place was throwing him off balance a little. He had never had a home. From childhood he moved from military installation to military installation. Heading up the U.S. Army Delta Force training program had made Fort Bragg, North Carolina, his base of operations but not a home. Now the cabin on Lake Miasalaro was his new base, but it still wasn't a home. There was nothing permanent in his life, and maybe that was why events had to be. He needed to secure his environment because there was no place to retreat to, no touchstone. Home was wherever he was, and his home had to be clean and right.

Or maybe that's just a way-tired brain talking bullshit, Lewis told himself. Maybe he just resented having to let scubas off the hook. *Resented?* he thought. Hell, he loathed it.

The colonel closed his eyes, exhaled slowly, and imagined a different scenario. A scenario in which he had gone to the Front Street garage with a different goal. He wouldn't have had C-4 or even lead styphnate, mercury fulminate, tetracene, or any of the explosives he would traditionally employ in guerrilla attacks. Instead, he would have picked up butane lighters, paper towels, gravel, and mud along the way. He would have snuck in the same way he had, up the staircase. Furtively, he would have opened the gas tanks of the Moonshot cars, inserted tightly rolled lengths of paper towel—just enough to let him get back to the nearest concrete pillar—and set the towels ablaze. Then, if anyone had emerged from the cars alive, Lewis would have had a surprise for them. Butane lighter hand grenades in a plastic grocery bag. He'd have manufactured those before heading over to the garage. They were easy to make: You just punched a hole in the plastic casing, flicked your Bic, and tossed. The leaking lighter fluid caught fire and blasted the gravel and mud that had been packed around it. Moonshot death-peddlers fell to the concrete and bled to death before help could arrive.

That was a fulfilling scenario. And as Lewis thought himself through it, he eased into a fitful sleep. . . .

Thirty-nine

**Arlington, Virginia
Tuesday, 1:35 A.M.**

There were times in the laboratory when a test or experi-ment spiraled out of control so fast that there was just one thing Dr. Fraser could do. He would shut down his equipment, all of it, before the materials and the machines ate each other up. He was usually quick to hit the panic button; he would rather have to reset a sequence or series of sequences than recycle the entire experiment. He had once told a coworker that it was like going for the world domino-fall record. Better to knock a few from the middle than to watch everything come down.

The situation with General Anastasia had gone south faster than any undertaking in which Fraser had ever been involved. The scientist found himself mentally paralyzed as General Anastasia and his team marched him to the basement elevator. Fraser made his living by sitting back, reviewing data, and *then* moving on. Here, now, he couldn't get his mental footing and figure out what to do next. There was no fuse to pull, no panic button to slap. He was *part* of the damn experiment and not an observer.

Almost as bad, Fraser could barely keep his physical footing as they ushered him along the corridor.

"You have no right to do this," Fraser said lamely, "hustling me along like I'm a felon."

"You're the one who said it," Anastasia told him.

"Said what?" Fraser asked. Then he realized what. "You know what I mean," he muttered.

"All I know is that we're hurrying to get answers from this box," Anastasia said. "You are the least of my concerns."

"Obviously."

When he was at bay a few minutes before, Fraser had been panicked. Now that he was out and out trapped, he was amazed at how pissed off he was. He really wasn't sure the president would come to his rescue, and he cursed himself for having agreed to undertake this charade. What was he thinking? This wasn't a musical. This was reality. He wasn't a spy. He was a scientist. Over twenty-year-old visions of Lieutenant Colonel Oliver North taking the hit for Iran-Contra flashed through his brain as he doubted that President Gordon would come to his rescue for trying to steal the space shuttle's flight data recorder.

What were you thinking when you said okay? he screamed at himself. *When did the electrical spirit energy of "Wild Bill" Donovan ease into your body and make you think you were an OSS master spy?*

They reached the elevators and one of the colonels jabbed the button. They'd need Fraser's badge to activate the basement button. He should have dropped it somewhere. That would have bought him time. Maybe more time than the general was willing to invest in him.

The door opened. The elevator was too small to hold seven men.

"Wait here," Anastasia said as he got in with Fraser and

the MPs. "I'll send one of the guards back with the doc's badge."

The colonels acknowledged the order. The elevator door slid shut. Fraser felt as if he was being led to the lethal injection chamber.

A moment later the car stopped.

And dominoes flew.

Forty

Cape Canaveral, Florida
Tuesday, 1:39 A.M.

"Who the hell are you and how did you get in here?" a shocked Suze Samuels demanded. She picked up a heavy sky-blue Air Force mug and began backing away, alongside the desk.

At first Holly thought that he had screwed up big time. Maybe he'd lifted a disk or moved something on the desk while the woman was looking. To her, the object would have appeared to be floating. It wasn't until the woman spoke that Captain Holly knew the situation was much worse than that. He looked down at his left hand.

The glove of the stealth field uniform was no longer a smoky gray mass in the polarized lens of his faceplate. It was solid and clearly defined. He was visible.

His mind worked like it did in the cockpit, automatically and immediately searching for reasons something had gone wrong. Perhaps it was due to a combination of the cool air in the room and the condensed perspiration inside the suit. Or maybe a circuit had simply cut out on him. Not that it mattered. DARPA hadn't built a diagnostics system or repair kit into the SFU. There weren't even backups to speak of.

At least the woman was startled and not horrified. She saw him there, but she hadn't seen him actually materialize. If she had, her reaction would probably have been a lot different.

Yet even if they just thought of him as a specially suited infiltrator, a spy, or someone who might have had a hand in bringing the shuttle down, Holly couldn't allow himself to be caught.

Holly looked at the computer monitor. The data was still downloading onto the disk.

"Diaz, I'm in serious trouble," Holly said into the subvocal.

"What happened?" Diaz asked.

"My SFU just went AWOL," Holly told him. "The people in the room can see me."

Holly didn't move. He watched through the visor as the woman slid to the other side of her desk, perhaps for protection, and simultaneously reached for the phone. She was probably going to call the guard. Her companion was circling wide toward the door. The man had picked up a letter opener and was wielding it like a knife.

"Did you try shutting your suit down and rebooting?" Diaz asked.

"No—"

"Do it!" Diaz insisted. "The startup charge may muscle through the impendance."

"Not yet."

"What?"

"I'll try that when I'm alone," Holly told him.

"Why wait?"

"Because I don't think they saw me materialize and I don't want them to see me go invisible!"

"Captain, this isn't the time to be cautious," Diaz said. "You can't afford to be caught."

"I won't be," Holly said. "If you're right about the reboot I may be able to get out of this."

"I'm going to look for a way in," Diaz said.

"Don't do anything!" Holly hissed. "Just stand by."

The red bar showing the download status told Holly that less than a minute remained until he had all the ESP map files. He had to eat up some of that time and hope that what he was planning worked.

"We have an intruder!" Suze said emphatically over the phone. "He may be armed. Send assistance now!"

Holly had known that was coming, but there was nothing he could do to stop her. Even if he could have gotten around the desks, he hadn't wanted to attack the scientists. He would not strike at law-abiding people. Never. He wasn't even sure he could do that in this suit. So much for emulating go-get-'em Lewis and the other Stealth Warriors. It was tough enough just moving his arms. Still, whether he attacked or not, he had to make his move before guards came with firearms. The SFU wasn't bullet-proof.

Holly wished he could have dropped his face mask and talked to these people, told them that he was on their side. Even if they didn't believe him, a short conversation would have bought him time to finish the download. But there might be security cameras somewhere in the room. Holly didn't want to risk being identified and tracked to the DARPA field tests. That might lead to Langley, Captain McIver, and the Stealth War unit.

That left him with only one other maneuver. And its success depended on Diaz being right.

Holly moved away from the desk toward the door. He counted his footsteps, measuring the distance carefully. He was very good at marking distance that way and remembering it "in his bones." It had been part of his survival training, in case he ever had to bail out over enemy territory and move around at night, without flashlights that might give him away.

"Keep your distance," the man said.

The scientist's hand was shaking. He was scared. That was good. As long as Holly didn't attack him, Matt probably wouldn't act. Holly moved slowly toward the door. He hunkered a little lower, leaning toward his target. He wanted the man to be intimidated, just a little. Just enough.

Holly was seven steps, eight steps, nine steps from the computer. The man and the door were just over three yards ahead with nothing but open space between them and Holly.

"Do you understand English?" the man demanded. "Stay away from the goddam door!"

"Matt, get away from there!" Suze shouted. "Let security handle this. He won't get out of the building." She looked at Holly. "You hear that, Batman? If you don't give up you'll be Deadman."

Holly continued to approach. After a brief hesitation the scientist started backing from the door.

That was what Holly had been waiting for: room to move. The pilot bolted forward, but not toward the door or the scientist. It wasn't a pretty move in the big suit, but he reached his target: the light switch. Holly snapped it down. At almost exactly the same instant he activated the stealth function of the SFU while also turning and making his way back to the desk in the dark. He reached the computer and popped the disk.

Suze was shouting. Matt was bumping into desks as he made his way toward her. The door opened. Two men were crouching behind the jambs, weapons pointed into the room. Two other men were standing above and slightly behind them in support.

"Dr. Samuels? Dr. Mazer?" one of them shouted.

"Here!" Suze shouted. "To your left!"

One of the crouching security guards swung a large flashlight toward the doorway and shined it in. The fat white beam rippled across the computer monitors until it found the two scientists.

"We're okay," Suze said. "The intruder's on the other side—he put out the light!"

"You two stay down," the man with the flashlight said. He began moving the beam slowly to the left. "This is Corporal Hyams. Whoever you are, there is no way out of this building. I want you to rise slowly with your arms fully extended above your head."

The order was greeted with silence. The corporal's flashlight beam finished its sweep.

"He's gotta be behind one of the desks in the back," a guard whispered to Hyams.

"Yeah," Hyams agreed. "Brophy, get the light switch."

"Yes, sir."

The guard crouching on the other side rose slightly and reached in. He kept his fifteen-shot Beretta trained on darkness ahead. His hand snaked up the wall. He found the switch and flicked it. Light filled the office.

Except for the two scientists the room was empty.

Forty-one

Arlington, Virginia
Tuesday, 1:40 A.M.

In the Catholic faith there is a concept known as Adapta-
tion. It was defined by the Second Vatican Council in 1962
as a legitimate adjustment of principles to accommodate unusual circumstances.

Striking a superior—striking any good soul—was wrong.
But the circumstances did not leave Evans any options that
he could see.

Evans had gone to the Pentagon and parked his van in
the unmarked DARPA officers' section, which was practi-
cally deserted at this hour. He climbed into the back of the
van, put on his SFU, and went to the basement. Finding
that Fraser was not in his office, Evans headed toward the
Air Force intelligence wing, where he heard muffled shouting in the room the black box had been taken to. Instead of
going in, Evans waited for the occupants to come out, then
followed them to the elevator. It was easy to slip inside after them, hit the stop button as they neared the basement,

and go a little wild on the passengers. Evans used a palm-heel strike against the general's chin to weaken his hold on the box. The palm-heel was designed to drive the head back fast and far enough to stun without actually snapping the neck. Evans applied a little more force than he usually did to compensate for the weight of the glove. The box came free, and Evans grabbed it as he simultaneously struck the other men. He raised his right forearm and hit one man with a ridge-hand strike across the eyes while the other caught his elbow across the eyes. As both men slumped down, joining the dazed general on the floor, Evans handed the box to Fraser. Though startled, the scientist obviously figured out what was going on, and protected the flight data recorder while Evans hit the three men on the temples with his knuckles. That finished the job and left them unconscious.

"They're going to blame me for this," Fraser grumped as the elevator started up again.

Probably, Evans thought. But the security investigation unit that looked into this attack was also going to be very confused. They were going to wonder how a scientist with no combat training whatsoever managed to overpower a seasoned officer and his military police escort. They'd probably reach the conclusion that Fraser had secrets. Obviously he did, if he had disappeared from the Pentagon with the shuttle's black box. Evans hoped that finding the real perpetrators would take the heat off Fraser. If not, at least the scientist would be hidden up at the base. Perhaps this was part of the price team members had to pay to help maintain the liberty of others.

The elevator reached the bottom floor. Evans and Fraser left the car as the door closed.

"What took you so long?" Fraser muttered. "I know, you can't answer with that outfit on. I just want to let you know that you *did* take too long and I almost blew it because of that."

Actually, Evans had got there as fast as he could. And he'd made good time, considering that he'd had to load his stealth field uniform into the van and drive from the lake.

Fraser hugged the black box to him as they walked briskly down the corridor toward the exit. Evans reached out and touched him on the shoulder to slow him down. He didn't want anyone to stop Dr. Fraser and ask what was wrong. Fortunately, the hallways were relatively deserted at this hour. The few people who did see Fraser apparently thought there was nothing unusual in the eccentric man's wide-eyed demeanor.

"I assume we're not staying here, that we're going to the officers' exit," Fraser said. He was silent for a moment. "I assume you're still there. Tap me again if I'm right about where we're going."

Evans touched him again lightly.

"Good," Fraser said. "No guards there. I've done all the bullshitting I care to do for one day. And I didn't even do it well, which really galls me. I had the blessings of the president. I thought I'd be better at talking my way into things. Well, that's not quite right. I talked my way into it just fine. It was talking out of it where I screwed up."

For all his angst Fraser was probably in scientist's heaven. He was free to complain and expound with no one to answer back. Which was fine with Evans. He needed to vent.

The men reached Evans's van and got in the back. Evans sat on a rubberized tarp to keep the SFU from picking up stray fibers that would not become invisible if he did. Then he removed the SFU and told Fraser to stay there with the black box. The commander then climbed behind the wheel, flashed his credentials to the guard, and drove out. Evans took a few minutes to brief Fraser, after which the scientist was silent. Evans had experienced that many times in the field. After passing a crisis point, working at such a high with adrenaline racing, the body tended to shut down completely, almost as if it had been drugged.

As they made their way back toward West Virginia, it began to hit Evans himself exactly what they'd done. They'd stolen the evidence that could lead to whoever brought the shuttle down. That suddenly bothered him. Even though they'd been sent there by the president, it was a hell of a responsibility. But the possibility that something could have happened to that data at the Pentagon was very real. So was the price of failure: the fall of the United States government, of world governments. Evans wished he weren't so tired. Things always seemed confused and negative enough in the small hours of the night.

Evans glanced at the phone below the dashboard. He wished he could call Victoria to ask if she had heard from Holly and Diaz. But he couldn't risk phoning her on an open line. After the theft of the black box, the Pentagon's MoCSU—Mobile Communications Surveillance Unit— would be scanning the airwaves looking for any wireless calls that might lead them to whoever stole the black box. They'd be paying particular attention to cars heading away from the area at unusually high speed, which they could determine by a Dopplerlike shift in the strength of the radio signal. The faster the signal receded, the faster the caller was traveling. Aerial units from local police forces were probably already airborne awaiting a MoCSU report. Sharpshooters were almost certainly on board those choppers to make sure the thieves did not get away.

Evans could only pray that Holly and Diaz succeeded at the Cape. Without the ESP map data, whatever information Victoria might be able to pull from the shuttle's flight data recorder probably wouldn't be enough to let them zero in on the perpetrators.

The troubling aspect of these parallel missions was how inefficient they were. What the Stealth Warriors were doing to try to stop Estate struck him as a metaphor for the transitional age between the analog and digital worlds. He, Holly, and Diaz had to go out and get the information by hand, then physically *bring* it to a place for analysis. The Estate people simply had to press a button and digital signals accomplished the same kind of data-research. One method was slow and painstaking and had to navigate the ups and downs of earth terrain. The other was lightning-quick and flashed through the atmosphere oblivious to walls and other impediments. Evans felt prehistoric.

But there were many occasions when he had gone into battle armed with little more than morality and faith. The day those didn't give Evans an edge was the day he would hang up his suit.

It was nearly four A.M. when he reached the mountain base. Dr. Fraser had gone to sleep in the back. He was startled awake when Commander Evans popped the side door.

"Are we okay?" Fraser blurted.

"We're fine," Evans assured him.

"Thank God," Fraser said as he stepped out. He was still clutching the black box.

The parking area of the Stealth complex was off a short, private dirt road. It was just an oval of dirt up the hill from what was originally the only cabin up here. Commander Evans had added a tall iron gate at the foot of the road located between two high and wide outcroppings of granite. Three rows of razor wire were stretched across the top of the boulders. It would be extremely difficult for anyone to approach the cabin. If they did manage to get by the barrier, a small video surveillance camera would trigger an alarm inside both the main cabin and the com-shack.

Victoria was asleep in her chair when the men reached the com-shack. She was slumped low in the swivel chair, her legs straight before her under the desk. The woman's hands were folded on her lap and her head was leaning to the right. On the computer screen saver, colliding atomic particles were causing little nuclear explosions here and there.

She awoke slowly, dreamily as the men entered the cabin. Victoria looked soft and approachable in her white sweater and jeans. After a moment she was fully awake. She sat up sharply.

"Wow!" Victoria said. "I'm really sorry. My eyes got heavy and I must have—"

"It's okay," Evans said.

"What time is it?"

"Nearly four o'clock," Evans told her.

"Damn." Her glance drifted to Fraser and what he was holding. Her eyes were no longer heavy. "You got it. You got the shuttle's black box."

Evans nodded.

Victoria looked at Fraser, who was half-hidden behind Evans. She rose and came around the desk with her hand extended. "Dr. Fraser. It's good to see you again."

Fraser was holding the black box in his right hand. He twisted his left hand around to shake hers. "We had some disagreements about the SFU, didn't we?" he asked.

"Yes," she said tensely. "You called my idea for molecular microchips a 'stupid interim technology.' You were pushing DARPA to develop microchips made of DNA."

"For human interface," he said. "Well, if you're looking ahead you should be ambitious."

"I'm only looking ahead an hour or two and we're going to need some answers," Evans said. He pointed to the black box. "Dr. Fraser, do you have any idea how to open that?"

Fraser turned the solid-looking box over in his hands. "No."

"I can," Victoria said. She walked over, took the box from Fraser, and set it on the desk. "I used your security code to pull up the specs from NASA's on-line shuttle specs," she said to Evans. She slid back a narrow, nearly invisible panel that stretched the entire width of the topside of the box. There was a numeric keypad set into the slot with a keyhole beside it. "The only way to open the box is by inputting the launch date."

"It's that simple?" Evans asked.

"Everything's simple when you know how." Victoria tapped the access code on the keypad's small, black keys. "They used to have a key system, but the *Challenger* explosion melted titanium into the lock and they had to use a diamond drill to clean it out."

When Victoria was finished, the entire keypad flipped up. There was a small metal knob beneath it. The young woman turned the box onto its end, then simultaneously twisted and pulled the knob. It slid from the box along with a tray. A compact disc sat in the tray. When the tray was removed, another one popped up and took its place.

"There are sixteen stacks of trays in the black box," Victoria said. "Each one is designed to contain a half day's worth of data."

"Unencoded?"

"Apparently," Victoria said as she gingerly removed the disk. "I guess if you got this far, NASA pretty much assumed you belonged here."

"It may be different for an Air Force–managed flight, though," Evans pointed out. "If that's the case I'll ask the president to get us the data."

Evans and Fraser gathered around the desk as Victoria slipped the CD into her computer. She accessed the "run" menu and told the computer to read the disk.

The light came on under the drive door. The room seemed supernaturally still as the disk turned.

The screen went blue and numbers immediately began appearing in short rows:

| 182900-05 | 182910-15 | 182920-25 | 182930-35 |
| 182940-45 | 182950-55 | 183000-05 | 183010-15 |

"Is this what we want to see?" Evans asked.

"I think so," Victoria said. She moved the cursor to the first set of numbers and clicked on them. "The shuttle took off at 8:30 yesterday morning. I think each group of numbers represents the day—which is first number on the left—the hour, the minute, and the seconds of the data recorded during that particular ten-second block, starting one minute before liftoff."

The numeric screen was minimized as columns of headings began to download:

Solid Rocket Boosters

Hold-Down Posts
SRB Ignition
Electrical Power Distribution
Hydraulic Power Units
Thrust Vector Control
SRB Gyro Assemblies

External Tank

Liquid Oxygen Tank
Intertank
Liquid Hydrogen Tank

"There's no point in continuing with this one," Victoria said. "Clicking on the headings will give us all the systems status reports at that time. That's not what we want."

Victoria asked Dr. Fraser to remove the trays until they

got to the last data-bearing disk. When he handed it to her, she popped it in the player and went immediately to the last block of time recorded on the disk. She clicked on it, then clicked on the heading *ESP Download*. From there she went to the *Antenna Status* and selected *Coordinates*.

Within moments Victoria had the data.

"Good work," the commander said softly.

"Thanks."

Victoria split the computer screen vertically and brought up figures she had downloaded earlier from the space shuttle's classified flight plan. Commander Evans looked over her shoulder. The two blocks of copy consisted of nearly one hundred numbers and letters. These represented both the longitudinal and latitudinal alignment that had been programmed into the ESP along with the position it had actually locked into.

"They're definitely very different sets of data," Evans said as he compared the two sets.

"Yeah. Too bad they're in code instead of Mercator language or whatever normal maps are written in," Victoria said.

"Didn't you just say you have a security code to get what we needed from the files?" Fraser asked.

"Not information this sensitive," Evans told him. "Air Force intelligence data is stored in dedicated systems at the Cape Canaveral air base. You can only get to it on-site."

"I see. And what are we doing to get to it?" Fraser asked.

"Two of our people are down there," Evans said. "We should be hearing from them soon."

Very soon, the commander hoped.

After Victoria had downloaded and saved the ESP antenna coordinates, she took them back to the Estate home page. Thanks to strategically placed links and banner advertisements, over nine thousand people had visited the site in just four hours, according to the hit-counter. And all

Forty-two

Cape Canaveral, Florida
Tuesday, 2:20 A.M.

Because he was afraid that his SFU would short-circuit again, Captain Holly wasted no time trying to get out of the Air Force intelligence center. He waited until the guards left the room, taking the two scientists with him. Then he left and immediately made his way to the stairwell. Not only would he be able to bypass the guard at the elevator, but he knew exactly where the fire exit would leave him. As soon as he was inside he got in touch with Diaz.

"Are you still there?" Holly asked.

"Of course!" Diaz said. "What's going on?"

"I did what you said," Holly told him. "I rebooted the suit and it went invisible."

"Thank God!"

"I also got the data," Holly went on. "I'm in the stairwell heading down and—shit!"

"What?"

Holly looked down. He saw his legs and arms beginning to solidify. "The suit's shorting again!"

"Damn."

"It has to be the combination of the temperature and sweat," Holly said. "I'm moving more, sweating more."

"You're going to have to nurse your way out of there," Diaz told him. "Don't reboot the suit until you absolutely have to."

"Right," Holly said. "I'm going to kill the genius inventor who didn't see this coming!" The pilot wanted to keep talking, just like he did whenever there was trouble in the cockpit. Flying was lonely work. Talking reminded Holly that there were people below, that even though he was close to heaven, that wasn't necessarily the next stop.

"That's why we were field-testing these suits, remember?" Diaz asked. "We weren't supposed to be going out on missions."

"I know. But you'd think they'd've checked sweat and temperature swings out in the lab."

"Even if they did, scientists can't anticipate every situation," Diaz pointed out. "Body heat, perspiration, cold, the length of time you're in the suit. There are too many variables."

"Maybe. But I've still got a foot with someone's rear end written on it," Holly said as he reached the top of the stairs.

Holly was so arm-and-leg-weary that all he wanted to do was get out of the SFU and leave it on the landing. His neck hurt too. Just holding the headpiece and the heavy visor erect took muscle power. When he wore his flight helmet, at least he had the back of the seat for support. He had absolutely no intention of abandoning the suit, of course. But he also knew that if he got out of the SFU, dumped it, and told the guards who he was—Captain Peter Holly, USAF, who had been hit on the head by a costumed intruder and then stripped of his uniform—they would probably let him go and keep looking for the individual who had been in the map room. He didn't know which was more important at the moment: saving the suit or downloading the disk to Victoria Hudson. It was like the choice any test pilot had to face when his plane was in jeopardy. What matters more: your survival, your aircraft, or your honor? In the end, a pilot worked like a sonofabitch until the last possible instant to preserve all three. That's what Holly was going to do now.

The captain reached under the armpits of the suit. He activated the knobs that controlled the stealth function.

The suit phased out for just a moment and then shut down again.

"Crap!"

"It didn't work?" Diaz asked.

"It came on for a second and then it died," Holly said angrily. Perspiration was beading on his forehead.

"Are there any other exits?" Diaz asked.

"From here? No."

"There's got to be a roof exit," Diaz said. "What if there were a fire and the first floor was full of smoke?"

"Hold on a sec," Holly said. He looked around. "No. I don't see another way out."

"Wait," Diaz said. "You may not see it because you've got your faceplate down."

"Huh?"

"The emergency lights where you are may not be white light."

"Right," Holly said, perking. "They'd be infrared so you could see whatever it was lighting *through* smoke."

"Exactly."

Holly quickly slipped up the faceplate and looked around. Being polarized, the faceplate would not allow infrared light to pass through. "Bingo!" he said enthusiastically. "I'm on my way!"

The stairwell was lit by a pair of battery-powered black-light spotlights. There were white lines painted on the floor. They were glowing brightly. Directly behind Holly, also painted white and shining in the dark, was a ladder. There was a trapdoor directly above it.

Less than two minutes later Holly was under the trapdoor. He pushed it open. It seemed heavier than it was and his arms trembled. An alarm sounded. As he stuck his head through, he saw that spotlights had come on all over the grounds. Guards were heading toward the area from surrounding buildings. Struggling through the narrow opening, he started running toward the side where Diaz was waiting. His steps were sluggish and he was panting hard. The perspiration from his forehead dripped and blurred his vision.

"Diaz, I'm going to toss you the disk," Holly said. "If I'm caught you can still get the data to base."

"You're not going to get caught," Diaz said.

"Why, you got a bailout plan?"

"Yes," Diaz said. "Put your visor down."

"What?"

"You're heating up again," Diaz said. "Put the visor down and try going invisible."

That made sense. Holly stopped and slid the faceplate down. Christ, he sucked at this cloak-and-dagger stuff. Holly had felt himself warming and hadn't thought to try the damn controls again. He reached under his arms and pressed again. He disappeared. And stayed that way.

Moving quickly to the edge of the building, Holly spotted a ladder and hurried to the side. Diaz met him at the bottom and together they made their way back to the astronaut living quarters.

Forty-three

Cape Canaveral, Florida
Tuesday, 3:30 A.M.

MCPO Diaz had never heard someone beat himself up so fiercely as Captain Holly did when they returned to their quarters. Anyone listening to him would have thought he'd failed to carry out his mission.

The men climbed back through the window and stripped off their SFUs. The SFU trunks were lying on the floor between the beds. Diaz finished first. He put the stealth suits away, then shut the case and moved it into a corner. The entire time the airman stood there muttering, "I fucking screwed the goddam pooch, man. I fucking screwed the fucking pooch."

"You're wrong," Diaz told him.

"No, man," Holly said bitterly. "Don't soap me."

"I'm not," Diaz insisted. "You broke into a secure military building, figured out how to get downstairs, and obtained the data you were sent there to obtain. I don't call that screwing the pooch."

"I do," Holly said. "I froze in the headlights."

"No," Diaz said. "You got out of there without hurting anyone. That's a hell of an accomplishment."

"It was three-quarters of a goddam job." Holly looked down at the suit. "All right. Priorities. I wonder if I should leave this thing out, let some of the sweat evaporate."

"I wouldn't," Diaz said. "If anyone comes in—"

"They'll recognize it," Holly said. "Fucking duh. Damn, I'm dumber than toast tonight."

"Listen, you've got to stop this—"

"Bullshit," Holly said. He finished packing his suit. After removing the disk from his equipment pouch, he latched the case shut. "When I got to the stairwell I stopped fucking *thinking*!"

"Hey, I didn't even get inside!" Diaz said. "You did. It was teamwork. Didn't you ever have anyone on the ground talk you through a blow during one of your test flights?"

"That isn't the same," Holly insisted. "The answers were all there tonight, in front of me. I just didn't think of them. I couldn't. My brain locked up because I was tired and scared."

"Jesus," Diaz said. "Sometimes one person just can't see and do everything. That's why we have teams and coaches, pilots and navigators."

Holly shook his head as he handed the disk to Diaz. "I just hope I didn't fuck this up," he said.

"Me too," Diaz told him. "I don't want to have to listen to part two of this rant."

Holly didn't seem to have heard. Diaz walked over to the desk and booted his laptop.

"I really don't get it, Captain," Diaz went on. "You weren't going in there to prove anything. We went to get something and we got it."

"Yeah," Holly said. "That's what we went there for."

"You're not used to being on this kind of team, where

everyone's equal," Diaz continued as he booted the disk. "You're used to hotdogging, being a soloist playing a concerto."

"I don't understand that, but it doesn't really matter," Holly said. "You going to call the commander and tell them we're back?"

"When I'm sure that we have it I'll call," Diaz said.

Diaz was about to jack in the computer when he heard footsteps coming toward the room. Diaz immediately diminished the screen while Holly flopped on the bed and slipped under the covers. Obviously, security was either doing a bed check or making sure that anyone who showed up on a base security camera over the last few hours hadn't suddenly left.

There was a knock on the door. Diaz wiped his sweaty palms on his underwear and went over. He opened it. Captain Ryan was standing there with a pair of military police. She didn't look happy.

"You're up," she said.

"Sure," Diaz replied. "Would you believe I had to get up to answer the door—"

"Your light was on and so's your computer," she said.

"Well, *I* was sleeping," Holly said groggily.

Ryan looked at the open window. "Warm?"

"No. It's just that we don't get the sea air up at Langley," Diaz said. "I miss it. Captain, what's going on?"

"Security matter," she said. "You two have been in here all night?"

"Is that a question or a statement?" Diaz asked.

"A question, Mr. Diaz. Just answer it."

"Yes, we've been here all night," he said. "Captain Holly was tired and went to bed early. I'm working on data so we can be ready to start our investigation tomorrow."

The woman glanced at the computer. "Your drive is operating."

"So? I was about to load data I have to study," Diaz said. "Captain, is there something going on that I should know about?"

"If there is I'm sure you'll be informed," she said. "May I see the disk you're using?"

"Sure, if you have an order from Rear Admiral Todd in Maintenance and Logistics Command," Diaz said easily.

"And I would need that because . . . ?"

"There's eyes-only data about shuttle recovery procedure during classified missions," Diaz said.

"A disk was stolen from intelligence," she said. "I want to make sure that isn't it."

"Get the approval and you can have the disk," Diaz said. "Use my phone if you like. I'll wait here while you wake the admiral's aide, wake the admiral, and register a formal charge of suspicion of possessing confiscated goods. With any luck, he'll let you take it without asking to see any paperwork."

The woman glared at him.

"Look," Diaz said. "We haven't been out of the room. I'm sure you've got security cameras—check. Besides, Captain Holly has alpha-level clearance. If we needed Air Force intelligence he could have gotten it at Langley."

Ryan's tired eyes showed defeat. "I'll be in touch if there's anything else," she said.

"We'll be here," Diaz said.

The officer shut the door. When Captain Ryan's footsteps receded, Holly came over.

"That was some kinda B.S. you were shoveling," Holly said.

"Some guys kill to get out of trouble," Diaz said. "I talk to get out of it."

"I believe that," Holly said. "I would've choked if Ryan had asked me all that shit."

"Like I said, teamwork," Diaz told him. The Coast

Guard SHARC sat back down at the desk. "And if you need any indication of how well you succeeded back there, that was it."

"Maybe. But I feel bad for her."

"Me too," Diaz said. "But I'm glad it went the way it did."

Diaz opened the download from Holly's disk. The screen filled with columns of hundreds of numerals, punctuation marks, and letters.

"Shit," Holly said. "That looks like a lot of gibberish."

"Patience, Captain," Diaz replied. "Have you ever worked with encoded files before?"

"Never," Holly said.

"The encrypted data always comes up first," he said. "In case anyone does hack into a system, they may only take a second to react the way you did and move on."

Diaz jumped to the bottom of the file. After approximately two thousand lines had downloaded, a new set of data began appearing. They were longitudes and latitudes. Before each one was a number, letter, or combination thereof that corresponded to similar assignations above.

"That looks good," Holly said.

"It looks great thanks to you," Diaz said. He reached for the phone. "Now we can call Commander Evans."

Forty-four

Lake Miasalaro, West Virginia
Tuesday, 4:17 A.M.

Evans opened the cabin door. The hinges complained just enough to remind him of the imperfections inherent in what men did. At least, that's how it sounded to his tired mind. And he was tired, not just from the long hours but from the mental application. His body was handling it okay, but his brain seemed to lag about three or four paces behind.

Evans stood there, facing the lake. The cool breeze that came off the water and up the hill was invigorating. He took a step outside and drew a long breath. The early morning air was crisp, clean, and invigorating. He needed that. More than the day before, he needed a taste of Eden. More than the day before, this place seemed like Eden. Since yesterday morning the world outside had become a darker, less welcoming place.

"Commander, we're getting something!" Victoria said urgently from behind him.

Evans turned back to the desk. Dr. Fraser had been standing in a far corner reading data Victoria had printed out. He continued reading as Evans walked up beside Victoria.

"From Holly and Diaz?" Evans asked.

"Yes," she said. "The download is being cycled through Langley so it isn't traceable."

"Then they have something," Evans said hopefully.

"It looks like it," she said.

An airman and seaman had done their job on land, and in suits that were still basically prototypes. At that moment Evans was extremely proud of his team. He wished he could call and tell them that, but the fact that they didn't call him suggested that they had no way of knowing if the lines were secure. Obviously, they didn't want to take a chance calling over the cell phone.

The data was going to take nearly ten minutes to upload. Until then it would be inaccessible.

"You know, there's something troubling about this list from that Atlantic City conference," Dr. Fraser said.

"What conference is that?" Evans asked.

"I was pulling together the names of people who had worked with Dr. Gregg," Victoria said. "These were names from a major scientific conference he attended several years back."

Evans glanced over at the list. "What's the problem?" the commander asked.

"I don't know," Fraser said. "That's the problem."

"Excuse me?" Evans said.

"It's these names," Fraser told him. "I encountered them somewhere, but I can't remember where."

"You mean you encountered the names or the people?" Evans asked.

"Just the names, I think."

"Professionally?" Evans asked. "Perhaps you attended a convention or seminar with them—?"

"I don't go to those. Too many disputatious personalities," Fraser said.

"What about on a personal trip? At a party? Socially?"

Fraser shook his head.

The download finished just then and Evans looked back at the monitor. He couldn't decide whether he was intrigued or frustrated by Dr. Clark Fraser. Back at DARPA the scientist had always spoken his mind about science. But he was always well-informed and usually correct. Evans had very little experience with him in the outside world. Victoria shot the commander a look that told him which side she came down on.

Victoria engaged a search program. She inputted the coordinates that had been recorded in the shuttle's black box data, then told the program to find those coordinates in the new list.

The response was instantaneous.

"We've got our antenna realignment," Victoria announced. "It's 151° 289' west, 57° 316' north."

"That's pretty specific," Evans observed.

"All of these Air Force coordinates are," she said. "I guess that's how they can pick out individual houses to spy on."

Victoria went to the Internet and browsed longitude and latitude. She came up with a United States government census gazetteer site that allowed her to look up zip codes by map coordinates. She input the figures. A few seconds later she had the zip code.

"Those coordinates are for the zip code 99619. Not one I'm familiar with," Victoria said.

"A 9 would place it on the West Coast somewhere," Evans said.

Victoria looked the number up on the Internet. "Right," she said. "It's in Alaska. Kodiak."

"Kodiak?"

"You know it?" Victoria asked.

"That's where the Air Force had their White Alice Communications System until about eleven or twelve years ago," Evans said. "It was a communications support system to all the elements of the DEW line."

"What's the DEW line?" Victoria asked.

"The Distant Early Warning line," Evans said. "It was a string of radar stations near the seventieth parallel across the North American continent. The United States maintained it jointly with Canada to warn against Soviet attacks over the North Pole. That, the Pinetree Early Warning Line, the Mid-Canada Line, and others were pretty much replaced by satellite and aerial surveillance after the collapse of the Soviet Union."

"You say the Air Force gave it up years ago?" Victoria said.

"Yes," Evans told her. "I think they leased the Kodiak site to a radio station which used one of the fifty-foot dishes for a while. The dish was finally going to be dismantled. At least, that's what the Air Force planned."

"How much of the DEW line is still in place?" she asked.

"Probably most of the facilities, though I imagine they've also been decommissioned like the Kodiak site."

"But maybe not dismantled," Victoria said.

"That's right."

"And if they weren't, it might be possible to communicate with other dishes and other satellites," Victoria said. "There's your simultaneous world access. From Kodiak."

"Perhaps," Evans agreed.

"We should try and find out who bought or leased those sites," Victoria said. "Maybe they're still using them."

"I wonder," Evans said.

"Wonder what?"

"If anyone really did buy or lease them." Evans looked at her. "I mean, look at what we have here. A rogue Air

Force satellite retargeted to communicate only with a former Air Force radar station."

"Are you thinking that Dr. Gregg had an accomplice in the Air Force?" Victoria asked.

"*That's* where it was," Fraser said. "That's what he was talking about before. A meeting."

"Who was talking about what?" Victoria asked.

Evans regarded the scientist. "Dr. Fraser, do you mean the names?"

"Yes," Fraser said.

The scientist was thinking. Much too slowly.

"What do you remember?" Evans pressed.

"The first and only time I heard them was at a meeting at DARPA about four or five years ago. I was approached about going to work in a new division. It was all very hush-hush, even by DARPA standards. That's where the names came up."

"Who was it that came to see you?" Evans asked.

Fraser replied, "General Anastasia. The man you left on the floor of the elevator."

Forty-five

Arlington, Virginia
Tuesday, 4:35 A.M.

If there was one thing General Rudolph Anastasia should have learned during his nearly fifty years in the Air Force, it was this: Never underestimate the resourcefulness of men.

Machines were predictable. Barring structural flaws in the materials or an act of God, if you did everything right they worked. If you didn't they failed. Dr. Barry Gregg had done everything he was supposed to do before the ESP was released. And the satellite had worked: It had killed the space shuttle. The dead shuttle was then supposed to kill Gregg. The scientist had agreed to that. Gregg felt that the goal of the group was worth the sacrifice—to establish the on-line government Estate. To create one world, a world where the tools of war could be shut down and science could be adequately funded, where humankind could move forward under a single guiding vision. The vision of General Anastasia and Estate. But people were not predictable. Who could have imagined that Commander Boring would be able to bring the stricken shuttle back to earth? That Anastasia would have to scramble to find a way to silence Gregg, to make sure that if he were drugged or delirious he didn't talk to investigators.

I *should have imagined that,* Anastasia thought. Even though NASA studies and even Dr. Crabbe had said it was impossible, the general should have had a contingency in place.

Then there was the surprise from Clark Fraser. General Anastasia had woefully underestimated the scientist. Fraser must have wanted the shuttle flight recorder bad to turn on them the way he did in the elevator. He turned on them fast and brilliantly. Even the men Fraser hit didn't see the blows coming. The officers still couldn't believe that the scientist didn't have an accomplice, but they were definitely in the elevator alone.

And why did Dr. Fraser want the shuttle's black box? Why did the White House back him? Did they know or suspect that the position of the ESP's antenna was recorded there? Even so, why send *Fraser* to get it? Why not dispatch a multiforce team from the Execom Security Division of the Joint Chiefs of Staff? It didn't make sense.

Not that the data would help Fraser or the president. There, at least, Anastasia and his team were covered.

Anastasia still wasn't sure. He had just finished checking Fraser's file. There was nothing in it to suggest combat training. Or a special relationship with the president or the Joint Chiefs or any watchdog group such as the CIA's Directorate of Science and Technology, which had overseen the background checks on everyone involved with the ESP project.

But then, Anastasia knew that not everything was in a person's file. His own file, for example, contained nothing about his work against anti–Vietnam War students on the Berkeley campus during the 1960s. He had worked in Air

Force intelligence in Vietnam until 1965, when he was sent to oversee security for the 60th Air Mobility Wing at Travis Air Force Base north of Sacramento. According to his dossier, that's where he remained until 1972, when he was transferred to Air Force Intelligence in the Pentagon. In fact, in 1967, as student protests threaten to undermine American support for the military, Anastasia was asked to infiltrate the Berkeley campus and watch radical activities there. Then-Lieutenant Anastasia recruited a young scientist named Charles Shannon-Crabbe. Crabbe had an overfondness for young women that Anastasia exploited. The officer helped to keep Crabbe's trysts quiet in exchange for information about campus rabble-rousers.

By the early 1970s Vietnam was over and Anastasia moved on. However, as technology boomed in the middle 1970s thanks to spinoffs from the American space program—calculators, personal computers, satellite communications, and the dawn of the Internet—the Pentagon began to feel that strategic alliances with key technology players in private industry could be vital in information-gathering. Especially as budgets were slashed after the war. ELINT, electronic intelligence, was deemed more practical and was far less expensive than HUMINT, human intelligence, which required personnel in the field and support personnel around the world. Anastasia saw to it that Crabbe's liaisons were discovered by the authorities at Berkeley. The teacher was forced to resign, whereupon Anastasia hired him to work for his small Office of Technology Development—a cover operation of ten people who established information partnerships with American businesses. There was very little that a frightened man with a sex scandal in his record wouldn't do to continue to earn a living.

It was a good relationship. Crabbe helped OTD update its equipment and Anastasia gave him a place to put it. To keep an ear on partners and potential allies, OTD took over the decommissioned radar and radio stations of the DEW line. Anastasia automated the system and ran it entirely from his office as a black-ops surveillance project, eavesdropping on phone calls, faxes, and satellite signals. He was happy to do the work until he saw his government lose its way, becoming mired in long wars and then lying to the American public—and to themselves—about the effectiveness of the war machine. That had really hit home in Kosovo before the turn of the millennium. After seventy-eight days of around-the-clock NATO bombing consisting of 38,000 sorties, the Air Force said they had destroyed 110 Serb tanks and 153 armored personnel carriers. In fact, the numbers were fourteen tanks and twelve APCs destroyed. It was the bombing of factories and bridges that had finally brought Serb strongman Slobodan Milosevic down. To admit that the high-tech weapons had failed to strike with overwhelming precision would have been a disaster for the Pentagon budget and the next generation of weapons. The same percentages were repeated in Iraq several years later. Yet what bothered Anastasia most wasn't the lie to the taxpayers. It was the failure of the technology. What if American soldiers had been exposed to that Serb artillery? What if the war had really mattered to national security?

Just as HUMINT was inefficient, General Anastasia came to realize that war was inefficient. There had to be a better way to manage world affairs. Anastasia found it when the ESP was first proposed. He made sure that he was given jurisdiction over the security of the project. But it was not the same project the Pentagon had envisioned. Not at all.

Less than fifteen hours ago it seemed as if Anastasia, Crabbe, and the general's partner in Estate had achieved their dream. Not world domination, but world redirection, the means to focus most of the world's five billion people on the things that really mattered. Not war, not partisan bullshit, not geographical boundaries, but progress. Now, as he sat in his office and looked at top-secret e-mail from Captain Jessica Ryan at Cape Canaveral, it seemed as if that goal were in jeopardy. An individual wearing what was being described as a "bulky wet suit" had broken into the map room at the Air Force base and stolen data. According to the download file, what was taken was a decoding folder for encrypted map coordinates. Security cameras offered no clue as to how they got in or out.

Assuming these were the same people who had taken the space shuttle's black box, they now had the ability to pinpoint where the ESP signal had been directed. Anastasia was going to have to act quickly on two fronts. First, he had to move the ESP link. Estate had a backup system ready in case the main antenna in Kodiak went down. The general had to contact his partner and have the signal switched before the president could send military personnel to Kodiak. Calmly, he placed that call. Then he had to sever all ties with the White Alice Communications site. When OTD took charge of the system, Crabbe had installed a "panic code" that would erase any evidence OTD had ever been there. Anastasia raised the site on his computer and inputted the code. In an instant, the WAC died.

When he finished, General Anastasia sent a third message. This one was an e-mail to the President of the United States. And it was much different from the last message he had sent to President Gordon.

Forty-six

Lake Miasalaro, West Virginia
Tuesday, 4:38 A.M.

Evans and Victoria spent a short while researching the current status of the White Alice Communications base. They could find nothing to indicate that any group had assumed responsibility for the facility after the short period it was leased to a Canadian broadcast group and then was closed down. However, while they were searching the Pentagon files, they came across a top-secret Air Force research file labeled MTL. Fraser asked to see it.

A short time later Evans received a call from Captain McIver. Like so many Air Force personnel who knew the shuttle crew or support personnel, or who simply followed the work of their colleagues, she had not gone to sleep. The stealth team's Langley liaison called to say that the Cape Canaveral Air Force base was heating up with investigators searching for whoever had broken into the map room at Air Force intelligence.

"I don't know what Captain Holly and MCPO Diaz

were doing down there," she said on the secure line from Langley, "but this might be a good time to pull them out."

"I was going to call you in a while about bringing them back," Evans said. "I didn't think they started flying again until around seven."

"They're running up shuttle investigators at 5:20," she said. "I can probably get them on that plane."

Evans thanked her. He was grateful for her vigilance.

Shortly after speaking with Captain McIver, Commander Evans received a call from the president. There was an urgency in Gordon's voice that Evans hadn't heard there before.

"Commander, Estate knows exactly what we're doing," the president told Evans.

Evans looked at Victoria's computer. He did not understand how that could be. The data they'd uncovered was all here, but there was no way Estate could have gotten it.

"I just received an e-mail from Estate," the president went on. "The message said they've switched their signal from their original site to another location. They're not happy that we've been investigating them. They have no intention of leaving themselves vulnerable. And one thing more, Commander. There have been repercussions."

"What kind, sir?" Evans asked.

"They've used the ESP to shut down the Wadi installation in northern Saudi Arabia," the president said.

"I never heard of that one," Evans said.

"Few people have," the president replied. "It was set up post-Iraq as our first line of defense against an attack from Iraqi insurgents who reportedly have SCUD missiles and are looking to spread unrest to the south."

"If they can slip those through, it will embolden rebel fighters," Evans said.

"Exactly," the president said.

General Anastasia would have known about the Wadi

base. First the shuttle crew, now American servicemen. Estate was willing to spend the lives it took to realize their
goal.

"I understand," Evans said. "Mr. President, there may be
a connection between Estate and one of the men who was in
charge of the shuttle mission, General Rudolph Anastasia."

"Anastasia?" the president said. "He's got top-level security access. We should get security people over to the
Pentagon and talk to him."

"I wouldn't, sir," Evans said. "We don't know what kind
of trip wire might be set out for anyone who comes after
him."

"Does it matter? If Anastasia is connected, he's a greater
danger on the loose."

"Perhaps. But if he is tied to this, there may be a way to
get to him quietly. I'd like time to look into this a little
more."

"Fine, Commander. But I'm going to tell you what I just
told the National Security advisor and his team. Get back
to me with something we can *use*."

"Yes, sir," Evans replied. He hung up the phone and
looked at Victoria. "Estate switched antennas. They also
gave us a parting shot."

"A bad one?"

"Very. They shut down an Air Force base in Saudi Arabia, near the Iraqi border," Evans told her.

"No more closing down federal offices to make a point,"
Victoria said.

"Apparently not."

"Do you think they're still using the other dishes from
the DEW line?" she asked.

"Probably," Evans said. "That would give Estate a clear
shot at the skies all across the Western Hemisphere. They'd
never be out of communication with the ESP and whatever
other satellites they've commandeered."

"Then why doesn't the military just destroy all of those relay sites?" Victoria asked.

"Estate is probably watching them, either from other satellites or through ground-based security systems," Evans said. "Besides, they chose the Saudi Arabian base for a reason. It's on the other side of the world. If we take the DEW line sites out, they're telling us they still have resources elsewhere."

"Without telling us *where* elsewhere," Victoria said.

"Right. They could cripple us in the Middle East. Take out the Israeli military, our own forces, leave the region open for Iran to hit a struggling Iraq over oil." He paced the cabin. "If General Anastasia and Estate closed down the White Alice site, he still needs a powerful antenna that can reach at least one of the sites in the array to relay data to the others."

"How near does the main antenna have to be to the other dishes?" Victoria asked.

"Eight hundred miles or so," Evans said. "Chances are good the antenna would be located to the south, since antennas to the north of the DEW line are extremely scarce."

"So we're still looking at what—over three thousand miles long by roughly eight hundred miles wide? Twenty-four thousand square miles is a helluva lot of ground to cover, especially if we're talking about Air Force as well as private resources."

"Private resources?" Evans muttered. "I wasn't thinking about that."

"Maybe we should be," Fraser said. He was still reading the Air Force MTL file.

"Why?" Evans asked.

"This file is fascinating," Fraser said. "General Anastasia was one of the officers in charge of a project that used a laser beam to position atoms in new patterns—Microscopic Tunneling Laser."

"Why were you involved in a physics project?" Victoria asked.

"Because they wanted to know if it could be used to simulate strokes in personnel," Fraser said. "Long-distance assassination."

"Lovely," Victoria remarked.

"I'm not following what this MTL project is or why it matters," Evans told him.

"As I recall, the idea was to hit a missile or aircraft guidance system using a laser beam that was so faint it couldn't be detected," Fraser said.

"Similar to quantum cloak technology," Victoria said. "I was thinking about that earlier."

"I believe they're very similar," Fraser remarked. "The beam would then be used to pick up atoms in memory systems, place them in a new position, and literally rewrite programs."

"Attacking onboard computer systems," Victoria said.

"Yes," Fraser replied. "The problem was they could only make this work with xenon atoms at temperatures near absolute zero. I'd heard the project was abandoned, but apparently it was outsourced—to Oxford University in England."

"What happened there?" Evans asked.

"It doesn't say. But I remember from the list I was reading before—Dr. Crabbe lived in England for a while. The times coincided. If the MTL was perfected, that technology could have been incorporated into the ESP system and used to rewrite earth-based computers—given new commands to shut down or do God knows what else."

"You mean they may have the capacity to turn our computers *against* us?" Evan asked.

"It's possible."

"So shutting computers down may only be the first step," Victoria said. "They get millions of people to join Estate, let them vote, conduct finance, whatever—all the while manipulating data or e-mails or whatever to their advantage. This could get really ugly."

"Doc, you said that Anastasia approached you to work on his team," Evans said.

"Yes. It was a good team too," Fraser said.

"We have a list of scientists Gregg and Crabbe were both involved with," Victoria said.

"We've got to find that backup dish," Evans said. "Is there anyone on that list who might have been an expert in radio communications or had access to—"

"Shit," Victoria said. "Shit shit shit."

"What's wrong?" Evans asked.

"They don't have to be experts," she said. She began typing.

"Why not?"

"Because I know where he might have picked one up," she replied. "Someone with access to satellite dishes around the world."

Forty-seven

**Germantown, Pennsylvania
Tuesday, 5:17 A.M.**

Major Taylor woke when he heard a soft click. It took him a moment to remember where he was. He was in his mother's bedroom, dressed in his briefs and lying on top of the bedsheets. The window was open and the air was still. The sun had not yet risen.

He lay there for a few seconds. The click had come from the hall. It was followed by soft footsteps.

Taylor swung from the queen-sized bed and moved toward the bedroom door. He peeked out. There was no one in the hallway. It was still dark outside and he headed toward the living room. He stepped low through the blackness so he wouldn't cause the floorboards to creak. He heard springs groan. He knew that sound well. It was the sofa bed. He couldn't believe that someone might have come in to attack Colonel Lewis and had gotten that close—

They hadn't. Colonel Lewis was sitting on the foot of the old bed. He was dressed and staring down. His normally rigid shoulders were uncharacteristically rounded.

"You okay, Colonel?" Taylor asked.

Lewis glanced over. "Yeah, I'm fine. Did I wake you? I tried to be quiet when I came in—"

"I was close to getting up," Taylor replied. "All those months of up-at-dawn have rewritten my sleep patterns." Taylor came closer. "So—what were you doing?"

"Walking," Lewis said.

"Trouble sleeping?" Taylor asked.

"Fell asleep after a while, then something woke me up," Lewis replied. "Not sure what it was—decided to go for a walk."

"Where'd you go?" Taylor asked.

"Just out. Around." Lewis glanced at the kitchen clock. "Look, we've got another hour or so before we have to get up. I'm going to grab a little more sack time. You want to do stuff, go ahead. It won't bother me."

"Sure. You need anything?"

"No, thanks. I'm fine."

Lewis removed his work boots. There was dirt caked in the smaller treads. There was no dirt anywhere around the fully paved apartment complex. He had gone somewhere else. Taylor decided not to say anything. The colonel didn't appreciate being pressured about anything. Whatever Lewis's reasons were for going out and wherever he went, they were none of Taylor's business. Not unless Lewis wanted to tell him.

Taylor turned and went back to the bedroom. He lay down on the bed. But he didn't go back to sleep. Something didn't sit right about this. It was more than just the dirt. It was the man himself. He seemed spent. Taylor had never seen him looking so beaten. After training or a work-out, as tired as he was physically, he always seemed ready for more of the same.

Unless it's an emotional crash, Taylor thought. That

was possible. Lewis had to have been affected by the stress of protecting Taylor from his own desire for revenge, of planning an operation behind his back, of actually running the attack on the Moonshot people, then getting back and talking Taylor down again. It was a long hard day. And from all Taylor knew about the colonel, compromise wasn't what Lewis knew best—

Taylor's brain suddenly stopped, locked on a target, and looked down the barrel.

No. Compromise was *not* what Lewis knew best. What Lewis knew best, better than anyone on the Stealth Warrior team, was finishing a job with terminal prejudice. When Commander Evans had hesitated to kill Axe, it was Lewis who did the job. If having let the Moonshot boss go was what was eating the colonel up, Taylor wanted to know about it.

Fuck this, he thought. If something was going on, Taylor wanted to know about it. Lewis had pushed him before, outside Independence Hall. Rank or no rank, Taylor was going to push back.

The major turned and went back to the living room.

Forty-eight

Lake Miasalaro, West Virginia
Tuesday, 5:26 A.M.

Victoria went to her browser and input a name. Then she crossed her arms and sat back.

"You going to tell me what's up?" Evans asked.

"A once-only event that might have some bearing on what we're doing here," she said.

Two minutes before, Victoria had been ready to go to sleep. Her eyes burned and her head was fuzzy. She just couldn't do the all-nighters the way she did even five years before. But this had energized her, the realization that Estate might have failed to cover its tracks entirely and that she had been the one to find them.

"Marcus Forte," Evans said as he read the name she'd input. "The media big shot?"

"Yes," Victoria said. "He's got a head and wallet the size of Mt. Rushmore—I don't think there's a major electronics communications market he doesn't have access to in some way."

"There are a lot of guys like that," Evans said. "Big egos and international access."

"Yes, but Forte sponsored a technology symposium a couple of years ago. Crabbe and Gregg both attended."

"That's still a reach," Evans said.

"You think so?" Victoria replied. "Forte was also the first media entrepreneur to finance and launch his own communications satellites."

"Okay. He's got money and reach. But why would he have agreed to join something like Estate?" Evans asked.

"Because not everyone acknowledges that there's always going to be a higher power than themselves," she replied.

Evans looked at her. "Touché."

"There are advantages to being a godless cynic," she replied. "I'm wondering if maybe Forte didn't just join it but started it. Maybe he's the one who put the pieces in place, possibly after that symposium. Maybe during it, using it as a cover."

Victoria started scrolling through the headings of the thousands of web articles that mentioned Marcus Forte. She had a gut feeling about this. DARPA had come to her looking for help with the Stealth Field Uniform project. Half the scientists and academics she had known at NYU were working with government agencies or Washington think tanks. Outsourcing was cost-effective and allowed generals or department directors to build their own loyal bands, making them difficult to replace. At the same time, men like Forte loved getting into bed with powerful government allies. It helped to short-circuit regulatory changes that might hurt them. In this case, an alliance between Forte and the Pentagon, even a rogue element in the Pentagon, might have been too much for him to resist.

Victoria stopped and clicked on an article that discussed his satellite holdings. "Here, look at this," she said as the article from May 2002 appeared. "Forte used French and

Chinese rockets to launch Forte Apache and Forte Bravo. One satellite to cover northern Europe, one to cover the Far East. It says here, 'This is in addition to the partnerships he has in seven satellites in geosynchronous positions ranging from northern Canada to Fiji.'"

"So those plus the DEW line stations could constitute the basis for Estate's global span," Evans said.

"Absolutely," Victoria told him. "And if the satellite was equipped with the MTL technology, it can rewrite the programming of other satellites. Maybe it already has."

"But all the signals going to the satellite still have to originate at a single source," Evans said.

"Yes. *Those* commands were originally being sent via the WAC site," Victoria said.

"But not by personnel based there—"

"No," Victoria said. "That was simply the amplifying antenna. They needed that for the signal to reach space. Here's the scenario I see. Someone, somewhere would send a command to the WAC. Maybe dish-to-dish, maybe over a fiberoptic line."

"Crabbe would be the one to do that," Fraser said as he continued to read the MTL report. "He sold out. He stopped caring about science."

"I agree. Crabbe also had the programming skills," Victoria said. "So a signal goes to White Alice, which would then relay that signal, probably scrambled, to the ESP."

"Scrambled digitally, so we can't see it," Evans said.

"Correct. The satellite would then use its onboard program to send a kill signal either directly or back along the DEW line to other earth- and space-based satellites, like light bouncing along a mirror. Send it right to whatever computer they want to kill. So now White Alice is shut down. Another antenna has to take its place relaying scrambled signals to the DEW line."

"Which means we have to find that backup antenna and shut it down," Evans said.

"Yes."

"But without knowing where within that twenty-four-thousand-square-mile area it could be," Evans went on.

"Maybe not," Victoria said. "What I'm thinking is that Estate would want to replace the WAC with another private antenna," Victoria said, "a site that no one else would go near."

"One of Forte's broadcast antennas within reach of the DEW line," Evans suggested.

"Exactly," Victoria replied. She continued scrolling through the articles on Marcus Forte. "And when we find it, I bet we're going to find Dr. Crabbe close by, keying in Anastasia's commands and making sure that nothing happened to the backup site."

"You've got Colonel Mustard and the candlestick," Fraser said.

Evans and Victoria looked at the scientist. "What?" Victoria said.

"I play Clue with my nephew," Fraser said. "You need three things to solve a crime. Name, weapon, and place." He looked up from the MTL data. "I can tell you where that antenna probably is."

"Where?" Evans asked.

"My wife and I once went to a black-tie 'Dinner with the Stars of Broadway' event in New York City," Fraser said. "Forte Communications was the broadcast sponsor."

"Where was it held?" Evans asked.

"In Manhattan, at the 1776 Tavern—"

"Of course!" Victoria said. "On top of the Freedom Tower. Tallest building in the world. That would be a perfect spot to broadcast from." She went to the on-line yellow pages. "And here they are. Forte Communications. They've got the entire one hundred and sixth floor."

"The question is, would someone like Forte risk everything to be involved in something like Estate?" Evans asked.

"Yes," Victoria said. "He doesn't have 'everything.' He wants respect. He wants power."

"And he's got Anastasia to take the fall if all of this doesn't work out," Evans said. "All right. Let's assume he's our man and we commit our resources. All we've got to do is cut the power to the building, have a SWAT team move in, and seize the offices," Evans said.

"No," Victoria told him. "Shutting down the Freedom Tower site would only kill Estate's access to the DEW line."

"Isn't that what we need?" Fraser asked.

"Not entirely," Victoria said. "They'll still have access to Forte resources like the Apache and Bravo satellites to hit other countries."

"Which gives them coverage of parts of Europe and Asia," Evans said.

"And whatever dish systems those satellites are linked to elsewhere, plus any other satellites they may have co-opted. No," Victoria said, "the objective has to be the computer they're using to run the operation. Unless we can talk to the ESP, give it new instructions, they can still use a wireless modem to send the program somewhere else."

"Well done, both of you," Evans said. A moment later, he reached for the phone.

There was no satisfaction in Evans's voice, and Victoria knew why. Because as difficult as it had been to get to this point, going the distance was going to be even more difficult.

Forty-nine

Cape Canaveral, Florida
Tuesday, 5:44 A.M.

Diaz was pleased to see that the Air Force 737 was far more comfortable than the cargo plane he and Holly had flown to Cape Canaveral. The two men were exhausted. Diaz was glad there was insulation that keep things relatively quiet inside the cabin. He also enjoyed the fact that there were real seats that reclined—four of them, all first-class-sized. He didn't even have to sit next to Holly since the other seats were empty. That was a good thing. At least at sea, even on a small ship, there was always water around for washing. Neither Diaz nor Holly had had a chance to shower. After a night in the hot suits they needed to.

But there was quiet, there was comfort, and there was one other thing. They were getting out of there safe and with a successful mission behind them. This kind of drama, of being both the hunter and hunted in the same night, was new to Diaz. And frightening, despite the front he had put on for Holly.

Diaz glanced across the aisle at Holly. Behind them were about three dozen bags of mail and material in white leather pouches.

"You think they'll be serving us beverages?" Diaz asked.

The Air Force officer shook his head.

"That was a joke," Diaz pointed out.

"Sorry."

"What about all those bags?" he asked. "Don't they just mail the stuff from a U.S. post office?"

Holly shook his head again. "They go to Washington. The Pentagon keeps track of the addresses in case anyone mails out secrets. We're not supposed to know they do that, but everyone does."

"So then what jerk would send secrets that way?" Diaz asked.

"Well, you hit it on the head. Foreign governments don't always go after the brightest bulbs in the billboard."

"Of course," Diaz said. "What about the pouches?"

Holly craned around and looked along the aisle to the bins that lined the sides of the cabin. "There's no black ones. Not a one."

"Meaning?"

"Times're changing," he said. "White pouches carry time-sensitive material that's not top secret. When I first joined I pulled mail-loading duty once a week. We all did. There used to be hundreds of whites a day plus black pouches with top-secret stuff and armed couriers cuffed to the handles. Now most of that stuff is transmitted electronically. Those whites are probably just hard copies of orders or contracts from private industry that were already sent on-line."

"Everything's on-line and vulnerable," Diaz said. He looked at Holly. The captain was looking at him. "We did good," Diaz said. "Believe that and *remember* it."

Before Holly could say anything the door of the cockpit

opened. The copilot leaned from her seat and turned around.

"Captain Holly?"

"Yes?"

"We've got a call coming in for you," the woman said. "We'll put it through on the cabin phone. It's in the back—"

"I see it," Holly said.

The captain looked at Diaz, then made his way back through the mail bins. Diaz watched as Holly went to the phone, which was located between the fuselage door and the lavatory, near where they'd stowed the trunks with the SFUs. Holly covered one ear as he listened.

Diaz knew it was either Commander Evans or Captain Ryan calling. They had not notified her when they left. Captain McIver had arranged for a driver to run them over to the airstrip and they'd departed immediately. Though it was a breach of protocol to leave a base without notifying the officer in charge or his representative, Holly and Diaz had felt that the less contact they had with Ryan the better. So either she was angry and wanting them to come back for questioning, or else Evans had news.

Holly came back after about two minutes.

"It was the commander," Holly said as he dropped into the seat. "He says we're to head up to McGuire Air Force Base in New Jersey."

"What's happening there?" Diaz asked.

"It sounds like they've got a lead on Estate, thanks to the map coordinates we got him," Holly told him. He smiled slightly when he said that, obviously pleased with the news—and with himself. "Commander didn't want to say more on the open line, but said we'll get an update when we reach Langley. Captain McIver is arranging a transfer to McGuire."

"Did it sound like McGuire is the target?" Diaz asked.

"I don't think so," Holly replied. "He said that we should be ready to move out quickly."

"With or without the suits?"

"Without," he said. "Sounds like we're going to have to be mobile."

"Sounds like we're going to be busy," Diaz said. "I think we better get a little rest."

Diaz settled back in his seat and Holly did the same. Diaz noticed that the smile on Holly's face didn't disappear. Whether it was because of what Evans had said, because Holly would be flying again, or both didn't matter. It was good to see his partner happy.

That was the last thought MCPO Diaz had before passing out.

Fifty

Germantown, Pennsylvania
Tuesday, 5:49 A.M.

When Taylor went back to the living room he found Lewis asleep. The colonel had obviously just lain back and crashed. Lewis actually looked peaceful, and Taylor tried to make sense of that. He wondered if the things Sensei Ruiz said had made an impact on him. Maybe it was a revelation the same way that—what was his name?—Father John, Father Joe, had been to Evans when he was a teenager. *Sensei* had pointed out a different way to approach a conflict, one that Lewis had tried against Moonshot. It had worked to defuse the situation and protect "assets" Taylor and Lewis. Maybe it had also brought peace to Lewis. There was something satisfying about that, the fact that he had introduced Lewis to someone who might have had a positive impact on his life. Evans said that God had a plan for everyone, and maybe this was part of it.

While the major was standing there, the phone rang. It was the house phone, not the cell, and it woke Lewis with a start. Taylor hurried around the sofa bed into the kitchen and answered it.

"Taylor residence."

"Major?"

"Yes—"

"It's Evans. Sorry to wake you."

"I was up," Taylor said.

"Is everything all right?" Evans asked.

"Yes, sir."

"Good. I need you and the colonel to go to New York."

Evans told him why. That was obviously why the commander had called on the house phone; it was a ground line, unlikely to be intercepted. The news from the past twenty hours was astonishing. Taylor was sorry they'd missed the stealth penetrations at Cape Canaveral and the Pentagon. The commander assured him that there would be more to come, perhaps the most critical part of all—actually shutting Estate down. Evans said they'd reserved seats for the two officers on the Acela leaving 30th Street Station at seven A.M. and arriving in New York's Penn Station at eight-fifteen A.M.

"Where are we going when we get there?" Taylor asked, checking the clock on the stove.

"To the Freedom Tower," Evans told him. "Your target is going to be Forte Communications. They have the entire one hundred and sixth floor."

"What's the game plan?" he asked.

"We're still working on that," Evans said. "It looks like you're going to have to locate and commandeer the ESP control system."

Is that all? Taylor thought. It would have been nice to have the SFUs for that. Or at least a gun.

"We've pulled blueprints from the Homeland Security skyscraper database," Evans went on. "Dr. Fraser is looking to see whether there's some way to get into the offices via air vents or a private elevator shaft. We're also trying to get Holly and Diaz up there to help you, but we don't know how that's going to pan out."

"Those guys'd only get in the way," Taylor joked.

"Major, I know we're dumping a lot on you," Evans said, "and we're going to get you all the intel we can. But our backs are really up against it."

"I understand," Taylor said.

They agreed to talk again when Evans had more information. Taylor hung up and looked over at Lewis. The Delta Force leader was awake and lacing his work boots. His movements were sharp, his eyes intense, and his expression alert. Whatever peace there had been in repose was gone.

"What's up?" Lewis asked.

"We've got an assignment in New York," Taylor said. "Train leaves in an hour."

"Recon or takedown?"

"The latter," Taylor said. "A big one."

Lewis listened as Taylor told him about the call. There was no change in the colonel's expression. When Taylor was finished, Lewis stood, emptied his duffel bag, and went to the kitchen.

"You have tennis balls here?" he asked.

"Regular old tennis balls?"

"That's right. And binoculars or opera glasses in case we need them?"

Taylor nodded and went to the hall closet. When he came back, Lewis was busy loading the toaster into his bag. He asked Taylor for matches, razor blades, and tape. Taylor got them as well.

Lewis put the items into the duffel bag along with sandwich-size Baggies. "Do you have any more matches?"

"Yes—"

"I want as many as you have. Also, any spray paint or a can of WD-40?" Lewis asked.

Taylor said there was. He got the spray can of oil from under the sink. "Bomb-making equipment?" he asked.

"In case we need it," Lewis told him. The colonel examined the butcher knives in the wall rack. He selected the two sharpest blades. "There's a pool here, isn't there?"

"Yeah, out back. Didn't you see it on your walk?"

Lewis didn't answer. He took a small flashlight from its hook over the kitchen counter. He checked it, then put it in the bag. "Get the matches, call a cab, and meet me by the pool in ten minutes."

"Sure," Taylor said.

Lewis hurried from the apartment.

Taylor placed the call, then walked to the foyer. He got a small backpack from the closet. Beside it was a small table with a vase containing his mother's collection of souvenir matches going back to the Brass Rail in New York. He dumped the matches into the backpack, then locked up and went to the stairwell. He rushed out to the gated pool. There was a small wooden shed near the shallow end. It was still dark out and Lewis had the flashlight out. He had kicked in the door. Taylor entered. Lewis was busy putting chlorine tablets into one of the Baggies.

"Got everything you need?" Taylor asked him.

"Unless you've got an AK-47 hidden somewhere," Lewis said.

"The pool guard prefers Uzis," Taylor said. "Deeper penetration in water."

Lewis grinned at that.

So much for the colonel's newfound pacifism, Taylor thought ironically. Then again, the Stealth Warriors were back in business and this was the kind of man you wanted to run a field op.

The major pulled the door shut. It took a moment to work it into the cracked jamb, but he didn't want to leave it open. Thugs did that.

As the men left the pool area, the top windows of the apartment complex were glinting with the first light of day. Taylor was not as combat-experienced as the colonel, and decided to follow Lewis's lead. He looked ahead and focused on the job at hand.

However, there was one other irony that Taylor couldn't shake. The very nature of what they were about to do.

They were preparing to attack the Freedom Tower to *save* the Free World.

Fifty-one

Lake Miasalaro, West Virginia
Tuesday, 6:15 A.M.

After talking with Taylor, Commander Evans left the com-shack and went to his cabin. He brought the TAC-SAT with him; until this crisis was over the phone would never be far from his side. He joined Dr. Fraser, who was already working on the commander's computer. Victoria had accessed the blueprints archive and sent the hyperlink to Evans's PC. Though Fraser was not a computer expert, he knew enough to find, download, and print a detailed layout of the Freedom Tower.

This idea was madness and Evans knew it. Two men, no SFUs, no handguns, attempting to infiltrate a heavily armed office, seize a computer, and hold it long enough for Victoria to figure out what to do with it. Though there was no one he trusted more than Matt Lewis to lead a mission like this, there were some missions that didn't have a prayer. Missions where the participants wouldn't be coming back were one thing. "Suzies," the SEALs called them, for "Suicide Missions." But at least those had a chance of succeeding. Missions where the probability of accomplishing the goal were virtually nil didn't have a nickname. "Stupid" and "Messed-up" usually sufficed. And that just applied to achieving the goal. They didn't know what kind of security Forte had up there. It was conceivable Taylor and Lewis might not get out of there alive.

First things first, Evans told himself. *Get your men a vantage point.*

As Fraser looked over his shoulder, Evans studied the plans to see what kind of obstacles the team would be facing. There were air ducts but no private elevators. Evans would have to direct the men to the ducts. It looked like they could enter them through an air-conditioning room that was accessible from the roof, just beneath the lighted 200-foot-tall spire. He started looking for ways to get his people up there. The staircases were probably accessible only to security and maintenance personnel. But that shouldn't be a problem for Lewis. He had experience getting in and out of secure facilities.

"Commander, I've been thinking," Fraser said. "What's the nearest relay station in the DEW line system?"

"I believe that's Mt. Reed, about two hundred miles north of Quebec," Evans said. "The station is a relay point for a dish to the far north, on the Hudson Strait."

"Why can't we just shut down that DEW station there and cut the relay?" Fraser asked. "Canadian Air Force activity could be kept from our bad boy in the Pentagon."

"The dishes are all located on the tops of mountains protected by radar," Evans said. "The dishes are linked by their own early warning system whose signal is fed into both Canadian Air Command's National Defense Headquarters in Ottawa and the Pentagon. I'm sure General Anastasia has arranged that EWS to alert him in case anyone approaches by air."

"At which point he'll shut them down," Fraser said.

"Exactly. And shift somewhere else. That might not give him full coverage of North America, but he could still do a lot of damage."

Evans returned to the blueprint. He thought about security cameras on the 1,776-foot-high deck. Going up there in daylight when security cameras on the spire might see them clearly. Wind as a factor, and noise. The wind probably wailed like a banshee coming off the Hudson River.

He wasn't liking this. Not at all. In the past, whether it was believing in God or that a mission in Iraq could succeed or trusting that a stealth suit that worked in a computer simulation would work in the field, he'd had faith. At some point in any process, after logic and sound reasoning had been thrown at the problem, you had to make that jump. Usually Evans was able to do that. Not this time.

The phone beeped. It was Victoria.

"There's good news and bad news," she told him.

"What's the bad news?"

"I hacked the payroll of Forte Communications," she said. "He's got forty-six security people working around the clock, three eight-hour shifts. That's up from twenty-three people just two years ago. I checked two other broadcast setups in New York. Those places have less than half that number. And according to paperwork filed by Forte Communications, every one of his security people is licensed to carry a firearm."

"What's the good news?" Evans asked.

"Obviously, they've got something to protect," Victoria replied. "Whatever it was got ratcheted up over the last two years. And it wasn't just security concerns following the World Trade Center attack and the construction of the high-visibility replacement tower."

Victoria's finding eroded what little weight remained behind Evans's faith. In addition to everything else, Lewis and Taylor would be going in without firearms. Unless Major Lewis somehow managed to pick them up on the way. Evans wouldn't put it past him, but he wasn't counting on it either.

"I'll pass that information along to the team," Evans said. "Thanks."

"You're welcome. I'm sorry the news isn't better. How're things going over there?"

"We've got the plans, but they're not as detailed as I'd like."

"You don't sound hopeful," she said.

"Frankly, I'm not," Evans admitted. Just thinking it was bad. Saying it was deadly. "There's got to be some other way to do this."

"I'll play devil's advocate," Victoria said. "Walk through the alternatives. I'll give you the worst-case-scenario response."

"All right. We cut the power to the building. Electricity, phone lines, everything."

"Estate loses the Freedom Tower transmitter, but their computers probably have battery backups and wireless modems," Victoria said. "They slip control to another site and lean on the president to restore power."

"We teargas the floor so no one can see or do squat."

"The computer isn't there," she said.

"What?"

"The computer controlling ESP isn't located at Forte Communications," Victoria said. "We're pretty certain Estate is using one of the tower's antennae, but maybe they have another office just for this system somewhere else in the building. Or maybe there's a guy with a laptop and a wireless modem sitting in a stairwell and sending up commands."

"Wait a minute," Evans said. "How do we even know the ESP computer is in the building? If what you say is true, Estate can be modeming instructions from another building. Hell, from another country."

"That's not likely," Fraser said.

Evans looked at him. "Talk to me." He put the phone on speaker so Victoria could hear.

"I'm looking at the electrical schematics," Fraser said. "In 2005 the Port Authority of New York and New Jersey installed a buffer to keep television broadcast signals from being pirated off their building. The buffer services the main antenna and all the small antennas and dishes—according to the plans, they're all run through it except for the PBS signal."

"Meaning?" Evans asked.

"They scramble the outgoing signals to satellite systems nationwide," Victoria said. "That's why we need decoder boxes for cable."

"Okay. I still don't see why the computer would have to be on-site," Evans said.

"It doesn't," Victoria replied. "But at some point the data being sent to the ESP has to go through the scrambler."

"And *that's* located in the building," Evans said.

"Right," Victoria said. "The buffer looks like it's built into the main antenna. Signals come in, get scrambled, then are sent up to the various communications satellites. If a signal isn't hardwired in the building, it has to be in a line-of-sight to the antenna."

"That could be anywhere in New York City or eastern New Jersey," Evans said.

"No, it would have to be very close," Victoria said. "Estate has got a heavy data stream going up to the ESP."

"Probably one hundred times the information Bravo or one of those services sends up," Evans said.

"At least that," Victoria agreed. "The farther you get from the buffer the more the signal would be degraded by buildings, birds, even rain and smog. That's the reason I'm still betting Estate would want to be hardwired into the antenna from the Forte offices."

"It's also probably easier for security, to protect the data," Evans thought aloud.

"No doubt about it," Victoria replied.

"Which puts us back to infiltrating the site," Evans said.

"Sorry," Victoria told him.

"Don't be," Evans said. "You were a good devil's advocate."

"Look, I'm going to get to work," Victoria said. "If Taylor and Lewis can seize the link, then we've got to have something ready to send up and poison the ESP."

Victoria got off the phone, and Fraser continued to study the diagram. He was quietly humming "Send in the Clowns."

Evans wondered if he was making a statement.

As the commander was digesting the logistics of what needed to be done, the TAC-SAT beeped. He answered.

And things got a little worse.

Fifty-two

Philadelphia, Pennsylvania
Tuesday, 6:55 A.M.

There is a form of chaos that is uniquely Amtrak's. It's called boarding the train. Taylor always hated that about the Washington–Philadelphia–New York corridor.

The Acela gets to the station five minutes before it's due to leave. The track isn't announced until the train is about to arrive. Then dozens of people try to squeeze down a narrow escalator onto a narrow platform, and then get onto a train that's already crowded with early-rising Washingtonians and will be pulling out before you can find a seat.

Lewis and Taylor arrived at the station fifteen minutes before the hour. They picked up the reserved tickets along with coffee and muffins. They hadn't eaten dinner and Taylor was hungry. He was also looking forward to getting another hour of sleep. When the train finally arrived Taylor's phone beeped. He answered it as they headed down the escalator.

It was Evans.

The commander told him to call back using the train's phone as soon as possible. That meant security was a concern to the commander. On the Acela the signal would be stronger than his own cell phone, he'd have relative privacy in the small booth, and because the train was moving it was unlikely that anyone with a cell phone in a passing car could accidentally hear more than a few words of their conversation. The only risk they ran was being intercepted by cell phones in another part of the train. Obviously, given the current situation, that was a risk Commander Evans was willing to take.

On the way down the escalator, Taylor noticed a businessman holding a copy of that morning's *USA Today*. An under-the-fold headline said that an unmanned Predator drone had disappeared over the border between Saudi Arabia and Iraq. He wondered why drones were on patrol in a noncombat zone. He also wondered whether its disappearance had something to do with Estate.

When the men entered the train, they couldn't find seats together. Not that it mattered. Lewis told Taylor that he had work to do in the bathroom. He said he'd be moving from lavatory to lavatory so as not to attract attention and would find Taylor when they reached Penn Station. Taylor didn't have to ask what the work was. He had a very good idea. Colonel Lewis would not be using the chlorine to sanitize the Acela toilets.

Heading directly to the phone cubicle, Taylor punched in his calling card number, entered the commander's direct phone line, then took a bite of his bran muffin.

Evans picked up at once. "Major?"

"Yes, sir."

"Here's what I can tell you so far, and it's not the kind of assignment I'd like to be giving you," Evans said. "As I said before you'll be going to the Freedom Tower, to the

Forte Communications offices. We need you to get in there and find and seize the ESP master program.

"We've confirmed that there are ventilation ducts accessible from the roof, so that's where you'll be starting out," Evans went on. "You'll be looking for an area that's probably secured by armed guards. Victoria is writing a new program for the ESP. I know that you and Colonel Lewis are not computer people, so once you get control of the computer station you'll have to contact us. We'll send the program over and tell you how to upload it. Hopefully, we can get it up to the satellite and kill it."

"Sir, I'm not questioning orders, but why aren't they turning NYPD or FBI SWAT teams loose on this problem?" Taylor asked. "At least those people know the building and they have the manpower and weapons to take what I assume is a pretty large office. I mean, the colonel's off in the rest room putting together some armaments, but it's all low-yield stuff."

"It may come to that, but as soon as the White House starts talking to law enforcement agencies they open the door to leaks," Evans said. "Estate is certain to be watching every computer and phone list they can to monitor possible threats to protect this site. The big advantages you and Lewis have is that he's done infiltrations and no one knows about you. There's no way Estate can be forewarned. Even the president's advisors haven't been told about us."

Remaining Stealth Warriors in plain sight. Master Ruiz would have enjoyed that concept.

"I wish we had more intel, but we don't," Evans went on. "I also wish we could get Holly and Diaz up there in time to help you, but that's not looking likely either. The problem is time. Estate has already used the ESP to shut down American bases in Saudi Arabia—"

"That would explain the newspaper headline I saw in the train station," Taylor said.

"We got shut down, sent up a new source for intel, and it apparently got shot down," Evans said. "The president just phoned to say that Israeli radar has also just been blinded. We've got to shut these people down."

Taylor understood.

"Major, I wouldn't ask you to do this if we had another option," Evans told him.

"Sir, I knew what the dangers were when I accepted the uniform," Taylor told him.

"But there are risks you may not have considered," the commander pointed out.

"If you mean PTO—"

PTO was personnel takeout. It generally applied to innocent people being lost in an operation.

"The mission may require that," Evans agreed. "But—and I'm going with full disclosure here, Hank—if you do what I've asked and you're taken, I can't guarantee a pardon. The president said he might not want the back-story known about how we were on the verge—how we *are* on the verge of an international disaster."

Evans was right, of course. If Taylor and Lewis succeeded in stopping Estate, the commander in chief was not going to admit that the world's computers were nearly taken out of circulation by an American Air Force general who had hijacked an American spy satellite.

Evans said he would update them over a landline when Taylor and Lewis reached the city.

Taylor hung up the phone and sat in the cubicle for a moment. He was suddenly very much aware of the forward momentum of the train. That was how his life felt at that moment. Surging ahead and carrying him to a place, to a resolution, to a possible ending over which he had no control. The only control he had was over the responsibility.

Taylor thought about the last few hours and those hours yet to come. He had absolutely no reservations about doing what was right for the country no matter what the cost to him personally. If he had to take a fall for the president he'd do it. So would Lewis. What bothered the major was how his mother would fare when she was released from the hospital. If there was lasting damage from the attack, someone would have to take care of her. That would be tough for the independent woman, but she'd learn to deal with it. She was also strong and realistic. What would be more difficult for her to handle was the idea that her son had died or was imprisoned for an apparent act of terrorism.

Hopefully, Commander Evans will tell her the truth and help her through that, he thought.

He hoped Evans would somehow let his fellow officers at his former base, Camp Pendleton, know the truth as well. For a Marine, dishonor or even the perception of disloyalty was worse than death.

But worse than all of that was if anything happened to the United States of America. And with that thought firm in his mind, Major Hank Taylor left the cubicle and went to find a seat. He found an open table in the café car and, feeling surprisingly at peace, he finished his coffee and muffin.

Fifty-three

The President of the United States walked into the conference room in the Old Executive Offices across the street from the White House. The green walls, green carpet, lighting fixtures, and even the green upholstery of the chairs were unchanged from the days when strategies for winning the Second World War were discussed in this windowless chamber.

The vice president, Joint Chiefs of Staff, National Security Advisor, and his chief of staff were already seated around the long mahogany table. Their expressions told Gordon that the news was not going to be good.

"Let me have it," the president said even before he sat down. A male assistant brought coffee in a blue mug with the presidential seal in white. Gordon was glad to have it. His head was a mass of cotton.

"We underestimated the power of the ESP," Joint Chiefs of Staff Chairman Jesse Rogers said gravely.

Sadly, that didn't surprise the president. He'd had a feeling the bastards at Estate still held trump cards. In a battle of this size and scope, they'd need the equivalent of an Enola Gay to send against the still-determined enemy.

"We designed the ESP to read computers," Rogers said. "Estate somehow redesigned it to shut down computers. We thought they were doing it by impeding the program somehow. That isn't the case."

The president suddenly thought of the computer in the Chicago hospital. "They're able to rewrite programs," the president said. He should have realized that sooner, not that there was anything they could have done.

"Yes, sir," Rogers said. "They've apparently done more than just shut down computers in the Middle East. We just heard from Israeli military intelligence, Aman, that their nuclear missile launch codes have been rewritten. They're working hard to try and regain access. But right now, someone on the outside is in control of the atomic arsenal."

To raise the ante in case there are any further moves against Estate, the president thought. If the United States moved against the ESP antenna, Israel would be made to make a "preemptive strike" against one of its regional foes. Gordon was sickened at how apt the Enola Gay metaphor was.

And that was just one spot on the globe. Estate could do this anywhere, with any nuclear power. India and Pakistan. North and South Korea. The United States and China.

The president was about to make the most difficult decision of his life. Perhaps it was also the most fateful decision since Harry Truman elected to drop the atom bomb on Hiroshima. Evans and his team were good, but they were also working in the dark. He needed to have a fallback position even if that position might lead to disaster.

Commander Evans had phoned with an update on their intel efforts and said his people were due in New York at a little past eight with a plan to stop Estate. The president would give them a head start, but that was all.

"Gentlemen," the president said, "I just received another communiqué from Estate." That was a lie, of course, but he didn't want to tell them how he knew what he knew. "They want to meet me at their headquarters in New York."

"Where in New York?" General Rogers asked eagerly.

"At a financial district location," the president said. "I want you to think out a joint NYPD-FBI SWAT attack on top skyscraper-level offices."

"Can you tell us which offices?" Rogers asked.

"I've not yet been informed," the president replied. He didn't want to say more in case Estate had informants on hand or some means of eavesdropping. "Plan for an SAS and also an SAD. But until I OK it, I do not want that plan to leave this room."

Seize and Seal was a hopeful idea. Seize and Destroy was what his gut told him they would have to go for. Whether it succeeded or failed, he couldn't even contemplate the ramifications of that.

"I assume we have to stay off-line," the vice president said.

"Off-line and off the phones," the president said. "You men know your business. Put it on the table and we'll talk again in an hour or so. If I give you the go-ahead, contact the appropriate people on a need-to-know basis, and get the operation moving."

The mood in the room was immediately energized. It was the rush that came from doing something other than fretting. The president was glad to see that. He wished he shared their enthusiasm.

The president left to go back to the White House. He prayed that Evans's team was able to move quickly, quietly, and effectively.

And that they somehow managed to hit a home run. Because despite what was going on in the conference room, the president didn't think they were going to get a second turn at bat.

Fifty-four

**The Northeast Corridor
Tuesday, 7:57 A.M.**

Colonel Lewis had been pleased to find that the lavato-
ries on board the train were large, wheelchair-friendly facilities. That gave him room to spread out on the floor.
Lewis visited three separate bathrooms on the train, spending an average of twenty minutes in each as he prepared
the materials that he and Taylor would need to do the job.

The first thing Lewis did was use the razor to make a
small slit in each of the tennis balls. Then he put the balls
back in the duffel bag and pulled a piece of paper towel
from the dispenser. He sat down on the floor, his back to
the door, and opened the paper towel on his outstretched
legs. He used the razor to shave the heads off dozens of the
matches. When he was finished, he recreased the towel and
used it to pour a little of the powder inside each of the tennis balls. Then he used his Swiss army knife to remove all
the screws and nuts he could find under the sink.

Moving to the next bathroom, he used his fingers to

crush the chlorine tablets into the paper towel. He added this powder to the inside of the tennis balls. Finally, he used the tape to seal the balls shut. He had created very powerful concussive "cherry bombs." Not only would they explode, but upon igniting, the sulfur from the matches would cause the chlorine to burn and release caustic smoke. The colonel would stop at the station and buy several bags of peanuts to add to the mix. Not only would that pad the ball so that the concussion would travel from one side to the other, but they would serve as painful but non-lethal shrapnel. Before leaving this bathroom he collected more nuts and screws.

In the third bathroom Lewis removed more screws and nuts. He took the remaining matches and cut off the heads. He placed these between the nuts and bolts and screwed them tight. When thrown, the explosion of the match head would blast out the screw with the force of a BB pellet. Finally, the colonel used the knife to slice off the remaining match heads. He tore off six-inch lengths of tape and placed two rows of five match heads in the center. When taped to an object and struck by one of his cherry bombs, the "flash tapes" would cause powerful, very concentrated explosions.

For Matt Lewis this process was vital, the equivalent of primitive peoples applying war paint or a Buddhist in a Zen state of meditation. It "brought him to center," as they said in Delta. Made him one with the mission and the tools he'd be using, gave him time to become familiar with the balance and texture of the equipment. Even when he was using handguns or rifles, he would disassemble and assemble them before going out on a mission. Become a part of them. Lewis didn't know how and why that worked. It just did.

Making the little explosives also allowed Colonel Lewis to take his mind off what had happened the night before. Unlike Commander Evans, Lewis didn't believe that evil men who repented sincerely deserved a place in heaven.

He wasn't even sure he believed in heaven. But Lewis did believe they could change if they wanted to. The big, fat operative word was "if." Lewis didn't know whether that applied to him. The evidence seemed not to point in that direction.

When Lewis was finished, he carefully replaced everything in the duffel bag. He used paper towels and toilet paper to cushion the explosives. Though they weren't likely to blow from jostling, there was always a possibility that the duffel bag strap could snap. He left room to tuck the toaster on the side of the bag, where he could get to it without disturbing the tennis balls. He packed the remaining chlorine tablets inside the toaster slots. There were usually electrical outlets in sites he infiltrated. Plugging the toaster in and letting the coils heat gave him a few seconds to get away before noxious, blinding gas spilled from the machine. It was a great way to cover one's retreat.

The train was already passing under the Hudson River as Lewis finished his preparations. He didn't bother trying to find Taylor. Passengers were already lined up in the aisles waiting to get out. The men met on the platform, where Taylor took a minute to brief his partner. As they talked, they made their way to the pay phones in the food court. Since they were now on a mission and he wasn't otherwise engaged, Lewis, as ranking officer, would place the call to the base.

The commander answered the phone. There was tension in his voice and no exchange of pleasantries.

"Colonel, has Major Taylor briefed you?"

"He has."

"We're working on getting more intel about the site," Evans said.

"Which still isn't going to tell us exactly where the target is," Lewis said.

"Probably not," Evans admitted.

"Sir, excuse me for asking the obvious, but has anyone thought about sending a Tomahawk missile in from McGuire and just taking the top of the goddamn tower off?"

"That was considered and rejected," Evans told him. "Given what happened at the World Trade Center, the death toll and local trauma would be horrific. Media scrutiny alone would undermine future special ops activities in the homeland. Even if the president were willing to suffer the collateral damage, air traffic would have to be stopped over the city. Estate would be sure to hear about that, which would give them time to spot the missile, rewrite the program, and sent it to Times Square or some other site."

Lewis wasn't sure he agreed. National defense wasn't always clean and it certainly wasn't easy. The greater good had to be what guided them. But Evans was right about one thing: Lewis's plan could leave them with the messiest victory since the Union defeated General Lee in Antietam, at a cost of 6,400 soldiers.

"We're trying to get you other support from McGuire, but we don't know how the timing's going to work out," Evans said. "You'll know when you see it. Now, Major Taylor said you have some armaments."

"Yes, sir. Mostly cherry bombs filled with peanuts and WICO."

WICO was an old, politically incorrect acronym for "Wife's Cooking." Homemade tear gas.

"That should help you get to the guards," Evans said. "They all have handguns."

"How many guards are there?" Lewis asked.

There was silence on the other end of the phone.

"Sir?" Lewis said.

"Colonel, you just gave me an idea," Evans said. "Get down to the site and call me from there."

Lewis said he would. He hung up and joined Taylor,

who was on another phone. The major had called the hospital for an update on his mother's condition. Taylor got off the phone moments after Lewis did. The major's expression was grave.

"What did the commander say?" Taylor asked as the men started walking toward the stairs to the subway.

"We're still a 'go,' but he's looking into something," Lewis said. "He wants me to call when we get down there. How's your mother?"

"There's no change," Taylor said. "I was hoping for something, a little thing, *anything*."

"Give it time," Lewis said.

"Sure," Taylor said. "And just how much of that do you think we've got, Colonel?"

"That's a damned good question and I'll be damned if I know the answer," Lewis admitted.

The men reached the bottom of the stairs. Then they waited on the brightly lit downtown platform for either the number one or the number nine train. The Freedom Tower was at the heart of the financial district. The stop was jammed with commuters heading to Wall Street.

He was sure that none of them had any idea what the world was facing. Not just a nuclear conflagration in the Middle East, but a hostile takeover of every government and institution on the planet. He wondered how amazed—and how frightened—they would be to learn that.

And to learn that the only firewall was two quiet men standing among them.

Fifty-five

**Lake Miasalaro, West Virginia
Tuesday, 8:23 A.M.**

When he first came to DARPA, Evans had gone to a mandatory series of seminars on various aspects of science, mathematics, and logic. One of the most fascinating lectures was Permutations and Combinations, the study of techniques for handling probability problems. A permutation pertained to the manner in which elements could be arranged in any given group. A combination meant the selection of elements from a larger group. The way in which these elements affected one another often appeared infinite and daunting. The trick to handling them was to imagine the desired end and work backwards, blocking or cutting away components that were extraneous. Even if they were present, they should be ignored in theory.

What had started Evans thinking about Permutations and Combinations was what Lewis had said about launching a Tomahawk missile at the tower. That was the "Muscle" way of dealing with an obstacle. According to what they taught in P and C about eliminating unwanted elements, Muscle often required too much effort and put a strain on resources. The "Dagger" method was better, finding a weak spot and thrusting your force through that way. What Lewis and Taylor would be attempting was a Dagger thrust, though not an ideal one: They didn't know what the target's weak spots were. According to P and C training, that left the third and preferred approach: "Distraction." That had evolved from the techniques used before the D-Day invasion.

In order to neutralize much of Hitler's army in the region, the Allies had made it appear they were going to invade France at Pas de Calais. That was the logical spot with the shortest span of English Channel to cross. A fake army of wood and canvas was constructed on the beaches in and around Kent, along with dummy railroads and headquarters. The Allies even "lost" a body at sea, "the Man Who Never Was," a corpse ID'd as an officer with fake plans on his person. To German agents outside the carefully guarded perimeter and spy planes taking high-altitude photographs, the preparations there looked like the real thing. Meanwhile, the real invasion force was secretly being amassed to the southwest, ready to assault the Normandy beaches between Cherbourg and Le Havre. While bombing runs were conducted against installations in Normandy, fully twice as many sorties were flown to the northeast. The deception was so effective that even when the Normandy landings had begun, Hitler still believed the main attack would come at Pas de Calais. He refused to allow troops stationed there to be moved to the besieged beaches.

Evans realized that the elements were in place for a Distraction maneuver. The key to making it work was precision timing.

The commander had to call the president. First, though, he looked at the blueprints. He found what he wanted.

Then he phoned the com-shack. He needed to ask Victoria a question.

"If the scrambler weren't an issue, would we be able to block a signal from Estate?" Evans asked.

"If we knew where the address was going, yes," she said. "We could use undertow."

"What's that?"

"A nanosecond before the electrons that make up a signal pour into a system, the passageway is opened by subatomic particles," Victoria said. "If you send out a stronger signal, the electrons of the original signal get pushed back. As they move in reverse, they actually drag the impeding signal with it, telling it where to go. That's basically how people hack broadcasts, put their faces on stadium scoreboards, and that sort of thing."

"And we can't do that with Estate because—"

"The impeding signal, the one we'd send out—from the Israeli computers, for example—won't be able to see the Estate signal coming," she said.

"Because of the randomness of the digitization, the scrambling," Evans said.

"Exactly," Victoria said. "Unless you have the descrambling code, you won't be able to see the incoming signal. All you'll see is a billion disorganized flakes coming at you. You won't be able to hit the signal square and force it back to create the undertow."

"But that process doesn't take place in the Estate computer," Evans said. "It takes place in the antenna itself."

"Well, in whatever box controls the signal going into the antenna," she said. "But even if you knew which of the antennas or dishes belonged to Estate, you said they'd know if you went near it."

"Maybe not," Evans said. "Thanks for your help. Work on your poison program and I'll fill you in later."

Evans hung up and picked up the TAC-SAT. It took a

minute for the president to answer. It was the longest minute of Evans's life.

"Yes, Commander?" the president said.

"I think there may be a way to snare Estate," Evans told him.

"I'm listening," the president said.

The commander was excited, hopeful, but he was careful not to let it show in his voice. What they had was better than nothing, but it was still a long shot. He didn't want to build the president's hopes up.

"Sir, there are fourteen antennae and dishes on top of the Freedom Tower," Evans said. "We don't know which one Forte Communications is using to send out their broadcast signals, but they would have to have registered for a license with the Federal Communications Commission. Can you get that information for me as soon as possible?"

"Yes," the president said. "But I thought the problem with attacking the antenna is that Estate would detonate the Israeli nukes."

"We believe we can make sure they aren't able to do that," Evans said. "But I'm going to need you to do three things for me, Mr. President."

"They are?"

"First, I want the Israelis to be ready to send a signal that Victoria is going to feed them. Tell them they're to use 'undertow' when the signal from the ESP comes in. It won't be scrambled."

"'Undertow,'" the president said.

"Victoria described the process. It should work. Second, sir, I need a distraction."

"What kind?"

"A SWAT attack against the Forte offices. Preferably NYPD. Something small, local, and quiet. A group that can get to the building without attracting too much attention up front."

"I thought you were worried that SWAT activity will show our hand," the president said.

"We want to, but at the right time," Evans said. He looked at his watch. Taylor and Lewis would be reaching the Freedom Tower any moment. "Ask them to be ready to move on the offices in exactly one hour."

"That's not a lot of time," the president said.

"New York can do it," Evans said.

"What's the third thing?"

Evans replied, "I want Anastasia to hear about the attack in fifty-nine minutes."

Fifty-six

**New York, New York
Tuesday, 8:59 A.M.**

Taylor and Lewis rode the subway to the newly completed Freedom Tower. It let the men off in a shopping center located beneath the skyscraper. Colonel Lewis found it strange being in a mall that had no sunlight at all. He found it strange being anywhere that had no sunlight.

And he felt moved to be standing on the site once known as Ground Zero, home of the World Trade Center.

They went to the nearest pay phone and called Evans.

"We've had a change in plans," the commander told him. "There should be a large cable box in the northwest corner of the tower deck. You're going to have to open it and do some switching."

"Will we need additional equipment?" Lewis asked. If they did, there was no point wasting time. He would send Taylor to one of the shops down here to try and get it.

"No," Evans said. "The success of the operation is going to depend on you finding the key to the box. There are cameras on the roof and an alarm in the box. If you try and break it open, alarms will probably go off. There's a maintenance office in the tower basement. I suggest you start there."

"All right," Lewis said. That didn't bother him. He had ways of making people tell him things he needed to know, such as where keys were located and what combinations opened doors.

"When you get to the deck we need you to switch some cables," Evans continued. "According to the schematics we have, the cables inside that box are jacked in, not spliced, so it shouldn't be a problem. One of the cables will be labeled 'AM-5-25.' That leads to an unscrambled PBS dish. We don't have the number of the other cable yet, the one that Estate is using. Call me when you're up there and I'll give it to you."

"When we make the switch, won't they notice what we're doing?" Lewis asked.

"We hope not," Evans said. "We'll be sending up a SWAT unit to distract them. Estate will think that's the main assault. You'll have a one-minute window to execute the change while we distract them. What time do you have?"

Lewis looked at his digital watch. "Nine-oh-two and forty-five."

"Tell me when you hit nine-oh-three and we'll synchronize," Evans said.

Lewis did. It had been eight or nine years since he'd had to synchronize watches for a field mission. It felt good.

"Sir, are we taking pieces in this game?" Lewis asked. The chess euphemism pertained to whether Evans would accept civilian casualties if necessary. The killing of reluctant guards, for example, or security personnel that might respond to their presence on the roof.

"Protect the pieces if you can, Colonel, but we need to win this one," Evans said. "Be ready to move at nine-five-oh."

"You get us the information and we'll do the rest," Lewis said.

The colonel hung up and while he briefed Taylor, he looked for signs that would take them to the tower itself. The men reached the escalator, and as they rode it to the lobby, Lewis made sure the major's watch was synchronized with his own and that his cell phone was turned on.

Like the night before in Philadelphia, Lewis was calm, psyched, and ready.

The bastards weren't going to win this one either.

Fifty-seven

New York, New York
Tuesday, 9:01 A.M.

Hulking forty-nine-year-old Lieutenant Bryan Orjuela, City
South supervisor for the elite Special Operations Division
of the NYPD's Emergency Service Unit, did not know for
sure why the President of the United States had selected
One-Truck for this assignment. They were not directly affiliated with Homeland Security the way the FBI was.
Maybe it was because they knew the target better than the
FBI. Orjuela's One-Truck division spent every minute of
every day patrolling the southern half of Manhattan, from
59th Street to the Statue of Liberty, including the Freedom
Tower site. Or maybe it was because their vehicles were a
familiar sight around Wall Street and wouldn't attract un-
due attention.

Or maybe the president simply thought the men and
women of One-Truck were the best people for the job. It
was true. They could dust the ceilings with those bushy-
topped G-men over at Federal Plaza.

Regardless, the Chairman of the Joint Chiefs of Staff had spoken with Orjuela personally. He asked him to take whatever force he needed to the Freedom Tower, wait for word from General Rogers himself, and then take and secure an entire floor in the tower. He would not be told which floor until it was time to go. All they had to do right now was get to the building with as many fully crewed REPs—radio emergency patrol vehicles—as it would take to seal off a floor, then wait on the street, in the vehicles, prepared to move when they got the word. Orjuela was told to be ready to face armed, possibly barricaded resistance, though no "silent puppies" as far as the general knew, attack dogs whose voice boxes had been surgically removed so police wouldn't be aware of their presence. The week before, a successful drug bust in the East Village had put two of his people in the hospital with serious bite wounds from silent Dobermans.

The possibility of armed resistance meant suiting up in bullet-proof tactical vests, "body bunker" ballistic shields that were carried by selected "point" members of the squad, and tools including sledgehammers and hooked pry-bars. Weapons had to be heavy-caliber for the job, and ranged from .50-caliber Desert Eagle pistols to heavy-duty Ithaca 37 12-gauge shotguns.

Since the shift had changed at eight A.M., Lieutenant Orjuela was faced with a command of rested and potentially overeager officers pumped from a hit of morning coffee. Assaults didn't typically come this early in the shift; there was usually time to plan and review tactics and get to a calm psychological place.

Not this time. Orjuela and his chief, Captain Toroian, would have to manage and direct the energy as they went along.

The REPs were already loaded and moved out silently,

as ordered. Lieutenant Orjuela had the unit of twenty-four officers on-site at 9:38.

Few people in the street broke off their cell phone conversations to give the REPs much of a second thought.

Those whose cell connections were broken by proximity to the building's powerful antennas were too frustrated to notice the REPs at all.

Fifty-eight

New York, New York
Tuesday, 9:10 A.M.

According to the Freedom Tower directory, the building's maintenance and security office was located in the uppermost of the building's four basements. Different elevators visited different blocks of floors. Taylor and Lewis showed their military creds to the security guard who took a cursory look through their bag. Taylor said that the tennis balls were being distributed to former grunts who were new in the private sector.

"To relieve tension," he said, squeezing and opening his fist.

The guard let them through. They took the only elevator that went down.

"Hey, you see that?" Lewis gestured up with his thumb.

Taylor looked where he was pointing. There was a dark, hemispherical lens in the corner. "A security camera," Taylor said.

Lewis unshouldered his bag and pulled out one of the

tennis balls. He pretended to squeeze it. "We'll check it out, but that's not good," Lewis said. "Even if we get what we're after, they can probably watch us from other stations and shut us down before we reach the sky deck."

"This can't be the only way up," Taylor said. "There's got to be a freight elevator."

"Even if we could find it, I'm sure it's got a camera too."

"How about the stairs?" Taylor asked. "It's a hike but we can do it."

"Not in thirty-five minutes," Lewis told his partner. "Even if we could get there, when they find out which passkeys we've taken, they'll know where we're going. By the time we get to the roof, the police would have choppered SWAT teams to the rooftop. And that'd be a double whammy. Estate might think the choppers were targeting them—"

"And they might switch antennas before we can finish," Taylor said.

"You got it."

"I can't believe Commander Evans wouldn't have taken this into consideration."

"You can't, not on a quick-plan mission like this," Lewis said. "That's why you need experienced personnel in the field, to make these calls."

That was the first time he'd ever heard the colonel defend the commander, and it surprised and pleased him.

"If we go for it, you take care of any security personnel while I make for the office," Lewis said. "You move when I do."

The elevator door opened. Lewis stepped out. Taylor followed immediately behind, but kept his foot in the elevator so the door wouldn't close.

An African-American security guard was sitting behind a small desk in the corner. He was reading the *Daily News* and drinking coffee from a thermos. Beyond the big man were the security, communications, and electrical of-

fices. A small black-and-white monitor sat on the side of
the desk. Because the desk was in the way, Taylor couldn't
tell whether the guard was wearing a gun. His no-bullshit
eyes said "yes," and only his left hand was on top of the
desk.

"Can I help you gentlemen?" the guard asked.

Taylor was ready to follow Colonel Lewis's lead. He
had the entire attack worked out in an instant. If the guard
had a gun, Taylor would go low, use the desk for cover, and
use a zujitsu strike to disarm him—either "patting" the gun
hand, repeatedly slapping at the forearm to push it away,
wherever it went, or using a knife-hand to snap at the wrist
from left and right simultaneously. That usually stunned
the hand and caused the gun to drop. Then he would get
behind the guard and choke him unconscious. It would take
less than five seconds for the guard to black out as long as
Taylor maneuvered the man's chin into the crook of his elbow and was able to pull his fist back toward his own chin.
That maneuver not only closed off the victim's oxygen supply, but also the blood supply to the brain by shutting down
the carotid artery.

"We're looking for the Freedom Mall," Lewis told the
guard.

"Go back up, take the escalator at the north end of the
lobby, and go down one flight," the guard told them. Emphatically.

"Oops. Thanks. Sorry to bother you," Lewis said and
ducked back in. He pressed the lobby button and put the tennis ball back in the duffel bag. "That wasn't going to work."

"Why not?"

"Did you see under the desk?" Lewis asked. "The guard's
foot was on the alarm button. He must have watched us
come down and saw the duffel bag. He was eyeballing us for
a handheld trigger mech. He was ready."

"Then what do we do?" Taylor asked.

"We don't have a choice," Lewis replied. "We're not going to score the keys in the time we have. We need to get to the target as soon as possible and go from there."

Taylor wasn't sure he agreed. Evans thought they needed the keys and so did he. But then, he was just a medical officer. He didn't have enough field experience to intuit invasive actions the way Lewis did.

The men exited the elevator and made their way to the bank of elevators that went to the top of the tower. Lewis didn't want to go near the Forte offices or directly to the top of the tower. Instead, they took the high-speed elevator to the 106th floor, where they looked for a stairwell.

There were surveillance cameras in the corners of the hallways here. Lewis pulled the train ticket from his wallet to make it look as though they were searching for a specific office. When they spotted the stairwell, Lewis stopped and looked at his paper. His back was blocking the view of the camera. He tried the knob. Because the door led to a firewell, it was not locked. The men moved quickly up the concrete stairs.

"We've got to assume they saw us," Lewis said as they ran. "When we get to the roof I'm going to give you my Swiss army knife. You work your surgical magic on the cable box and I'll cover the entrance."

"I'm there," Taylor said.

The men reached the end of the stairwell. The door leading outside was open for roof rescues in the event of fire, a lesson learned in the World Trade Center attack. They could hear the wind roaring outside even before they cracked the door. Lewis gave Taylor his Swiss army knife. Then he turned to the door. He had to push hard to get it open. When he did, the suction nearly dragged them both out.

Lewis hurried out and put his duffel bag on the roof. He unzipped it while Taylor looked around.

The commander had gotten it wrong. Except for a helipad in the southeast corner—another lesson from the 2001 attack—there were literally dozens of antennas here, most of them just a few feet high and sapling-thin. They reminded Taylor of antennae he had seen on military bases, and he imagined that they were point-to-point relays for police and fire dispatchers throughout the city. There was no confusing them with the TV broadcast and satellite equipment, all the larger dishes and antennae. Through the skeletal forest of metal, Taylor saw the large cable box. He hurried toward it, picking his way through the fishbonelike antennae. As he neared, he noticed the security cameras bolted to short, stocky poles in the corners of the tower.

Taylor reached the cable box and knelt beside it. The box was squarish, about the height and length of a kitchen oven with a pebbled pea-green exterior. The molded one-piece covering was riveted at the bottom with bolts. The heads of the bolts were nearly two inches in diameter. Taylor tested them and swore. The bolts weren't budging without a heavy-duty wrench. He rapped on the box casing on all four sides. It didn't seem very thick, maybe a quarter to half an inch. The eastern side seemed most hollow. The major rose and raced toward Lewis. The colonel had found an outlet, plugged the toaster in, and set it inside the stairwell.

"This isn't going to do it!" Taylor yelled, waving the pocketknife. "I need something heavy-duty!"

Lewis turned on the toaster and shut the door. Then he reached into the duffel bag.

"How many bolts are there?" Lewis asked.

"Three on the long side," Taylor said.

Lewis withdrew six tennis balls. "These don't have

shrapnel," he said. "Put two next to each bolt and hit them with one ball each."

"I don't think that'll do it," Taylor said. "Let me have the bag. I've got to go through the casing itself."

"That's going to leave us pretty naked if we're attacked."

"Then we'll spit at whoever comes after us," Taylor said. "If I can't blow the casing, we might as well leave now."

"You sure that much pop won't blow the box *and* destroy the cables?" Lewis asked.

"I don't think so," Taylor told the colonel. "The east side of the box sounds hollow. I'm guessing the cables come in through the roof there and plug in to a master board on the west side. If I can blow the east side I'm hoping I won't damage the cables."

"But the explosion will blow the metal in," Lewis pointed out. "That could sever the wires."

"Colonel, we're not getting in that cable box otherwise," Taylor said. "I'll use the bag and spread the balls out inside to focus the blast along the entire side. I should be able to peel back the cracked metal. I didn't spend years breaking boards for nothing."

Lewis thought for a moment. "All right," he said. He kept a few of the balls, then gave the bag to Taylor. "Keep one ball, stand back about five yards, and heave it hard. Don't miss."

"Thanks," Taylor said.

Thick, greenish smoke had begun to curl from under the door to the stairwell as the men stood there. Lewis backed away and took up a position behind a small dish as Taylor rushed back to the cable box. He removed the binoculars, flashlight, and other items and set them aside. Then he placed the bag against the base of the box and lined the balls up inside, along the wall. He shut the flap, kept one of the tennis balls, and stepped back. He was going to have to throw it very hard to compensate for the wind blowing in from the river, which was to his left.

Taylor wasn't thinking about anything other than getting that side of the box open. He wasn't thinking about the possibility that he could be injured by the blast or killed in a raid that was sure to come. He had no doubt that the NYPD would be sending up a chopper with snipers before very long. Like performing surgery, this was an immediate need that shut out all others.

Now the medic stopped thinking. He just stared at the bag and threw the ball as if he were skipping a stone across a pond. That gave him the most control and speed. The ball sped toward the target and struck it square. For the next few moments everything seemed to be happening in slow motion. There was a small yellow flash as the tennis ball flew apart. If there was a sound, Taylor didn't hear it because of the wind. The blast hung like a starburst as the fabric from the ball hung in the air for a moment. Then it vanished, swallowed by a much larger explosion. Taylor heard this one. There was a clanging pop and the bag was simultaneously lifted up and back as the blast tore through the opposite side. Yellow-red spikes of fire shot from the side. The bag came down about a yard from Taylor, yellow smoke still coughing from the rips in the fabric. The major moved forward holding his breath and waving his hand from side to side. The wind disbursed the smoke quickly. After a second, he could see the cable box clearly. There was a long horizontal tear in the end near the base and vertical cracks in the center and on the sides.

He shook a fist triumphantly and ran toward the box, picking up the remains of the duffel bag as he passed. As he did so he glanced at his watch. In just over two minutes the SWAT raid against the Forte offices would begin. The broadcast to Israel would probably begin soon thereafter. The counterattack, the poison, would follow within moments. The security of the Middle East and the end of Estate depended upon him getting to the cables and hoping that Commander Evans could tell him which ones to switch.

Taylor took the cell phone from his pocket as he ran. He wanted to have it ready.

When the major reached the box, he dropped to his knees and looked inside. The edges of the cracks were blown in, but the cables were about six inches farther in. They seemed to be intact. Eagerly, he wrapped the remains of the duffel bag around his hands and began to pull upward, as though he were lifting a car by its fender. The metal groaned and gave. All he needed to do was separate the side from the bolts. If Taylor could do that, he hoped he could roll the rest of the casing back. It wasn't as thick as he thought, less than half an inch.

The wind blew so hard that his windbreaker seemed stuck to his arms. It heightened his awareness of the muscles there, of how taut each of them was. He needed to make his mind as taut. He thought about his mother, about the guys who beat her, about how scared she must have felt. He thought about himself not being there.

He thought about the shame of failing here.

Rage flowed from his brain down his shoulders and into his hands. His fingers felt like cables themselves. The metal began to move. He focused his energy, his *ki*. The lid came up higher and Taylor switched positions, crouching so he could push upward, get his strength beneath the metal. He felt the burn in his thighs as he held his torso straight, his arms cocked at the elbows pushing up.

The cover suddenly bent in the center and stood straight up. The other half was still bolted shut.

"Shit!" Taylor said.

He grabbed the flashlight and looked inside. He could see where the cables jacked into the board. There were seven of them lying side by side, all different colors. The colors matched marks on the base of the satellite dishes and at certain junctures on the main antenna. The cables were also labeled with white letters on the side. He found the one belonging to PBS. He'd be able to pull that cable out, and also the Estate one when they knew which one it was, but he didn't see how he'd be able to plug them into their respective slots.

Taylor looked around desperately. Lewis was standing back from the door, watching him through the forest of antennae.

"What happened?" Lewis yelled.

There wasn't time to answer. Taylor didn't think that having them both pull on the metal would help. He needed something else.

Then he saw it. The small antennae.

The major jumped to the nearest one, a three-footer with small fine spines on the top half, like fishbones. He snapped it off at the base and swung back to the box. He removed his belt, then set it and the antenna down. Then he picked up the phone and called the base.

The call went through, but all Taylor could hear was static. The Marine tried again. The same thing happened. And in a horrible flash he realized that the call would never go through. Not here, not with a wall of microwave signals spilling in every direction.

"We've got company!" Lewis yelled. The colonel stepped back from the door. "We're also at the thirty-second mark! We need things to happen!"

Taylor stood and looked around. He couldn't get the intel he needed. It was as if his patient had just flatlined. He needed to do *something*. He began moving among the dishes. Time seemed to have slowed down again, or maybe it was his mind that had kicked into supersonic. There had to be something here that would ID the dish or part of the antenna that belonged to Estate.

Something, he thought. Some. Fucking. Thing.

And he had to find it fast.

Fifty-nine

**Arlington, Virginia
Tuesday, 9:51 A.M.**

General Anastasia hadn't felt this energized in over six years. Not since fliers in his squadron had helped tenderize Saddam Hussein before his ouster.

It had been a long night, sitting at his desk and watching sign-ups flood the Estate line. Though he had been alone, he hadn't felt alone. Forte and Crabbe and all the others who had taken part were in his thoughts. Forte in particular. He had joined with Anastasia because he believed in a future guided by a few men with a shared vision. They even agreed that sexual repression was a bad thing. They were willing to bet that, in time, freed of national and religious prejudices, their new Estate society would be much more tolerant. That had happened on the Internet even before the founding of Estate.

The thousands of people who had signed up to become part of Estate during the night were also there with him. They were at the forefront of a revolution. They were the first citizens of a new world order, an on-line government that would end war by making the e-state he had created the only effective, functioning world government. A government that didn't concern itself with boundaries, only with the progress of humankind. Its expansion to the edges of the solar system and beyond. The elimination of disease and ignorance. There would be a flowering of all the wonders that partisanship and small minds had blocked for millennia, from the Dark Ages to the present. And anyone who disagreed with this humanistic goal, who put "the self" above "all," would be shut down.

It was happening. Right before him. All around him. Hit-numbers were rocketing up on the website, and most were signing up for the concept. Soon they would begin to refer to the memberships as what they really were.

Citizenships.

Anastasia's only regret was that Dr. Gregg could not be here to see this. The scientist who had been his partner, the man who had given everything to make this a reality.

Anastasia's private phone beeped. It was a level-three TAC-SAT secure phone linked to Forte Communications in New York and to Forte's villa in the south of France. He picked it up.

"Yes?"

"General, something has gone wrong."

It was May Scott, Forte's executive vice president. The fifty-six-year-old woman was the only member of the Forte Communications board who knew about ESP and the true nature of Estate. Her voice, normally soft and composed, sounded urgent.

"I'm listening, Ms. Scott," Anastasia said. His voice was low and rough, as thick as tree bark. He hoped the president hadn't done something stupid. He didn't want to have to do what he said he'd do.

"An NYPD SWAT team is moving through the office,"

she said. "We don't know who ordered the action or what they want. The officers who moved in aren't talking. They're just positioning people throughout the office, making sure people don't leave, and they're keeping us from computers and phones. They haven't reached the back room yet."

The back room was the locked area of the office suites reserved for Estate activities. Until six months ago they were Forte's private office. Employees were accustomed to not being asked there. Only a handful of people were allowed there now, and of those only Scott and Crabbe knew what really went on.

"Do the police have a warrant?" Anastasia asked.

"They haven't produced one," Scott said.

That meant they were probably there for the only reason anyone would think was urgent enough to circumvent the law. To shut down Estate in a lightning move. Maybe the president thought that Anastasia would e-mail him again before acting. That would give the police time to seize the computers and stop Estate from broadcasting the launch code to the Israeli missiles.

The president was wrong.

"Stay calm, Ms. Scott," Anastasia told her. His voice was low, soothing. It displayed none of the rage he felt. "Don't resist and don't cooperate. We'll take care of the target. Then we'll move the antenna and deal with the strike."

"Yes, General. Shall I tell Mr. Crabbe to proceed with his action?" the woman asked.

"No. I'll call him directly," Anastasia said. "You just remain at your desk and go about normal Forte business."

"They'll have to drag me out," she promised.

"Good woman."

The general hung up and punched in Crabbe's number. Anastasia did not tell the scientist what was happening. Crabbe might panic. He simply told the scientist to send the new program to the Israeli site, then shift to antenna three, the cell phone tower Forte had bought on the coast of Connecticut in Westport. Unlike the Kodiak site, which was being accessed through a direct cable in Anastasia's office—a holdover from the Cold War days—Crabbe needed line-of-sight contact with the other antennae.

Crabbe acknowledged the order. When Anastasia hung up, his mood had changed. He was no longer luxuriating in a job well done, but in the hurdles that obviously remained ahead. Hurdles that should not have been, save for the shortsighted and reckless behavior of career border guards.

They were about to learn, most definitively, that their time on earth was over, their kind headed for extinction.

Sixty

**New York, New York
Tuesday, 9:54 A.M.**

They were four minutes past the deadline when the switch was supposed to have been made. The SWAT team would be on the move and, if they hadn't done it already, the Estate megalomaniacs were probably getting ready to nuke the Sinai and turn the sand to glass.

As Taylor stood there, looking around for clues or inspiration or even a thread of hope, he noticed a dish that was actually two dishes. One was six feet in diameter and the other, located at the base, was about two feet wide. They were conjoined. The larger dish was turned to the sky and the other was turned streetward: Taylor leaned over the side to see where the smaller dish was pointing.

It was aimed to the west, toward the Hudson River. Toward the yacht basin at the World Financial Center almost directly below.

Quickly, Taylor scooped up the binoculars and looked down at the basin. Either a signal was being beamed down there, or it was being beamed from there. He could think of reasons for the latter. One in particular. Taylor scanned the line of yachts in the small artificial inlet. Many of them had satellite dishes. But one of them, larger than the others, stood out. It was the name that caught Taylor's eye. The *Ticonderoga*. The Forte satellites were Apache and Bravo. Legendary forts. So was Ticonderoga.

Taylor looked over at the dish. It was marked with a yellow swatch. There was a yellow cable in the box. He dropped beside the cable box, picked up the broken antenna, and used his belt to lash the antenna to the yellow cable. He didn't hesitate. There was no time. He pulled the cable from the PBS satellite, then pulled out the yellow cable. He held the flashlight in his left hand and the broken antenna in his right. Using the antenna, he moved the Estate cable over the others to the PBS slot.

Whether it was his own determination or the hand of Evans's god who helped him, Taylor guided the cable home, into the vacant slot. The PBS dish immediately began to turn so that it was pointing the same way as the other dish.

He'd made the switch. Now Taylor prayed that it was the right dish moving into position.

A moment later, he heard a noise that wasn't the wind. It was the sound of an explosion. He turned and saw Lewis throw one of the "flash-bang" tennis balls at the partly open door. Taylor caught a glimpse of the distinctive powder-blue shirt of a tower security guard before the door shut again. He unstrapped the antenna to bring with him and use as a whip if need be. He picked up the phone and opera glasses and stuffed them in his pocket. Then he raced to join Lewis at the door. There wasn't even time to savor the accomplishment. The chlorine smoke was thinning. The walls of the Alamo would be breached before very long.

"Everything all right?" Lewis asked.

"No problem," Taylor replied.

"Good work," Lewis said.

"Are we going to fight our way out of here or stand down?"

"I want to get past whoever's coming up here without hurting them," Lewis said. "Then we head back to the station. Did the commander have anything else to say?"

"I didn't talk to him," Taylor said.

Lewis looked at him.

"There was too much interference. But it's all right. I got the dish. They were wrong, Colonel. The instructions weren't being broadcast from Forte Communications headquarters. They were coming from a yacht in the river."

"A yacht?"

"The *Ticonderoga*," Taylor said. "There was a little receiving dish pointing directly at it."

"Fuck," Lewis said, and made a face. "We should've been looking for something like that. Is it still at anchor?"

Taylor said it was.

"Then the police won't be able to seize the program," Lewis said. "We *have* to get down there and get it ourselves."

"You don't think they'll listen to us if we explain—"

"We just blew the top off their cable system, on tape," Lewis said. "By the time the head of security brings in the cops and they let us come up for air, the yacht will be out of here."

The men suddenly became aware of another sound. A drumming from the east, from over the city. They looked over and saw two police helicopters, one coming from the south, one from the north. They also heard muffled voices from the stairwell. The security team must have sent for gas masks.

"We're going to have to go in before they can set up to

take us," Lewis said, a new sense of urgency in his voice. "You remember the layout?"

"Yes," Taylor replied.

"We'll go down two flights," the colonel said quickly. "I'll hold them back with flash-bangs while you find a fire alarm. We'll move out with the crowd, and if we get split up we meet at the yacht. If it starts to move out, whichever one of us is at the site gets on board."

Taylor acknowledged the order. The men were about ten feet from the door. Lewis put the last of the tennis balls down and gestured for Taylor to pull the door open while he got in position to move in. The colonel had his arms crossed in front of him, elbows out, obviously intending to bowl the men over. Under the circumstances, that was probably the best tactic.

Taylor reached for the knob. As he did the door suddenly flew open. The major jumped back as a canister rolled toward them, spewing a blinding cloud of tear gas as guards wearing bullet-proof Kevlar vests and gas masks rushed through the smoke.

Sixty-one

New York, New York
Tuesday, 10:03 A.M.

The MH-60G Pave Hawk helicopter is a variant of the Blackhawk tactical transport. The fifty-foot-long aircraft is fast, able to cruise at speeds approaching 190 miles an hour at sea level—twenty miles an hour less traveling "hot and high"—and it can hover as high as four thousand feet. Though there are seats on the flight deck for a pilot, copilot, and crew chief, the Pave Hawk can be flown by a single operator. The chopper can fly nearly nine hundred miles without having to refuel, and the cabin is equipped to hold from seven to twelve people.

As he sped northeast with MCPO Diaz in the copilot's seat, Peter Holly hoped he would be collecting just two people: Major Hank Taylor and Colonel Matthew Lewis. He wanted to be able to pick the men up, get the hell out of there, and head back to McGuire. But in his short time with the Stealth Warrior team he'd learned that nothing went as planned. Which was a compliment, in a way. If the job were easy, the president could have sent someone else.

After Commander Evans determined, shortly before nine-thirty, that he would need the rest of his team on the ground at McGuire AFB, he notified Captain McIver to find a bird Holly could fly. The captain's records showed that he was flight-certified for all variations of the Black-hawk; McIver made sure there would be one at his disposal when he and Diaz reached McGuire AFB. She was able to get him one of the Air Force's specially modified Search and Rescue Blackhawks. The two men were on the ground, out of the mail plane, and up again in the Pave Hawk within five minutes.

Captain Holly had always loved the Sikorsky-made chopper. The headway was "strong," which meant that the helicopter's streamlined contours allowed it to slip neatly through head winds and turbulence. Holly had been warned he would face both the closer he got to Manhattan, since he would be coming in over the windswept bay, which was at the confluence of two rivers and the Atlantic Ocean. The ride was already bumpy, since he kept the bird cranked to the maximum in order to cover the sixty miles from the base as quickly as possible. The faster the chop-per went, the shakier the ride became as faster airflow caused the two General Electric turboshaft engines to fire less efficiently.

The men swung over Lower New York Bay. They crossed the Verrazano Narrows Bridge, which connected Brooklyn with Staten Island, and continued up over Upper New York Bay toward Manhattan Island. The water was glistening and rippling below them. Ahead, the Statue of Liberty seemed small compared to the giant towers that rose beyond it in the hazy morning sun. The Freedom Tower was the nearest of those skyscrapers. Holly had never flown here, and the view was breathtaking. If they weren't flying into the sun, he would have taken off his sunglasses. The colors of the different metals, stones, and glass were probably dazzling.

After crossing the bridge, he descended from two to one thousand feet. They were now in the flight path for jets coming into JFK International Airport, and he wanted to make sure he was well below their approach floor.

The radio buzzed as they passed Liberty Island.

"This is Captain Holly."

"This is Evans," the commander said. "What's your ETA?"

"Just inside of three minutes," Holly said. "We have the tower in visual, but can't see anything on top as yet. Any word?"

"None," Evans said. "We have to assume they were unable to reach the target. Which means you have to."

Evans had already briefed the crew about the target, including the code numbers on the two cables that needed to be switched. The last set of figures, the ones they were supposed to phone to Taylor and Lewis, had come in from the FCC just ten minutes before.

"We'll get there, sir—"

"Captain, look over there!" Diaz said suddenly. "Northeast, around one o'clock."

Holly looked past the chopper's black, starboard 12.7-mm machine gun to where the Coast Guard SHARC was pointing. He didn't see anything. Then the captain lowered his sunglasses slightly. In the natural light he saw what Diaz was pointing at.

"Commander, we see smoke around the top of the tower," Holly said. "Just can't tell if it's coming from the top or from a smokestack or something behind—we're a little lower than the tower is. I'm going to top off at another three hundred feet."

Holly pulled on the stick and sent the chopper climbing quickly. He continued to peer over his sunglasses.

"That's on top," Diaz said.

"Sir, Diaz is right," Holly said. "The smoke is definitely coming from the top of the tower. And there are people up there. I'm not sure who's who, but it looks like there are about six or seven of 'em. There are also choppers hovering over on the east side—"

"I'll be damned," Evans said.

Holly shot Diaz a did-I-just-hear-the-commander-swear look. "Sir?" Holly said.

"I said, 'I'll be damned,'" Evans repeated. "Hold on."

The Pave Hawk continued to knife toward the tip of Manhattan. The smoke was beginning to thin out. It looked like there were a total of eight people on the roof. Two of them were moving backward, away from the others. It looked like they were down on the ground. The others were moving forward from a door of some kind.

Because Holly didn't know what they were going to do when they reached the target, the Pave Hawk suddenly seemed to be moving very fast. They swung over the shoreline and in toward the tower.

Then Holly saw a new problem that needed to be addressed at once, one that gave him an adrenaline punch that had him spinning as fast as his forward rotor.

Sixty-two

Lake Miasalaro, West Virginia
Tuesday, 10:06 A.M.

Amos Evans and Clark Fraser both looked over Victoria Hudson's shoulder. They were staring at her busy computer monitor. Evans was still holding the line that Captain McIver had run through the Langley com center to Captain Holly's Pave Hawk. Fraser was still humming his tune. Evans didn't know how Victoria felt, but he found the tune relaxing. Or maybe distracting. What Evans saw on the monitor was fantastic.

Ten minutes before, using data the president had obtained from the Air Force, Victoria had finished writing the poison pill for the ESP. One minute later, the data was on its way via hyperlink to Aman headquarters in Tel Aviv. Ninety seconds after that, the Israeli intelligence agency had loaded her program and was ready to undertow it back to the ESP. Meanwhile, the FCC had given the president the code letters of the Forte Communications cable. Everything was ready except for the unscrambled link to the satellite.

The 9:50 deadline came. When Colonel Lewis and Major Taylor finally telephoned the base—at least Evans assumed it was them—the signal couldn't get through.

And then, unexpectedly, a signal from the ESP came in to Israel's Air Defense Forces Missile Command Center at Haatzerim Air Force Base. Victoria's poison pill had been written to become active upon receiving an unscrambled signal from the satellite. Once it was triggered, the undertow pulled it into the Freedom Tower dish and sent it up to the satellite. Her program had also been designed to kickback the upload chart to the com-shack computer as her codes streamed into space. If there were a breakdown or impedance, the program would crash and she would know within a few minutes, as soon as the kickback cleared firewalls in the Israeli computer systems.

The computer scientist had explained all of this to Evans and Fraser as they waited.

Then, suddenly, at a few seconds after 10:03, kickback began pouring in from the Israeli computer. ESP had tried to send a launch code to the ADFMCC eight minutes before. When it did, the poison pill immediately blocked it and began sending itself to the satellite.

"We're in!" Victoria shouted. "They switched the dish!"

Evans got back on the phone at once. "Captain Holly, the mission has been accomplished! Evac our team immediately and report back the moment you've got them."

"Yes, sir!" Holly replied.

Evans kept the line to the chopper open as, in silence, he, Victoria, and Fraser watched five horizontal green bar graphs grow higher with every moment. Numbers and names of files flew by too fast to read. But Victoria knew what they were. Her left hand was a tight fist and she shook it each time some new plateau had been reached.

"Strike one against Estate," Victoria said. "The antenna realignment protocol has been blocked. The ESP is locked in place."

"Translation?" Evans said.

"Estate still controls the satellite but they can't switch antennas," she explained.

"Can they still send up a new scrambled signal?" Evans asked.

"Yes, but they have to realize they've been busted first," she told him. "They don't have feedback from the ADFMCC because the Israelis have firewalls on outflowing data. The ESP didn't bother erasing those. So the only way they'll know something is wrong is if they're watching the news and they don't hear about a nuclear exchange in the Middle East."

They continued to watch.

"Strike two," Victoria said. "The non-Estate schematic has been uploaded. That's the original Air Force design for the ESP. It's going to shut down everything that was Air Force–approved. When that's done, the final program will upload. That one's going to kill everything that's still standing. It's not as surgical as I would have liked, but it's the best I could do on short notice."

"You've got absolutely nothing to apologize for," Evans told her. He was extremely proud of her.

There was another long silence as the bars grew. More numbers and headings flew by.

"Strike three is under way," Victoria said, her voice tense. "Please let me have written the program right. Please."

Evans placed a hand on her shoulder. "I'm sure you did fine."

"No, you're not," she said. "*I'm* not sure!" She was anxious, scared. "This was rushed and I don't want to have screwed up."

The bars swelled at slightly different speeds. They were

heading toward thin black lines at the top of the monitor.

"We've got another twenty seconds or so," Victoria said. "If I didn't mess up and if Estate doesn't break the connection, they're dead."

"What if they do break it?" Evans asked.

"They can still talk to the ESP, break the connection with the ADFMCC, and send up a recovery program," she said. "I'm sure they have one."

When he was a kid, Evans used to watch the Gemini rocket launches on TV. He remembered that after one minute each second seemed to have a personality of its own. Fifty-nine was the top of the peak. Fifty-eight was like the queen of the deck. Fifty-seven and fifty-six were the last dominant parts of the fifties, and then you were at fifty-five and heading to the forties. The process was like the last two minutes of a championship football game. It seemed to last forever. Watching this process was like that.

Victoria's fist loosened. She reached blindly for Evans's hand and grabbed it tightly.

"What do Catholics call it when they request something from God?" Victoria asked.

"A prayer of petition," Evans replied.

"Right. Would you make one?" she asked.

"I will," he replied. "Will you?"

"I'm doing that now," Victoria said. "I truly am."

Suddenly, four of the bars surged toward the top of the monitor. One after another they began hitting the top bar. The fifth column was moving a little slower, but was almost there.

"There it went," she said as more headings flew by. "*Tertiary command link.* That was antenna number three, wherever that was. They've got no way to talk to it. We did it."

"No, you did it," Evans said.

Victoria watched as the last bar crept toward the top. "Come on, you bastard. Move."

Evans got back on the phone. "Captain?"

"Sir, I heard the news," Holly said. "Congratulations. Permission to take personal command of the mission."

"Reason?"

"No time to explain," Holly replied.

Evans quickly considered the request. When it came down to it, of course, he had to trust his people in their jobs. He had trusted Victoria. But he was still the commander of the Stealth Warriors and he would be answerable to the president and to his conscience for anything Holly did.

"Permission granted," Evans replied. As he glanced over at Victoria, concerns about Holly were nudged back by Victoria's sullen expression. "What's wrong?" he asked.

"I don't know," she said. "The bar stopped moving. I thought I covered everything. It could be a glitch or it could be something else."

"Such as?" Evans asked.

Victoria began typing. "Such as—that there may be something in the satellite we didn't know about," she said.

"Meaning?" Evans asked.

"That Estate may not have lost all contact with the ESP."

Sixty-three

New York, New York
Tuesday, 10:09 A.M.

MCPO Diaz was accustomed to working in big, open places, alone, and at a somewhat easy pace and usually without weapons. He was also not used to racing against the end of civilization as we know it.

As he listened over the headset to the exchange between Captain Holly and Commander Evans, Diaz felt as though he were in hyperdrive. He had been worrying about ESP and about Taylor and Lewis. Now that the ESP issue was settled, his concerns were solely about Taylor, Lewis, and whatever it was Holly intended to do. Diaz had no idea, but it wasn't looking good.

Holly maneuvered the Pave Hawk so that it was about 150 feet above Taylor and Lewis. A call from the president to the mayor of New York had ensured that he would not be shot at. As he settled into that position a new voice came over the headset.

"VG531, this is NYPD Precinct 1 command," said the

caller. "You are in a secure action zone. Withdraw immediately."

"How'd they get our number?" Diaz muttered. Obviously, they were permitted to be observers, nothing more.

"They know the Air Force frequency and probably sent this out over all the call signs," Holly replied. The pilot punched the reply button on the flight panel. "This is a military matter," he informed them. "We will take charge of the two men on the tower and then withdraw. Tell your fliers and the security personnel to back off."

"Negative," said the dispatcher. "We are authorized to move in to apprehend the individuals."

The president be damned, the NYPD obviously intended to protect their own turf. Diaz had heard they were tough. Apparently, tough enough to take on the U.S. Air Force. A few moments later, the two blue and white police choppers began nosing in from the northeast and southeast corners of the tower. They were approaching slowly, obviously trying to drive the Air Force helicopter back. Diaz was curious what Holly would do. He couldn't move forward or to the southwest, where there was a large antenna. If he went up, the police choppers would control the surface.

The men from the stairwell were moving toward Taylor and Lewis. They appeared to be armed. The two Stealth Warriors were on the ground, kicking backwards, into a grove of small antennae. They looked like they were struggling to get away and also to breathe. At least the prop-wash from the three choppers had helped disburse the tear gas.

"I wonder if our guys know we're here," Diaz said.

"Or that we're friends," Holly pointed out.

Just then one of the security people lobbed another gas canister at the fallen soldiers.

"Precinct 1, tell your helicopters and ground personnel to back off or we will open fire," Holly said. "They have a five-count starting with one—"

Diaz fired him a look.

"Two—"

The police choppers continued to move forward. So did the men on the top of the tower. They were just about twenty yards from Taylor and Lewis.

"Three—"

Holly began to guide the Pave Hawk toward the rooftop. He used the heads-up display to swing the twin machine guns toward the helicopters. He locked on his targets. Wherever the Pave Hawk or the police choppers moved, the guns would automatically follow.

"Four—"

The choppers continued to move forward.

Holly punched off the radio and threw the chopper forward. He accelerated so fast that Diaz was literally tossed back. Not against the seat but against the door, since Holly simultaneously banked sharply to the south. Diaz was glad he was wearing a shoulder harness. That kept part of him in the seat. Within moments the Pave Hawk was parallel to the converging police helicopters. Then just as suddenly, Holly swung the chopper to the north, jerking Diaz toward him. An instant later they were facing west and hovering behind the police choppers.

"No cop-copter fucks with me," Holly said angrily. He punched the radio back on. "Five!" he said.

There was a moment as long and thick and awful as any Diaz had ever experienced. He was watching Holly. The pilot had his left hand on the seat-side trigger that swung up from the armrest. Diaz didn't know if Holly was going to fire. Certainly they couldn't allow Taylor and Lewis to be arrested.

The police choppers stopped moving. The security personnel did not. The last blast of tear gas had put Taylor and Lewis on their backs. It was amazing they'd gone as far as they did, moving blind and gagging. The team on the rooftop was just a few yards away. Holly looked as if he were fighting the war between Heaven and the rebellious angels right inside his head, from the brow beneath his helmet to the taut line of his mouth.

Fast, very fast, Holly dropped several feet so that he was slightly lower than the police choppers. He tapped the target-lock button on the armrest to unlock it, used a tiny joystick in front of it to shift the gun sight to the skids of the helicopter on the southside. He fired a short burst.

A few bullets struck and sparked off the struts and padded landing gear. They flew away from the tower and the men on the roof. The helicopters immediately peeled off to the sides. Holly continued to descend. The security guards had stopped and were looking up. The pilot turned the guns toward them. The men called off their attack at once and retreated to the stairwell.

Holly turned off the radio. "They're men in uniform but they were in my way," he said as he pushed the chopper toward the rooftop.

Holly's expression and tone were both lighter now. The battle in Holly's brain was over. But not the one that started in Diaz's head. He wanted to know what Holly would have done if the choppers hadn't moved. Even more than that, he wanted to know something else.

What he himself would have done.

Sixty-four

New York, New York
Tuesday, 10:12 A.M.

For Colonel Lewis the worst thing that could happen right now was being caught by the Freedom Tower security guards and having to answer questions, possibly being put on trial. Almost as bad would be stumbling off the roof, and not because Lewis was afraid to die. He didn't want to have his body taken into custody and fingerprinted, thus revealing his identity. Either eventuality would lead investigators to his having been seconded by DARPA and sent to Langley. Though the paper trail ended there, good people like Captain McIver and possibly Commander Evans would fall protecting the Stealth Warriors and the black-ops unit the president had been running.

That was why he and Taylor had backed away and would do whatever they could to get past these guards and off the rooftop. Lewis had already slipped his knife from its ankle sheath. He was prepared to kill them if he had to. But his thinking now was to try and take one of the men hostage. At least that would keep any sharpshooters in the police choppers from firing. Given the wind speeds up here, those birds weren't steady enough for that kind of shot.

The colonel had been through lacrimator gas training. The greasy fumes hit the eyes like a strong onion, burning the insides of the lids both top and bottom and making it difficult to keep them open. Difficult but not impossible. If he pressed them shut and opened his eyes once every second or so, he was able to take a snapshot of his surroundings. Taylor had obviously been trained to do likewise. Since the smoke itself inhibited the security team, they were all pretty much paralyzed until it began to clear. Then he and Taylor were able to back away. They stayed low on the ground because the heat generated by the tower was causing the air above it to rise, carrying the tear gas with it.

The second gas canister thrown by the security guards did not change Lewis's plan. That only made it necessary for him to continue backing off until the smoke cleared.

And then, unexpectedly, the top of the building, every part of Lewis, even the air itself shook with a low, rumbling drone. As the sound rolled to the east, the colonel squinted up through the gas. He saw a black chopper angled steeply on its port side, charging behind the police helicopters in a tight arc. Lewis blinked hard and when he opened his eyes again, the black helicopter was braking sharply behind the two police aircraft. It did not look like it was there to back them up. If it were, the chopper would have stayed on the west side of the tower.

Lewis was unable to suppress a quick, involuntary smile. *"You'll know it when you see it,"* Evans had told him. The commander was right. From the pushy angle and speed, the urgent need to join the fray, that could only be Captain Holly at the controls. He and Diaz must have gotten to McGuire or another local field to attempt an airlift. First Major Taylor had been forced to improv a solution to the antenna problem, and now this. Lewis wasn't impressed by very much, but he was impressed by the performance of the Stealth team this morning.

Even though the security guards were approaching, Lewis stayed put and motioned for Taylor to do the same. If it were Holly, and he had a plan, Lewis didn't want to complicate things by moving.

Though Lewis's eyes were still bleary, the tear gas had begun to clear from the air around them. Sure enough, an instant later, the black chopper dropped and fired a short burst. The two police choppers veered away and the security men turned and ran for the stairwell. A heartbeat after that, the black chopper nosed down and sped toward the rooftop. It was about five feet above the surface. Just a few feet short of the forest of antennae, the chopper suddenly swung nose-south and stopped, like a skier putting on the brakes. It settled down quickly, gently, and the door opened. MCPO Diaz ducked out.

Lewis looked behind him. Taylor was about six feet away. He was also looking out at the chopper.

"Let's move!" Lewis shouted.

The major waved and got up. Lewis turned toward the stairwell as he rose. The security guards were huddled in the doorway, on the radio, awaiting instructions or reinforcements. The police choppers were also waiting, hovering off about a quarter of a mile south and north of the tower.

Because Lewis was closer, Diaz came to him first.

"Get him and keep your face down!" Lewis said. He didn't say Taylor's name in case the security cameras could see them. Computer enhancement might allow them to read his lips. That was also why he wanted Diaz not to let them photograph his face.

Lewis reached the helicopter and opened the cabin door. He jumped in, turned, and helped Taylor on board. Diaz hopped back into his seat and Holly was moving to the south even before the doors were closed. The Pave Hawk quickly cleared the top of the building and swung upward and to the east. Holly informed Commander Evans that they had retrieved the two men.

Diaz turned back. He was grinning broadly.

"The commander said you did it!" the MCPO told them. He had to shout to be heard over the rattling of the rotor. "Victoria sent a poison program up to the satellite and it swallowed—"

"We can't leave yet!" Lewis shouted back. He was still blinking out residual gas and sucking down the clean air.

"Why not, sir?" Holly asked.

"We think the program was being controlled from a yacht in the basin due west of the tower."

Holly immediately swung the chopper around. "Do you know which yacht, sir?" he asked.

Taylor was looking out the window. "Yes," he said. "It's the one running like a torpedo for the open sea!"

Sixty-five

**New York, New York
Tuesday, 10:16 A.M.**

Taylor watched the river. From the corner of his eye he saw
the police choppers circle wide to follow them. They were
certainly on radar from JFK or Newark, but these guys
were probably looking for a chance to box the intruder in
and maybe force them down.

Captain Holly would have to worry about that. Taylor
wanted the *Ticonderoga*. And right now the motor yacht,
about a sixty-footer, was tearing down the Hudson River toward the bay and the open sea beyond. He pointed it out to
Holly, who swung the chopper around while he corkscrewed
lower. In just a few seconds they were in pursuit of the sleek
white vessel.

Taylor had no idea who was on board. He also didn't
know whether they were fleeing because they knew what
had happened on the rooftop, or had been sent away because of the SWAT team's actions against Forte Communications. But Taylor believed that whatever evidence the

government needed to apprehend the rest of the Estate team was on board that yacht, either in data form—if it hadn't been erased or tossed overboard—or more likely, in the person of whoever had been manning the computer.

I don't know if evidence obtained like this will be admissible in court, he thought. Nor did he think the government would care. If the people behind this whole enterprise mysteriously disappeared, that would suit him fine.

Holly guided the chopper to within a few hundred vertical feet of the yacht. They were still about half a mile behind it, but closing fast. The police choppers were behind and above them.

"How do we want to handle this?" Holly asked.

"Short of shooting them out of the water?" Lewis asked.

"I don't have a problem with that," Holly replied.

"Mr. Diaz, if we get on board can you stop the boat?" Lewis asked.

"Absolutely."

"Then that's what we're going to do," Lewis decided. "We go down and secure the vessel, then grab whatever software and programmers are on board and bring them back to McGuire. The White House can deal with them and whoever's behind this."

The chopper continued to angle downward without cutting airspeed. Diaz pointed to a rope ladder that was rolled up inside a net hanging against the wall. Taylor reached back from his bucket seat and released the net from the hooks above. The ladder had latches on top that could be secured to eyelets on the bottom of the open hatch.

"I wonder where they think they're going," Taylor said.

"Outside U.S. territorial limits, I'd imagine," Holly said.

"Or maybe another antenna?" Diaz suggested. "We got their powerful primary antennas here and in Alaska. Maybe they have to be up close and personal with whatever backups they have."

"That may be," Lewis said. "Or it could just be that they're running scared. They probably had no idea anyone was after them till the SWAT team started moving in."

All of that was true. Taylor was not thinking as clearly as he should be. Or seeing as clearly either. He had to push the exhaustion and distractions aside. He had to center himself.

The chopper was less than a hundred feet above and behind the yacht and closing quickly. Taylor hooked the ladder in place. As he did he marveled at the poise and professionalism of their pilot. Outside the flight deck, Holly seemed like a good-natured, unsophisticated kid. Behind the stick, he seemed like a grandmaster. It was thrilling.

"Ladder lights are green," Holly said. That meant the latches had been correctly engaged. "You've got a yellow light on the door."

Taylor laid the ladder between the seat and the door and put his left hand on the large, horizontal door handle. A tug 180 degrees to the right and the hatch would slide open like a van door.

"Hold it!" Diaz said.

The Coast Guard SHARC was looking out the window at the yacht. The boat was pushing itself, traveling at nearly forty knots; the Pave Hawk was within twenty vertical feet of the vessel. In another ten seconds or so the chopper would be directly on top of it.

"What's the problem?" Lewis asked Diaz.

Diaz studied the yacht for another moment. "Captain Holly, get us out of here."

"What's wrong?" Lewis demanded.

"Captain, *now*!" Diaz shouted.

Holly swung up and away, toward the New Jersey side of the river. As he was rising, the yacht suddenly expanded in all directions and then evaporated in a blazing white fireball.

"Shit!" Taylor screamed as the shock wave hit the chopper. He let go of the handle so he didn't accidentally pull the door open.

The Pave Hawk shuddered in all directions. At the same time Holly turned the underside of the carriage toward the explosion to protect the rotor as pieces of the yacht flew by. They hit hard, like little bumper cars. Taylor heard and felt each of them. One piece of metal slashed through the cabin, embedding itself in the floor. Another ended up inside the coiled ladder. At the same time the sky turned gray as the explosion gave birth to an oil fire. Though the barrage lasted only a second or two, it felt much longer. Relatively intact, the helicopter continued its rapid westward ascent. If Captain Holly had blinked during the near-escape, Taylor had missed it. The major was a different story. He had been squeezing the armrests hard enough to crack the plastic.

"Jesus, man," Taylor said. He settled back in his seat as the ride smoothed. "Diaz, how did you know that was going to happen?"

"Boats like that have a very distinctive fire alarm," Diaz said. "It's very high-pitched and loud so you can hear it even if you're right next to the engine, using a winch, or raising anchor."

"What made you think the yacht was gonna blow instead of just burn?" Lewis asked.

Diaz turned back. "Because I saw a little bit of smoke coming from the stern, from the windlass port, and I *didn't* hear a fire alarm," the sailor said. "I figured it was a fuse of some kind. The smoke detector might not have picked that up, especially if the smoke was venting outward."

"That was a good get," Taylor said. "Really amazing."

"Thanks," Diaz said. "But you know what's really amazing? That those guys preferred to blow themselves up rather than get caught."

"I wonder," Lewis said.

"What do you mean?" Diaz asked.

"Let me borrow your headset," Lewis said as he reached across the seat. "I want to talk to the commander."

Sixty-six

Lake Miasalaro, West Virginia
Tuesday, 10:21 A.M.

As suddenly as it had stopped, the bar started moving again.

"*Yes!*" Victoria shouted.

Evans and Fraser watched with her as the bar edged closer and closer to the top. Victoria was relieved but baffled until she heard the commander talking to Colonel Lewis.

"They blew up the yacht?" Evans said.

"The yacht and the command center," Victoria muttered.

"I wonder if the explosion was a decoy," Evans said to Lewis. "Maybe Estate used it to buy time so they could move the real ESP command station. If we think the center has been destroyed, we'll stop looking."

"No," Victoria said emphatically. "The uplink commander center was definitely on the yacht."

Evans looked at her. "How do you know?"

"That's what caused the ESP to stop taking my commands for a moment," she said.

"I don't follow."

"It was receiving a final signal of its own. Dr. Gregg or whoever wrote the program built their own poison pill undertow into the ESP. In case the location of the uplink were ever discovered, they obviously felt they couldn't trust the operator to destroy the evidence."

"The operator—Dr. Crabbe," Evans said.

"Correct," Victoria said. "I'm betting the guy was blackmailed to be there. But Estate couldn't trust him, so they wrote a trigger into the ESP program. If the satellite were ever reclaimed, that reclamation process would automatically send a destruct code to the source of the Estate commands. In this case, to the computer and from there to a fuse linked to explosives that blew up the yacht."

"It's possible," Evans agreed.

"If you need further proof, all the satellite program bars are at one hundred percent," she said. "Now the fucker really is dead rising." She grinned. "Sorry, Commander."

"It's okay." Evans smiled.

The commander got back on the phone. He proudly informed the Stealth Warrior team that the ESP was history. Then he congratulated them on an exceptional job and told them all to come home.

Dr. Fraser had been standing quietly behind Victoria the entire time. As she slumped, ready to crash, the scientist gave her shoulder a gentle squeeze and walked away.

That was the richest compliment of all.

Sixty-seven

Arlington, Virginia
Tuesday, 10:53 A.M.

General Anastasia stood over his desk. He couldn't be- lieve it. It was there, in their hands, all of it. And then just as quickly it was gone.

The general was looking at the world map behind his chair. It was a mosaic constructed of photographs snapped by different space flights over the past forty years. Not just American space flights but Russian space flights.

World space flights.

The general's tired eyes turned from the mosaic to the phone on his desk. Just a few minutes before, the president had called, asking to see him. President Gordon had been blunt.

"I want to talk to you about your role in seizing the Electronic Surveillance Post satellite and the destruction of the space shuttle Venture," the president had told him.

The president had been impassive as he'd said it, like a jury foreman reading a guilty verdict. A verdict for "murder one." Gordon hadn't even said he was sending an armed escort to bring him to the White House. There was probably one waiting for him outside somewhere, not that it mattered. The president knew that the general would not be leaving his office. The activities of Estate were one thing. Orchestrating the destruction of the shuttle and its crew was another.

General Anastasia's eyes drifted to the back of the computer monitor. The president's reaction was predictable, even understandable. But Gordon didn't really get it. Estate had taken a few unfortunate, drastic, but necessary measures to ensure the growth and survival of humankind. As long as politicians ruled the earth, we would effectively be planet-bound. We would not survive a climatic change or collision with an asteroid the likes of which destroyed the dinosaurs. Not unless humans had cities in space and on other worlds. And we wouldn't have that as long as politicians controlled the purse strings. This was a chance to turn government back to the people, eliminate the extraordinary waste—especially of his own profession—and turn our eyes to the future.

Now that wouldn't happen. Even though one of the members of the shuttle crew had felt the sacrifice was a worthy one.

The general's red eyes moved to another object on the desk. His loaded .45 was sitting beside the mouse. Anastasia picked it up.

There was nothing else to think about, nothing else to do. Dr. Crabbe had called to say that the antenna had somehow been unscrambled, that the ESP had turned on them, and that he was getting the hell out of New York with the Estate software. He would head beyond U.S. territorial waters, where he expected Forte to meet him somewhere in a day or two in his personal yacht *McHenry*. The ultimate fort. The birthplace of "The Star Spangled Banner."

Poor Crabbe. He was motivated solely by personal survival. He never had the vision, shared the dream. Not that it mattered now. Nothing did.

That isn't true, Anastasia thought. This did. That he do it and spare himself a trial. Not that the general would feel humiliated by televised hearings. He believed in what he had done and a trial would be a forum to express his hopes and fears. But he knew that the public would view him and his beliefs differently. There would be a very strong backlash against the very thing he was trying to promote. This way, at least, the shuttle crash would be deemed an accident. It would set the space program back, but not destroy it. Insufficient as that was, at least it was *something.* God willing, fate would give the million-year-old human race some of the nearly four hundred million years it gave the dinosaurs and their predecessors before snuffing them out.

General Anastasia put the long barrel of the gun in his mouth. His tongue recoiled reflexively from the extremely tart taste, but he closed his lips around it. A kiss? A suckling? Both? He couldn't decide. The front sight scratched the roof of his mouth. Impulsively he tilted the gun back so the sight dug in harder. And then, without another thought, he pulled back on the trigger.

General Rudolph Anastasia never heard the awful crack as the single shot tore through his head, killing him before the sound reached his ears. The bullet exited the back of his head and slammed into the wall.

Right through a framed photograph of the *Venture.*

Sixty-eight

To Commander Evans the gathering on the shores of the lake had the feel of sitting around the campfire after a long, unusually hard forced march. Even though the campfire was a battery-powered lantern and the food had been heated in the mess cabin, the stars were out—he could see the faint sweep of the Milky Way—and the air was cool and the easy lapping of the lake water was relaxing. Everyone was "dead-dead" as one of his old SEAL mates used to put it, but no one seemed willing to go to sleep. For the past ninety minutes they had been basking in the lazy afterglow of an impossible job well done. With one exception, the members of the Stealth Warriors were seated on large stones, a tree stump, the pebbled lake shore. Even Captain McIver had stopped by the base to tell them that everything was back to normal in the Middle East, meaning that the region was merely as unsafe as before, no less. Only Major Taylor was missing from the group. He had gone to his cabin to call the hospital and check on his mother. Evans himself had just returned from a long talk with the president.

"He still can't believe we did it," Evans said. "He thought this was going to be a long, ugly battle."

"To tell you the truth, I had some long moments there at the end," Victoria said as she nursed a mug of tea.

"How so?" McIver asked.

"I thought they'd managed to get a foot in the ESP door somehow and were trying to push me back," she said.

"They weren't really equipped to push back," Diaz said. "Estate hadn't planned for every contingency. They only knew how to bully when they had the advantage."

"They were well-equipped enough," Lewis said. "They managed to push us against the wall a few times."

"But not for long," Holly said. "And when it came down to it, Anastasia took the doggie walk."

"Doggie walk?" McIver asked.

"That's what my mom used to call it when our terrier pooped inside the house and crawled off to hide under a bed or behind the toilet," Holly said. "Sheppie took the doggie walk of shame. He knew he did wrong and just didn't want to deal with it."

"You had a terrier named Sheppie?" McIver asked.

"Yeah," Holly said. "Why not?"

"No reason," McIver snickered. "No damn reason at all. I guess you could call a German shepherd Terry too."

They looked up as they heard boots crunching. Taylor had a flashlight and was walking back down the hill.

"Well, my attitude is up the general's walk of shame," Victoria said. "He was a killer, and I only hope they find something to pin on Marcus Forte."

"That's going to be tough," Evans conceded. "The president said the NYPD got a warrant to search the offices. They found nothing to tie Forte to Estate. The explosion on the yacht was apparently tied to a fuel tank. The first leak-age was what Mr. Diaz saw. The preliminary investigation suggests there was a chip inside that received signals from the ESP, but it was probably designed to melt in the fire. I'll be surprised if anything turns up."

"Speaking of the NYPD," Diaz said, "was there any fur-ther fallout from our being there?"

"The president phoned the police commissioner and told him the action had to do with the shuttle and its secret cargo," Evans said. "The commissioner accepted that and didn't press for more. Everyone likes to feel as if he's in on even part of a big military secret."

"Except me," McIver said. She was sucking on a Marl-boro, drinking Budweiser from a bottle, and looked the most tired of anyone there. "General Jackson has not been thrilled about giving me whatever I want when I want it. He keeps asking me what I've got going with the president to get me carte blanche like that. I told him it isn't what he thinks. If it were, I said I'd ask for a transfer to fucking Hawaii or something."

"Come on, you like working with us," Holly said.

"I like you all a lot," McIver admitted. "And I'd be sure to E-mail you every day from Hickam AFB, Honolulu."

"So the police are happy, Israel and the Saudis are safe, and Estate will get shut down," Victoria said. "It's too bad we lost Marcus Forte."

"And the shuttle," McIver said, raising her beer. "God bless Commander Boring and his copilot."

Everyone raised their bottles, cups, and cans as Taylor walked into the middle of the group. He didn't sit back down on the grassy edge of the foothills, but stopped a few feet before Colonel Lewis. The Delta Force officer was sit-ting against a tree stump working his way through a bottle of Southern Comfort.

"How's your mom?" the colonel asked Taylor.

"There's no change," Taylor said. "Can I see you please, Colonel?" His voice was steely. His eyes were even harder.

Evans was sitting on a flat boulder. He regarded the major closely.

"That doesn't sound good," Diaz said.

Evans hushed him with a gesture.

"You're seeing me," Lewis said.

"I'd like to see you in *private*," Taylor replied.

"Why?" Lewis said. "We don't keep secrets from our teammates."

"Apparently we do," Taylor said.

"Nondisclosure is not keeping secrets," Lewis replied.

Evans was completely lost. But he wasn't going to interfere. These men had been off on their own. He had learned from experience that whatever conflicts arose between individuals in the field were best settled by those individuals wherever possible. Peace mandated by a superior rarely stuck.

"I just talked to *Sensei*," Taylor said. "I wanted to apologize for my behavior at the dojo."

"That was the right thing to do," Lewis said.

"Right?" Taylor said. "Excuse me, sir, but coming from you that's fucked up. After everything you said to me about my responsibility to the team and its needs, about not risking my ass and upsetting my mother and *all* that shit, you went and did it, didn't you?"

Lewis looked at him. "I don't know what you're talking about."

"I think you do, sir."

The colonel looked past the major at the crescent moon. "Forget about it, Mr. Taylor. Let's toast the moon. A shot for the moon." He laughed. "Where are the missing parts? They'll return, I bet. They always do."

Openly disgusted, Taylor turned and headed back toward

the cabin. Lewis took another swallow of Southern Comfort and sank back staring at the sky.

Evans followed Taylor. He caught up with the major at the bottom of the path where it curved up the hill, away from the landing. They were out of earshot of the others.

"Major, I'm sorry to hear there's no change in your mom."

Taylor stopped. "Thank you, sir."

"Do you want to talk about the rest of this?"

"There isn't much to say," Taylor said. "My *sensei* just told me that the leader of the gang that hurt my mother was killed at his home last night," Taylor said. "Stabbed between the ribs and left to bleed to death."

"And you think Colonel Lewis was responsible?"

"He's a knife-fighter."

"Gang leaders have a lot of enemies. Those enemies carry knives."

"I'm sure they do," Taylor said. "But Colonel Lewis went for a walk last night. He didn't tell me where he went."

"And that makes him guilty?"

"No," Taylor replied. "Not denying it makes him guilty."

"I see," Evans said.

The commander hoped that Lewis hadn't committed a cold-blooded murder. That was the kind of action he'd sent the colonel to Philadelphia to prevent. But he knew that actions committed in the field were often determined by events that officers behind the lines were not equipped to judge. Evans wasn't going to take it further. Not unless he was invited to by Lewis himself.

"You know, we're all working under in-your-face close quarters and under pretty isolated conditions," Evans said. "We may not all be best friends, but we can't afford bad blood either."

"There's no bad blood, sir," Taylor assured him. "I'm

angry at myself for not following my heart, my instincts. For letting him do my job. Now I feel like I backed down for the wrong reasons."

"Backed down from taking revenge?" Evans said.

"Revenge, justice, whatever you want to call it," Taylor said.

"There's a big difference," Evans said. "Justice is impartial and righteous."

"Whatever it was, I wanted it. I didn't take it, and now I've got nowhere to put this," he said, shaking his fist.

"You just stopped an attempt to take over the world," Evans said. "I'd say you hit someone pretty hard."

"Yes, sir. Just not the right someone."

Major Taylor excused himself and started to walk away. Evans watched him go.

"Major?" Evans said.

Taylor turned. "Sir?"

"Colonel Lewis is not a drinker."

"I'm sorry?"

"Sometimes it takes more strength not to hit," Evans said.

Taylor stood there for a long moment. His posture seemed to change a little. His shoulders seemed a little less stiff, his neck a little less rigid.

"I hope you'll come on back and join our little party when you're ready," Evans said.

"Thank you, sir," Taylor said. "I will."

The major headed back up the hill while Evans turned and looked out at the lake. The air was fresh and brisk as it whipped gently under the sleeves of his uniform. And the vision ahead was beautiful. A cloudless sky with a glimpse of the Milky Way, a sliver of moon low above the black hills. At least Evans no longer wondered if this was what Eden might have been like.

For all their differences, and in ways Commander Evans was not sure any of them exactly understood, these men and women were all brethren looking out for one another.

With a grateful smile and a little prayer, Evans turned and walked slowly back to the campsite.

DAVID E. MEADOWS

JOINT TASK FORCE: AMERICA

Terrorist Abu Alhaul is bringing mass destruction to America's east coast. Alhaul says he is retaliating for the death of his family, which he blames on one man: U.S. Navy SEAL Commander Tucker Raleigh.

0-425-19482-5

"David Meadows is the real thing."
—Stephen Coonts

B136

Bestselling Author

JOE WEBER

"One of America's new thriller stars."
—Tom Clancy

PRIMARY TARGET
0-425-17255-4
"*Primary Target* is a chilling scenario of
global warfare. The suspense never stops."
—W.E.B. Griffin

DEFCON ONE
0-515-10419-1
"A gripping techno-thriller...
frighteningly credible."
—*Publishers Weekly*

**Available wherever books are sold or at
www.penguin.com**